BLOOD at the ROOT

BLOOD
at the
ROOT

LADARRION WILLIAMS

 LABYRINTH ROAD | NEW YORK

All rights reserved. Published in the United States by Labyrinth Road, an imprint of Random House Children's Books, a division of Penguin Random House LLC, New York. The Author's Note was originally published in different form as "When Black Boys Find Magic" in issue 21 of *FIYAH: Magazine of Black Speculative Fiction,* in 2022.

Labyrinth Road and the colophon are trademarks of Penguin Random House LLC.

Visit us on the Web! GetUnderlined.com

Educators and librarians, for a variety of teaching tools,
visit us at RHTeachersLibrarians.com

Library of Congress Cataloging-in-Publication Data is available upon request.
ISBN 978-0-593-71192-7 (trade)—ISBN 978-0-593-71194-1 (lib. bdg.)—
ISBN 978-0-593-71195-8 (ebook)

The text of this book is set in 11-point Adobe Garamond.

Editors: Liesa Abrams and Emily Shapiro
Cover Designer: Liz Dresner
Interior Designer: Ken Crossland
Managing Editor: Rebecca Vitkus
Production Manager: Natalia Dextre

Printed in the United States of America
10 9 8 7 6 5 4 3 2 1
First Edition

This is dedicated to the seventeen-year-old
Black boy who the world told he doesn't have magic.

Lemme let you in on a lil' secret: you do.
It is in your blood; it is nestled deep in your bones.
It is in the very soil you walk on that's been blessed
by the sweat and tears of your ancestors.
Walk in it with pride.

To Ashton:

This is for you.

AUTHOR'S NOTE

Wassup, *BATR* fam!

Yes, that's gonna be our slogan from now on!

Picture it: The world of *Blood at the Root*—or *BATR,* as I like to call it—first came to me in early 2020. It bothered me for years, but it didn't manifest itself until the entire world had to shut down due to Covid-19. For the first time in a long time, I had to sit around and think. Dream. Revel in my anger because this was when George Floyd was murdered for all the world to see.

In that fit of righteous rage, this was when Malik Baron finally revealed himself to me and told me to write his story. This beautiful Black boy has been with me since I was dreaming in my childhood home in Helena, Alabama. He told me to go against the grain and tell his story that will not be in death but in glory.

Far too often, I would see the death of Black people and not life. In plays. Films. Social media. And even in books. I came up and was in high school during the big young adult boom in films and television. *Twilight, The Hunger Games, The Maze Runner, Divergent. Percy Jackson & the Olympians: The Lightning Thief, The Vampire Diaries,* all of them.

However, those characters looked different from my friends. They didn't speak with that Southern twang. I didn't see my mama. My grandmama. My cousins and 'nem in those stories. Though I loved them, I felt distant from the stories and characters. And if we were in them, we were often relegated to being a side character to propel and humanize the white main character.

I'd always heard that Black boys don't read. Maybe that's why sports are pushed so hard on Black males or why so many educators push them through the system without proper accommodations. Maybe that's why publishers don't feel the need to create content geared toward them. But I must pose a question: Is it that Black boys don't read or that Black boys are just not interested in reading whatever is put in front of them? If you have young Black men constantly reading about white main characters, specifically white privileged male characters, that don't reflect their identity or that they simply don't relate to, it's going to make them reluctant to read.

The late, great Toni Morrison once said, "If you find a book you really want to read but it hasn't been written yet, then you must write it." I carry those words with me everywhere I go.

Black boys surely deserve stories filled with magic, wonder, and warm summer rain.

Black boys deserve to have their origin stories.

Black boys deserve to have the fullness of their power revered.

They need to remember that they are magic, that "Blackness is magic."

It's in the soil of the South. Beyond the Louisiana bayou, resting with the bones of our ancestors that triumphed over the Middle Passage. Where whitewashed Voodoo was called by its sweeter true name and werewolves were not diminished to lowly dogs. Where regal kings of the jungles and vampires were known by their original, melanated faces, that is where the magic is. The magic lingers at the harbor docks in Charleston, South Carolina, and in the bolls of cotton in Georgia, and it blooms in Alabama, a forgotten mecca of magical blackness.

Let Black boys hear the cicadas sing their songs to the Alabama sky. Let them feel that syrupy sweat sticking their clothes to their body. Let their stories be filled with the smell of the sweet corn bread and collard greens of their grandma's cooking. Let the words on the page reveal our young Black boys, who will be sitting at the feet of their grandparents and meet God.

Let them spin magic from their fingers.

Let them hold stars in their hair.

Let Black boys be the alchemists in their stories.

Let Black boys be seen.

Let them be colored softly.

Let them fall in love.

Let them have adventures.

And let Black boys be the heroes of their own stories.

More than having magical powers, I want Black boys to find themselves by establishing their roots. I want them to make mistakes and I want them to feel seen, something I so desperately hoped for when I was a youth in Alabama. I want them to unlock a world that tells them they can choose who they want to be. A world that tells them they deserve to be centered and loved, whether they decide to wield a magical sword, astral-project to another dimension, or find love in a whirlwind romance. When Black boys find magic, they find themselves.

Stay Blackgical, *BATR* fam.

Sincerely,
LaDarrion Williams

Life is your birthright, they hid that
in the fine print.

Take the pen and rewrite it.

PROLOGUE

BLACK BOYS LIKE ME DON'T HAVE MAGIC POWERS.
At least, that's what I believed growing up. I couldn't move things with my mind. I couldn't make the things that haunted me disappear in thin air or read people's minds. Hell, I couldn't even race against time to change things for the better.

Well, until the night my magic manifested.

And . . . when my entire world was turned upside down.

My auntie Denise had a get-together at her place on the Fourth of July. She had them every year. On the hill, right by her spot, people be popping off firecrackers. Uncle Butch played "Soul Heaven" by Johnnie Taylor over a hundred times from his raggedy speakers, trying to get all the old aunties and uncles to dance. It was a sad attempt, but he tried anyway. Their trailer rested on a hill, surrounded by thick trees, looming like they're guarding something that they don't want to let out. A corrugated-tin roof hovered over the slanted wooden porch with old furniture from Big Lots stacked sloppily everywhere. *Shidddd,* the trailer itself seemed like it was in a boxing ring with Mike Tyson. Dents, rusted fences, and all kinds of bedsheets made into curtains. Auntie had all the food, though. I'm talking about collard greens, macaroni and cheese, and sweet baby back ribs with the Dreamland barbecue sauce. Everybody could go and get themselves a plate and a cold Mr. Pibb to wash it all down.

When it comes to Black folks in Helena, Alabama, the Fourth of July ain't got shit to do with patriotism.

The dark Alabama sky exploded with different shades of reds, blues, and yellows. Bottle rockets whistled. Bombs literally burst through the thick, foggy air. The whole hood smelled like burnt gunpowder and barbecue, a scent that'll confuse your nose all day long.

All the kids who ain't had no business being around grown folks be outside, trying not to lose an eye, acting like they're wizards and shit with the screeching Roman candles. But what was supposed to be a fun and regular night was also the night my life changed to the point of no return.

After dancing the Cupid Shuffle, I felt something was off. Right in the pit of my stomach. That bad feeling tugged at me to go home. The more I ignored it, the worse it got.

Before I knew it, I was racing home on my red-and-blue bike. My legs burned as I pedaled against the sizzling wind. My mouth dried up as the aftertaste of soda settled on my tongue. Rubber tires slapped against the pavement while beads of sweat dripped down the side of my face as I dodged everybody dancing drunk in the middle of the street.

That's how it was in Liberty Heights.

The orange color from the streetlights spilled down, illuminating Timmy Billings and the fam hanging out, drinking, and hollering at one another while playing a game of spades. If you don't know how to play, don't sit at his table, because he's liable to cuss you the hell out. Mrs. Johnnie Mae sat on her porch, turning her nose up at people being in her yard, cussing and fighting while the nine o'clock news played in the background. Nessie, T-Lane, along with the older kids, be having a firecracker war by the basketball court, or they off somewhere, hunching on one another. TJ Bivins threw a Red Devil M-1000 at me and missed. He was always trying to take somebody's eye out. Ooooh, I couldn't stand him.

If I wasn't trynna get home, I'd light his ass up. But I kept pedaling, swooping through trees, dodging the Chinese cracker bomb, and almost hitting Cousin Jeffro. "You betta get somewhere and sit yo ass down, Bart!"

That ain't my name. It's Malik.

He just calls me Bart Simpson because he says I be bad as *heyell*. I ain't see him 'cause he's so Black, he looks blue at night. No time for that. I was like a thief in the night, bobbing and weaving through backyards. The light from the silver coin–looking moon lit my path. A symphony of loud pops and a ringing sounded off in my ears. My head began pounding while another flash of bursting light crackled above me. The more I pedaled, the more the tugging feeling rose like the tide—and the whole block turned into a color-filled blur as I pedaled faster.

I *needed* to get home.

Our house was the third on the left on Front Street, next door to Old Man Zeke, the neighborhood gossip. Mama said he gossips mo' than a woman at a beauty shop on a Saturday. Old Man Zeke would just sit out in his front yard, spitting tobacco into a Coke bottle. I swerved right, passing Ms. Doll's house. She used to sell all the kids Bebops, which are basically frozen Kool-Aid in white Styrofoam cups, salt-and-vinegar chips, and dill pickles, for a dollar. She also had all types of sweets. Fudge Rounds, Swiss Rolls cakes, and Sour Punch Sour Apple Straws. The word was Ms. Doll kept Helena's dentist office real busy with our cavity-filled teeth.

I threw my bike onto the grass, hopped onto the porch, and burst through the front door. First the cold air from the AC hit me. My nose flared up—a burning smell from the gas stove. I turned it off. Mama used to say I ain't had no business touching a hot stove. This time I ain't had no choice.

Walking through the living room, I felt the tugging gnaw at me, shredding my insides. My knees were about to lock up. Throat dry as the Sahara, chest heaving, and nerves strangling whatever bravery I had left.

At first, I didn't hear nothing out of the ordinary. The twisted shadow on the wall shifted and moved with rhythm. Firecrackers continued to whistle from outside. Mama's yelling pierced my soul as I edged closer to the end of the hall, so I darted down the hallway, rushing to the doorway that led into my mama's bedroom.

There she was, surrounded by four tall people in long black cloaks like Grim Reapers. I thought they got the wrong holiday. It ain't Halloween. Mama was on the floor, crying and yelling, tears falling out of her bulging light-brown eyes like a river. Her thick, curly hair was wild, like she'd been pulling on it from every direction. Her shrill voice screeched something I couldn't understand. I thought she spoke another language because I had never heard her talk like that before.

The chanting grew louder.

Right when I covered my ears, a powerful gust of wind almost knocked me down to the floor. Papers flew, walls cracked right down the middle, all that. Just like the silence before the storm, the glass from her window shattered, flying into the air in slow motion.

Suddenly, as if someone pressed play on a remote control, time resumed.

"Mama!" I remember calling her name under the loud chanting and the strange wind. "Mama!"

Her wild eyes cut to me. She kept chanting something weird. I reached for her, but the wind was too strong. It pulled me back toward the wall. I needed to get to my mama. Finally, the wind began dying down. I was still reaching for her, and somehow I seemed closer. That was when I realized I was the one controlling the current. None of this felt real, but somehow this was happening—I was the kid with the magic powers I'd always seen on TV. One of the cloaked people looked toward me. Face hidden. Darkness was all I saw when my tear-filled eyes landed on him. Maybe he was my archenemy, and I had to use everything that was in me to defeat him. Just like in all those stories starring white kids.

Mama's expression changed when she noticed me reaching for her, and she screamed so loud, it was like a blast of energy. From there I felt a tingling sensation right at the tip of my fingers—like little electric bolts flowing through me.

Magic.

Before I knew it, Mama was swallowed up in a bolt of green light. I screamed so hard, I felt like my throat was ripped open, bleeding. One of the cloaked people tried to grab me with a long stretch of finger. I screamed again, and a swirling ribbon of blue light shot from me, and just like the Alabama sky with firecrackers, everything exploded. Flames incinerated the whole room. Black smoke covered my vision.

When I could see again, I was surrounded by dead bodies mangled all over the floor, burned to a crisp. It took a literal minute for my seven-year-old brain to fully process what was going on.

My eyes wandered to the floor, seeing the crumpled bodies and shards of glass. A sudden coldness hit me right in my chest. My reflection from the slanted, broken mirror showcased a seven-year-old's face exposed to something dark. The innocence . . . melting.

Looking down at my shaky hands, I saw my palms still had little swirls of blue light creeping up my arm. In just minutes, my magic was here, and my mama was dead and gone.

Maybe there's a reason why Black boys like me don't have magic powers.

Because no good ever comes from it.

CHAPTER ONE

PRIDE IS THE DEVIL.

And it definitely got a hold on me because that's the only thing that gets me through. Walking through this ghetto-ass world, I have to pay an abundance of broken memories and pride to live and survive.

With a thickness in my throat, I have a storm gathering inside me. I mean, I don't know what it is, but all I know is that the weight of the world and past sins make my shoulders slump while I hustle my way into town. A whistle, then a loud pop, sizzles through the humid air. Right after, a trail of smoke follows. From my perspective, the Fourth of July ain't changed for real. People doing the same old, same old. Barbecuing. Drinking. Playing loud-ass music and popping firecrackers. Carrying on like their lives can't be destroyed in a single night.

Ten years later, and with fifty dollars and a few pairs of pants and shirts and my clean-ass Nike Dunks, I have nothing else but questions and pain—which is more than some folks got, I guess.

My phone vibrates against my leg.

> You still coming to get me?

It's a text message from my foster brother, Taye. He ain't supposed to have a phone. If he gets caught, I ain't buying him another one. It took me damn near three months of mowing lawns, cleaning up trash in the neighborhood, and low-key scamming and hustling just to get him that one. We needed to stay in constant communication because for the past few months, we've been devising a plan on how to see each other again. So that means *kidnapping* is on my agenda for today.

He sends a *hurry up* meme.

I click out of my messages, making my way deeper into town.

When I was first at the orphanage, I always wondered why I couldn't go stay with folks from the neighborhood. Everybody in Liberty Heights talked—and they were not trying to take me in after the fire, my mama's death, *and,* not to mention, me waking up surrounded by dead bodies. The rumors of me having something to do with my mama's death flooded Liberty Heights like a river of blood.

I can remember it still, the red-and-blue lights slicing the dark. Smoke rising to the sky while hungry eyes crawled on me as I was ushered out of the house, unburned and disoriented. Confused social workers and police scoured the entire yard, questioning everybody in the neighborhood, but all my neighbors ain't want that smoke.

Too many questions.

One of the questions being: *Did he really kill his mama?* Another one I heard whispered through the winds was how the hell did I make it out alive while three other bodies ended up crumpled under the debris, burned beyond recognition. Just catching the little conversations from the police and one of the firefighters, everyone assumed my mama was one of them. No matter how many times I told them there were five other people—my mama and those four strangers—in that house when the fire started. No one wanted to hear it. They told me I must have remembered wrong. I didn't want to believe my mama was gone or that it was my fault. I thought she must have gotten out somehow, that she'd come back for me.

But from the whispers from the cackling play aunties and uncles of the neighborhood, my mama was for sure killed that night. And with everything and everyone around me believing she was dead and gone, I guess I just got tired of fighting it. But that was a long time ago.

One thing I did know is those folks didn't want anything to do with me. So to the group home I went.

Do I blame them? Part of me did. But part of me kinda understood because my mama was everybody's friend and auntie in Liberty Heights, and they looked at me as her murderer.

Never thought I'd end up where I am now. No family for real, and with this magic that I don't have no idea about. I'll say this: it ain't like what people see on TV. It's lonely as hell, and when it comes to these powers, I'm still afraid to even show them to myself.

When I first arrived at the orphanage, I met this girl Alexis, and we were at each other's throats. Constantly fighting and bickering. Ya know, kid shit. Alexis always thought she was smarter than me and better than me at everything. Even for a little kid herself, she had the confidence of a grown woman. I couldn't stand her ass. After some months of me being there, she started playing mean jokes on me. One time she made a bucket of old rainwater fall on my brand-new Easter outfit. Another time she pushed me out of the swing. But there would be times when I was around her, I'd get this crazy feeling of, like, we were connected in some way. With my seven-year-old brain, I ain't really know how to communicate that.

But one night I saw her do magic. Bright purple and gold stretched from her hands like lightning and a gaggle of stars. It swirled and bent all around her, as if it was trying to protect her. She made the crummy backyard of our orphanage the most beautiful thing in the world. She made it our sanctuary.

She was just like me.

But she wasn't afraid of her magic, even though her birth parents abandoned her when they found out their little girl had it. For a few months, she made me less afraid too.

And then like always, my lil' bit of happiness got snatched away. Alexis was adopted and was gone. An older Black couple came in. The man had thick glasses. A scrunched-up face that reminds you of a pastor at a Baptist church. His wife was pretty, though. Young. I took her as an elementary school teacher. Not even an hour after they showed up, they decided to adopt Alexis and make her a part of their family.

My best friend, my first love, driving away . . . and never seeing or hearing from her again was the second heartbreak my young self experienced. Just thinking about it, I feel my heart beat faster and my lungs fight against my chest.

After that I tried to pretend my magic didn't exist. All it did was remind me of pain. But I couldn't always control it. Sometimes I managed to make little stuff fly, or make the channels flip on the TV without so much as a thought, or make the basketball go right in the net from half-court. Then Taye came to the orphanage and caught on fast to what I could do.

At first, he wasn't even supposed to know about it. I wasn't trynna show regular people my magic. I set those rules for myself because that's how it was in the movies and comic books. People ain't supposed to know you got magic powers, right? For their sake or whatever.

"I promise, I ain't gon' tell nobody," he'd say, like I was the biggest superhero.

Taye doesn't understand. He's young. But spending the past ten years trying to find the good in my magic and understanding the magnitude that it brings doesn't make me feel like nobody's hero.

I'm the villain in everybody's story.

Walking along the edge of town, I feel sweat ski down my neck. The oppressive humidity got my clothes sticking to me like syrup. I guess the old folks are right when they say, *Alabama got some funny-made weather.*

Speaking of funny-made weather, I twirl my fingers and manage to create a small breeze to cool myself down. That's pretty much the most I can do without tiring myself out anyway. The few little tricks make me feel groggy and sluggish. Like I ate a triple burger with cheese and extra pickles from Whataburger. Even after ten years, I'm still a lil' hesitant on using this magic stuff. I don't trust myself with it. Most times, I can't help it, but when I can, I try to avoid doing anything that'll get attention on me again. Or get anyone else hurt.

And the only reason why I do the small stuff like this is because I remember how back at the group home, Taye's eyes were cocked like a pistol whenever I did my magic.

He would say to me, *"You doing ya magic makes me feel safe."*

I suck my teeth just thinking about it. *My magic makes him feel safe.* . . . It shouldn't make nobody feel safe because it took my mama away from me.

When Taye got placed with the Hudsons two years after he arrived at the home, he held on to me for dear life, crying and begging them to take me with them. They agreed. Hell, that was an extra check for Carlwell from the state. His ass didn't mind none.

And I didn't mind either, as long as I was with Taye. I've been trying to get back to him since Carlwell kicked me out two years ago, and today it's finally happening.

Me and Taye low-key already decided on a place to go: Cali. It's far enough away for nobody to really notice us. This'd be our chance to start over. Hell, we deserve it.

So, on to part one of my plan: we need a car.

Which brings me to part two of my plan: I gotta *steal* one.

About two miles into town, things slowly become familiar. I come up to a bend that leads into a subdivision named Plantation South. A messed-up name, I know. It's a haven for rich white and Black folks who think they are better than everybody. That old family money that gave people an out on life's bullshit. Only in Alabama. Tall two-to-three-story homes. Autumn-baked streets paved with privilege and newly soldered tar. Stupid-looking yard gnomes and lawn chairs spread out in the manicured front yards, taunting us outsiders with a bullshit sign about ALL ARE WELCOME. Perched just right for everybody to see their fake-ass activism.

Just like the rest of the South, they try to hold on to things they should've let go of a long time ago. I guess we got shit in common.

On the left is a park full of exercise machines and a dog park. A small trail merges with the thick woods that bleed into Buck Creek, which runs through the city of Alabaster. Me and Alexis used to come here trick-or-treating during Halloween. I would dress up as a ninja, and Alexis would be a witch. They used to give out good candy: Reese's. Butterfingers. Green Apple Jolly Ranchers.

Even with magic powers, I'm still a nigga in the street, and I gotta be careful to not look too "suspicious." My face shifts from *intimidating* to jovial—to keep my ass alive. I ain't trynna end up like those people they post on social media. Nah. With me, I throw hands before I ever record a Karen or Dave with my phone for social media.

They got me fucked all the way up.

My headphones are wedged in my ears, blasting this artist called K. Starr. His EP bumping. Which helps me keep my head down, trying to be *incognegro*.

The front part of the neighborhood is pretty much out into the open. Walking along the road that curves before me, I hear kids in their backyards, sloshing around in their fancy pools and jumping on their trampolines.

A mixture of barbecue, chlorine, and sulfuric gunpowder makes my nostrils flare with curiosity. It's a funny thing about smells and how they can trigger memories you've tucked away for so long. I can't even lie, that night still claws at me, trying to pull me down to that darkness that I spent so much time climbing out of.

One sniff, and you're back to where it all began.

Nostalgia is a bitch, huh?

Soon as I find a hiding spot behind some of these bushes, I strip down to nothing but basketball shorts and a wrinkled T-shirt with Tupac from *Poetic Justice* that I bought from Walmart right when I left my last foster home, the Markhams', back in Georgia. I wrap my headphones around my phone and place them and my clothes in my book bag.

My eyes scan the neighborhood in its entirety. I'm trying to pick the best car I can steal. No cap, I gotta be strategic about this because it's something I gotta travel across the country with. Nothing too flashy, especially something the police ain't going to be too quick to pull over.

Several cars are lined up in formation. The first one: *Tesla.*

Hell naw. They got those fancy computers. With the Find My iPhone app, I'm caught before I even hit the freeway. Shit smooooth, though. But pass.

Nissan Altima. Damn, the way my reflection slides across the tinted jet-black windows. That's an automatic pull-over. So, I'm good on that one.

Dodge Avenger. Black. Not too decked out. Silver rims and a few dents decorate the side of the door. Also, the windows ain't tinted that much. Just perfect for my first try at grand theft auto.

Body crouched low, I sneak up to it and crane my neck to make sure nobody sees me. The closed doors and muffled haughty laughter from inside the homes let me know that the coast is clear.

My hands wrap around the handle, pulling on it to open.

And . . . it's locked.

Damn. A'ight. That means I gotta try the *other* way.

Like I said before, ain't no manual to this magic stuff. And I for damn sure ain't met nobody else since Alexis I can ask. I just know when I do use my powers, it's a rush. It feels like that moment you are on the Goliath at Six Flags. It was my first time going there with my senior class. The orange Goliath stood two hundred feet, and I felt closer to God more than anything. I felt free as the hot wind bit at my cheeks. I felt limitless when Downtown Atlanta glistened in the distance. And just like magic, trying to make stuff happen feels like slowly rising to the incline—you hold on to the handlebars, and you feel like you still have a little bit of control. Then the steep drop happens. A swooping feeling grows in your stomach when you know you gotta let go.

A deep breath meets adrenaline in my chest, and my fingers curl inward like legs on a spider. I tug on the energy that floods through me like an electrical current and try to open the car door.

And outta nowhere, the rain comes down in sheets, sideways. If there were an imaginary camera right now, my ass would look right at it like . . . *This is the shit I be talking about.*

Anyway, the countdown begins. One minute to get in this car, start it up, and dip out this bitch before anybody notices.

A'ight. Here we go.

Soon as I touch the door, the lock on the car instantly clicks to unlock. I hop in and close the door real soft. The rain continues to drum on top of the car, and now the wind whips around, blowing yard signs and leaves everywhere.

With my magic glitching, my time is probably cut in half.

On the passenger seat are a few candy wrappers, empty Gatorade bottles, and a durag. Oh, this a nigga car. I can tell because there's a red-and-white tassel and a Black Ice car freshener dangling from the rearview mirror, and a pile of nickels and quarters rests in the ashtray. A school ID. A pack of Backwoods and a pair of AirPods. Fully charged.

Hell to the yeah. I'm taking these.

A'ight, back to the car. Now all I gotta do is think about the car turning on.

But with this rain and misfire, I'm definitely on my Jimmy Neutron shit.

My fingers wrap around the steering wheel.

Then I close my eyes.

Think!

Suddenly, the windshield wipers cut on, swaying back and forth. Hot air blows from the air vents, and the radio blasts nothing but static. The speedometer rises, but the car is stationed right where it's parked. The sky even turns blue, clouds huddle in the distance, and the sun peeks out. Not even two seconds, sweat starts to drip from my forehead. My hands cramp up from frustration as I go for the steering wheel again. This time the turn signal clicks left and right. Radio going haywire from AM to FM, and the car finally sparks to life with a roar of an idle engine.

Why my magic acting up right now?

The front door to the house swings open.

From the corner of my eye, three dudes step out onto the porch. Two white dudes and one Black dude with eyes of an eagle, spotting my ass trynna steal they car.

SHIT!

A muffled voice barks from the porch, "*Aye,* who the fuck is in my car?!"

The Black dude, who looks like a fake-ass LeBron James, jumps off the steps and runs toward me. His white friends, with fresh fades—probably thinking they're Black too—straddle behind him. They all bang on the windows while surrounding the car, trying to get in.

"What the hell do you think you're doin'?!" one of the white boys spits.

Shit. Shit! Shit!!!

"Nigga, get yo ass out my car fore I beat yo ass!" The Black dude presses on the key, trying to unlock the car. But I lock it back. Us going back and forth.

Click. Lock.

Click. Unlock.

We stare at each other through the window.

"Muhfucka—" ole dude says.

Finally the doors unlock, and before I can lock them, ole boy pulls me out and starts to stomp a mudhole in my ass.

"Y'all niggas *allllways* trynna steal somebody's catalytic convert-ers and shit!" fake LeBron says.

"Get the fuck offa me!" I scream.

Kicks and punches land on me hard, making my entire body curl up against the damp and hot pavement.

C'mon, magic. Do your thing.

A firecracker sizzles in the sky. Then a jolt of energy swells around the palm of my hands. My fight-or-flight response causes a gust of wind, stirring the trees above.

Everything around us *slooooowwwsss* in motion. Hell, it's even like that moment just before the drop on a roller coaster. When you get that butterfly feeling in your stomach, and you have to let go.

One of the white dudes tries to kick me again; I raise my hand, and I swear to God, him and his other friend are flung all the way back across the yard. They hit the concrete hard.

Instantly, I stand up. In defense mode.

Adrenaline of fear and magic rushes through my veins. Just like clockwork, the memory floods my head like a basketball game on replay. My mama's screams. The cloaked figures reciting a chant that I've been spending ten years trying to decode. One of them lurching forward, trying to grab me. My seven-year-old self yelling, "Mama!"

As I slowly come back to reality, I clock ole boy coming for me with his whole fist. I juke left, doing a faux Euro-step move like we're playing a one-on-one game. He comes face-to-face with the pavement. *Oooooh. Dayyyyum.* Ankles prolly straight broke. Fingers spreading, I spot the ball of blue fire thinly flickering from my fingertips.

"What the hell?!" This white boy is petrified as hell. But to be honest, I am too from this blue light. "This freak is using some kinda trick!"

They all try to get up, legs wobbling like Jell-O. Fake LeBron holds his foot and swallows the pain.

I feel winded.

But I need that damn car. It's gonna help me get Taye. My eyes quickly scan left as one of the white dudes hesitates on coming for me again. I jump straight back into the car and slam the door shut, using my magic to keep it locked this time. I focus all my energy until my palms ring with heat and sweat drips down my forehead.

Using the high-stakes emotions, I wrap my fingers around the steering wheel.

As I think it, so it shall be.

The engine roars to life.

With my foot to the gas pedal, the gear violently shifts into drive, and the wheels screech against the pavement, lurching me forward. Like a dumbass, I crash straight into a gaudy-looking mailbox. Gray-and-white smoke clouds everything. *Fast & Furious*–style, I put this bitch in reverse and sharply peel out there faster than a runaway slave.

The revving from the engine matches my anxiety, rising with a crescendo to a new height. I'm not gonna lie; I feel bad. But Taye and I need a car to travel around. Being on a bus ain't gonna cut it. And I for damn sure can't afford to buy no plane tickets for the both of us.

When I get far away enough, about ten miles into the next town, I pull over on the side of the road beside an open lot to give myself a minute to let the adrenaline from using magic die down. I even hold up my hands in disbelief, trying to make the blue light appear again.

Where the hell did that come from?

The combination of mental and physical exhaustion turns into one of those hunger headaches, even as my body reflexively calms down, my heart rate slowly going back to regular.

Across the parking lot, a church Fourth of July picnic is happening. Music spills out of the building into the streets. That real Baptist church music too. It's the type where it ain't no instruments, just voices and the stomping of feet. I can remember the songs I would hear on Sundays at Mount Pleasant Baptist Church.

The doors to the church open, and a sea of Black folks flood out into the parking lot. They hug, talk, pray, and move slowly toward long tables full of food. They grubbing and having a good ole time.

I catch a little boy off on the side, playing with a lit sparkler. I can see him now, on Sundays, he pats his mama on the arm, begging for her to stop talking and get in the car. I find myself chuckling because he's probably been in there since this morning—you know how Black folks do when it comes to church. Be in there like an eight-hour shift at a job.

His eyes drift over to me, staring.

I stare back.

He waves to me. Slowly, I wave back as him and his mama make their way over to the table to grab a plate full of food. I flick away hot tears and exhale the dull ache that's bubbling up in my chest. But pain and grief gon' do what they do. Ignoring all your feels.

The memories of me and my mama at church pop in my head. They all move so fast, my brain itself can't catch up.

My mama's screams in a fevered pitch, rising like a tide until . . .

My eyes spring open.

Nothing but bombs bursting in the air.

I don't seize up or panic when I notice the orange-and-pink sun surrendering, letting the moon have her turn. Adjusting to the tilting world around me, I notice that the church parking lot is like a ghost town. A chorus of crickets, slob on the side of my mouth, and fire-crackers in the background remind me that I must've fallen asleep.

I pull out my phone to text Taye:

Wya?

Three dots appear on the screen.

Taye finally texts back:

Home. Carlwell doin' the most. Please come get me. They left to go to the store.

I'll be damned if I have to wait six more years for him to turn eighteen to get out. Ain't no telling what Carlwell been doing to him or how he treats him. Carlwell's wife, Ms. Sonya, wouldn't do shit. She'd just sit there. Hell, sometimes even watch.

She probably was scared of him too. But in my book, she guilty by association.

With one hand, I pull the seat up, and with the other, I text back:

Omw.

CHAPTER TWO

THE HUDSONS LIVE ON SIMMSVILLE ROAD.

Ain't much changed about this neighborhood. A slew of Section 8 brick apartments at the end of the cul-de-sac. Ghosts of graffiti markings on a fading green transformer. Toys and trash cans scattered like treasure from a lost empire. Clothes hang lazily from a saggy clothesline. In the distance, a Waffle House sign towers over the hood like a ghetto Statue of Liberty.

The house looks damn near the same. Creamy white. Chipped paint. Sloped wooden steps. The patchy grass ain't been cut in forever. On the outside of the gate, right in the front, is the rusty black mailbox. Carlwell's trifling ass used to beat the mailman to it every month on the third. That's when the checks from the state would come. He spends the money on bullshit, doesn't pay any type of bills, and from what I remember about staying here, barely gave enough to Ms. Sonya to even buy groceries.

After socking him in the face, I was met with two social workers before I could even say, "Fuck you." He called them so quick because one, he's scared as hell of what I can do. Two, he a mean-ass bastard with a shitty soul.

My last foster home was the Markhams'. They were cool. They ain't talked to me crazy or put their hands on me or nothing like you always hear with foster kids. Mr. Bill Markham did have a handful of rules, though. Basically, I couldn't be out all night, or he'd lock the doors on my ass. Do my homework and don't eat his salt-and-vinegar chips. That's literally it. I can still hear his loud-ass chewing like he ain't had no sense. The sound of licking his fingers still got me heated.

So after some finessing and testing out of high school this past May, I emancipated myself from the system and moved out.

And now my seventeen-year-old ass is officially an adult and committed grand theft auto and now kidnapping.

I text Taye back.

> Pulling up.

I park a few houses down to make sure there are no cars in the Hudsons' driveway. Everybody and they mama out tonight, partying and gliding back and forth from one another's yards with glistening bottles and aluminum foil pans full of artery-clogging delectables. Simmsville always hella lit on the Fourth.

A few seconds later, I text Taye.

> I'm here. But don't come outside yet.

> Bet. I'm ready.

With more firecrackers popping off in the distance, I remind myself I gotta make this quick. Can't get caught, or Carlwell will call the police on me. I am not trying to spend the first moments of freedom in a jail cell. Plus I don't know enough about my powers to even break out.

I lean back, slipping a hat over my head, and shift my eyes to my right. From what I remember, old-ass Mrs. Clara lives across the street; she will call Carlwell in a quick minute if she notices me. She's one of them nosey, *ain't got better shit to do–ass* neighbors.

Getting out of the car, I trek across the street. Back in incognegro mode. Cackling laughter of drunk aunties and uncles filters from the houses. Little kids float by with sparklers in their hands. One of them gives me an up-and-down, sticks her tongue out, and disappears down the street. *Lil' badass.* When I approach the house, I hop over the wooden fence and go to the back door. Damn. The shit is still locked. I almost forgot that me and Taye snuck away that one time. We got caught no less than a day later, and Carlwell had the back door sealed shut.

Wayment—the kitchen window is usually open. Soon as I make my way to the side and hop on the air conditioner, the whole thing cuts on, blowing hot air up my shirt. Stretching till I reach the windowsill, I try to look inside the house. The curtains block my view.

I text Taye.

Open the window.

...

Where?

By the kitchen. Hurry up.

A few long seconds pass by and Taye comes to the window, cheesing hard.

"Open the damn window!" I whisper under my breath. Fooling with him, my ass finna get straight caught.

Taye opens the window, allowing enough space for me to climb through. "Bruh, why you ain't use the front door?" he asks.

The look I give him is enough to make him think about what he just said.

"Oh, my bad." He reaches for me and pulls me inside the house.

It's wild. Taye has grown a few inches taller. I figured he'd be a late bloomer because the last time I saw him, he was running around the yard, short as hell. But now he's about tall as me. And I'm five-ten. He's still lanky, though. Big head and saucer brown eyes with a mischievous grin. Taye's twelve going on thirty, which means he thinks he knows everything. He's smart as hell and deserves so much more. We may not be blood, but we're brothers, and I have to protect my little brother from the bullshit this world got to offer.

"Malik . . ." His voice is deep, lips cracking into a childish grin. Lines riddle his forehead as he goes in to wrap his long arms around me. They're like branches on a tree. All I can do is hug him back. Take him in. It's hard, but I hold back thug tears. That guilty feeling of a year and a half not being able to hold him hits me hard.

The memory of that stupid cop and that social worker pulling me away from Taye's arm still haunts me to this day. I could kick Carlwell's ass for making me miss almost two important years of Taye's life. But hugging Taye and seeing him, this feeling right now, are better than using any magic.

When I pull back, Taye quickly hides his left arm. I grab it and notice a small bruise snaking on his forearm like a necklace. His brown eyes dance around awkwardly, and his body language stiffens.

"It's nothin'," he starts to lie, and pulls his arm back behind him. There's one thing Taye can't do, and that's lie to me.

"Where he at?"

His gaze falls, landing on the floor. "The store, remember? Him and Ms. Sonya went to Walmart."

Walmart ain't nothing but a mile away from the house. Usually they don't do too much shopping, the way Carlwell be getting on her nerves in the grocery store. They used to stay arguin' about her buying real expensive meat. He'd make her put a pack back and pick up one that's literally seven cents cheaper. They're probably already on their way back to the house.

"I'm so glad you're here." Another hug from Taye melts the steaming anger away.

"Me too," I say back, hugging him tighter. "I told you I was coming to get you."

The inside of the house ain't changed much. Nothing but two bedrooms, old-ass furniture, and a small flat-screen TV in the living room that Carlwell always watched the evening news on. In the kitchen, the dishes are put up. Clean and neat. This is Ms. Sonya's sanctuary, and you can tell. That's one thing she don't play. But the refrigerator got a damn lock on it.

All I can do is shake my head. "I see nothing's changed."

Taye laughs himself silly because he knows what I'm talking about. Taye don't take a lot of stuff seriously, either. Always have a reason to laugh. That's his gift. You can have the worst day, but when he steps in the room, his laughter fills you up more than any negativity that tries to weigh you down. I hope he doesn't lose that.

"Carlwell be trippin' all the time, Malik." Taye groans, bringing me back.

We both cross into the living room. "Well, get ya stuff, we ain't got long."

Taye disappears up the stairs, and I ramble through everything, filtering through unopened mail and cutouts of old Burger King coupons right by the front door. Sonya still on that. She's one of those types that'll do all that grocery shopping and stop on the way home and grab something at the local Burger King. She'd be like, "I ain't cookin' tonight, so y'all order somethin'."

I'm trying to look for cash, but it's nothing but past-due bills. Carlwell stays owing folks.

Cars pass by. I rush to the window to peek through the blinds.

It ain't nobody.

"Taye, hurry the hell up!" I try to whisper-yell at him from downstairs. Over by the window, I catch a glimpse of a dent that's in the wall. Something in me freezes. That's the same dent where Carlwell fell after I socked his ass in the face.

Another reminder of how fast my life can change.

Not even a minute later, Taye runs back downstairs with his whole world packed in one duffel bag. Everything on the outside gets louder as crackling fireworks blaze the sky.

"I'm ready." He starts zipping the bag up with a goofy-ass smile cresting on his face.

"Cool, let's go—"

The front door swings open. Taye jumps and falls back. It's Carlwell.

Haloed by the blues and reds from firecrackers. Tall. Scraggly, with a receding hairline and brown-stained teeth from that smelly-ass tobacco. Damn, he looks kinda old in the face too. I guess almost two years of being low-down will do that to you.

"The hell you doin' here?" He still sounds the same. A gruff growl of a voice.

"Wadup, Carlwell." I stand in front of Taye, acting as a shield. Just like when I was living here.

Carlwell steps more into the living room. "Thought yo ass was down in Georgia." One thing for sure ain't changed—that breath. Straight halitosis.

"I came for Taye."

He glances over at Taye, noticing the duffel bag in his hands. "Taye ain't goin' no gahdamn where with you."

No matter what, I make sure I keep my body between him and Taye. "You wanna bet? I'm takin' him outta here."

Carlwell's eyes flicker. Oh yeah, he's shaken but trynna hide it. One wrong move and I'll use my powers to break his arm, and me and Taye can dip out.

"You best get outta my house fore I call the police," Carlwell says, trying to make his voice sound all hard. Ain't nobody scared of his ass.

Ms. Sonya steps in with grocery bags in her hands. She looks more worn-out than the last time I saw her. A bit thin. Gray hair peeks from her pinned-up fake ponytail. A few wrinkles of that hard life dented into her face now.

"Malik, what you doin' here?" she asks, baffled as hell to see me.

"I came to get Taye. He ain't stayin' here no more." I turn to Taye. "Go wait outside."

He doesn't move. It's like he's frozen, looking at Carlwell like he seeing the devil himself.

"Taye," I say again, with a much deeper bass in my voice. His eyes finally shift to me. "Go wait outside like I said."

He starts to move. Carlwell goes to grab him. Taye screams—sending me all the way back to that night. It's my mama, screaming.

A jet of green light circles her, pulling her in. I see my seven-year-old self fighting through the torrent of wind, trying to reach for her.

"Malik!"

Taye's scream brings me back to the present, seeing Carlwell yoking Taye up.

Pop! Every lightbulb in the house explodes. Everybody stops, frozen in the darkness. The TV cuts on, providing a little light. Carlwell reels back, scared like heyell.

"Like I said, Taye is coming with me."

The seriousness in my voice gives Taye enough courage to yank himself away from Carlwell. He stalks toward the kitchen. Soon enough I hear him climb out the window. I turn back to Carlwell and Ms. Sonya.

"Malik, you need to get on outta here." Ms. Sonya looks real scared between Carlwell and me. "We don't want no trouble."

I straight ignore her ass.

"Yo lil' ass best do like she says and get the hell on outta here. Fore I—"

"Before you what?" I say back, grabbing Taye's duffel bag. My lips curl into a smirk. "Oh, you must've forgot."

He remembers. The twitching of his eye says so. All that weird shit I used to make happen around the house, scaring the hell out of him.

"Carlwell . . . ," Ms. Sonya nervously says to him. I glare at her, and she backs away, anxious. She remembers too.

That gives me enough credence to move toward them. "I told you, don't put ya hands on my lil' brotha."

"I'm callin' the police." Ms. Sonya takes out her cell phone and dials.

Before she hits that last number, my hand whips forward so fast, I don't even have time to think. The phone smashes against the wall.

"Oh, Lawd Jesus!" Ms. Sonya screams.

"Ain't nobody scared of you, lil' nigga. You ain't shit without dem powers."

I step up closer to him. Man-to-man. My fingers form into a

tight fist, making a swirl of blue light travel up and down my arm. *Oh shit. It didn't do that last time.* Quickly, I snap out of it and hold my hand up. Another pop, and now the windows in the house shatter. Even the house sways back and forth.

Something about this one feels different.

I don't know what it is, but it feels like I'm supercharged.

The more I focus, the more the blue light sparkles between the palms of my hands like a thousand stars. My breathing picks up as all I can think of is pain. A sickly sound of bones crunching. Carlwell stumbles, holding his twisted fingers. They snap like twigs. One by one.

"The hell you doin' to me, boy!" Carlwell groans in agony.

Everything is a blur. Like a rising tide, the energy flows through the house, making the lamps flicker and the walls shake from the volatile wind. Mirrors and cheap-ass decorations fall off the wall.

Shifting my focus back on Carlwell, I raise my hand. He's thrown against the wall, pinned like that picture of Jesus on the cross. My other hand points toward Ms. Sonya, and she dips to the ground, yelling. And then I glance over, shutting the front door in one motion.

"Boy, you betta put me down!" His ass is scared now. The ball of blue fire grows even more between my fingers.

Only thing is, it doesn't freak me out this time.

"Malik, please, just leave him alone; don't kill him," Ms. Sonya begs, and even starts to pray.

"Now I told you if I find out you put hands on my brother, I'd know. Didn't I?" I lean closer, making the ball of blue fire swirl around my arms. "Didn't I?"

The energy from my magic feels like tiny needles, pricking and centering to the palms of my twisting hands. Memories flash in my eyes. Taye crying. Me being thrown into the car, hearing Taye scream my name into the cold, crisp air. This pain, this hurt, it gives fuel to my magic.

And I'm ready to burn this bitch down.

An abrupt motion of my hand, and Carlwell starts to choke on his own spit.

"Malik, STOP!!!" Ms. Sonya yells.

But to tell the truth, something in me can't. And to be quite honest, I don't want to.

"You killin' him!" Ms. Sonya just keeps screaming.

With my magic wrapping around his neck, choking him, I can feel his throat close, and his heartbeat slows down to the point I could count it beat by beat.

"Malik, STOP!!!"

When she screams, images of that night pop up in my head, my mama yelling and me standing there—not knowing what happened—and those dead eyes, peering up at me.

A rush of guilt fills me like water in a cup.

The energy from this blue light flows right back to me, and Carlwell drops on the floor like a sack of potatoes.

Ms. Sonya crawls to him as he desperately gasps for air. She throws a glare at me with all the hate in the world. I look down to my trembling hands.

"Chile, you ain't nothin' but the devil! You already killed ya mama—now you gon' kill my husband!"

I absorb the sting of fear and resentment from her. My eyes drift over to the window, noticing the sky light up in red and blues from the fireworks. But a shadow rushes across it. I blink a few times, brushing it off.

"I'm taking my brother," I struggle to say, getting eye to eye with Carlwell. "You got lucky this time. Don't come lookin' for Taye, or next time I ain't gon' stop." I snatch Taye's bag from the couch from when I dropped it.

"Take him, and you get the hell out!" Ms. Sonya says through tears, cradling Carlwell in her arms. There is real fear glazed over in her eyes when I glare at her. The same look of fear that my mama had.

Forcing down the guilt, I struggle to keep my trembling hands steady. The blue light finally dies out. Ms. Sonya's whimpering makes me raw. My eyes welling up as the weight of my magic yet again destroying somebody's life.

The next thing I know, I step outside into the sweltering night heat. Taye is watching by the mailbox, nervously waiting for me. There's an unnatural wind whipping around us. "What you do?" he asks innocently.

"Don't worry about that. Let's go," I tell him, avoiding his gaze.

We run to the car. Taye stops to admire it. "Daaayyyuumm, this you?"

"Yeah, it is. Put ya stuff in."

Taye zips closed his duffel bag, throws it in the back seat, and gets in. I crank the car up and peel out that bitch in a hurry.

"Where you get this car from?" Taye asks, and we're not even two minutes down the street. That's another thing about Taye; he asks way too many questions.

"I got it from a friend."

He smacks his lips, laughing while plugging his charger up. "Why you lyin'?"

"Put ya seat belt on."

We keep on driving until we reach the Pelham city limits. These tiny towns around here ain't nothing but a few stoplights, restaurants, and a grocery store away from the next town. Hell, all these towns can be one big city. Alabaster, Pelham, and right into the backway of Helena.

All the streetlights in front of us turn green, and there ain't no police around to make this day worse.

"Just gotta make one more stop, though."

WELCOME TO OLD TOWN HELENA
EST. 1877

Nostalgia digs its claws into me as I cross into a town I tried many a night to let go. It's like my mind becomes a drone, taking stock of a town of Little League baseball and soccer moms fighting for a parking spot at the local Publix Super Markets. A town where you'd want to grow old or raise a family. But in my world, it's a place of pain, chaos, and broken hearts. Split by train tracks surrounded by old buildings. Driving over the bridge that overlooks a small bank that leads to the Buck Creek waterfall, I curve right onto a familiar street. Lawley Street. The trees, the train tracks where Ms. Freda Jackson's kids got killed, a cluster of brick project homes, and our neighborhood church all in my POV. The car slides to a stop as I put it in park on the side of the road.

A brotha needs a beat. A moment to breathe.

"You good, Lik?" Taye asks.

The tightness in my chest comes back, along with a wave of nausea. Everything is spinning, and my hands meet the steering wheel, almost breaking it off. Letting the seat back, I roll down the window to let the cool breeze in.

"Yeah, I'm cool, Taye."

And I go back to try to steady my breathing.

My childhood neighborhood surrounds me: Liberty Heights. This neighborhood used to be the most lit place in Helena, especially during the summertime: Dinky rolling by in his Jeep Cherokee, blasting some of that Drake. Old folks sitting on their porches, fanning themselves. Everybody ran to Ms. Doll's house, trynna get a pack of Skittles, dill pickles, and the coldest Kool-Aid Jammers you could drink. Knowing me, I would beg my mama for a few dollars. She would dig in her purse for folded small bills, and the pack of sour straws would be mine. Finally, Wayne Allen would come by, rolling on his four-wheeler, giving all of us a ride. Each house lined on the side of the road all had different worlds and problems.

Right by that church, we used to stand there for the bus to come. Bus 99-55, and Tick's old man was our bus driver—a man with a glass eye. We used to crack on him, saying his ass could see in the future and past. Of course, I'd be the one he'd sit in the front as punishment, making all my friends in the back of the bus bust out laughing. Mama cussed him out cat raggedy in front of everybody one afternoon, and from then on, he ain't too much bother me. Across the street is Ms. Linda Faye's house. We used to ride our bikes between hers and Mrs. Christine Billings's house. People used to say she did Voodoo, and she'd turn you into one of her little dolls if you pissed her off. I even heard Auntie Denise say she'd put period blood in her boyfriend's spaghetti to make him fall in love with her.

After getting out of the car, me and Taye keep walking up the street. I notice it all. A few people on the porch look to see this *familiar* stranger in their neighborhood. Kids play in the yard. The uneven pavement. A weather-beaten stop sign that leans to the left. The last time I was here, everything seemed so big. But now it looks as though it's just a tiny little corner in the middle of nowhere.

The memories flash like a camera.

Colors of ghostly indigo and violet mesh as I see my play-cousins Tanisha and 'nem, playing and throwing firecrackers or slinging rocks at the passing train. I try to reach for them, but they all fade away like wisps of cotton candy.

"A basketball court." Taye runs over and tries to touch the net of the rim.

The basketball court is right down the street from my childhood home, and it was a place where the whole neighborhood would play twenty-one. It's where we'd have our ghetto version of baseball games. Our asses would play with metal bats and tennis balls. I can feel and hear our laughs whistle all around me.

Me and Taye keep walking.

And there it is. The house where happy memories once lived. The place of laughs and good cooking and music. Now it's all boarded up. A metal fence barricades the entire property. I'm thinking maybe it's trying to keep people out, but nah. It's trying to hold the secrets and heartache in. Weeds grow around it so high, they're trying to kiss the sun. Right on the porch, the pink paint chips away to ten years of nothing.

There was a little hill that led to our house where I would swim right in my blow-up pool. Mama couldn't really afford much, but I remember the day she bought me that minipool and I stayed in that pool till my hands became wrinkly.

"What is this place, Malik?" Taye's voice pulls me from memory lane.

At first, I don't answer. That night where it all happened, where my mama died, where I was surrounded by bodies, constantly replays in my head.

The words spill out of me like water. "This is where I grew up. With my mama."

Taye's eyes land on me and then back on my old house. "For real?"

My feet reluctantly move along the dirt, walking up to the fence. My fingers curl over the opening of the twisted metal part of the gate. The house is only a few feet away from me, yet it feels like a million miles. Mama is on the porch, laughing, a comb in her head and hair parted. A jar of Blue Magic hair grease sits on the side of her. She's laughing with Auntie Denise while she smokes a cigarette. They both cackle like a pack of hyenas.

The sound of the coming train screeching against the tracks brings me back.

"You never really talk about her," Taye mumbles. "I mean, we always heard the rumors, but I never believed you killed your own mama. You don't have that in you."

I can't even comment on that. Because the one thing I ain't trynna do—what the world already tries with boys like us—is take his innocence away.

"Well, at least you got me," Taye reminds me.

I low-key wipe the tears from my eyes because he's right. There's no use in holding on to bad memories when you can make new ones.

"Yeah, you right about that," I say, wrapping my arms around him. "C'mon. Time to start over. *Our* way."

We hop back in the car. I look back at my house, my old neighborhood, and I give it one last good-bye as it morphs into nothing but a blur.

Good-bye, misery.

Hello, new life.

CHAPTER THREE

I GOT PAIN, ANGER, AND MAGIC INSIDE MY DNA.
Skipping over a few songs, I stop when the shuffle lands back on Kendrick. Him rapping his street poetry gives my mind permission to remind me that this magic shit ain't no joke.

My eyes feel like sandbags, and my hands tremble over the steering wheel. Swerving from lane to lane, I can feel that nausea sloshing in the pit of my stomach. That's why I roll the window down, inviting the cool night air to chill my bones and throbbing headache. After driving for a few hours, we're about to cross from Mississippi into Louisiana. The stars and bursting fireworks make themselves known in the inky sky. A slew of distressed billboards showcasing TRUST JESUS hang about on the side of the freeway, taunting us sinners. But little do they know, the world itself is hell.

It's funny how your brain goes on autopilot as you trek across the open road. You can think of a million things, and your body, your mind, keeps you from crashing against the guardrail.

Maybe I went a little too far with Carlwell.

Naw. Bump that. He put his hands on Taye, and I wasn't having that. But that doesn't mean I can use Taye as an excuse to hurt somebody or act out of character. I do think that he could seriously be hurt.

I switch back over to the fast lane, and it takes a few swerves of me trying to justify breaking that mofo Carlwell down just like he tried with me. And now I'm subconsciously flicking away my inner angel and demon that are weighing down my shoulders because I am really trying to turn over a new leaf.

Shit.

The gas pump light sparks on the dashboard, snatching me back to this cracked reality.

Welp. It was fun while it lasted.

As I swerve from lane to lane, the dial creeps toward the letter *E*. Honestly, the reality of us trying to get to Cali becomes harder and pretty much damn near impossible.

We're gonna need money.

And fast.

Taye's groan makes me look over. He's asleep, but sweat pours down his forehead. Under the passing orange light, I clock him holding his stomach like he's about to throw up. He even starts to shake and lick his lips like he ain't had water in days.

I press my free hand to his cold, clammy forehead. "Taye, you good?"

He grunts and twists over to the other side. Wait a minute. I wonder, did Taye forget his insulin back at the Hudsons'? Damn it! Taye's diabetic. Ain't no way he can go too long without his insulin. If he does, we in big trouble.

A sign that reads EXIT 42 comes into my view.

"Taye, hold on, a'ight," I tell him, veering the car off the exit ramp.

We come up to a bright red light. I run it, making the wheels squeal. It must be God or somebody, because a gas station is right by the off-ramp, at the edge of the road. Sketchy as hell, but oh well.

Through the rearview, no cars are coming on either side. With nothing in sight, I flip the bitch right in the middle of the road and speed into the parking lot, stop next to a gas pump.

Hopping in the back, I rip through the duffel bag, throwing

out clothes. Searching anxiously for the very thing my baby brother needs at this moment.

My heart drops. No insulin. I flash back to Taye running out with his bag still unzipped. Must have fallen out during the commotion before we left the house.

"You gonna be okay, Taye. I'm about to get you somethin'." He keeps groaning in pain.

I hop out of the car, nervous as hell. A quick look inside the store and my empty-ass wallet with a few crumpled-up bills. Hesitation glues my feet to the concrete. Fuck it. I cross through the parking lot full of grimy gas pumps, a muddy puddle, and overflowing trash bins. The doors slide open as I rush in. On the left, there's a white man behind the counter, watching TV, looking hella bored. I head toward the back, grabbing a pack of Pop-Tarts and some crackers. I thought about stealing them and then just paying for the gas somewhere else. But I see the dude watching me like a hawk on the camera monitors beside him.

From the TV: *"Local teen Katia Washington's disappearance sparks heated march at the New Orleans Police Department . . ."*

Out of nowhere, my hands feel like a thousand needles are pricking at the tips of my fingernails. Then my whole body vibrates. I felt this same feeling back when I was at the group home with Alexis. We ain't really think nothing of it because we both got used to it, but this prickling feeling—nah, I ain't never felt this before. When I look over at the window, it looks like a shadow gliding across the glass.

I jump back. Almost shit a brick, it scared me so bad.

Somebody walks into the gas station with rhythmic footsteps tapping against the tile floors. The smell of smoke makes me peer up, clocking a tall Black man in a top hat, holding a cigar in his hand. He gives off *"Ain't nobody comin' to see you, Otis!"*—type vibes, and his skin shimmers like a brand-new penny. He maneuvers through the aisles in a purple suit, gyrating and humming to himself.

"These last two dollars . . ."

That song, though. It reminds me of when Uncle Butch used to play Johnnie Taylor at every barbecue.

The way this dude walks, it's like he's walking on air. He strolls up to the liquor section, tapping his foot against the tile floor.

Ole dude continues to sing, his voice rising an octave. *"These last two dollars . . . I'm not gonna lose."*

For some reason, I get a whiff of chocolate. The man bends forward, fingers lightly caressing each section of the bottles. The tingle moves onto the palm of my hand and continues to shoot up my arm like icicles.

What the hell is happening right now?

My trembling hands grab a bottle of orange juice, the pack of Pop-Tarts, and some crackers, and I limp to the front cash register. The white cashier dude behind the counter looks at me suspiciously and takes the snacks.

The total racks up fast with each beep.

"Aye, how much y'all gas is?" I ask him, stretching out the numbness in my fingers.

The cashier looks at me, annoyed. He points to the sign that's outside: $4.85/GALLON

The sign is in bright lights. A strained reminder that I don't have enough to make it outside the state.

"Okay, cool. Can I get gas too? Umm, fifteen on pump two."

After he totals up the snacks, he looks up, waiting for me to pay. "That's gonna be $25.49," he says. I glance down at my fingers, wrapped around a crumpled-up twenty-dollar bill. It's all I got left in the world.

Welp, looks like I'm gonna have to beg.

I look back to the dude that's behind the counter. "Look, man, I got a sick kid in the car, and we trynna get to the hospital." I lie on the last part. "He's diabetic, and I need this gas, bad. All I got is the twenty."

"Pay full price or you ain't gettin' gas."

That cigar smoke assaults my nose and taste buds.

"Yo, please, I need the gas. I'll—"

"Hey!" the cashier screams after the man. "You can't smoke back there."

The man puffs a ring of smoke like he doesn't give a damn. The cashier walks from behind the counter and storms up to the dude in the back. They start to argue, cussin' each other smooth out.

Fuck it. I'm stealing it. As soon as I grab the shit to go, an image on the TV snatches my attention. A Black girl with her fist raised in the air like she about to lead the march to freedom. She looks hella familiar. I squint, trynna get a good look at her.

On her shirt is the girl that the news was just talking about: *Katia Washington.*

A voice from a reporter comes on with Katia's picture on the screen. *"After a recent investigation, the NOPD was notified that Katia was a troubled teen. She was into drugs and . . ."*

The rising cussin' from the back pulls my attention, and the convex mirror on the ceiling shows the cashier dude's face changing colors. "You need to get ya ass outta here! Right now!"

The man in the top hat voice sounds gruff and nasally. "Cheap-ass gas station ain't got what I want anyway!"

The Mississippi pimp makes his way to the front, puffing one last smoke. He looks at me, tips his hat, and then gets swallowed up in the darkness outside.

That was hella weird.

The white dude goes back behind the counter. Slicking back his mullet. "You gon' have ta pay," he says under his breath, looking outside.

Lemme soften my tone just a bit. "Yo, please—"

He snatches the food away. "Ya know what, get your ass out of here, now!!!"

It all happens in a blur. That same blue magic from before activates with a mind of its own and throws the cashier dude against the wall of tobacco products, my shaking hands extended toward him. The blue light crackles between my fingers. Now I ain't even mean to do that. Looking over the counter, I see his ass is knocked the hell out.

Damn it!

As the energy from my magic ebbs, the fluorescent lights pulsate.

Ain't gotta tell me twice. I stagger out.

"Taye," I say, hopping back into the car. He ain't say nothing.

He ain't even moving. My heart plummets as I speed down the road. Through the rearview mirror, I sneak a glance to make sure nobody's following me.

I pull into this dark spot, away from everything.

"Here, you gotta eat this, Taye." I break off a piece of the Pop-Tart and try to put it in his mouth. Then twist the cap off the orange juice.

Taye is out.

Not responding. He's not even moving at all. Is he—

No!

No!!!

He slumps over. "Taye, wake up!" I shake him, refusing to let the warm tears break through my eyelids. "Taye, please wake up!"

There's a knock on my window. It's the Black dude from the gas station. He has a smug grin through the dark window. "Fuck off, bruh, we ain't got shit," I tell him.

He knocks again.

"You can't hear good?!"

And his ass knocks again. A'ight. Gotta use my magic on his ass. I roll my window down and whip my hand toward him. "I said, fuck off—"

My magic fizzles. I try again, searching for the anger and fear I felt in front of Carlwell.

And again, nothing.

Ole dude looks at me, a rumble of laughter in his chest.

Oh shit. This is it.

We about to die tonight.

"Calm down now, youngblood," he says, as if he's read my mind. "I ain't here to hurt ya." His accent slips into a Caribbean sound.

He leans down, glaring into the car at Taye. "He looks sick. He needs a healin'." Ole dude's deep brown eyes dance over to Taye, then back to me.

"Yeah, he needs dat healin'."

The hospital would be a no-go. Since Taye is a minor, they would ask all kinds of questions, and then boom, we're straight caught. I'm going to jail and Taye back with the Hudsons, and I'll die before that happens.

"Go'n 'head, heal him." The man winks. "I know what you can do, *Malik.*"

I'm confused. Scared. Sad. All in one. It rushes into me like a wave as I look back to Taye, seeing his body slumped in the passenger seat.

But then I realize— "How you know my name?"

"Because I know everythin'," he says with a thick accent. "Go'n 'head, use that *majik* to heal him."

Shaking my head. "I can't."

Shit. But I gotta do something. Taye still doesn't move. Pulling him into me, I hold him like a baby.

A lump forms in my throat, and tears fall from my eyes. "I'on wanna hurt him."

"You won't. Trust me."

That's the thing. I don't trust nobody. Last time my magic affected somebody I loved, I hurt them in the worst possible way, and if that happens to Taye, I'll die.

My shaky hand hovers frantically over Taye, and I focus all my energy on imagining him being his goofy self again. Him laughing. Making me laugh. All those images pop up in my head, and then it manifests into an orb of blue light, engulfing the whole car. It shakes back and forth.

The blue light on my arm steadies, traveling up and down Taye's whole body. But it siphons back into me and snuffs out just as quick as it starts.

Everything around me starts to spin.

Nausea creeps up in me like a rising tide about to spill out on the dashboard.

When I try again, nothing.

A cloud of self-doubt hovers over me. How the hell am I gonna be able to take care of Taye and keep him safe? Maybe I'm in over my head. Maybe I do mess up everything. And I put this innocent boy in danger.

When I get out of the car, I struggle to keep my balance because my head spins fast and both my ears ring. A wave of dizziness hits me, and just like that, I'm on the ground.

Blinking through the brain fog, I see ole dude start to laugh, letting the smoke escape through his nostrils as he slowly walks around the car.

"You real funny, youngblood. Usin' all that majik, huh?"

I stare unblinking at my hands. "How did I do that?"

He ignores me and puffs on his cigar till the ashes fall on the door. Whirling smoke filters out of his mouth and stretches into the car like a pair of ghostly talons. It crawls hungrily all inside the car, licking the door handle, the steering wheel, the gear shift, and even over Taye's whole body.

My head still spins as I try to get on my feet and fuck ole dude up, but I can't.

"Taye!" I struggle to say.

This dude in the top hat shadow hovers over me. Smoke that escapes from his lips wraps around me, and everything on me feels brand-new. I spring up, fast.

When I make it back to the car, Taye sharply inhales and then goes back to sleep, snoring. I wrap him in my arms, feeling his skin warming up with each panted breath I give.

"How did you—how'd you know I got powers?"

The man takes out his cigar and chuckles. Again, there it is. The smell of chocolate. It permeates all around us. "You'd be surprised at what I do know, *Malik Baron*." My name rolls off the tip of his tongue like it's dipped in honey.

Something tells me this man is different. Different like me.

"Man, who are you? What you do to us?" I ask, shocked. I keep half of my body inside the car because even though he seems like he's here to help us, I don't know this dude from a can of paint.

Slowly, he turns to me, tipping his hat. His eyes suddenly turn crystal blue like ocean water, and his lips part, revealing a set of perfect teeth. No lie, they're so perfect, he looks like he swallowed a handful of stars.

My breath catches because I ain't never seen no Black man with crystal blue eyes before in all my life.

He laughs and coughs on the cigar. "They call me *Bawan Samedi*. But you can call me Sam. Or whatever ya like." He moves like a gliding shadow from the back of the car to the front.

A flame flickers from his thumb, and he lights his cigar back up. Nerves bundle up at the pit of my stomach when I hear his thunderous laugh rumble in his chest.

He puffs, creating a halo of smoke dancing across his lips. "You need to go see her."

"See who?"

Another puff. And *swish!* Out of nowhere, a red envelope falls on the windshield. It looks fancy as hell. On the back, a perfectly stamped seal, and right on the front is my name spelled in fancy gold ink that glints under the moonlight.

Could it be from my mama?

The question hangs on my shoulders. It even squeezes my heart. I don't know why I'm getting all worked up, because I'm a hunnit percent sure she's been dead for the last ten years.

I rip the envelope open, and a picture of me as a baby falls out. WTF? And just like that, words begin to etch themselves on the piece of paper in perfect cursive.

Dear Malik Baron,

I know you have nothing but questions, and you'll be happy to know I have nothing but answers. You may not remember me, but I am your grandmama Aya. The mother of your mama, Lorraine. I am writing this letter to tell you I am so sorry for not being in your life when I had the chance. But I am here now. I would love for you to come stay with me here in Louisiana. You have a home and a family waiting for you.

I do hope this letter reaches you. And just know that

I love you, Malik; I always have. I'll be expecting you soon, baby.

Love, Mama Aya

Mama Aya? A home?

In Louisiana, no less. The fancy-looking words dance in my eyes, and the paper almost flutters to the ground. I glance back at Taye, who's still sleeping in the front seat.

I try to process this shit. Part of me is pissed the hell off, because why she ain't reached out to me after all these years?

"Mama Aya. Ya grand-mère," the Samedi dude says in a puff of smoke. He looks to Taye with a nod. "Don't believe everythin' 'bout that night, youngblood. All the answers you've been lookin' for, she got 'em."

My trembling fingers grab the letter tighter.

I have a grandmama.

"Y'all don't need to be goin' to no California." I give him a look like, *How you know?* Maybe he's a mind reader or some shit. "Everythin' you wanna know is down in Dessalines Parish. With her. And she gon' help that boy."

Finally, I got enough strength to speak. "Man, I don't have enough money or gas to get to nowhere to be honest."

The words leave my mouth before my brain can catch up. *Am I really considering this shit?*

Shaking his head, he puffs a ring of smoke into the night air and chuckles to himself. "Yo worryin' 'bout da wrong *thang,* youngblood."

Just like that, he snaps his fingers, and the car instantly cranks up. I look inside, and on the dashboard, I see it has a full tank of gas.

Oh shit.

Magic . . .

"Address on the back of that letter," he reminds me, dabbing out his cigar. Ashes fall to the ground in slow motion. "C'mon, I'll ride wit'cha. Show you the way."

He heads for the back seat of the car.

"Aye, uh-uh. Nah. We don't know you."

Another lit cigar appears in his hands. "A'ight. I hear ya. Well, you'll be seein' me very soon. *Veeeeery* soon."

Swooosh. He's gone.

Whaaaaat?

I'm like them old cartoons when their jaws drop to the floor, because did this nigga just jump into the air and fly off like Superman?

After I get myself together, I find my fingers grazing over the gold lettering of my name again. But this time, it's a feeling in the pit of my stomach. Something pulls at me.

Telling me I need to go.

I climb back into the car, letting the trepidation and possibility cloud my mind. My fingers wrap around the steering wheel. Putting the car in drive, I let us get swallowed up by darkness, hopping back on the interstate.

I take a deep breath.

And the high-mast freeway streetlamps light my path as I go to meet my *grandma*.

CHAPTER FOUR

YOU WANNA MAKE GOD LAUGH, TELL HIM YA PLANS.
My auntie Denise used to tell me that whenever I told her I wanted be this or that when I grew up. An astronaut. A lawyer. Or maybe on TV somehow. But as the years went by, I learned you gotta put away childish things. Because in my world, Black kids ain't got time to just . . . be. We take two steps forward just to get knocked ten steps back. God forbid we be silly enough to offer up silly prayers that fall on deaf ears.

Maybe God does laugh at our pain.

As we drive on this dark-ass freeway, the red envelope that's stashed on top of the dashboard beckons every single curiosity I have in me. *Mama Aya*. First off, weird name. Secondly, if she really is my grandma, then why the hell did I have to spend the past ten years in hell, going from the group home to the Hudsons to the Markhams?

Why has she waited till now?

More importantly, why she ain't ask about her daughter? My mama . . .

The granite city skyline sparkles as we cross over a bridge under the morning sky. A yawn forms in the back of my throat, which got me stretching out my arm. Everything on my body hurts from yesterday's encounter. My head swims, full with questions.

The exit I'm supposed to take reveals itself a little too quickly, so

I swerve off the freeway until we float through a small neighborhood outside of town, deep in the countryside, where the city life fades into the distance. The lettering of this lady's address is tattooed on my brain as I move through the morning traffic. Under the harsh gaze of the sun, Black folks do what they always do and hang out in the yard, sitting on cars, observing as we pass by. Off to the side, a group of niggas is huddled on the street, playing basketball. One of them dunks in the no-net rim. Among them, a mutual acknowledgment of skills as they crack up, laughing and roaring cuss words at one another.

It is hot as hell. Muggy. Humid. That type of heat makes your sweat feel like syrup and build in places only God knows about. July in the dirty Souf ain't no joke. My hand reaches for the AC, turning the knob. The cool air hisses from the vents as we continue to drive. To my right, it's a little girl sitting between her mama's legs with a labyrinth of cornrows exposed to high sun. Her face scrunched up, looking mad as *heyell.* "Tender-headed self," Mrs. Arlene would tell my play-cousin Justina as she would get her hair done the day before school.

We pass by an army of construction workers in orange vests, zipping by, spilling into the streets. One of them steps out with a stop sign. This gives me a chance to survey the area a little bit more. On their dirt bikes, two boys right around Taye's age, popping wheelies. They soar through, buzzing like flies trying to outrun a swatter. They duck and dodge the construction while their laughter fills the morning sky. Then they get swallowed up in the rising dust.

Everybody seems like they're on their own beat here.

The hustle and flow of Black folks just . . . living.

We stop at a red light. The drum of thick bass from a chromed-out Escalade pulls up beside us, bumping some of that bounce music with a cloud kush blooming from the rolled-down windows. The spinning silver rims will make you hypnotized just by looking at them. A cross with red-and-black beads dangles from the rearview mirror.

The dude in the front seat lifts a white Styrofoam cup to drink while his other tattooed arm grips the steering wheel. His face is slender and his hair long, like twisted vines. If the Black Jesus posted on Black folks' wall went missing, he's driving this truck right now. His lips spread when he looks over at us, revealing silver grills. He offers up a *wadup* nod and speeds off when the light turns green.

Farther down, I keep driving until everything around us fades away into nothing but tall tangled bodies of trees and an open dirt road. An ocean of neatly groomed sugarcane and waist-high stalks surrenders to the stingy, lukewarm breeze. The land coils into a calm bend, and there are a cluster of rusted tractors and a gaggle of farmhands tending rows of emerald green fields. If anything other than rain waters the tilled soil, it's the sweat of their brows.

We turn off into a swampy-looking area where it's supposed to be Dessalines Parish. A small part of town where I'm not even sure if a gas station is nearby. The address on the letter and the GPS on my phone point straightforward. Secretive. I gotta be going the right way. Soon as we cross over, Taye's eyes spring open. He wipes the drool from the side of his mouth. My right hand meets the back of his head, relieved. "I'm glad you awake."

"Where we at?" he says as he scratches his throat and jams his index finger in his ear to relieve an itch.

"We ran into somebody," I tell him. The red envelope resting on the dashboard, posing as a sharp reminder that I'm probably making a big mistake. "Ya insulin must've fell out when we was back at Carlwell's house. But there was this guy back at the gas station said he's gonna make you all better."

Taye rolls down his window. The sweltering heat and the smell of peppery air assault my nose. After a beat of recollection, his eyes land on the letter. Instantly, he grabs it to read.

His face twists in confusion. "A grandma?"

Yeah, the words sound hella foreign to my ears. So much so, I can't even bring myself to answer.

"Don't worry. He said she can help you feel better. After that, we on to Cali."

A small corner turns into a long stretch of trampled ground, deeply rooted with dips and patches of grass. Overarching Spanish moss and oak trees bend above us like they're trying to hear our thoughts and deepest secrets. Dust rolls across this beautiful, endless swampy land. Somewhere in the distance, we see rows of sugarcane. The ground, deeply rutted with tread marks, slopes itself into the marshy Mississippi River. Right at the edge of the bank, the glimmer from the sunlight reflects off the rippling surface of the water.

When Taye lets down the window even more, I get a whiff of the musty compost and the smell of the gulf. He snaps a picture of tall white birds taking flight, and I wrap my fingers around the steering wheel, trying not to turn back around and say to hell with this. Instead my stomach churns tricks, letting me know that we are edging closer and closer.

Chairs, a collar of a vegetable garden, and an old chariot wheel melted into the earth comes into view like a mirage. Surrounding the chariot wheel are tangling weeds that seem to dance along with the soft breeze. I pay attention to everything, except for what's before us. And that's a big-ass tree. I mean, this tree looks tall enough to touch the feet of God. On the branches are blue rusted bottles hanging down.

That's weird. . . .

The closer I drive to the front yard, the more my hand tingles. Just like last night. My whole body is on vibration mode. My head starts to hurt too. Tapping my foot on the gas, I force myself to take a deep breath. My hands meet my forehead, flicking away sweat. I'm not sure if that was the magic or the nerves because I'm about to meet this woman who "claims" to be my grandmama.

"You all right?" Taye asks.

"Yeah," I say all breathy.

Out nowhere, the car stalls, losing power. We both get out of the car.

Up ahead in the middle of the clearing stands a faded white plantation-style home. Two stories with a big screened-in wraparound porch. Two rocking chairs angled to face each other. Big plants are placed on each end. White clapboard siding, tin roof. Weathered shingles and hung shutters. I can't tell if it's the front or the back. Obviously a bit ramshackle because vines and roots snake up and down the side of the house like it's been here for damn near a hundred years. A brick stepping-stone path leads to the screened door. A black—wayment, black roosters shoot across the yard?

Me and Taye immediately stop in our tracks. Exchanging the same look. *I know that ain't . . .*

We keep walking. Right off on the side, a little garden area. Purple and yellow flowers spring up. Tomatoes, watermelon, all kinds of vegetables stick out.

Like distant shadows, two people dancing from one side to the other. A few steps more, I immediately recognize one of them.

Ah, hell naw! That's the dude from last night.

He twists a woman around. Moving and shaking, they both grind up on each other. The old folks where I'm from would say they're basically hunchin'.

"Whew, chile!" the woman dancing with Baron Samedi shouts. Immediately, I can tell her vibe is a dignified type that'll make you believe God is a Black woman. A scarf wraps around her head as if it's a crown. Sharp features. Very regal. Her silky brown skin beams under the sunlight while she holds a mason jar in her hand.

Music spills out from the house through the windows. One of them old-sounding songs that are played on a record player.

Time is on my side . . .

"You betta quit," she says, and shimmies her shoulders. They start grinding on each other again. "Doncha start nothin' you can't finish."

Samedi burst out laughing, with a plume of smoke leaving his lips. "Oh, I can finish just in time. 'Cause"—he starts singing—"*time is on our side . . .* yes, it is!"

The woman finally notices us walking up. Her hands glide over her eyes to shield them from the unrelenting sun. "Oh, hey, baby . . ." Her high-pitched voice doesn't have the same accent as the Samedi-whatever dude. She sounds just like a Black auntie in the middle of Louisiana. She cracks a smile at Taye. His excited and confused ass waves back and then slaps his leg, killing a mosquito.

"How you doin', youngblood? This my sweet laaaaady, Brigitte," the Samedi dude says to me, and kisses the giggling woman until she's helpless.

All of us meet in the middle of the yard.

"Have mercy on me; it's good to finally meet ya." *Brigitte* pulls me into a tight hug that'd make a church lady jealous. You can just smell the mango shea butter coming off her skin. "Chile, you real handsome."

"Brigitte," a stern voice shouts from inside of the house. "Come turn dis music down and peel these shrimps."

Brigitte rolls her light eyes and winks at Taye. "Yes, Mama Aya." She starts to leave, but not without kissing the Samedi dude all over. "You betta be ready," she tells him, and disappears behind the screen door.

"Hot damn, woman! You gon' rock my whole world." Samedi turns around to look at us. A toothpick swivels at the corner of his mouth.

"Mhmm. That's a woman for ya right chere. Y'all don't know nothin' 'bout dat. That cat'll make that dog go buck wild." He hops back on the porch, laughing and landing with a thud on the creaky step. "*Gen ou ye*. I knew you was gon' find it. About damn time y'all showed up."

"Yo, you ain't trick me, did you? You said my—you said this Mama Aya can help Taye."

He takes the toothpick out his mouth. "I know what *I* said."

My suspicion rises. "Who is you, man?"

"We been over this, youngblood," he says, snickering to himself. "You can call me Sam. Uncle Sam. I don't give a damn." He places the toothpick back in his mouth. "Ah, shit, that rhymes. Ayyye, Brigitte, I'm a gahhhdayum poet!"

His words from last night still ring in my ears. And his eyes, his crystal blue eyes. That still got me wilding.

"You made da right decision," he says. With a quick turn to Taye, he nods. "Wassup, kid?"

Taye shyly waves and gives him a half-hearted smile. "Hey."

From the inside, the music fades into stillness. This Samedi dude cuts his eyes at me and Taye and then back to the opening screen door. From it, an older woman steps out on the porch with her clenched hands on her hips. She isn't taller than that Brigitte lady, but she seems like she runs things around here. It's the way she steps on the porch like it's a platform. She got that boss energy. Her hair is wrapped in a shiny black scarf that looks like diamonds in a midnight sky. The sun glints off her mahogany skin as she steps off the porch, meeting me and Taye in the middle of the yard. For a minute, we just look at each other. Taking each other in. Her deep brown eyes flick from me to Taye, then back to me as if she's taking a mental picture.

Something inside me knows.

This is my grandma—Mama Aya.

"Well, hello there." The way she talks, it sounds like she's not even from this time.

"Who is you?" I ask, trying to get her to say it out loud.

Her lips curl like she's one of the old ladies at a church revival who made the collard greens and potato salad. "Most folks call me Mama Aya. But you . . . well, you can call me Grandma."

My bullshit detector tweaking.

The Samedi dude bursts out laughing. "Look at him, Mama. All shooketh."

She notices the letter that's clutched in my hand. "I see you got my invitation."

I give Samedi a deadpan look. "He said you wrote this for me."

"'Course I did, cher. I told ya, you're my grandbaby."

"I ain't nobody's baby," I snap.

That lands for a beat. She and Samedi trade a *who the hell he talkin' to* look.

"Well, you ain't no baby no mo', that's fa'sho," she comments while circling me.

"What you want?" I ask, keeping my eyes on her. "Why you write me this letter?"

51

She takes another deliberate step around me as if I'm on the chopping block. I can feel the vibrations all over my arms, tugging at the palms of my hands. Something tells me she feels them too.

"Come on in dis house. I know y'all hungry, and I know I got some explainin' to do."

No muscle in me moves at her command. "Wayment—he said you were gonna help my little brother."

Taye presents himself right beside me. She throws a grin his way. "Oh, you ain't got to worry about that," Mama Aya says back.

"Hold up—I need you to heal him."

She sucks her teeth. "That chile don't look broken to me."

"He got real sick last night, and if you ain't gonna fix . . . heal him, then we can be out."

The adults throw each other a subtle glance.

"Look, I ain't trynna be disrespectful." I feel Taye's hand on my arm, signaling for me to calm my ass down. "But I don't play about him or his health. Plus, you can just be anybody."

Mama Aya steps forward. "Malik Jaques Baron. Ya just had a birthday on June thirtieth, and you were born right here in this house. Slapped ya on yo naked ass myself." She points to her house. Nothing about it feels familiar. "You moved around a lot; your last foster parents were the Markhams. You had that lil' run-in with a gas station attendant cuz you were tryin' to save this sweet baby. Am I right?"

The skepticism antennae on a thousand right now.

Maybe Samedi ass told her?

My eyes land back on her. And my silence is confirmation to her question.

"Now come on in da house like I say. Get on out dis heat." Mama Aya glides back into the house. Hesitation glues my feet to the ground.

"Come on in here; don't be scared." Samedi's hand lands on my shoulders, pushing me toward the mouth of the house.

Soon as we step inside, we enter a whole different world. It's the smell that hits me first and makes my toes curl. Activating some blurred memory I had stored away as a baby. It's that good cooking, peppery and fishy, making my stomach touch the back of my spine. I'm hungry as hell.

Through the foyer and into the living room, this seems like one of those houses that creak so much, you'd think it's singing something scary. It's old. Like time itself stood still right in this museum of a living room. The couches even look like they ain't been replaced in over twenty years. Adorned with doilies, a wooden coffee table, and when it comes to old Black folks' homes, they gonna have pictures of a Black Jesus and plastic all over their furniture. For the life of me, I never understood that shit.

Pictures of the family and mirrors grace the walls that ascend to the upstairs area.

One picture catches my attention—and that's my mama. She smiling and wearing a maroon-colored sweatshirt with a circular symbol on it that has a pair of hands, a book, and a flower, and gold words that read CAIMAN UNIVERSITY. The hell is a Caiman University? I never heard her say nothing about that. Then my eyes drift to the bottom of the wall, and there she is again, when she was little. Big smiles. Long pigtails with purple bows at the end. She's standing next to a little boy who gives a hard look. The pictures look kind of grainy. I turn away, feeling the hole in my heart getting wider.

"You're really Malik's grandmama?" I hear Taye nervously ask Mama Aya.

The word still makes every muscle in my body tense. She steps up to him, giving him a smile that's filled with so many unspoken words. "I am. And who might you be?"

He does that thing of putting his arm behind his back whenever he gets shy.

"I'm Taye," he tells her, then timidly corrects himself. "Ma'am."

"Well, nice to meet ya, Taye. You can call me Mama Aya." They shake hands. Taye lets out a sharp breath, and his body tenses. Mama Aya stares deep into him, like a snake hypnotizing its prey. "You hungry, sweet baybeh?"

"Yes, ma'am," Taye answers back, mystified.

"Taye, you good?" I ask. "Aye, what you doin' to him?!"

She lets him go. Taye blinks, relaxing and cheesing like he ain't got no sense. Breathing all kinds of crazy like he's high on life. "Malik, it's all gooood."

Mama Aya turns to Samedi, nodding. Both of them do that old people type of laugh where it rumbles in their stomach and chest before letting out. "Sam, take this chile into the kitchen, get him some of that bone broth that's been cookin' since last night. I'mma pick some of them milk thistles in the mawnin'."

They start to go. I step between Taye and Samedi. Taye turns to me. "Malik, chill. I'm hungry and tired. They seem cool."

"I wanna be able to see you."

I find this Samedi dude leaning against the wall. He winks at the both of us.

Taye says back all loud, "Talk to your grandmama. I'm good."

This Brigitte lady comes back in, peeling shrimps. "Doncha worry 'bout a thang. We'll take good care of him. Put some food in his belly. Make him feel all betta."

Me and Samedi clock each other. A nod. I guess he's keeping his word on this lady healing Taye.

I wanna argue back. But I let it slide. Taye shakes his head and disappears into the kitchen with her.

"C'mon, chile. Lemme explain myself," Mama Aya says, making her way down a long, dark hallway.

Through a white door, it's like we're back outside again. A sunroom. Flowerpots are splayed thoughtfully around the room. Mason jars full of dirt and springing flowers. I mean, there's a lot of them. Like I stepped back in Ms. Doll's candy shop in the back den of her house. Only thing is these jars that rest on Mama Aya's towering shelves aren't candy. With name tags plastered on the front of them, they seem like they're jars of dirt. ALLIGATOR FEET. RED DUST. ALFALFA.

What kinda shit is this?

I turn around, and I about jump out of my skin because on the far back wall are weird-looking masks. Over in the small corner is a table with a white linen cloth draped over it. On top are two long white candles that are lit, and factions of small pieces of food and water.

"You a devil worshipper or something?"

"Chile, ain't no devil worshippin' here." She continues to laugh one of them old people kinda laughs where they cough uncontrollably. "Whew, chiiiiile, you funny. This here is my ancesta altar."

What the fuuuuck?

Purple flower petals sprinkle from her hands. She starts to hum as she methodically places them in a grayish bowl on her *ancesta altar*.

An overworked ceiling fan raining down lukewarm air. From the outside, a loud whizz of the bugs singing their tune. A chair sits in a small corner, away from the fading sunlight.

"This is my lil' sunroom, where I keep all my flowers and thangs. My apothecary." Mama Aya walks up to one of the clearly slumped-over flowers, dried up in a brown jar. Dead. Her hand hovers over it. A whisper from her and the flower springs back to life. Just like that. She then goes over to a big bowl and pours in some liquid from a glass bottle.

I stand in the middle of the room, incredulous.

"You got magic powers too?" I ask, staring blankly at her as she put a white candlestick in a bowl full of water. It just floats. "You seem like you into somethin'."

She just keeps on humming as she waves her hand over the candle. Out of nowhere, it sparks with an orange flame.

"Oh, we all into a lot of sumthin'."

The cushion of a seat folds me in as I sit down. Questions flood my mind but dry up when they make it to my tongue. I'm still in shock by everything. I found out I got family in this world not even twenty-four hours ago. I glance up, seeing Mama Aya smiling as if she's holding the biggest secret in the world.

Bump this. "If you're really my grandma, how come I never know about you?"

"Me and ya mama, we had a real bad fallin'-out right when you were born."

I press for more information. "What kind of fallin'-out?"

To be honest, I ain't never even heard my mama talk about this woman before. After arriving at the orphanage or during nights staying with the Hudsons or Markhams, I always wondered what other family I had. My daddy, my grandparents, everybody on his side. I mean, growing up, people in Liberty Heights were considered family.

"Who's that chile with ya?"

"He's Taye. My little brother," I say back quickly, trynna get her back on topic. She looks hella confused. "My foster brother."

"And you's takin' care of him?"

Is she really asking *me* questions? "Now I do."

"And what about them folks he was stayin' with—"

I cut her off. "He doesn't need to be with them."

Another tense beat.

She walks over from the flower that she healed and sits down in the chair on my right, all calm and collected. Studying her, I see she really does favor my mama. They both do this thing with their eyes like they're staring at you deep in your soul. Like they know everything about you, more than you do yourself. This woman that sits in front of me doesn't even look the age to be a grandma. The ones I know got wrinkled skin, salt-and-pepper hair. Nah. "That Samedi dude said you'd help him if I come here."

I can tell she lets that settle. It's in the way her eyes shift and her lips crack into a smile that holds a thousand secrets. "He gon' be just fine," she says under her breath. *"Fais dodo, Colas mon p'tit frère."*

The air is sucked outta the room.

Tears well in my eyes because that song strikes a chord in me. "I remember that song."

"Because I used to sing it to ya when you was a baby." She pauses, then places a jar on a shelf. "You look just like ya mama. Them eyes. They so deep, chile. Deeper than the ocean itself."

The direct mentioning of my mama feels like a healed wound just been ripped back open. Because day by day, her face fades from my memory.

But alla this gives me ammunition.

"Why haven't you come for me? I mean, all those years, where were you?"

"We gettin' into it, I see."

I angrily pull the letter from my back pocket. "Yeah, in your letter, you said you had answers. I need some of them before I head back out." No lie, I still got Cali on my mind. To start over with Taye. "Why you ain't reached out sooner?"

"There was a lot of things at play, Malik. I made a lot of mistakes, especially with ya mama. You wasn't nothin' but a few days old when she took you, and me and her were just on two different pages. But I can assure ya that I thought about you every day for the past seventeen years and fought long and hard to get yuh back."

"This don't make no sense."

"What don't?"

"All of it. Look, I ain't trynna come at you like this, but you owe me. You owe me for the past ten years because I've been through hell."

"I know, baybeh, I know," she says with a hint of guilt in her voice.

"Do you?! Nah. You don't. And now you wanna come in and claim—" I'm trying not to get mad. But the more I look at her, the more I do. Those lonely—and I mean lonely—nights in foster care. The confusion and fear I had when it all first happened. My magic . . . sweeping over me like a blanket. Seeing all this, I now realize there were so many things I could have avoided.

"I know you're angry, Malik—"

"I'm too tired to be angry." The words themselves even catch me off guard. I guess that's some heavy truth for the both of us because she blinks back shame. "Do you know what happened the night she died?"

Mama Aya takes in this question silently. A look of concern flickers across her face. But she remains silent, which pisses me off.

"Look, if you ain't gonna be straight with me, then I don't need this."

As I head for the door . . .

"Your mama went down a different path."

My mind is telling me go, but my body is telling me to stay and listen.

"I ain't think it was right for her. But yo mama, she had a mind of her own. She thought she knew everythin'. Hardheaded self. Lawd. She was so headstrong. Kinda like how you is right now."

Tears well up in my eyes. Mama Aya looks to the floor for a moment. Something stirring . . .

"All we did was argue. . . . I was angry. She left. Took you with her. And I ain't seen her since."

The image pops into my head. It's like I'm inside the memory itself. Like a mighty storm, my mama stomped toward the door with me as a baby cradled in her arms. Tears and anger flash in her eyes.

"You can't control me no more!" my mama says.

"Well, you go on, then! You can't stay in my house no mo'! I can't believe you was at that school doin' alla that!" Mama Aya yells back at her.

They both look like they have a world of pain set in their eyes. Mama steps out into the sunlight, and the memory snuffs out like the light from a candle.

Mama . . .

"Like I said, I made many mistakes, baybeh. But if I had known what was going to happen . . . that you were left on your own . . . I ain't sensed none of that. Because if I did, I would've saved my baby girl and you."

Her words force me to pull the letter from the side of the chair I was sitting in. The picture of me as a baby falls on the table. Both of us are rocked to stillness as we stare at it.

"This is one of the only pictures I have of you," she whispers. Her deep brown eyes land on mine. "You grew up to be so beautiful. I know it don't feel like it, Malik, but I was there with you the whole time."

Another question dances on the tip of my tongue.

"If you're really my grandma, and you got magic just like I do, why you ain't come for me?"

"Baybeh." She stops, then continues. "I was angry, and stubborn, and scared. I missed my daughter, and more than anythin', I wanted to have you in my life. But I let her go, and I didn't look for her . . . for seven years. I could feel her out there the whole time, but I let her—you—go. All that time wasted. And then ten years ago, out of nowhere, our connection was just . . . gone. She was gone."

The memory comes to me. My mama screams, she looks at me, and the bright light blinds, and *boom*. My entire house and childhood blow up in my face.

"I tried to find you as soon as I felt it, but it was like you were hidden from me. I thought she must have cast a root, done something to keep me away from you."

My face scrunches up on the word *root* as I try to follow along. "Well, what changed? I mean, how did you even find me?"

She stretches out her hand. And I swear fore God, it's like a thick cloud of blue light swirl around her fingers. Out of nowhere, there is a small gust of wind in the room.

A pang churn in me. The same blue flame I used at the Hudsons' . . . the same flame, I now realize, that caused the fire that night.

"What . . . what is that?"

"That's that Kaave magic. It's how I finally found you."

Her fingers morph into a closed fist, making the Kaave-whatever-the-hell disappear.

"When you used it, it was like a signal calling out to me. First just a whisper, and then a few hours later, when you used it at that . . . Carlwell's house . . . it was like a shout. I heard ya heartbeat for the first time in ten years. It was enough to grab on to, to fight with everythin' I had to follow that thread and find you. And I did."

It takes a lot to slow my breathing. "But not my mama?"

She falls silent.

Too silent. Because it low-key confirms what I already knew was true.

"I would've felt her light leave this world," she says, clocking the disappointment on my face.

"How?"

Her eyes meet mine, focused. "Because a mother knows. A mother knows."

It takes every mental muscle I have to lift the heaviness of those words.

"You're saying . . . you think she's alive?"

The burned dead bodies. My childhood home on fire.

And me, on the outside, unharmed, as the fire department rushed in.

All of this got me thinking back how when I was at school, without the computer teacher knowing, I would check out the missing persons website. Because in my heart of hearts, there was a part of me that didn't believe she was dead. Some small, shrinking part of me knew she was out there somewhere, that there was a reason she hadn't come back for me. I can still remember that cop's confused face. And how I had to tell him, in my own words, that it was four strangers that attacked my mama. Four strangers and only three bodies. Everyone told me she was one of them, and even though I didn't want to believe it, I stopped fighting it years ago. But now . . .

Mama Aya eyes shift, her own personal grief kept at bay.

"Listen, baybeh, I don't wanna get ya hopes up. My daughter had her ways, and she—" Mama Aya pauses. Swallows the next set of words she was about to say. "I told you; I haven't been able to feel her in ten years. And usually when that happens, it means—"

The pause in her voice makes me sit back down. "It means what? You just said she wasn't dead."

"I know—"

I spring from the chair. "Look, don't shatter my hopes. Is my mama alive or not?"

"Ever since that night I stopped sensing her, I've cast so many spells to try to feel her, to try to find out what happened to both of you. I haven't been able to sense either of you, no matter what I tried. And even now, with you here, she's still lost to me," Mama Aya admits. "But if she was dead, I would know. I truly believe that. I don't understand it but— Baby, tell me what happened that night. What did you see?"

The weight of not knowing makes me fold over, frustrated.

"I rushed home, on my bike. It was the Fourth of July." The memory of it all slams into my head. "And I raced home so fast, I thought my legs was gonna fall off because I had this feeling at the pit of my stomach, and when I finally reached my mama—there was this wind, this light, and they were chanting some weird stuff, then *boom*. Everybody in my old neighborhood was convinced that I killed my mama. Like I was this bad seed or something. I spent these years trying to make myself not believe that I did it. But when those people in those long cloaks came, I—I really don't know what to believe."

Her eyes drift to the altar that's on the right of us. "If my daughter was truly dead, baybeh, her spirit would be here. Because no matter what, a spirit would return home to complete their unfinished business."

"So, I didn't . . . I ain't killed my mama."

Her eyes drift to my shaking hands. "Baby, you don't have a bad bone in ya body. Look here; I want you to stay with me. You and that precious boy, Taye."

"What's the catch?" I ask her.

"Chile, ain't no catch. I see you have trouble harnessin' that power inside ya. You only havin' trouble because you's afraid of it."

"I ain't afraid of nothing." I try to sound confident. She gives me one of those old people laughs again. Her age definitely shows in her voice.

"What you have, Malik, it's generational. It's a part of who we are. And as the *old folks* say, we are descendants from a mighty tribe. Your great-grandma Miriam, a powerful slave woman, had the magic ways of Kaave too." Her hands circle over me, and she looks at me, deep. Her eyes are like a thousand mirrors.

"You soundin' all mystical," I say, slipping out a laugh.

"Oh, you think that's funny," she says, smiling. "Lemme guess, you probably was 'bout seven years old when it revealed itself to ya, huh?" she asks, seeing that I'm sporting a confused look on my face. "Ya magic?"

All I remember is when my magic activated, there was fire and the dead bodies. I've spent so long running from the memory of that night. But what if it holds the answers I've been looking for? What if it holds the key to finding my mama, if she's really still alive?

"You're special. Our bloodline is special. When you *fully* learn, you'll be able to conjure the Kaave by will alone." So much emphasis on the *fully* part.

Her hand extends toward me. Her magic hums around the room in a slight breeze. It's as if she's holding purple-and-gold diamonds between her fingers. Beautiful. Something I've never seen before. The dust particles flutter around the sunroom and turn into shapes of butterflies flying out the open window.

I can't help but look impressed. I mean, it's hella dope.

"Go ahead and try." A quick move with her hand, and the candle that's floating in the big bowl goes out. "Show me ya *àṣẹ*."

My face twists up. "My what?"

Another one of those laughs. "Ya magic, chile."

Hesitation settles into me.

Her hands clasp mine, and a surge of energy courses through me like electricity. Suddenly, the blue light from before swirls around my arm. This time it's stronger.

"Ban mwen limyè ashe . . ."

The candles sitting on top of the shelves and in the bowl light up with orange sparks. The flickering flame spirals down, glittering into more dust. It takes shape. Like little black butterflies, floating toward the ceiling.

The energy inside me becomes stronger and stronger. I feel it all over me. Deep inside. Her magic. My magic. All of it. It feels like my skin is stretching from my bones.

A clash of sounds. Thunder. Wind. Blowing around everything in this room.

"Pour in everythin' you got, baby. Your love, your hate, your fears. Your dreams . . . feel it in your bones, in your soul. Ha-ha!" Her voice echoes as if she's speaking into a thousand microphones.

Mama Aya snaps her fingers, and just like that, the whole sunroom disappears into nothing. We're in the middle of the sugarcane field, where the weeds twist in a coiling motion. The sky becomes the ground, and the ground becomes the sky. Everything around us is tilting, shifting. I see fleeting images of us in long white clothes, with white powder on our faces. There are people behind us banging drums. They're all in white garments and start to dance in a circular motion.

"You got a right to the tree of life. . . . Ups and downs, but you got a right to the tree of life. . . ." Everything around us is so beautiful. To be honest, I don't even know if we're in Louisiana anymore.

Mama Aya gazes at me and says, "Ya magic is ancient." Black folks take flight around us. Their bodies move and twist like they're possessed. All of this reminds me of when Ms. Pauline would catch the Holy Ghost in the middle of church, and her whole body would fall on the ground, shaking. Her wig would fall off, making all of us almost piss on ourselves, laughing.

The air around us bends.

Thunder crackles in the distance.

Inverted clouds spread, revealing nothing but mountains. Even the moon and the sun surrender themselves to the darkness of night. The same tall tree in Mama Aya's yard swishes and sways, and it's like somebody's whispering inside the blue bottles. Branches spread out, twisting up like they're reaching toward the sky. Dust of magic flutters around the bottles, lighting them up like Christmas lights. People circle around the tree, dancing. When I look up, I see nothing but a constellation of stars shining like tiny diamonds in the sky. Something in me steps forward to get a better look.

Suddenly, light bursts in a whole buncha colors that streak across the sky like a summer thunderstorm. And then the stars fall right into a bowl where dirt is thrown on the inside. Flames sparkle like tiny embers, overflowing out of the sides. The people in the white clothes do their circle dance, lifting the bowl to the sky.

"What is this?" I ask Mama Aya.

She doesn't answer. She just starts walking, making the water and soil from the ground rise slowly in the air. The twisting dirt and water loop around each other, turning purple and blue. On instinct, my hands rise like I'm in church, making my magic ripple in small vibrations. The people all surround me, the drums and singing become louder.

Mama Aya's voice echoes inside my head. "You come from a powerful tribe of Vodun priests and priestesses."

And the people around us continue to sing . . .

"You got a right to the tree of life. . . . Ups and downs, but you got a right to the tree of life. . . ."

The water that floats in midair lands, drifting into a globe shape. It drops down to the ground, spreading itself out into a lake. Mama Aya leads me to the edge. The manifestation of my magic wraps around it like it's giving it a hug. *Whooosh!* Something outta nowhere whirls around me. Power. Power I never felt before.

Àṣẹ . . .

The word explodes into my mind as if I've been speaking it all my life. The edge of hearing, and it sounds as though it's coming closer. Muffled. Like water sloshing around inside my head.

Up ahead, right by the tree, is a woman in a long dress. Her gold locs fall down her shoulders like a sheet of rain. As she cracks a smile, the creases fold in her Black skin. I don't know whether to bow or back up. She reaches for the sky as if she's picking stars like plums from a tree. She forms and molds the stars with her hands. And on everything I love, the stars turn into a small Black boy that looks exactly like me when I was little. He gazes up at me, smiling. Brown eyes. Innocent. Don't know a lick of pain yet.

"What—" I say in disbelief. The little boy reaches out his hand, guiding me toward the water. I can't help but tear up when I look at him. Given what happened that night ten years ago, I know that smile is gonna be lost forever.

The sound of laughter sings into the air. My own laugh from when I was a kid. Memories flurry around just like those black butterflies. It grows and grows the closer we get to the water. My feet are the first to dip into the stinging cold water. A sharp breath forms in my throat as the water rushes around my ankles. One of the people places their hand on my chest. The other behind my head as if they're about to baptize me.

I'm fully submerged. Everything becomes stifled, but I can still hear them chanting. It's like my primary urge to breathe or fight to the surface goes away as I sink deeper.

My memories flash before my eyes, memories of Mama Aya holding me as a baby, her and my mama fighting, yelling while she stomps away. The memories switch in my mind like I'm flipping through TV channels. Me at school. Me looking out the window, feeling alone when I first arrived at the orphanage. Me and Alexis. All of it.

Then, at seven years old, I biked home to save my mama. Firecrackers pop in midair. Then I see my mama on the floor, crying as the men in black cloaks surround her. Her screams are swallowed up, and she continues to scream those words I can't understand. A green light and the explosion. Glass shatters. Walls cave in.

As if a rock has been thrown into the water, the memory ripples right in front of me, and I see my younger self's big brown eyes staring at me from the surface of the water. He smiles.

The surface changes, shifting into a familiar shape . . . my mama. She stares down at me with a strange-looking necklace dangling from her neck.

I reach out for the necklace, my finger touches the pendant, and suddenly, the water rushes into my lungs, making them feel like they're being incinerated.

Everything crashes into me as if I'm drowning.

I'm lifted out of the water and back into Mama Aya's sunroom, coughing up my lungs.

"There ya go, baybeh . . . ," Mama Aya says, wrapping her arms around my shaking body.

I gasp for air. My heart sinks.

Once again, my mama is taken away from me.

CHAPTER FIVE

PICKING UP THE SHARDS OF MY HEART, I REALIZE SOMETHING.
I'm afraid that, with each passing day, the memory of my mama is gonna fade into the distance. And that I will forget her because grief is squeezing the good times from the corners of my mind. When I think of her, I only think of her screams piercing through my chest, shattering every little hope I had left of helping her.

For all these years, I thought those screams were her last, that she was gone. I wanted to believe she was alive, but I had no reason to, and now there's a real chance she is. But if she's alive, why wouldn't she have come for me?

Only one reason I can think of. She's in trouble. More than I ever knew.

It's a whole new kind of helpless feeling now, not just wishing I could change the past and that one night but thinking maybe all this time my mama's been out there, needing me.

At least there's one person I care about who's right here under this roof.

When I open the door to his room, Taye is laid out on the bed like he is staying at the Four Seasons. He scrolls through his phone, playing videos and dozing off at the same time. A part of me hates it because I don't wanna get his hopes up in case we don't stay here long. I still don't trust Mama Aya.

"Yo, this is so dope, Malik. I mean, dude, our own rooms. It's like they knew we were comin'," he says, looking hella sleepy. It's definitely time for bed.

I look around the room. It sharpens into focus. Taye is right—it does seem like this is tailor-made for somebody that was accepting visitors. There is a large bed with fresh towels and linens. Sheets wrap the mattress so tight it'd take a man of steel to pull them off. Over on the right, a wooden door creaked halfway open leads to a bathroom with a pearly white sink that meets cream-colored tile floors. No lie, it's bigger than the one I had at my last foster home. Hell, if you even call that a room that I had.

"That food was good as hell too," Taye says, rubbing his bulging stomach. "They say this was your old room when you were a baby."

"So, you good?"

"Auntie Brigitte said I ain't gotta be worried about nothin' no more with this diabetes. She's gonna take care of me."

"What you mean?"

"All she said was that I'm not broken, so I don't need fixin'."

With a sheepish grin, he crosses over to this tall white dresser that's propped against the wall by the window. He starts putting his clothes inside. "Auntie Brigitte says I still have diabetes, but that stuff they cooked up will always make me feel a thousand times better."

I don't say nothing back. A shift in energy. Taye got a worried look washing across his face.

The question finally spills out of him. "You think they gonna send me back?"

"Hell naw. That ain't never gon' happen."

His eyes wander to the floor, and his shoulders slump, processing this new situation.

"If they find out about the Hudsons, you know they gonna call the police or somethin'. Especially if they find out what really happened."

"Taye, you ain't got nothing to worry about. Chill. You here. With me."

"I mean, this is your family, man. I don't know where I fit into all of this—"

I cut him off. "You're the only family I need. Don't you ever forget that."

He nods, and I pull him in for a tight hug. "I love you, bighead."

"Yeah, I love you too."

"A'ight. Enough of that mushy shit. I'm gonna check out *my* room."

He's mindlessly back on his phone.

"Get some sleep."

Pushing the squeaky door open to my room, I see a queen-sized bed cornered right by the window. Old vintage lamps cast a pool of light into the shadows. From the top of the wooden posts, a thin sheet rains down toward the mattress, spreading like it was made for royalty. Bare walls and no remnants of anybody ever staying in here. But something inside me tells me this was my mama's room.

It hasn't been touched in all these years.

I ramble through the drawers, closets, and hanging there in a closet is the same maroon-colored Caiman U sweatshirt I saw from before. The words CAIMAN UNIVERSITY stitched right on the front of it in gold. I pull my phone out, typing the very letters that stoke my curiosity. Hold up—that's weird. Even Google don't recognize this school. Tapping on hella tabs, but nothing is popping up. I'm too damn tired to fight with this phone.

Snatching the sweater off the hanger, I pull on a dangling string to turn on a low-dimmed light. Old clothes and dressers are lined up on each side.

From the top of a shelf, I pull on a brown wooden box. It falls down, spilling all its contents on the floor, including a small silver jewelry box. The weight of it feels like I done found the jackpot. I cross back into the bedroom, over to the door, and lock it.

I lay the Caiman University sweatshirt right on the bed and then I immediately crack open the silver box. It's full of pictures from the past. I flip over one of them that's a bit torn, and it's my mama. Younger. Pretty chestnut skin and long, thick hair. She stands in front of a tall tree with that same sweatshirt with weird-looking buildings in the background. Around her neck is this long gold necklace with something hanging at the end of it. The same necklace that was in the vision with Mama Aya.

This is my mama's stuff, and it's more precious than gold.

Looking back to the silver box, I shift one of the small trays around, and I find a list with baby names written on it.

Ephraim I.I.
Tomas.
Malik

Here it is. Every laugh. Every song she used to sing around the house. Every dance she used to make me do, all reduced to this silver box full of stuff I'll never know about.

I do find myself laughing at this one picture of her making goofy faces in front of that tree. Then I notice a folded scrap of paper with a different kind of handwriting that's not my mama's. When I unfold the small piece of paper, I see that it's a note—one she scribbled a response to but must never have returned.

> *If you keep sneaking into the classroom after hours, you're gonna get in trouble. You need to stop it, Lolo, before you're expelled!*

From what my mama writes back, her handwriting swooping and swirling toward the edge of the page, she doesn't seem to care:

> *I'm sorry. But something in me can't. Bane magic is tempting me. Please, I need your help.*

First of all, what the hell is *bane magic*? Secondly, what does she mean, she needs help? And what was she addicted to that could get her expelled?

It's gotta be connected to whatever happened to her that night ten years ago, and maybe to where she's been since then.

I tug tighter on the Caiman sweatshirt, using it as comfort as I lie down.

Me and sleep have been strangers, but tired as I am, I'll be surprised if I don't stay awake for the next three days. That same feeling I had when Samedi first came rises back up. I hold on to the bed, closing my eyes and taking a deep breath to let the spinning subside.

Soon as I close my heavy eyes, I see the mental picture of the three burned bodies being pulled from the house on gurneys.

My eyes pop open.

The early morning sunlight takes flight around me before anything else, dissolving the dark memories trying to level their claws in me. My hand meets the back of my neck, rubbing out the kinks of the tossing and turning. Me and sleep gon' fight if we can't come to an agreement. I'm sick of this shit.

Ain't nothing like the South and this humid weather. After using the bathroom and putting a warm rag to my face, wiping off the sticky sheen I accumulated overnight, I walk down the hall to Taye's room to find him sprawled all over the bed, with his clothes on and shoes hanging half off his feet and his phone smacked on the floor. I bend to pick it up, hearing him snore. Lil' brotha tired. I'mma let him sleep a little bit more.

Down the stairs, there's an unfamiliar voice. "I don't know, Ms. Aya. He's reckless."

Reckless?

"Taron, he's strong." Mama Aya argues like she's pleading a case.

Taron?

Well, whoever the man is is saying back, "Since you've found him at the gas station, I've looked into what he's been up to, you know? First it was the young men from the University of Alabama, and him stealing the car outside. Then the Hudsons. He almost killed the man, Ms. Aya. And not to mention the gas station attendant. He could've exposed everything, implicating him and that young boy."

Wayment—keeping tabs? On me? I listen even more closely. "How did you find him after all these years?" he asks Mama Aya. "I thought you tried everything. You said he'd gone invisible. Seemed that way from all I could tell too."

She changes the subject. "Does your mother know about this?"

"I erased their memories and all video footage from the gas station."

Mama Aya releases a sigh of relief.

"But if she did know, the Kwasan tribe would get involved, stripping him of his magic."

No lie, I'm kicking myself, because I should've known there was gonna be a video at the gas station. But with Taye being sick and Baron Samedi coming outta nowhere, I was in the heat of the moment.

"I know," I hear Mama Aya tell him. "I need you ta let him into Caiman."

Hearing that word, my mind goes back to last night, finding my mama's college hoodie. The way they're talking about it makes it seem like it's University of Alabama or Auburn University.

There's some shuffling around from one end of the living room to the other. "That I can't do, Ms. Aya. The summer term has already started. He'll be way behind. Besides, it's a lot happening right now, and tensions are rising with several faculty and departments. Dr. Akim and the Deacons of the Crescent are demanding answers involving the missing children."

Missing children?

"Do this for me, please," Mama Aya pleads one more time. "We're runnin' outta time." I catch the tail end of that statement. "And it'd be good for him to learn his way. Be with folks his age and not be reckless, as you say. Think about it: he'll be more of a liability out here in the real world than he would at that school."

A couple of sighs come from this Taron guy. Then all I hear is some more shuffling, and the closer I get to downstairs, the more my hands tingle with irritation.

Magic.

Does that mean there's more folks like me out there besides Alexis, Mama Aya, and Baron Samedi?

Soon as I hear footsteps, I dart back to the lower steps, acting like I didn't just listen to them talking behind my back. They both drift toward the bottom of the staircase. Mama Aya clocks me first and falls back, putting on one of them *we got company* smiles. This man that's in front of me is probably six foot four. A little on the lighter side but still on the edge of not having light-skinned privilege. The way he has his hands in his pockets, he looks like he stepped off *GQ* magazine or a pulpit at the church. As he grabs the coffee mug from Mama Aya, I notice the ring on his finger. The ring is gold, with a raised surface revealing some sort of engraving.

"Nice ring," I tell him.

His haunted eyes travel to his ring finger. "Thank you." Ah, hell. I know this type. He's definitely like one of those school principals that already hate me. Growing up the way I did, you can detect that type of tone a mile away.

"Who is you?"

"I am Taron Bonclair." He doesn't have an accent. Just proper as hell. "A friend to your . . . grandmother."

That word feels like prickly thorns. "Oh, okay. Cool."

Mama Aya steps in between us, interrupting our silent battle. "Baybeh, I got some grits, eggs, and sausage on the kitchen table."

"Yes, you should eat," this Taron dude says. "Expending a lot of energy can be . . . exhausting."

Every muscle in my hand pulsates.

Mama Aya grabs this weird-looking broom, and she starts to lay down what looks to be cinnamon on the floor. Then she sweeps from the back of the house to the front, and out the door.

"Why you doin' that?"

"She's sweepin' away the bad energy and juju," Taron answers.

I wasn't talking to you.

"That's right, been this way for generations. You don't sweep right to left or east to west. You sweep out dust and all the bad energy." She sweeps all the way out on to the front porch.

Me and Taron look at each other.

She comes back in, wiping the bit of sweat off her forehead. "Where's that sweet baby at?"

I tear my eyes away from Taron. "Uh, yeah. He's real tired. I ain't wanna wake him."

"Lemme go wake him up. I know he is hungry. You and Taron talk. I'll be back down directly."

"He's gonna need his insulin soon."

She stops by the edge of the stairs. "Doncha worry 'bout that," she says. "I'll be makin' him take some herbs, and Brigitte gonna make him take some of that burdock root."

"What's that?"

"It's an antidiabetic," this Taron guy answers, all smug. "It not only cleanses the blood, but it purifies it. In that young man's case, it won't cure it but will treat it, and he will be perfectly fine."

"I'll leave you two to talk." Mama Aya smiles and then disappears upstairs.

Taron has his hand out like he's leading me to the kitchen. We both walk in there, and the plate of food sits on the table, fresh. The twisting steam comes off the buttery grits. Soon as I bite into it, everything else melts away. I may not trust this lady fully as my grandma, but this food is the one thing I can count on from her.

"So, Mr. Baron," Taron starts, sipping his cup of coffee, "you finally made it to Louisiana."

No answer from me. I just keep eating my grits and sausage. My fingers tingle even more, and I massage the sharp feeling from my fingertips. Taron notices it too.

"You sense me, don't you?"

I summon a confused look. "What?"

He points to my shaking hand. "Your magic. You sense me. I'm sure you did when you first met Samedi and your grandmother, of course. Sensing is when a conjurer recognizes another. It's— Well, you feel it. I'm sure you've been baptized in your magic, no?"

Slurp.

The way he's speaking sounds hella foreign. The only thing I can offer up is a look of confusion, because what the hell is he talking about? No lie, last night with Mama Aya still got my head spinning.

"All conjurers with abilities possess this. No matter the skill level."

I continue scooping up more hot eggs and grits. Finally, the tingling subsides. He sits down right in front of me. "You are very gifted, Mr. Baron. I can tell." He says it like I'm part of the X-Men. "You manifested your magic at, what, around nine years old?"

"Seven."

"Impressive. That's not a typical age for boys like you."

Boy?

It was the way he said it for me. There was some shade hidden in his tone. I know it. He leans forward. "There is a school for people like you."

School? *Tsk.* Man, I knew it. You can always tell a principal or teacher type. They stay acting judgy. But, then again, maybe there is a manual for this type of shit.

"You're talking about Caiman University, ain't you?"

He puts on the Malcolm X thinking pose. "Yes . . . and it's a school for those who can practice magic. Caiman University—"

"I tried googling it last night. Nothing came up."

His hand reaches his tie, fiddling with it. "As I was saying, it's a historically Black college—and your grandmother Mama Aya wants me to admit you for admission. Even though the summer term has already started."

That last part was definitely shade.

"She feels that you would excel there."

"But you don't?" I say, grinning. "Yeah—I figured that."

However, I don't really care what this Taron dude thinks, because Caiman U is a tie to my mama.

"Caiman University is not some party school, Mr. Baron. The courses there are very rigorous. And as I stated before, you'd be very behind. Seeing all the other students who grew up training in their powers with *proper* guidance advance while you'd have to play catch-up could be a distraction to your learning experience. But Mama Aya feels that you must attend school. Get acclimated with those who are just like you. Learn to *control* your magic."

"I can learn."

"Can you?"

I fight the urge to sink back, letting the cloud of doubt hover over me.

"If my mama learned all that at this school, then so can I."

"Your mother was one of the best students at Caiman University," he says, then clenches his jaw like he didn't mean to let the words out.

So he knew my mama, huh? Could he know something Mama Aya doesn't about what happened since she left?

"According to Mama Aya, no one's heard from her since I was born, basically. None of you Caiman folks know what happened to her?" No response. A dead end if I've ever seen one.

I make my way out of the kitchen. His alligator shoes clomp against the wood floor, trailing right behind me.

"You know what? I don't go where I'm not wanted."

His tone is laced with irritation. "It is very evident that you are not in control of your magic. For example: the car that's out in the front yard, your old foster parents Sonya and Carlwell Hudson. Oh, and that clerk from the gas station."

"I—"

He interrupts. "I know everything, Mr. Baron. You've been irresponsible, and it's our job to keep people like you safe and keep magic in secrecy."

He talks so fast, I can't even get a word in.

"And if you really want to protect that young man who's upstairs, you will need to learn the essentials of your magic. The basics."

"I'm good on protectin' Taye."

Another round of slurps. "Are you? What happened at the gas station last night? You couldn't help him in the midst of trouble."

He got me on that one.

"We had to erase the memories of all those people you encountered. And that . . . Carlwell, Malik. You lost control."

"If you knew they were hurting Taye, you know I ain't had no choice." That part slips from me before I can even catch it.

"I know if you ever get caught, it wouldn't be good for you or that young man upstairs. You must—"

"I ain't got to do shit."

"That air of defiance you have reminds me of your mother."

CRACK!!!

Both of us turn. The cabinets in the kitchen all burst open, and some dishes fall to the floor in shattered pieces.

"You didn't mean to do that, did you?" Taron asks. Suddenly, I feel like shit because I just gave in to this dude and the way he thinks about me. But I keep up my guard.

Taron shakes his head, waves his hand, and the broken pieces all lift in the air, assembling back together in the cabinet. The light from the sun glints off his gold ring as he holds his hand to the mirror for a second.

"Just as I suspected. Reckless."

Mama Aya and Taye travel down the stairs, hearing the commotion between me and Taron.

"Clearly, Caiman University would not be a good fit for you. Have a good day, Mr. Baron." Putting his hands back in his pockets, he marches out the front door.

I turn to Mama Aya, furious. "Next time, don't offer me to go to no school. You don't know me like that, and I can handle everything on my own. Just like always."

I storm the hell out, all the way off the porch, and pass the car that I stole. In a few long strides, I end up by the tall-ass tree.

I lean against it, exhaling, trying to calm down.

The sunlight shines through the branches, crystallizing the swinging blue bottles. The leaves tremble from the blow of the generous breeze. Something about it is so peaceful, the storm of anger passes over.

I walk around, getting the whole scope of the yard. Up ahead is a small clapboard house. More gardens with fruits and vegetables growing. The land meets the swampy water. Around the corner are a few wooden shacks laid out in a row. *Slave* shacks. When I step inside, a heavy feeling weighs down on my shoulders. Blood, sweat, and tears stain these walls. Light slashes in through small slats crudely made in the wood. The dirt floor feels cold. Off on the side, collections of straw and old rags, thrown down in the corners and boxed in with boards. I look up, and there's a soft breeze swaying the bottles hanging from the trees.

Stepping back out, I see the land. It's so secretive and beautiful even though it was built on pain. Pain builds everything in this world, and pain is all that's left when everything's been stolen from you.

Low-key, this place feels like home. But it's not. I ain't got no home in this world. I lost it, right along with losing my mama, that night ten years ago.

• • • •

Next day.

This time, I kinda get a little bit more sleep. But of course that shit is interrupted when I hear "All aboard!" blare from a loud-ass trumpet.

I jump outta the bed, scared as all get-out, thinking the world is ending.

Now I know my ass ain't dreaming.

More trumpets and horns blaring from the outside.

When I crawl to the window, I see the yard full of Black folks dancing, carrying on like it ain't nine o'clock in the morning. Over on the right, by the tree, is a ministage with a jazz band. From downstairs, I heard Samedi singing at the top of his lungs:

Oooooh, far away in Africa
Happy, happy Africa

The door to my room burst open, and Taye appears in the hall, excited. "Malik, come on, get up. Yo, it's a party for you!"

Before I can say anything, he's gone, running down the stairs.

A party? At this time of the morning? I climb out of bed with a groan and wipe the crust from my eyes. After a quick change and brush of my teeth, I wobble down the stairs, and judging from the noise, a party is kinda an understatement. Before I hit the last step, the music warbles through the entire house, and I clock Baron Samedi drifting from the living room to the foyer with Auntie Brigitte. They on they shit, dancing and swaying like they trynna rock boats.

In the middle of the living room, a group of them old types slam dominoes on the table. One of 'em cusses the other out, saying he's cheating. A man and woman lean against the wall, sucking on each other's faces. Everybody on their own chaotic beat.

Before I make it to the kitchen, I'm greeted by an army of folks. First, it's a lady that peels herself from one of the barstools. Her hair is silver and shaped in crochet braids. She has on an outfit that's obviously too young for her—and a glass of some kind of liquor in her hand. You can tell she's the "bougie auntie" at the family reunion. You know, the one that got all the money and is down to show everybody just how much she has. Her arms wrap around me before she says anything.

"How you doin', baby? I'm ya auntie Caroline on ya great-uncle's side." She glides back, pulling her bougie-looking shades down to the bridge of her nose. I picture Mo'Nique when I look at her. "Whew, chile, you a handsome young man. Elroy, ain't this chile handsome?" Whoever she's talking to moves through the busy kitchen. Elroy fixes himself a plate full of crab legs, potatoes, and corn on the cob.

"Yeah, lookin' just like his mama. Woman, pass me that butter over dere." He sounds like he lives in the back of a bayou.

She passes him the butter. "Welcome home, young buck," he says, flying out of the kitchen, chomping on crab legs.

"Thank you?" I say, trying to slip away.

She spins me back around and takes another look at me. "Whew, sha . . . They right 'bout you. I feel that majik runnin' right through ya." Then she mutters something in a language I never heard before. *"Ou yon bagay pwisan, Chili."*

Pwisan chili—what the fuck she just say?

"Well, welcome home, sweetness." She struts off, already hugging somebody else.

The entire house swells with folks running in and out. Some on the phone kiki-ing. A woman who looks like she's in her midtwenties chases after two little badass kids coming down the stairs. "Y'all stop runnin' in this house like I said. Actin' like y'all ain't got no home-trainin'." She looks me up and down. "Hey, baby, I'm Gutchie. Ya cousin twice removed. We heard so much about ya."

"Nice to meet you too," I say to her.

The kids run up to her and shock her with little electric currents from their fingers. But, oh wow, they got magic too.

"They gonna sign you up for classes at Caiman next semester? Mama Aya been sayin' she wants ya to go. You should, even though folks ain't sending their kids there. I'm like, the school grounds would be safer than here."

"Safer?" I ask.

Oh yeah. I quickly remember the convo between Taron and Mama Aya about the missing kids around here.

"Aye, yo, there's really folks out there going missing?"

"Yeah, it's all over the neighborhood," she answers.

One of her kids knocks a statue to the ground, shattering it into pieces. She waves her hand and the statue assembles itself back to normal. "Cuzzo, lemme go. These kids gon' tear up Mama Aya's house." She disappears outside, following her kids. Throughout the house, I meet more of my kinfolks: Cousin Johnny, who nearly tipped over the table after a few too many drinks; Cousin Sierra, who's around Taye's age; and Ms. Taylor, an elderly woman in her nineties. She's not a part of the family, but she says she and Mama Aya are good friends.

Taye is in the kitchen, helping Brigitte with the food. He pulls hot corn bread from the oven and places it on the counter. Hanging back, I'm noticing that smile he does. That type of smile when I do magic. He is having a grand ole time, recording himself on his phone, cooking.

Outside, the band switches songs, just playing random notes, improvising. "You really do look just like Lorraine," one lady says to me under the soulful vocals. Spent years hearing that; also spent years trying to remember what she looked like. Ten years is a long time to hold on to an image of somebody that was sucked in by the green light.

"You hungry?" Brigitte's voice rises over the loud music. "We makin' gumbo."

"Nah. I'm good."

I don't know why, but everything is about to boil over in me. A pressure radiating from my chest. Seeing everybody in here, vibing, laughing, drinking, and having a good time. These people say they're my family. But I think of those lonely nights at the orphanage, or me sitting on the back of the fire truck talking to the police, and seeing that white lady caseworker. Pulling me away from Taye. Or when I had questions about this damn magic. And they were all here. Laughing. Partying. Happy. It's becoming too much. Too fucking much.

"Come on over, baby, we family! We ain't gon' bite," Auntie Caroline says.

"Y'ALL AIN'T MY FUCKIN' FAMILY!" I snap.

The whole kitchen goes dead quiet. You can hear a rat piss on carpet. Auntie Caroline clutches her "pearls" and whispers, "Chiiile." Hands are on my shoulders. It's Mama Aya. Everybody straightens up as if they were about to be caught with something.

"What's goin' on in here?" Mama Aya asks everybody.

Without a word, I storm out, busting through the screen door, out to the back of the veranda, facing the bayou. I lean against the rail. Trying my best to calm down. Right under the loud whizz of the bugs is slow music, a serenade from a woman onstage, pressing her red-stained lips to the microphone as she sings. People making their way to the middle of the yard, dancing and having a grand ole time. They're here for me, for my *welcome home* party.

But they don't know me.

Nobody here does.

The screen door opens. Before she says anything, I sense Mama Aya. "Baybeh . . ."

"Look, I ain't mean to snap or disrespect your people, a'ight?" She doesn't say anything. "I just . . . All of this is happenin' way too fast."

"I know it is. It's been so long since this side of the family saw ya. I just figured to throw ya a little welcome home party, is all." Everybody comes out of the house, filling the yard even more. Some stop laughing when they see me.

I glare at Mama Aya with a flash of vulnerability. But I snatch that shit up and place it behind my emotional walls. "You know, when me and Taye were staying in the same foster home, I found out that mutha—I mean, our old foster parent was puttin' his hands on him. And yeah, that Taron dude was right. I nearly killed him." The words just pour out like lava. "When he called the social workers, and they snatched me from Taye's arms—it broke me. After my mama, it was the worst day of my life."

"I truly wish I can make it all better for you, I really do."

My eyes land on the folks back on the yard. I even notice Taye, talking and sheepishly grinning at Sierra. "I tried every day to get back to him. And I wasn't no more than two hours away." I pause, trying to bite back the crumbling command in my voice. "I did good in school, made sure I got straight A's. I didn't get into too much trouble. Because as soon as I turned seventeen, I emancipated myself from the system and planned to get him back. He may not be blood, but he's *my* family. The only family *I* got in this world. And if I can help it, I never want him to think the same thing that I'm thinkin' right now lookin' at you."

"Malik—"

"That I abandoned him." The words feel like arrows shooting from a bow. "And I be damned if I break everything in him and expect him to pick up the pieces. Nobody deserves to go through life thinkin' that. Nobody."

I hop off the porch and storm off, maneuvering through the swaying crowd, ready to get as far from this place as I possibly can.

CHAPTER SIX

MAYBE JAY-Z SHOULD'VE SAID NOBODY WINS WHEN THE family reunites.

Because what I experienced today is what they call family. But all I saw was a hundred and one strangers.

Family should've been there. Family should've wrapped me in their arms when I saw my childhood home go up in flames and watched paramedics drag out those dead bodies. Family should've been giving me the answers that I needed.

Where was the "fam" at then?

I close the door behind me and plop down on the bed. The exhaustion from so many different energies got my social battery on a negative 150. Struggling to keep my heavy eyes open. This is where my mama once lived, and now it's kinda my own little corner. Even though questions bleed from every item. From every bedsheet to the door that leads to the bathroom.

This is a life I never knew.

That she never talked about.

Only remnants of her past life. I can't even lie, the only thing that gives me comfort right now is the box I found and the CAIMAN UNIVERSITY hoodie. Her letters. Mama was a whole student at a magical HBCU out here.

The more I think about this discovery, the more questions I have.

Even though that asshole Taron dude don't think I belong there, my mama did. This school was a big part of her life, and the more I learn about her, the better the chances I have of finding out where she is now, if she's really out there somewhere.

A soft knock on the door, and Mama Aya peeks her head in.

"Hey, baby. Comin' to tell ya good night."

"Oh, hey," I say back.

She comes in with my clothes folded and places them beside me on the bed. "I figured since y'all leaving in the mornin', I do ya laundry and fix you some food for the road."

"Thanks," I say slowly.

She nods, then edges closer to the door. "I sure wish I could convince ya to stay. You welcome to, you know that?"

I really don't say anything. Just hold out the picture of my mama while she was at Caiman University.

"Lawd. I ain't seen these in a while," Mama Aya says, taking the picture. She rubs her thumb on it thoughtfully. "Tell ya the truth, I don't come in here much."

Together we flip through the pictures in the box. There's one of my mama right in front of a tall building. It's a candid photo showing how the wind tousles her hair. She's looking off in the distance like she's posing for someone. "She loved goin' there."

"Yeah, I can tell. But she never told me anything about this."

"I missed a lot," Mama Aya says to me as she flips a picture. It's another one of my baby pictures. "The school was supposed to help your mama too. She was around people like her."

The question dances on my lips. "If she's not dead, but we're not entirely sure she's alive, either, why did she just disappear off the face of the earth? What did those men in those cloaks want when they came to our house that night?" My voice almost cracks. All these emotions hit a brotha out of nowhere.

"I wish I knew, chile. Your mama, the kind of magic she was doin' . . . if I'm bein' honest, I'm not surprised it got her in some kind of trouble. Maybe it's best you focus on your future."

"But if she's out there somewhere, then maybe . . ."

My eyes land back on the picture of my mama at Caiman University. The only place I feel like I can get real answers is at that damn school.

"Well, since you got a early mawnin' tomorrow, I'mma let you get some rest. Can I say good-bye to that sweet baby in the morning before y'all leave—"

Even though I hate saying this next part with every fiber of my being, I'm confident on this decision and whatever may follow. "I'm gonna stay, and I'm gonna go to this school to find out what happened to my mama. If you really don't know about that night, then I gotta be the one to find some answers."

As I slip into my sleepiness, the real question slithers back into my mind. This picture and the letter got me going over every possibility: I didn't kill my mama ten years ago; she disappeared. So that means she's out there, and I gotta find her.

And this *Caiman University* is gonna give me the tools to help me do it.

ACT II

CHAPTER SEVEN

THIS COUNTRY BOY FROM HELENA, ALABAMA, AIN'T NEVER teleported a day in his life.

From the mouth of Taron, apparently that's how we gonna get to Caiman University. *Teleporting.*

Of course, he said it with a bougie-ass attitude.

Me and Taye stumble out onto the front porch, chopping it up. Sweat pours down both of our faces soon as we hit the harsh light. Taron lingers by Mama Aya's tree, hands in his pockets, waiting like he got a stick up his ass.

"Yeah, you sure you gonna be good here?"

"Malik, yes." Taye closes the screen door behind him, scoffing with preteen annoyance. "Me and Auntie Brigitte gonna go out to this marketplace, she said." He's cheesing so hard you'd think he won the Powerball lottery. "She real cool, Lik. I really like her."

It's the way he said it. The hope springing in his voice just the same as when we were back at the group home and prospective parents would come. He'd smile, bat his eyes real innocently, and try to give strangers a show.

But reality hit.

And no adoption.

"If anythin' happens, you call me, you hear me?" First-day jitters got my voice all shaky.

I mean, it's not like I'm going to a regular-ass college.

I'm going to a *magical* college.

Just thinking about it makes the humid breeze turn cold and got my stomach all in knots—bringing me back to a time when I was in school. I'd make sure Mama would lay out the freshest clothes for the first day to show off to all my classmates. Everybody'd be making excuses out the ass to go to the pencil sharpener just to show off the newest sneakers. I ain't had no money for clothes this time, so I just ironed my Aaliyah shirt and a pair of ripped jeans and called it a day.

"Look at youuuuu," Taye says, play-punching me. "Got that college bwoooy grinnin'."

I smack my lips. "Don't do too much."

Taye's laugh melts away any hint of doubt and hesitation. "Dude, you gon' be a'ight. Don't trip."

"And how you know that?"

"Because you my big brother, and I believe in you." His confidence makes me feel like I can lift a million pounds. "And you're like Miles Morales, but with magic instead of spidey-senses."

His hand reaches out to me. We do our handshake and wrap each other in a tight hug. "Fa'sho. Love you, boy."

"Mr. Baron," Taron calls. He taps his hand on his wrist, annoyed. "We do not want to be late."

Taye hugs me tighter. "I love you too. Go. I'mma be cool."

I hop off the porch, glancing back at Taye. He mouths a cuss word at Taron and disappears behind the screen door.

"So, how does this work, anyway?" I ask as I drift over to Taron. "The whole teleportin' thing."

Without an answer, he steps closer to the tree that rests in Mama Aya's front yard. Up close, it seems like the branches stretch out, trynna reach the highest clouds. The Spanish moss drapes down like curtains. After a moment, he inhales and closes his eyes. Focusing and touching the bark with the tips of his fingers.

Shifting my weight between my feet, I study just how he does this magic stuff. He doesn't seem to do anything grand or big. It's just simple, calm breathing and focus . . . and touching the tree.

At first, nothing. A split second goes by of us standing in silence. Taron's shoulders rise a bit, and a soft breeze whips around us like a tornado.

I step back, freaking out a little bit.

The wind grows strong. Taron mumbles something weird under his breath.

He lets his head loll back, whispering, *"Gbe ibori soke."*

From there, a slight exhale leaves his lips as if he's breaking through the water's surface. Energy swells around us, causing the earth to sing with a groan. Spiraling from the ground like a double helix, a flash of royal purple smoke swirls around us. It feels like cool mist against my skin.

One quick look back at Mama Aya's house as it fades like a rippling memory. My body itself feels like it's lifting off into space.

"Whoa, shit!"

Everything accelerates and becomes a blur.

And then a chorus of voices, yells, and laughter all fading in like someone's turning up the volume on a remote. As the spinning smoke thins out, everything before us appears like a watery mirage right before my eyes.

A WHOLE COLLEGE CAMPUS.

Suddenly, a wave of nausea washes over me, and my throat widens, prepping for the stomach acid sneaking up.

"What the hell? Why am I feelin' sick?"

"It'll pass."

It's the nonchalant voice for me. Swallowing the upchuck, I steady my heavy breathing.

Taron's ass is all regular. A bell tolls in the distance, sending a chime across campus.

"Let's take a tour, shall we?"

Slinking into view are acres of domed buildings scattered evenly across the green grass. Like with a fortress in the middle of a field, the longer you stare and take in these tall buildings, the smaller you feel. On one building, the arch on top meets the dipped sunlight, raining down shade around some oak trees. Right around the corner, there is a set of maroon-colored buildings with ornate, high walls and names etched into the stone outside the main entrance: THE SCHOOL OF MAGNIFICENCE, MANCELL HALL, ADMISSIONS, STEPHEN ROBINSON SCHOOL OF LAW.

A couple of "Watch it" and "That shit fire" are hoisted into the air as an army of folks zooms by, riding bikes and scooters, rushing to class. A Black girl with long blonde braids flips on a skateboard and zigzags across the sidewalk. She catches air, landing with a flourish, and disappears into a tall building with a golden swinging pendulum at the top for a clock.

We pass by one student painting a mural of Kobe Bryant with the words LEGENDS NEVER DIE. Over on my right, a stone bridge curves about twenty feet in the air that says CAIMAN UNIVERSITY in deep shades of purple and gold and shrouded by deep foliage. It has an emblem that looks like a purple flower rising out of an open book. It's supported by two hands in a praise gesture. It also has white-gold linings on the edge and a slogan at the bottom:

~WHERE OUR ROOTS ARE DEEP, NUMEROUS, AND VIVACIOUS~

"Whoa!" I say aloud, soaking in this place. "This is wiiiiiiild."

Tucked away in a small patch of grass is a phone hovering in midair. Two people stand right in front of it, dancing. A few of their friends hype them up with some "Ayyyyeeeees." Another group is lying in the grass with some headphones wedged in their ears.

In this world of extraordinary shit, that's the most ordinary thing I've seen so far.

Continuing through the campus, there's a courtyard full of drums, tables, and students. We walk deeper through the pearly gates of niggas doing magic. It's honestly giving *Stomp the Yard* mixed with *Drumline* vibes. My head swivels, surveying a basketball court, catching a game of twenty-one. The players move in a dizzying blur, passing the ball to one another. Just like that, one dude jumps so high that he's flying. He dunks the ball right into the rim with a style that'd make Michael Jordan himself question life.

I reel back, impressed. "Dayyyummm!"

His showmanship sends his homeboys into a series of frenzied daps and adoration. Just like back in Liberty Heights. On my right, a couple of baddies strut by, looking me up and down, smiling. I nod a *wadup,* trying hard not to look at them jeans, hugging them in all the right places.

They giggle and press on.

"People from all over come here to learn their magic," Taron explains, as if he's been paid lower than minimum wage at a touring museum. "Each is gifted with special abilities."

One dude in a cool-looking wheelchair closes his eyes, levitates. Another girl opens the palm of her hand, literally creating a mini tornado. It grows a few feet tall. Papers fly everywhere. She closes her hand, making the tornado disappear just like that.

All this got me stretching my fingers because that tingling feeling is on a thousand right now.

Taron glances at me, clocking the shade of uncertainty on my face.

I force myself to act like I'm all right.

A student, no more than twenty, comes up to him and does this movement with her hands. She looks hella frantic.

Taron signs and speaks, "You won't get pulled out of school, I promise. I will talk to your parents and get this straightened out."

The girl signs, clearly a bit frustrated.

"I know," Taron signs and speaks. "All is safe. They don't need to worry. You're almost to the finish line, and I want to personally hand you that diploma."

The student smiles and motions with her hands. Letters appear as if they're being written in pencil. The words **Thank you so much, Chancellor Bonclair** dance in midair and then dissolve.

The student walks off.

"What was that about?"

"Nothing that concerns you." He starts to walk. I follow. "The more you practice, the more your magic sustains and does not become *erratic.*"

I'mma keep it a buck, a bit of envy seeps into my bones, even though I stole a car without hot-wiring it and almost made a low-down bastard choke on his own spit. But here, everybody seems like they do their magic without effort. And they don't seem to be scared or ashamed of it like how I was with mine for all those years.

Taron's annoying voice pulls me back. "As a conjurer, you practice magic from the earth. From nature. Not only that, but your magic is also ancestral. So, when you conjure, you are blessed by the ancestors. Spellcasting, which you'll learn all about in your Intro to Black Magical Studies class. More higher-level classes are justice majik, which are spells for protection, and vindication."

Taron points to a grand rectangular building that features a steeply sloped, peaked roof supported by a central pillar. "This is the humanities building. This is where you'll learn history, religious studies, English, and literature arts."

My fingers wrap around the strings on my book bag straps. "Bet."

The path ahead snakes between another catacorner, and we come upon a building that shimmers in gold from the sun and has celebratory banners that read DANCE and THEATRE and MUSIC. On the side, it reads CHADWICK BOSEMAN SCHOOL OF THE PERFORMING ARTS. A thin wall of rain falls, magically creating a dope mural of Chadwick and the Black Panther with a quote from the movie. No lie, his sudden passing still kinda hurts. My arms cross over my chest, and I make the *Wakanda forever* move.

Rest in power, my king.

"Mr. Baron." Taron struts off, impatient. I'm trying to match stride to keep up. The music and voices around campus grow, yanking my unfocused attention a million directions.

"We have over ten thousand students from all across the globe here at Caiman University. Students who are of the African diaspora. Students come from the Caribbean islands, Africa; you know the rest."

"Is this, like, the only school around?"

"We have sister schools across the globe. Caiman has a top-notch student exchange program. There's Aganju University off the coast of

Africa—that's one of the oldest magical and academic institutions in the world. And for the younger students, there is Atwell Prep for the Gifted in New Elam, Alabama."

He walks off, leaving me stunned at *New Elam, Alabama.*

"We're community-driven. We expect excellence, integrity, and most importantly"—another round of shade-filled glares— "honesty."

"Sounds . . . very college-y."

He doesn't smile. Just keeps walking.

This dude rude as hell.

Clear across the campus, tables and tents are set up by a wooden gazebo and are crowded by a buncha people like it's a Sunday afternoon at the Golden Corral. It's giving me Black flea market vibes. A group of girls with long, thick curls wrapped up like crowns is exchanging bottles of what look like perfume and essential oils. Stations lined up selling candles, on-the-market handbags, all of that. Other tables include a dude pointing at a blank canvas. He moves his finger in a weird motion, and I swear to God, an array of colors and shapes appear on it as if he's Van Gogh or some shit.

Right behind them is a grocery store cornered in a small plaza where a chain of restaurants sits, offering an assortment of soul food and Jamaican and Ethiopian food.

I'm still stuck on the fact that places like this exist. Honestly, you only hear about shit like this in fairy tales. And judging by how Black this place is, we're definitely not in Kansas anymore.

". . . over two hundred courses, seventy undergraduate studies. You will get a well-rounded education in math, science, literature, history, Black magical studies. Some students apply for work-study. We also highly value extracurriculars."

Taron keeps talking, but I'm looking everywhere else, seeing all these Black folks doing their magic.

"Everyone is baptized in their ancestral magic," he continues, "which is the basis of all our abilities."

Folks are walking by, tapping on their phones and taking selfies doing magic.

Seeing this, I turn to Taron. "So, selfies are okay as long as you're not posting them?"

Detecting the sarcasm in my voice, he twists his gold ring on his finger and eyes the group of students filming. "It's all filtered through the cloud. The students upload, and whatever they share is only available here. On this campus. Outside, pictures with magic automatically get deleted. Of course, you can use your phone to contact your family if need be." Taron starts forward, passing by more club sign-up tables. "Let's keep walking, Mr. Baron."

This part of the campus is a bit quieter and laid-back. Park benches, a full garden. I see a student dig into the soil, letting it trickle between her fingers. She whispers into the palm of her hand, and a plant springs forth from the dirt.

"So, where exactly is this? I mean, how—"

"This campus is built off magic and blessed by our ancestors. Dimension casting—a very powerful spell that's taken generations to perfect. This school"—he points to the quad-looking area where more students linger and frolic like they're in the damn *Sound of Music*—"this is a safe haven."

"Safe haven," I repeat back. "So, everybody here doing magic, not scared, just magical vibes?"

Taron looks out to the campus. We both clock a student putting up posters. The posters read VOTE FOR AIDEN DUPONT!

"Caiman University is for people like you, me, and every Black person with special abilities. It was created as a place to come and be who you are." We pass by several more buildings. "There are clubs, organizations you can join. Of course, we have the Caiman University Marching Band."

I can't help but feel . . . I don't know the feeling, but I bet it's like going to Disneyland for the first time or something.

I mean . . . it's so much energy here, I can tell the leaves that's arching over the students shiver. Two Black dudes stand at a duel, whipping their hands back and forth. One of them spits out a chant. The other dude twists sharply, turning into a blinding, frantic, buzzing cyclone of leaves. It engulfs both of them.

Back to his regular self. They laugh. Hug it out.

Black joy at its finest.

"Everything all right, Mr. Baron?"

That cloud of self-doubt I was trying to avoid done found me.

Everything that's come at us so far has been like a movie. Like a fever dream that I don't wanna wake up from.

Me and Taron end up on a balcony overlooking the entire campus. "This is Congo Square. Students typically gather out there between classes. They study, do all sorts of things." He turns to look at me with those beady brown eyes. "You'll be starting off as a freshman and will be limited to beginning courses to learn and control your magic. You must pass all classes to move to the next level, you understand? Each professor has their own attendance policy. But don't be fooled; you can fail out of Caiman University if you do not take your studies seriously. And we do take it seriously. Summer term, it is best to get your core classes out the way. Math, science, history. By the fall, it would be best to declare your major. Dependent on your abilities and grades, you will be given access to upper-level classes."

Inside a breezeway that stretches across the quad into several residence halls and different departments, I look up at a wall full of pictures. Seems like old alumni and teachers. Hold up, is that Dr. Martin Luther King Jr. and a woman who has on a graduation cap from Caiman? The colors move as if they're first taking the picture together. Then it freezes again, kinda like a live photo on a phone.

"So, this is real? Like, no cap?"

"I beg your pardon?" Taron asks.

"I mean, this." I point all around us. "It's a whole campus full of magical niggas."

He stops dead in his tracks, tensing his jaw, and his eyes burn into mine for a second too long. "Please refrain from using that word around me. But to answer your question, it is indeed real."

In a blur, he snaps his fingers. My phone vibrates in my pocket. I pull it out to see a **CAIMAN UNIVERSITY** app home page on the screen. "That has your schedule for the rest of the summer semester. Take a good look at it. Be sure to have your advisor sign you up for

English class next semester because you obviously lack in that department."

I smack my teeth. This nigga . . .

"So, what are you? I mean, are you, like, some glorified campus tour guide?" I can't help but laugh.

With a glare, he steps up to me. "No, I am your chancellor. Meaning I run things around here, and you will address me as Chancellor Bonclair. Let me be very clear: there are rules to ensure the safety and well-being of our students. You will not go off gallivanting and perform your magic in front of everyone outside of this school. And you will certainly NOT cause a disruption to the Caiman way, or I will personally and delightedly expel you. Do I make myself clear?"

I ain't answer.

"I said, do I make myself clear?"

All I do is think to myself, *Chill, Malik. You're here for a purpose.*

"Yeah, whatever, man." Then, as he starts to walk off, I add, "Um, *Chancellor* Bonclair?"

He turns to face me. "Were you and my mama classmates? What kinda student was she here?"

A tense silence. Chancellor *Taron* clears his throat and buttons up his blazer.

"I'm just trying to get to know what she was like here," I say, trying to sound all innocent. "I just wanna make her proud, wherever she is."

His eyes shift from me back to the campus. "Focus on your classes. Grow in your magic and don't be reckless. That's how you make her proud. Professor Kumale, your advisor, will show you the rest," he says, tapping me on the chest. "Good luck in your studies, freshman."

I know this nigga did not just—

Suddenly, he disappears into a cloud of royal purple smoke, abandoning me to roam around this whole campus by myself.

My phone buzzes again, and I look down to find an official acceptance letter to Caiman U:

Dear Gifted Conjurer:

Congratulations! It is with great honor and pleasure that we inform you that you have been accepted into the early admittance of summer sessions here at Caiman University. This new journey will be prestigious and life-filling as you learn to grow in the excellence of Hoodoo and Vodun majik, integrity, and honesty. Your exceptional gift was selected from a very competitive applicant pool of conjurers, and we are confident that you will contribute to the Blackgical culture and thrive here at Caiman U.

Please download and refer to the CAIMAN U app for your official acceptance package, club sign-ups, campus life, and all pertinent logistical information about your admission to Caiman University.

Once again, welcome to Caiman University, where you will join us for the summer term. I commend you for your notable accomplishments. You are valued and worthy and belong here at Caiman U!

Let us all lead with love and know our roots are deep, numerous, and vivacious.

Sincerely,
Chancellor Taron Bonclair '00
Dr. Elesha Barnett '97, Director of Admissions and Recruitment

In all honesty, I just stare at it. Because back in high school, I ain't never really considered college. Again, I did the homework, but I never thought this was possible. Man, I wish I could shove this shit in Carlwell's face for all those times he called me stupid.

But most importantly, I wish I could show this to my mama.

I envision myself running to the mailbox when the mailman drives off, grabbing the college letter. Me and my mama jump up and down and go out and get cake and ice cream and eat till we're sick, because I got into my dream school.

So much for wishful fuckin' thinking.

Clicking over on the app, I see my schedule.

Intro to Black Magical Studies: M, W, F 9:00 a.m.–10:30 a.m.

African Diaspora History: T, Th 2:30 p.m–3:30 p.m.

Algebra: M, W 11:15 a.m.–12:15 p.m.

Since it's Thursday, I have history. Wherever the fuck that is.

Trying not to get lost, I linger in one spot, edging closer to a few benches. From a distance, I hear a voice filled with passion and anger. A mountain of steps meets an amphitheater. That voice. Calling to me like a siren at sea.

Onstage, with the microphone in her hand, is the same girl from the protest on TV at the gas station. And now, seeing her in person . . .

Seeing this girl with the microphone, I feel something I haven't felt in ten years. Warm summer nights looking up at the clear sky. A bed of flowers blanketing the ground and a rope with a tire hanging from a strong branch.

That familiar feeling of butterflies at the pit of my stomach. Like dopamine filling a brother to the rim, and I'm tasting the sweetest candy. My fingers stretch themselves, and I'm overwhelmed as hell. That tingling feeling got me feeling some kinda way.

"Over two hundred thousand girls went missing in the past few years. And the percentage of those who are Black and brown girls is astronomical. The recent missing victim is Katia Washington, and I feel like the police department is covering it up. Keep posting, keep hashtagging her name. And I know some of y'all have friends on the outside. We cannot let this girl's family down, y'all."

She continues. "With the strong ring of trafficked Black girls—we have to keep the pressure on the entire faculty here at Caiman U to do something about it. Especially since the local police won't help. Just because these girls don't have magic doesn't mean they don't need our help."

Under the sun, her beautiful brown eyes meet mine, and she

stops in the middle of her speech. The crowd looks around, confused. But she ain't care.

Ten years apart have come to an end at this very moment, happening before me in slow motion, like in a movie.

She jumps off the stage, and people part before her like the Red Sea. We meet each other in the middle, and everything around us fades into silence. I get a good look at her, and damn, she's definitely not the knobby-kneed little girl that used to run around causing trouble. Naw. She's all grown-up.

First I notice her jeans, flannel shirt, and black boots. Her luscious coal-black hair coiled in an updo, showcasing the beautiful mahogany face that's been getting me through my darkest of days.

"Alexis," I say, trying not to drown in her eyes. She glows with melanated tenacity.

"Malik," she says back.

A levee of feelings floods inside my mind as I hear my name finally spill from her mouth for the first time in ten years.

CHAPTER EIGHT

THEY SAY LOVE IS LIKE THE SEA.

Because of its vastness, we really don't understand it fully. But we know it moves with a rhythm, and it's deeper than anything in this world. It's endless, and it always comes back to shore. But how can you love something that's been away from you for so long?

For the past ten years, I held on to the ghosts of memories. Not only my mama, but Alexis too. Shoot, I remember the day like it's nothing. Her playing with her magic, seeing her laugh and smile whenever she had bursts of colors from her hands.

My seven-year-old brain was so shook, I didn't believe that it was another person just like me. Back then, for the first time under the moon's silver light, our hands touched, and both of our eyes locked in wonder. As our fingers tangled, a gust of wind ruffled the leaves. The sparks of light that burst from her hands engulfed everything around us, shining on our faces. Both of us were surprised that we had these powers, and we instantly bonded.

I sensed her before I even knew what the hell sensing was. Her magic didn't feel prickly like needles. Naw, hers felt like the sun finding me in the darkest of shadows. It felt like a Spring Fling Fair on a Saturday night where you ride the Ferris wheel. Or dipping into a pool and floating for the first time.

Her magic felt like the city lights kissing the belly of the stars, and Christmas morning, waking up to a pine tree swollen with presents.

In her own words, her magic was like believing in the impossible again.

Back to reality. A shift in the light, and now she is standing right in front of me.

Without a word, her arms wrap around me, pulling me into a warm embrace, and all the heartache and problems in the world seem to melt away. Her scent takes me back to that one time back in August when we played in the rain, and to the smell of hot, wet pavement. Her thick curls gently brush against my cheek. Hugging her here now, I just think back to summer in Bama. Us drinking frozen Kool-Aid slushes, scraping our knees from riding bikes. Or sneaking on the roof at night to watch the sky turn into the sunrise and eat sour apple straw candy till we got stomachaches.

Me and Alexis are like the sea and the land. Distant for a while.

But always meet at the edge of the world.

"Oh my God—what are you doing here?!"

My tongue feels like it's twisted in a million knots. "I found out that I had a grandmama, here in Louisiana."

She turns to the crowd, and everybody starts to go on about their business, lining up and going toward a table full of sign-up sheets for petitions.

"Wait, your grandma?"

"Mama Aya," I answer back. "She's—"

Her beautiful almond-shaped eyes are like the galaxies above, and her skin is like the starless midnight. A well of tears breaks through the disbelief that this reunion is really happening.

"Wait, you're *the* Mama Aya's grandson?!"

She acts like I said I'm the grandson of Oprah or somebody. "Yeah, I am. This shit is crazy, right?"

"Random as hell, more like it."

Her voice. Her half smile and gentle and measured breath. They carry me to a place beyond this world. My arms wrap around her once again, silently praying that this moment is not some trick or dream. If there is a God, he'll let this last for forever and a day. Fuh real.

"I missed you so much, Lex."

"I missed you too, Malik." Another round of studied glances. Alexis runs her fingers through her field of curls. "I'm sorry, I just can't believe this."

"Me either."

We both sit on a step, watching the campus life fight and fail to steal our attention from each other.

"Did you know her?" I manage. "That Katia girl?"

"I didn't know her personally." Her face splits, blessing me with that smile that still gives me a case of sweaty palm syndrome. I know we were young the last time we saw each other, but it's always been something about Alexis. She just makes me feel like no bad or wrong can ever happen in my life. "I just wanna bring her justice."

One of the girls comes up to her and hands her a clipboard. Alexis says something to her under her breath. The girl instantly runs off when Alexis low-key shoos her away.

"Dang, I see you kinda a big deal around here."

"Just doing what I can for the community on the outside. With the recent disappearance of Black girls in the Lower Ninth, everybody on the outside needs our help."

"You talkin' about . . . people like us?" I ask, referring to the magical side.

"If you ask the Kwasan tribe, 'people like us' are the only ones who matter. They're up in arms about some Caiman legacy kid going missing, and meanwhile, they ignore anyone without the gift of what we can do. Katia is just the last disappearance in a suspected trafficking ring right in the council's backyard, but they're not doing anything about it. Basically saying she's probably a runaway. Malik, she's only sixteen."

A little older than Taye. If he went missing, I'd scorch the earth just to bring him back. So the energy she got right now, I understand it one hundred percent.

But I'm high-key stuck on what she just said. The *Kwasan*—

She interrupts my train of thought. "I'm trying to get all the students to rally and offer their resources. Especially their folks and friends on the outside."

"Why won't they help?"

She pauses before answering. The expression on her face darkens. "This side of things is complicated. It's kinda like that old generation versus the new generation thing. But they have to realize that Black lives can't matter if *all* Black lives don't. Everybody deserves our help." A thought lingers between the both of us. She hugs me again, which makes me melt even more. "Anyway, I really thought I'd never see you again, Malik."

I flash a smile. "Yeah, it was hard for a long time after you got adopted. I ain't had nobody. Well, until Taye showed up."

Her eyes mist up a bit. "Taye?"

"Yeah, my lil' brother. He came to the orphanage a little while after you left, and he knows what I can do. He's everything to me."

Her hands grace the sides of my face. "You always had a heart of gold. Even though you were annoying as hell when we were kids."

A soft laugh from the both of us.

From a distance, there's a toll of a bell. Everybody that's down in this amphitheater starts to pack up their stuff.

"Damn." Alexis groans, wiping the tears from her eyes. "I have to get to class."

"Oh, uh—"

"Take my number. We can meet up after, I promise. I just can't be late."

"Fa'sho."

We exchange numbers.

"It's so good to see you, Malik," she says, hugging me again. I get a whiff of her perfume, and my heart stutters against my chest. "Let's meet after class."

I drown in her brown eyes. I'm breathless. "Okay."

Another toll of the bell.

And just like that, I'm the only one left in the amphitheater.

. . . .

Seeing Alexis was a distraction, to say the least, but now that I'm alone I might as well start following whatever trail my mama might have left behind here. I take out the picture I found of her right here on campus. What her first day like? How did she grow in this magic I never knew she had?

Popping in my *new* AirPods, I cue up that new Victoria Monét album and journey through the spots me and Chancellor Taron covered. The more I walk, the more it seems like the world around me grows.

Slowly, I drift through several buildings. ADMISSIONS. SCHOOL OF BUSINESS. At what feels like the edge of the world, I finally find the tree that's in the picture. It looks the same, just without my mama in front of it. Tall, overarching. My hands land on it, feeling the rugged edges of the tree bark scratching my palm. Instinctively, I inhale. This is where she stood and smiled.

This is where she got to be a college kid. But it's also where she started down the path that took her away from Mama Aya. Toward *bane magic,* according to that letter. Everything around me quiets as that familiar feeling begins to claw at me. . . .

I hear somebody scream into their phone behind me. "Ma, I'm not comin' home!" Some girl paces back and forth with her book bag hanging off her shoulders. "It doesn't make sense to do that when I'm safe here. They are not back; that's just a rumor." She rolls her eyes as she catches me spying on her conversation.

Shit . . .

"Ma—lemme call you back." She hangs up and storms past me. "Can I help you?! Starin' at folks and shit."

I shake my head and look on, fighting the urge to cuss her out.

My eyes scan the campus in front of me. The hustle and bustle of professors and students moving across this magical oasis on their own beat.

A voice comes from behind me. "You must be Malik Baron?"

I turn to find this dude standing right behind me with his glasses perched on his nose. He gives off a young professor vibe, like he belongs on an Instagram post more than in a classroom. His low-top fade is fresh, though. Clean lineup with a thick beard. He's a shade darker than I am and low-key doesn't look much older. His fancy draped cardigan got me feeling extra hot in this humid-ass weather.

"I'm so glad you're here to join us. I've heard a lot about you."

I pause my music. "Who are you?"

"Ah, forgive me," he answers with the same accent as Baron Samedi. "I'm *Professor* Kumale. You have me today for class, and I'm also your advisor."

"Oh, okay. That's wassup."

We shake hands.

"Did Chancellor Bonclair give you the rundown of the campus?"

Pshhh. A couple of eye rolls is my answer. *Professor* Kumale laughs.

"Come on, I'll give you a real campus tour," he says. But I stay put. Another chuckle from him. "I won't bite. I promise. I just . . . I know what it's like to be the new kid that everybody deems as 'falling behind' because you started late."

I scan the campus even more, and this world definitely gonna swallow me up. "Yeah, already feel like a fish out of water."

"Then let me show you around so you won't feel that way."

I slip my mama's picture in my back pocket. "A'ight."

In the middle of the other side of campus, you can see the sunlight's tip reflecting the burgundy brick buildings cornered in a tiny section with ivory and arches. Evergreen flowers with purple-and-blue petals just like the ones I saw on the Caiman University sign blanket this tall marble wall full of names. One in particular catches my attention. IN LOVING MEMORY—DR. ALISTAIR MCMILLAN.

"It's the periwinkle flower," Professor Kumale says. "It's a symbol of remembrance of the *enslaved* ancestors. They used it to record and locate their unmarked graves. It's Caiman University's way of honoring those who fought, bled, and died for our rights today. That's why it's our official university sigil."

I absorb the names.

So many generations lost.

Next up, we reach this one building that hides in the cut. LEWIS LATIMER SCHOOL OF SCIENCE & TECHNOLOGY is etched into the brownstone. A familiar smell hits me like a freight train, the smell of that good *ish*.

Through the cloud of kush, lying in the grass, students are in the heavenly blaze.

My eyes widen. Yo . . .

Professor Kumale starts walking without reprimanding them. "Don't worry, you can smoke here."

"Aye, for real? That uptight nig— I mean, *Chancellor Taron* ain't gon' say nothing?"

"Only for upper-level students, and it's grown here. It's from the chem lab. Hoodoo majors are smoking it up. As the students say. Also, we are not in the business of criminalizing marijuana."

We press on. Taking in different buildings. Tall ones and even small ones.

"The campus is quite magnificent, isn't it?" he says, pointing to another building. It's a pavilion shaped like a rectangle and set on a podium with a reflecting pool. The roof is holed around the edges, allowing a constant play of light and shadow below. The dope-looking arches are mirrored in a raised grid pattern of elongated hexagons. Damn. It looks top-notch as hell.

One dude tosses a deck of cards in the air. They swirl and assemble into the Eiffel Tower. His friend, laughing, speeds through it, knocking it down.

"So, like, we can do *anything*?" I ask.

"Whatever is in the means of majik, sure."

"Time travel?"

He raises an eyebrow. "Possibly, but temporary. Time is tricky as well, and you don't wanna get stuck, let's say, during the plagues."

"Immortality?"

"You can prolong life, but everything must die. But never say never."

His eyes land on mine; he can tell the wheels are turning.

"Matter is neither created nor destroyed. I'm sure you heard that."

I nod.

"Well—you can tap into that energy, but change is inevitable. Magic always comes with a price. When you get better in classes, you'll learn all about shadow work, protection, and even banishing."

Right in front of us is a sign with the letters BCSU. The building itself is brick, two-stories high, with big translucent windows at the front, and seems like it's in the middle of the entire campus. A slew of celebratory flyers are stuck on the sliding entry door: FALL CLASSES SIGN-UPS DUE! RA APPLICATIONS DUE 8/1.

"BCSU. The Bonclair Student Union." Professor Kumale opens the door, and we hustle into another world of chaos. It's like Walmart on the first of the month. *Bussssy as hell.* People studying, cracking their books open. Others lounging around, laughing with their little friend groups, drinking lattes and shit. In the corner is a place called Ground 'n' Pound Coffee Shop.

Then you got Rude Boy's Grab 'n' Go Sandwich Shop.

"Anybody ordered a Ain't Shit po' boy sandwich?" a cashier screams out, holding a wrapped foot-long sandwich in his hand. Somebody grabs it from him quick and darts back to their study group.

A few giggling girls pass us with glazing adoration in their eyes. They all say in unison like they're in an episode of *The Parkers,* "Heyyyy, Professor Kumale."

"Ladies," Professor Kumale chimes back, all *professionalllll.* "Remember: your history reports are due. It's worth twenty percent of your grade."

They giggle and bobble their heads even more and bound outside the door.

Hell naaaaah. I shake my head, stifling a laugh.

"Let's get you some books," he says, playing that shit off.

In this bookstore, a mountain of shelves is lined up against the wall. They're full of candles, incense, shiny-looking rocks, and books on shadow magic and astrology. It's like a whole candy store up in here, except no candy. It smells good as hell, though. Very sweet. Like cinnamon.

A book catches my attention: *African American Folktales: Magick in the South.*

Professor Kumale slowly goes up and down the aisles, pulling out books. They float behind him like they're trailing to see where he goes next.

One book zips right by me. I dodge it by mere inches.

We approach the cash register with hella books. My phone vibrates as the cashier rings up the items. The Caiman app has already been opened. My thumb swipes up and taps on the dollar sign icon. My eyes go buck wide: $2,500.

"Hold *the* hell on, what?!"

Professor Kumale throws back a laugh and grabs my phone. "Yes, it is. The dollar symbol is your Caiman Bucks, so aside your regular meal plan. This is extra for essentials and renews every semester."

"Bet!"

"You must be a lucky one. The chancellor doesn't admit late students, so Mama Aya must've pulled some heavy strings."

I can't help but roll my eyes. "Yeah, I guess she did."

"We at Caiman University want to set our students up for success. You don't have the stress and worry that regular college students have regarding higher education."

"You ain't gotta say nothing but a word." Shit, I can buy myself some real clothes. Shoes.

And a new phone because I am due for an upgrade. Taye too.

The cashier slides the books, in a CAIMAN UNIVERSITY bag, over to me with that customer service grin. I lift the bag off the counter, feeling the weight of unlearned knowledge that I'm gonna have to flip through.

"You'll make a good student. Good to know another Baron is here," Professor Kumale says as we walk back outside. I give him a look. "Apologies. I just meant because your mother, Lorraine, was a top student here."

So I've heard. Thinking to myself, *She really must have been famous or something around here. So how come no one knows what happened to her?*

"My mother who ran away with me when I was born and hasn't been heard from since, you mean?"

Professor Kumale presses his lips in a tight line. "I'm sorry. Chancellor Bonclair told me you've been on your own for quite some time. I didn't mean to pry."

"Nah. It's cool. She ain't never mentioned this place."

"Maybe she wanted you to have a normal upbringing."

"The way my childhood was set up, I wouldn't call that normal."

My eyes shift to the floor, deep in thought and putting up my guard.

"Look, sensing your magic, I can tell you're gonna do well here, Malik. Plus, you belong here. Our relationship with our magic is our own, and I believe Caiman can help you navigate it."

I suck my teeth. "What makes you think I need help navigating my magic?"

"Because I know what it's like being afraid of something about yourself that you don't understand." Professor Kumale's hands land on my shoulders, reassuring. "Glad to have you here at Caiman University, *Malik Baron*. See you later for class?"

We dap each other up.

"Appreciate it. Oh, and yeah, fa'sho."

Professor Kumale disappears in a cloud of maroon smoke.

Well, okay, then . . .

My phone buzzes in my pocket, and when I look at it, my heart almost leaps out of my chest.

It's a text from Alexis.

> Meet me by the quad.

• • • •

The quad is full of folks, resting between their classes. Sitting on a bench is Alexis with a few other people. They all just chillin'. "Hey, Malik."

I pull my newly filled book bag from my shoulders and sit next to her. "Wadup."

"Malik, this is my . . . this is Donja Devereaux. Second year. Donja, this is my childhood friend Malik Baron."

"Baron?" he says in a strange-ass tone. Then he switches to another language that sounds like French. *"Sa ki nan moute."*

Oozing with golden-boy privilege, Donja is clearly one of those light-skinned niggas who can go for a discount Drake. Straight hipster vibes with one earring dangling from his left ear, colored fingernails. A beanie curved on his head, with a beaded necklace hanging out from his half-buttoned shirt, his chest all out. His beard doesn't even connect for real, and his head is full of curly brown hair.

"Hey, wassup?" he says real dry in English.

A question burns my tongue. I even point to Lex and the Donja dude with a raised eyebrow.

"Wadup . . . aye, y'all—"

"No. No," Alexis replies, throwing ole boy a dagger-heavy stare. "Donja can't keep up with his escapades. Me and Donja kinda grew up together. Dating him is definitely not on my to-do list."

He playfully swats her.

I clench my teeth because who is this dude and why is he all up on Alexis?

Alexis looks at me, giggling. "And I'd also like you to meet—"

SWOOOOSHHH!

Two dudes appear out of nowhere, breathing hard. One of them is short, dark-skinned, with fresh waves just like mine. Wide, goofy-ass smile. The dude next to him seems more in his feminine bag. Sheer confidence radiates from him with his drawn-on eye makeup, lip gloss, and different-colored nails. Each of them has on a black CAIMAN UNIVERSITY shirt with the same periwinkle flower being held up by two hands.

"Wassup . . . I'm Elijah, and this is my twin—"

The twin brother with colorful nails steps in front, clearing his throat. "Umm, I can introduce myself. Wassup, cutie, I'm Savon. Pronouns they, them, and that Bitch."

Alexis pulls Savon back. "Elijah and Savon Carrington are annoying twins. Savon is studying and cultivating the Black Queer Conjurer Initiative and business essentials. And Elijah is in sports medicine."

"Oh, that's wassup. I'm Malik Baron. Nice to meet y'all."

"Oh, we know. Trust, we heard soooo much about you." Savon shifts their eyes to Alexis. "You ain't tell us he was this nineties fooooiiiinnne, girl. You've been holdin' out."

They laugh like they're on their own beat.

Elijah steps up to me. "Forgive my thirsty-ass twin. Welcome to good ole Caiman University."

"Appreciate it," I say back to him.

Savon cuts in between Elijah and Alexis, staring me up and down. "Surprised they let you in, though."

"Why you say that?"

"Summer term already starting . . . shoot, Caiman don't play when it's late enrollment."

"Ah, yeah, well, my grandma talked to the chancellor."

"Oh, the chancellor?" Savon throws a look to Alexis. "Well, shit, then you guuuud."

"Good thing you are starting in the summer, though." Elijah digs in his book bag, taking out his phone. "Because the summer term is how you can get all your core classes out the way so in the fall we can get to the fun shit. I'm talkin' block parties, capoeira classes, potions, all that shit."

"It's realllll triflin' how Caiman still make Kneegrows with magic take algebra and science and shit," Savon chimes in.

"What are you complaining about?" Alexis jokes. "You're passing all of it with flying colors. Professor Edmunds in Advanced Calculus is hard as hell."

Savon clicks their nails. "Told you to drop that class like a bad habit. 'Cause Professor Edmunds had me bumped!"

The way they act, it's wild. Like, all of this is just so normal to them.

I had friends when I was living with the Markhams, back in high school. Not many, though, because I wasn't trying to make friends and then have to leave or be transferred to another family. That shit hurts the most.

I kinda kept to myself most of the time, focusing on graduating and emancipating out of the system to get Taye.

"Group photo!" Savon says, holding their phone up. "Ummm, you too."

I awkwardly pose right beside Alexis as Savon snaps a picture. "Lemme see," Alexis says, leaning over him. "'Cause you like to send people out, posting photos, having folks looking all crazy."

"Girl, bye. You look *guuuddt.*" Savon taps rapidly on their phone. "Okay, Malik, with the sexy eyes. Male model. All the gworls gon' be fawning after you. You downloaded the CaimanTea app?"

"Uhhh," I say, pulling out my phone.

"That's our social media app," Alexis says. "You get all the tea with Caiman."

Savon jumps in and says, "Yaaas. The technology Blerds created our very own social media app, since we can't have the regular ones due to our . . . ya know, magic."

"Bet. I'll download it."

Seeing Alexis be so natural with these folks got me feeling some type a way. In the past five minutes, I gathered that they all grew up way more privileged than I ever did. They probably had their first magical lesson, being surrounded by people that looked and had the same *abilities* as them, at that fancy school Chancellor Taron mentioned earlier.

Damn. It must be nice.

That same bell tolls in the distance. Everybody groans. Alexis turns to me, shrugging her shoulders with a smile that can make any girl jealous. "We have to get to class. Please tell me you have Professor Kumale?" Donja walks through us. All rude and shit.

"Yeah, I got him."

Alexis takes out her phone. "Good, this class is dope. It's not like regular history class."

Elijah turns to us. "It's a *Magic School Bus*–type of class. Ooh, I wonder where we finna go this time?"

Savon steps in. "Probably the sixties. Maybe the Harlem Renaissance. You know I looove me some Langston Hughes. And I heard they was thotin' all up in those hotels, chile."

Elijah playfully slaps them upside the head. "Yo nasty ass—" They both speed off like lightning.

Alexis holds out her hand. "Give me your hand."

I'm a ball of confusion the way I'm looking at her. "Man, all this teleportin' . . . Y'all ever heard of walking?"

Even though I can't wait to touch her hand. No lie, I dreamt about this moment since she left.

She laughs. "Boy, give me your hand."

Our hands become tangled, sending a jolt through me. I rub my thumb over hers. A small enough gesture to make goose bumps dance across my skin. Her starry brown eyes are locked on mine.

"Ready?" Alexis asks.

"Yeah, I guess."

She leans in slowly. Instinctively, I do too.

Another *whoooosh!*

We disappear into thin air. Below we can see the whole campus going by in a blur. Then, instantaneously, we drop right in front of a building. Alexis goes up to a scanner–looking machine and scans the palm of her hand.

"Teleporting is fun once you learn it," Alexis tells me through my wave of dizziness.

A gust of wind blows against the back of my neck. Elijah and Savon appear right behind us.

"Yeah, if not, you can do it and drop down on a sharp-ass spire. So be careful."

All I can do is shoot a glance at Alexis. The three of them burst out laughing. Donja appears in swirling orange smoke and walks past a group of students, putting his hand on the door.

I look at it, confused as hell. "You have to scan your hand," Alexis says. And damn, I feel like a dumbass. "It's for attendance. Oh, word of advice: don't be skipping classes. Caiman U do not play that."

"Cool, I got you," I say, taking in her warning. I go up to the scanner and wave my hand. It turns green, making the doors slide open.

Taking a deep breath, collecting myself, I'm officially ready for my first class at Caiman University.

CHAPTER NINE

IT'S A WHOLE LOTTA WITCHCRAFT AND NIGGATRY IN THIS BITCH.
The state-of-the-art classroom opens to us through the double doors, like a big lecture hall or more like a movie theater. A whiteboard is stationed in the middle, right behind a mahogany desk. Cushioned seats are tiered up several rows. Big square-shaped windows that allow a whole buncha sunlight to creep in are placed on each corner of the paneled walls. Right above are fluorescent lights throbbing with a buzz.

No cap, this *shiiiiit* is on a whole other level.

"I'm sure you got the grand tour," Alexis says while we walk toward the middle three rows. If it's assigned seating in this class, I'mma go off because I wanna sit by Alexis. We go up a couple of steps, maneuvering right to the middle of the curved part of the assembled seats.

"Yeah, Chancellor Taron kinda gave me one, and then this Professor Kumale came in. He showed me some dope stuff."

Savon and Elijah park themselves right beside us, pushing Donja's raised feet off the back of a seat. Savon, Elijah, and Donja cut up, laughing.

"We thought we were gonna be late," Savon says, out of breath. "Somebody just had to go back to the dorm."

Elijah pulls out a bag of chocolate-covered pretzels. "Now you know I get real *hangry* around this time." He looks at me, licking the chocolate off his fingertips. "Low blood sugar."

Alexis rolls her eyes. "You made it just in time."

Elijah hops over a chair and turns around to face us. "We made a bet: ancient Rome."

Alexis leans forward. "Hmmm, I'm thinking North Africa or Spain, 'cause I wanna see the Moors. Ooh, maybe ancient Australia to see the Aboriginals?"

Savon shakes their head. "Australia? Hell to the no, chile." Low-key, they're kinda funny. "All those spiders and big-ass bugs? Count me out."

Alexis turns to me, beaming. "So, Professor Kumale is like the Black Ms. Frizzle, and we get to go to different time periods to learn about the history."

"Wait—like actual time travel? Professor Kumale told me that's temporary?"

They all bust out laughing. My face is on fire, but I hide it by forcing a smile.

"Aww, he's too cute," Savon utters. "Nah, we just use our *magic* to tap into the past."

"It's like our own lil' field trip," Elijah adds, holding up his hand like he's John Singleton.

"IMAX-style," Savon says.

Alexis takes out her thick notebook full of jotted notes. "Yeah, it's not like you're *really* there, but you do get to experience it in, like, 3-D."

"Bet," I mumble, a bit nervous.

The door flies open all dramatically. Professor Kumale strides in with his bag attached to his shoulder. He has a different type of swag to him when he steps over that threshold. He's in full-on professor mode.

"*Bon maten, klas.* I know you've all been waiting to see where we will go to next." He stops, making everybody hella nervous with his teasing pause. "Pop quiz first."

The class groans and throws up their hands.

"Just one question, and I'll tell you all, I promise. Who were the first ones to abolish slavery?"

A random hand shoots up. It's a girl down in front. "Abraham Lincoln, right? He started the abolishment of slavery in 1863."

Professor Kumale shakes his head, then looks for another answer in the crowd.

Savon shoots their hand up. "The first nation to actually abolish slavery was Haiti in the Haitian revolutionary war in 1804."

Professor Kumale grins.

A knowing gasp ripples from everybody except me—my ass is still confused on how we finna do this.

"Wait, Professor Kumale, are you serious?!" Elijah daps up this dude next to him. "Oh, this is about to be everything."

"Yes." Professor Kumale throws his head back. "I figured I'd take you all to *my* homeland so you can learn the history of Haiti. See how one of the bravest revolutionaries, Dutty Boukman, incited a rebellion that changed history forever."

He claps his hands. Out of nowhere, a projector on the ceiling cuts on, rolling like a countdown of a movie. From it, a picture of a Black man with scars running down his face like tears appears on the board.

"Dutty Boukman was a warrior. A powerful Voodoo priest and a leader of the Maroons who led the charge in 1791 that birthed the very genesis of Haiti."

"Professor Kumale," Donja speaks up, "is it true that Dutty Boukman was a part of the Bokors and sacrificed a young conjurer to win the war?"

Bokors?

Nothing but stressed whispers fluttering around the room. Folks looking on edge. Professor Kumale tries to regain the attention of the class.

"Interesting question, Donja. There were rumors on that. However, Dutty Boukman was a hero that held a ceremony at Bois Caiman, and he, along with many elders in our magic, sacrificed a great deal to lead their people to freedom. Even if it meant bloodshed."

Donja twists his lips, writing something in his notebook.

Another round of whispered *"Bokors."*

"We are ready." Alexis bats those beautiful brown eyes at me. Random bouts of fluttering butterflies are back in the pit of my stomach. "Don't worry. You'll see why we all are doing the most right now."

Professor Kumale crosses to the board to write: HAITIAN REVOLUTION. The words start to jumble, glowing like they got hooked up to some neon lighting.

Titters and whispers sweep the room.

"Who here can actually tell me about the Haitian Revolution?" Professor Kumale's accent is deep in his Kreyol. "Mr. Baron?"

Nothing but quiet, and everybody turns to me, waiting for me to say something. My body reacts in a learned response, and that's to sit up in my seat. The answer lingers on the tip of my tongue. "It's when they went to war in Haiti."

A beat. Damn, was that the wrong answer?

"Yes, that is correct. Good job, Mr. Baron. And why isn't it widely taught?" He points to Savon. "Savon Carrington?"

Savon leans forward. "Present, Professor?"

"Care to add?"

Savon's mood completely changes. They're in smart student mode. "Well, we know why. It's political. Just like everything in this world. Because the normal boring-ass American school system is racially biased. Also, they feel that didn't have much to do with America herself. But the reeeeal tea is that Thomas Jefferson felt that the revolution happening down in Haiti was going to cause an insurrection against slavery here in America. Thereby threatening America's economic interest. Hmph. He didn't want that smoke. He surely did not. . . ."

A few snaps from Alexis's crew.

All of this got me redoubling my focus. My eyes pan the room, taking in every point of view. Professor Kumale then points to a dude in the front.

"Whew, he is foooine as all get-out, and thoooose lips," Savon faux-whispers to Alexis.

"Chile, he got a girlfriend . . . or *boyfriend*?"

"Yo ass just need to ask him out," Elijah tells Savon.

"I heard he likes both," Alexis utters. "Had Antoine in his dorm room a month ago. Chiiiiilllle."

Under their breath, I finally hear them say his name. D Low.

"Well, Professor," D Low begins. "Let's be honest, it's some Black folks hackin' white Frenchmen's heads off. You know they don't wanna teach none of that. I mean, look how they're actively banning books down here in Louisiana. Florida. Alabama. Texas. They're erasing our truth. Our trials and tribulations."

Savon throws a praising hand. "America got ninety-nine problems, but the truth ain't one."

D Low and a couple of dudes dap one another up.

A girl in the front raises her hand. She's baaaaadddd as heyell. Long twisted braids. Pretty melanated skin. "Yeah, unless it has something to do with slavery, they always gotta add a white savior in the story."

Everybody in class offers their *chile*s or *you better say that*s.

My knee bounces up and down.

A bit wound up.

So much knowledge.

Alexis doesn't even raise her hand. "The Haitian Revolution was a successful insurrection led by Toussaint Louverture. It was the only revolution or rebellion that led Haiti to be free from slavery. It was against white supremacy. Against all that they'd ever known. That is the real reason why it's not taught. It's also how we got our name for the university. The war was fought at Bois Caiman, and word on the street is that's where they performed spells to call on the orisha Ogun to help them fight for their independence. The elders decided to name this very university after it to pay homage to those who fought in the war."

Okay. Alexis be on her shit.

"This is why the Catholic and Christian missionaries made it their mission to demonize Haitian spiritual practices. Spreading misinformation about Haitian Vodou. Villainizing Black magic," she continues.

Another hand shoots up. It's the girl with the long braids. Professor Kumale clocks it. "Yes, Dominique."

Dominique swishes one of her braids to the side. "I'm piggy-backing off Alexis. It's the American media's false portrayal of West African Vodun for me. Making white women victims or heroes in magical stories, while Black witches are nonexistent or are sacrificial lambs to save the white main characters."

Her homegirls snap their fingers in agreement.

I clock Alexis throwing hella shade.

The competition and tension between them are thick like expired syrup.

"Chile, the way they be portraying Black witches on TV is atrocious," Savon comments, holding a fist in the air like a revolutionary. "Hashtag-justice-for-Bonnie-Bennet. 'Cause they won't see heaven for how they did my girl."

Professor Kumale steps from the board with a dry-erase marker twirling between his fingers. "The passion in this room is inspiring. It's the same passion that inspired warriors in Haiti in 1791."

"Okay, can we go now?" Savon is about to bust out of their seat.

"I guess I can show you better than I can tell you. This here is the psychometry spell. We can tap into the past. It's a very skillful spell. Now, remember, this is a mere memory. Nothing or no one in here can touch or harm you. But I must warn you"—his eyes scan the entire classroom—"you might not like what you see. So, I urge you to be careful whenever and wherever you are venturing off to."

Professor Kumale turns toward the whiteboard. The numbers 1791 start to jumble. Vibrate. Making themselves into little ripples.

"Repeat the chant with me." Professor Kumale whispers in Kreyol, *"Moutre m' sot pase a . . ."*

The whole class repeats in unison: *"Moutre m' sot pase a . . ."*

I attempt to do the same.

Instantly, I feel Professor Kumale's energy. His magic pulsates and billows around the whole room like electric currents. The projector on the wall shifts like it's rolling the credits to the greatest war movie ever seen. The way we all move and zip is different this time; it's more so the building itself is collapsing and disappearing. The tile floors instantly turn into wet, mushy grass. The wall panels shift and move so quickly that they turn into arching trees. Swirling all around me is a plume of thick, burning smoke as the world sits on a tilting axis.

A cacophony of banging drums.

Pounding like heartbeats against someone's chest. A war call.

BOOM. BOOM. BOOM.

A shudder runs through me, blood pounding at my temples. It then turns into a sharp ringing in my left ear. It's like somebody placed the wrong plug in an amp, and the feedback from the mic is on a thousand.

The wind blows against my skin, making all the hairs stand at attention. The sound of the drums rises and falls, fading into the distance like soft thunder receding in the sky. The grass crunches under my shoes when I stalk off into the deep green foliage. Alexis and Donja go off, disappearing through a cloud of smoke.

"Alexis?" I call out. But the thick air instantly makes my mouth dry as the Sahara.

I'm left alone.

And woozy, trying to catch my breath.

The angry sky bleeds red, and the loud boom feels like it's only inches away.

Everything goes quiet. Still. Just the sound of something flapping through the darkness. I turn to find a flock of birds taking flight from a nearby tree. Right in front of me, there is a patch of woods, and grassland stretching in every direction. Gunshots ring through the air, but they're far away enough for me to revel in this otherwise dead silence.

Out of nowhere, a white woman and a little girl whip past me, coughing and stumbling across the field. Their dresses billow in the dark as they take cover. Behind them, a man with a longsword comes out with the bloodied and severed head of a white man. Right at his side is a tall Black woman with wild eyes. Ridges of muscles and tendons bulge beneath their midnight-blue skin. Both of them march with a vengeance. The woman locks eyes with me, and from her pocket she pulls out an oiled machete and hurls that bitch right at my face. Oh fuck! I duck, and I hear the piercing of flesh. I pivot my body to see a white soldier screaming from the pain.

Oh hell naw! Elijah and Alexis were right. It is like I'm in a personal IMAX theatre or some shit.

A battle ensues. Nothing but ass-kicking happening right in front of my eyes. The woman storms past me and grabs the machete from ole dude's chest and marches up with a ferocious stride to another soldier with a musket. I don't know how the hell she does it, but when he points it and shoots, she quickly dodges the bullet and the smoke and swings down and drop-kicks his ass right to the ground.

All in one motion, the woman uses her frame to dance around punches, overwhelming men twice her size.

Through the ghostly ring of light, I see more white folks getting their heads cut off and pummeled to the ground. My whole body seizes up, and the woman's face turns into my mama's—yelling and being swallowed by blinding green light. Right there in the middle of the memory, I see my younger self open his eyes, and the three burned bodies are crumpled on the floor. I let out a ragged breath and jolt back, scared.

More yells make me move my feet. Then I start to run, trying to avoid getting trampled. White women in fancy dresses running around, wild and screaming, and right in front of me, one of them gets sliced and diced with a long machete.

Crimson blood stains the grass, and her body drops to the ground, killed by the warrior that was walking beside the woman a few seconds ago. We look at each other, his Black face wrought with confusion.

Is this the Dutty Boukman that Professor Kumale showed back in class?

Out of nowhere, a white Frenchman on a spooked horse rears up and gallops toward us with a vengeance. The Dutty Boukman guy spins with an unnatural speed, throwing me to the ground. And like Spider-Man to his Green Goblin, Dutty twists in midair and mounts himself on the back of the horse. With a swift motion, he slits the white Frenchman's throat. His pale body lands on the ground in a bloody, lifeless heap.

The Haitian warrior with the cold eyes pivots the stallion, and the horse lifts up, neighing into the sky. Behind him, hellfire drifts across this land, burning up the entire soil. After a chaotic beat, he barrels right toward me. And as I was taught back in Helena in case of a drive-by, my ass duck for cover. Don't ask no questions. Just get yo ass out the way.

Soon as I hit the ground, everything changes.

Dust swirls in the fog.

Nothing but a dark void.

Before I know it, I'm deep off in the woods, somewhere far from the battlefields.

Through the pitch-black, a haze lifts, but now a thick nest of bushes and branches obscures my view. Sparks of fire split the darkness, showcasing a group of old Haitian men in a semicircle, dressed in white robes. They stealthily dance around the flames, shouting like they're in a church revival.

Goose bumps prick my skin from their magic.

A loud scream rips from behind me. I about jump out of my skin. One of the men comes through, carrying a . . . a little boy no older than Taye. His guttural screams tear at me like a predator's sharp teeth. Everything in me wants to walk up and snatch him away and tell him go run, but I know this isn't real. It's of the past. And one thing I learn, ain't shit you can do about the past.

From what I can tell, one of them walks up to this Black man with a long-curved knife. He's clearly the leader because they all bow, paying their respects to him. They're all lit by a single torchlight and stand next to a soggy swamp. The men crane their necks, staring up at the sky. Ceremoniously, they click their tongues. The leader of the tribe twirls his fingers as if he's finger painting.

In an instant, the light from the moon shifts, snaking through the pines, casting a ghostly silver light. A strange geometrical symbol appears in the grass. It glimmers with a red light. Another man on the side places a bowl on a tree stump. His face lifts, tightening with resolve.

"*Oya—Ban mwen pouvwa lavi ak lanmò.*"

All the men circle around the young boy, chanting the same words in Kreyol. "Papa!" the boy cries out in desperation. "Papa! *Tanpri sove m!*" The riotous sound of the drums grows as the man in the white robe stabs the young boy in the chest. A prism of light explodes, engulfing the entire woods.

My hands meet my eyes, shielding myself from the blinding light.

A powerful gust of wind snatches me up and throws me back to the ground. I spring up, meeting the leader. His eyes blink with a film of red, and his crinkly finger points toward me.

Another gust of violent wind blows in response.

I don't breathe.

As he steps forward like a rabid animal, I inch back. His lips twist, mumbling something under his breath. Instinctively, my hand goes up, and he stops in his tracks. The moon above us is darkened by a shaft of light.

Another exchanged glance between me and the leader. Fear fliting across his face.

A deadly cracking sound. It's bone, shifting and protruding from ole dude's body. He yelps in pain, and his head bobs from side to side like he's possessed. Oh shit. Under the harsh gaze of the moonlight, I get a good look at the folds of all the men's Black skin stretching from their bones.

An erratic death croak repeats from their mouths.

"*Ki sa nou tout te fè?!*"

Pain shoots through me as I scramble to my feet and out of the woods. I turn back, seeing them materialize from the woods. They're marching. Gliding across the field as if their feet don't touch the ground. A deep, dark dread shoots through me. With each step, a ghostly wreath of light showcases their curling white cloaks becoming black with long, flared sleeves.

Beneath them, the ground quakes, like tectonic plates separating. I clock one of them reaching and inching toward me.

The man's sunken mouth cracks open to say, *"Yo ap vini."*

He contorts in pain, dematerializing. From the tip of his finger, a green jet of light lasers right at me.

Before I'm pulverized . . .

We're right back in the classroom.

The sound drowns in, and the whole classroom erupts in applause. Except me. My hands are wrapped around the corners of my seat handle, bound to break it off. Beads of cold sweat slither down my forearm, and a sharp pain clamps my heart.

"Oh hell yeah, that shit was dooope!" the D Low dude at the front says. They all talk about how cool this "field trip" was.

I look around, confused and choking back the gravity of what just transpired. Dope? I just saw a lil' kid get murked in the middle of the woods.

"I mean, it felt soooo real," I hear Savon say to Donja.

All their voices crash into me like a wave.

Professor Kumale appears at the front of the room in a cloud of smoke. "And there you have it, folks, an up-close look at one of the most important battles in world history."

"And can't forget it was because of a sista, Abdaraya Toya, an Amazon woman who raised Jacques and made him into the warrior we all love. Also, she was a beast on that battlefield," Alexis says. "Watching them fight side by side . . . I can't believe we really just saw that."

I think back on the man and the woman with the swords. That must have been Jacques and Abdaraya Toya. But who was the leader of the tribe I saw while everyone else was watching the rest of the battle?

Alexis turns to me and asks, "Malik, you good?"

With everything I just witness, I can literally feel my heartbeat against my chest, and my throat feels like it's about to close.

To answer her question: hell nah, I ain't good.

CHAPTER TEN

THIS IS TOO MUCH. ALL OF IT.

Again, I'm left with more questions than damn answers, because who the hell did I see, and why the hell do they look so much like the strangers who showed up at my house ten years ago in those black cloaks?

At night the BCSU gives these cool spot vibes. String lights wrapped around tree limbs. Outside on the lawn, a sea of tired students meander around the food trucks. The smell of spicy oxtails wafts through the air, making my mouth hang on its hinges. And the way this stomach is touching the back of my spine, I'mma have to cop me a plate.

Drifting inside, I see a girl with an Afro and thick glasses sit on a stool and play the guitar right by the computer lab. She kind of reminds me of Summer Walker a little bit, singing some neo-soul while everybody else rests their faces between pages of thick books.

Familiar voices of jokes, shit talk, and bravado pull my attention to a table somewhere in the back. It's Alexis and her crew.

"Malik!" Alexis scooches over to the opposite end of the booth with half-eaten fries and a cold sub sandwich. I sit down, and they all look at me except for Donja. "So, how was your first day?"

"It's cool. Everything's cool."

"Well, glad *you're* having a good time," Savon grumbles, drumming their fingers on the table. "We thought you ran away, freaked out by all of this. 'Cause the way you disappeared after class—"

"Aye, yo, don't mind them." Elijah nudges Savon. "They're just mad that we are on campus lockdown."

"Lockdown? For what?"

"A couple of conjurers went missing in the Tremé," Savon says.

Elijah starts to chew on his straw. "The chancellor is trippin' and doin' the most, so we can't leave campus. And damn, did y'all hear, Akiyah ain't comin' back next semester."

Alexis adopts a real look of concern. "Whaaaat? You heard from her?"

"Yeah, she said her parents won't let her come back to campus. With everything that's going on, they wanna keep a close eye on her."

A collective "damn" escapes their lips in a single breath.

My mind immediately goes back to that girl Chancellor Taron was talking to earlier. She was real upset about possibly not coming back. And Alexis mentioned a magic kid going missing. Chancellor Taron and Mama Aya were talking about it too, and that cousin of mine at the party . . .

Savon cuts in and says, "Girl, you better be careful because Chancellor Bonclair already on edge; he'll expel that ass."

Alexis sips from her straw, blinking back shame. "Malik, you want anything from the trucks outside?"

"Naw. I'm good," I say back. I'm trynna get back on subject. "So, you can get expelled here?"

Savon picks up their phone from the table. "Hell yeah. We're not supposed to use our magic outside in the 'regular' world. Especially if it reveals or causes harm to regular folk."

I remember Chancellor Taron told me that earlier. "He ain't serious, is he?"

"Like a damn heart attack," Elijah answers bitterly. "It's the rules, hell, basically law around here. The Kwasan coven don't play. Especially the chancellor's mother, Empress Bonclair."

Savon clocks the *who's that* expression on my face. "If bougie was a person. Picture the *fabulous* Lynn Whitfield and Diahann Carroll. Boom. You got Mrs. Empress Bonclair. As in the Bonclair Student Union? Head of the Kwasan tribe."

"And it doesn't help that she's the chancellor's mama, either," Elijah adds.

Donja grunts and shifts in his seat, annoyed.

"Maybe that's the problem." Alexis leans back, continuing her thought. "Too much control on what we can and cannot do, but they're ignoring the fact that young Black girls are going missing at an alarming rate."

"Lex—" Savon starts.

"No, I can't. Look, Katia Washington is still out there and may be in trouble. A lot of girls have been going missing, and I know some of the folks in Lower Ninth and Tremé been asking for the conjurers to help. It's a shame that Caiman University and the other tribes are turning their backs on them. Now they're locking down the campus because folks with magic are going missing. But Katia doesn't have magic to protect her, wherever she is. So, what about her?"

"Lex, I hear you." Savon places their head on her shoulder while simultaneously texting on their phone. "But we are not trying to get expelled or get our magic revoked."

"Surprised the Deacons of the Crescent wasn't there; you already know how they be," Elijah comments, and turns to me to explain. "Deacons of the Crescent be on some Hotep fuckery. There are rumors that the Bokors are back, and if they are, they gonna try to expose our world to everybody else."

"The Kwasan tribe is not gonna let that happen," Savon quickly responds.

A grim beat among all of us as I try to keep up and collect the info.

"What happens if it does?" I ask.

"We're all in trouble. Our safe space would not be safe again." Alexis whips out her phone. Types rapidly. "I'm gonna email Madam Empress one more time to set up a meeting."

"Now you know that woman is not gonna meet with you." Savon

cracks up, grabbing her phone, and places it on the table. "She don't like you."

"I don't care. It's not right how we just sit here and do nothing."

"It's a lot you gotta catch up on, freshman," Elijah chimes in, reminding me that I am a fish out of water.

Can't even argue with that. Magic here apparently got rules. Even though I never been really good with rules or following them. And judging by the day I had, you'd think everybody had free rein to cast whatever spells they wanted. But nah. I think of Chancellor Taron when he was back at Mama Aya's house.

Reckless.

"Well, Lex, you just trying to help people," I say, breaking outta my deep thought. "You shouldn't let anythin' stop you."

"Thank you, Malik." She sticks her tongue out at Savon. "I mean, what's the point of having these abilities if we can't help our own out there? Those who truly need it."

Donja slams his phone on the table, interrupting the flow of the convo. He mumbles in his Kreyol language under his breath. "Ugh, can we please talk about something else? I'm hungry, and this stale salad is not doing it for me."

The hell is his problem?

"So, where you from, Malik?" Elijah asks me, changing the subject and ignoring Donja.

"I grew up in Alabama, and then I came here when I found out I had some family. I was supposed to be in California with my lil' brother."

I can feel Alexis's eyes shift to me. "Really?"

"Yeah, I wanted to start over."

Savon raises their coffee cup in the air.

That's all they're getting outta me. No cap, I learned the hard way about spilling your whole life story to people you barely know. Niggas love to throw shit in your face when you are no longer of use to them.

"His grandma is Mama Aya," Lex says.

Steeling myself for the questions, I play it cool.

"Wait—are you serious?" Savon leans forward and smirks. Like they're being let in on the biggest secret. "No wonder Chancellor Bonclair got you in so late in the semester. What's the tea behind that, chile?"

"She's my grandma."

Everybody goes quiet at the tone of my voice.

"Naw. Naw. You can't drop that bomb with just a shrug," Elijah says. "I mean, that's a pretty big deal."

"I literally just met her. I didn't even know she existed."

All of their expressions read the same.

Shock. Confusion. More shock.

"That's wild, yo. You do realize that Mama Aya is a living legend, right?" Elijah asks.

"Okayyyy, we *looove* a nepo baby, honey," Savon throws out.

I shake my head with a flair of nonchalance. "Nah. I ain't know that."

"Hell, she is the definition of royalty. They say she used to run with Marie Laveau and even Tituba. She's so old that she knows the wisdom of God."

I laugh. "Y'all wildin'. She ain't that old."

"We for real," Savon blurts out. "She's over a hundred years old—"

I let out a chuckle of disbelief. "She ain't a hundred years old."

From the looks on their faces, these mofos ain't playing.

"From the stories we've been hearing about her," Elijah adds. "I'm tellin' you, Mama Aya is a whole savage when it comes to this magic thaaannng."

"You really didn't know?" Savon asks me.

I blink down the awkwardness and interlace my stiffened fingers as a means of defense.

"Like I said, I don't know her for real."

"Well, some conjurers are able to live for hundreds of years, maybe even be immortal." Alexis bats those beautiful eyes at me. "That's why they say Mama Aya lived that long."

Elijah grabs the last of the cold fries on the plate in front of us. "And she, like, wiped out all the Bokors at once."

The expression on my face instantly slides into confusion. That's the third time that word has been mentioned, after Donja in class and Elijah just now. "What's a Bokor?"

"You don't know none of this?" Savon asks in disbelief. "Chile, they didn't teach you that in Alabama?"

Alexis throws a look of daggers at Savon, shutting them up.

"Kinda been doin' this magic thing on my own. So, all this kinda new to me," I admit.

Awkward silence.

It's like that time I was the only Black kid in a classroom full of white kids watching a movie about Dr. Martin Luther King Jr., and they all look at you with guilt, hella awkward.

"Rumor has it that the Bokors could control and make zombies, and Mama Aya killed all of them using a ouanga, a powerful talisman."

"Get the fawwwk outta here?" I say, laughing. "Zombies. Wayment—they exist too? Like the *Walking Dead* type of zombies?"

Judging by the tense shift in the atmosphere, they're not playing.

Donja interrupts. "The Bokors not zombies; they're more like enforcers. Protect villages from sickness and war. During the Haitian Revolution, they did some dark magic to help win the war, pissed off some powerful beings. But all the Bokors wasn't bad. And some say Mama Aya didn't defeat *allll* of 'em. Some people think they're still around, biding their time."

He throws a look of shade my way.

I prop myself up, about to give him the business, when Elijah chimes in. "Yeah, some folks don't feel the same way as the Kwasan tribe do," Elijah says. "I ain't gon' hold you, they kinda look at the Bokors as martyrs."

Nah. From what I'm hearing, these Bokors are the same tribe I saw in class. Martyrs? Not the way I saw them killing an innocent kid. *Do I tell them I saw them?*

Nah. I'mma let them spill all the tea.

Donja continues. "The Bokors were shunned by mambos, which

were the priestesses, and oungans, who were the puritans of the practice, for their use of bane magic. The Bokors were known to summon dark magic that can sometimes beckon the daka—demon. They steal your soul, your magic, memories, and everything about you. You know, they were the main tribes in our world that practiced duality. Both good and bad magic."

Elijah leans in. "Look up Madame LaLaurie . . . fawwwked her ass up."

The whole table goes quiet. Low-key, all I can focus on is Donja talking about bane magic. Which apparently has something to do with the Bokors. Then my mama getting tempted by bane magic connects her to this somehow? Could it really be the same Bokors I saw that attacked her? Sure looked like them with those black cloaks. It's not like that idea is not supported by the way Mama Aya be talking about my mama and how she got into some shit she ain't had no business getting into.

But hold up—if they were eradicated over a hundred years ago, who the hell brought them back to destroy my life?

"Chile, they said with some goofer dust, the conjurer who cast the spell can raise the dead and come get ya, like THIS!" Savon's scream makes Alexis jump, breaking me out my thoughts. Then more laughter spills out on the table. "Don't be messin' with them haints."

They break into a cacophony of *hell nah*s and *you a damn fool*s.

"But like I said, it was just stories that the adults would tell to get us to act right," Alexis jumps in.

Is it, though? Either way, I'm mentally taking notes.

Donja chimes back in, "The Kwasan tribe didn't like they were doing all of this, so over a hundred years ago, they rose up and overthrew them. If you ask me, Kwasan just wanted them out of the way so they could take power. . . ."

Elijah jumps on that real quick. "That's a cute story, but you're forgetting the fact that when the Bokors were around, they literally sacrificed conjurers to steal their magic. That's why even now when kids go missing and shit like what's been happening lately, you get all these rumors about a Bokor resurgence."

Donja shrugs like he ain't got a care in the world.

"Black-on-Black crime even making its way into the magical community," Savon comments, shaking their head. "Had the Divine Elam all up in here, canceling Bokors. After everybody ganged up on them back in the early 1900s, they had to take the L and be gone."

Savon leans in and says, "Except everybody don't believe they should've been. You have some 'sympathizers' out there, following their lost cause, hoping they'll be restored to justice."

Elijah says, "Oh yeah, you talkin' about Damone and them?"

While the swirl of their conversations keeps on, full of more names I don't understand, my mind instantly returns to what I saw in the woods in class. The woman and the man, chopping and killing folks. And then the eyes of the leader piercing into me, and then the screams.

Yo ap vini . . .

Just thinking about it makes me ice-cold.

"It was one of the bloodiest wars in our community. It set a precedent on how things are run now," Donja says. His eyes shift over to me, then back to Lex. "The Kwasan coven decided they were going to be the top dogs, setting rules and shit."

There's a bitter edge to what Donja just said.

"See, that's why we say your grandmama is hella powerful," Elijah says, interrupting my lingering thoughts. "She led the charge when they went against the Bokors. Man, our mama and daddy used to tell us that one look from Mama Aya, and you just disintegrate."

That make Mama Aya sound like some sort of hero. But I learned that heroes don't just hang you out to dry or abandon you.

"A'ight, y'all, I'm ready to head back to the dorm. This night has been *uneventful.*" Donja sounds even more annoyed. He gathers up his stuff.

"Yes, 'cause I'm about to crack open this bottle of wine and watch me some reruns of *P-Valley.*" Savon starts to get up, clearing the table. "And then run me a cleansing bath and spray on this Florida water."

Elijah playfully jabs them on the shoulder. "How many times you gon' watch that shit?"

"You know I can't get enough of Uncle Clifford and that fine-ass Lil Murda."

We all get up from the booths, and we make our way outside the student union, right onto the sloping steps.

"Malik, you have a way home?" Lex asks.

Damn, I ain't think about that. "Uh . . . I came here with Chancellor Taron. We teleported here, and I guess he figured I can get myself back home."

She chuckles to herself and tells her crew, "I'll catch up with y'all later."

"Cool," Elijah and Savon both say.

Donja looks hella pressed. "Lex, you know there's a buddy system on campus."

"Donja, tomorrow. See you in class."

Donja rolls his eyes before disappearing into thin air.

Alexis turns back to me. "Don't worry about Donja; he just has a mood."

"Nah, I ain't even worried about him." We keep walking for a bit until the BCSU starts to fade in the distance. The pavement shines like silver as we make our way through the small park area in the middle. "So, this is, like, a real HBCU? Like classes, parties—"

"Everything. Okay," she says, getting excited. "There's the Divine Ten, which are the House of Transcendence; that is a safe space and all-inclusive fraternity for Black Queer folx. Then you have your Oyas. The Daughters of Oshun. Now they in competition with each other. This coming fall, I'mma pledge the Daughters of Oshun."

"Oh, you are, huh?"

"I am. I am. Okay, so there's the Jakutas and the Yemojas. All of them fall under the different tribes and the Yoruba cosmology of African deities."

"Tribes?"

"The Kwasan tribe are the main ones. I mean, *the* tribe. They basically funnel money and magic into this school. Rumor is they can take your magic away if you cause too much trouble or reveal yourself—and I gotta be careful now because Chancellor Taron is not too pleased with me."

I take a mental note.

"Then there is the Oasis tribe across the pond," Alexis adds, faking an English accent. "They are over at our sister school in Europe. Some of the greatest go there. Descendants of the Moors. Children of literal kings and queens."

"Dang, all that?"

"Oh yeah, they don't play. Okay, you have the Domingo tribe; they're the Caribbean tribe. They practice Christianity and Vodoun. . . ."

"Don't most Christians believe magic is from the devil?"

"That's a whoooole other story," she says. "The ones who are lost. The Domingo tribe, you see, they use the Psalms as spells, and it is dope. Also, Santeria for our Afro-Latinx folks. But you gotta have that strong African in that bloodline!"

"You cappin'?"

Alexis is too hyped right now. "I wish I was! Then there is the Mojani tribe. They're on some next-level shit. You don't wanna mess with them. They study majik at the oldest university to mankind. Aganju University."

Aganju University.

I remember Chancellor Taron saying that.

"Listen, I'm trying to get into Dr. Honsou's cross-cultural class for real. To go to the motherland and study the ancient majik of atari. . . . You gotta be a senior to take that one."

She closes her eyes and falls quiet.

I do the same. We both listen to the cicadas around us, singing their nightly tunes. It low-key reminds me of those summer nights back in Alabama at the group home, when we'd sneak a couple of dill pickles from the fridge and go outside in the backyard.

"And the Bokors?"

She kinda exhales and then continues. "Yes. It's these scary stories we used to hear all the time. Stories of practitioners who, unlike oungans, are not chosen by the spirits. Who take their magic by force. You see, the Bokors weren't always bad. Some did money work, healing, love work. But a particular group in the tribe of Bokors who wanted so desperately to win the war, they turned to bane magic, the darkest and most powerful form of conjuring. They stripped the magic of a young conjurer who was just coming into their prime."

I don't need her to remind me—the young boy's haunting cries still linger in my ears.

My mama's letter pops into my mind. *I'm sorry. But something in me can't. Bane magic is tempting me. Please, I need your help.*

"So, the Bokors started bane magic?"

"Nope. Bane magic is ancient. Just that a lot of conjurers don't tap into it. When the Bokors did it, the goddess Oya punished them. Legend says that's why they have to steal magic from others—cursed to a monstrous form, doomed to repeat their horrific crime over and over again. Creepy, right?"

A flash of them and their bones cracking and breaking and their cloaks turning tattered and black.

"But why, though? Why they turn on them?"

"When you're like us—you know, conjurers—and don't be baptized in the fire, you pay your way in, but when you sorta renege on the deal, just like the Bokors did, consequences. Magic is wild, right?" It's just like Kumale said: magic always comes with a price.

"Yeah, I had no idea."

"Legend has it that you trade all of yourself for more power. Your memories, your happiness, everything that makes you *you*. The Bokors are said to practice evil and benevolence. Mostly evil, though. They serve the Loa—spirits in Haitian Vodou—with both hands." She could tell that I was thinking about this hard. "Like Baron Samedi."

"Wait, Uncle Sam?"

"Oh my God, you know him, don't you?"

I nod. "Hell yeah. He cool as fuck, though. So, he's one of these Loa?"

"Everything we knew or come to believe, Malik, especially when we were young, is not so black and white. There are things out there you can't even imagine. Things that were kept hidden from us."

We pass by a slew of dorms. Under the moonlight, people are hanging out, talking, or rushing back through the door with their late-night snacks. Others are sneaking in that *see you tomorrow in class* kiss and good-bye.

The Bokors *have* to be the ones I saw in Haiti. And maybe they were the ones at my house when my mama disappeared. So now I gotta figure out what the Bokors have to do with my mama's disappearance.

Lex's face spreads into a small smile at my furrowed brow. "You're gonna catch on, I promise. Plus, with a grandmother like Mama Aya, which I still can't believe . . . you're gonna be, like, the most famous kid at Caiman U."

"Appreciate that, Lex. You know, it's not just Mama Aya. . . . It seems like everyone here knows something about my mama."

We keep walking, passing another area for sitting. "You never talked about her at the group home."

"I always assumed she was dead, but then I find out about this whole new world and . . . I'm not so sure. Everyone seems to know her, but no one knows what happened to her."

"She won all kinds of awards here, you know. Her name is over display cases and on banners. She dropped out her senior year. . . . Well, some people say she was kicked out. But everyone agrees she was one of the smartest students Caiman has ever seen. I think . . . I think she'd be happy you were here."

I should be taking mental notes, trying to figure out if my mama really was expelled and if it had something to do with bane magic. But instead I just hold Alexis's last words in my mind, savoring them in grateful silence.

We move slowly, tracing the paths of this empty campus.

"Let's get you home."

Alexis holds out her hand. I ain't trynna be all gushy, but I take it with a quickness. Her magic takes me back to when we were kids outside, hearing the cicadas late at night. Those summer nights . . .

"What are you thinking about?"

"Just sensing your magic. It's wild. You know, Malik, your eyes, they tell a thousand stories even without a word being uttered. They can rewrite history if you let 'em. You've always been like that."

Her words got my cheeks feeling all kindsa hot.

"And he's blushhhhhhin'. Awwwwww."

"I never forgot you, Lex. I held on to what we had when we was kids. Where we felt safe. Where we—"

"Had each other."

Alexis takes a moment to gather her thoughts. Suddenly, she closes the space between us, wrapping her fingers around mine. Her breath cools the heat off my skin.

"Hang on."

On instinct, I give myself over to her, and it's like God himself cut off the gravity, and we're at Mama Aya's house in 0.5 seconds. It's that quick. My head still spins as a wave of nausea rushes past me as me and Lex step from a cloud of magic.

"You're going to learn the teleportation-and-projection spell when you get into your Intro to Magic class, and also get over that vertigo you're feeling."

Swallow down the upchuck. "Ah, that's what that is."

Her hand lands on my cheek, and instantly I feel a thousand times better. No motion sickness or nothing. *Her magic . . .*

She walks a few steps ahead of me, her beautiful brown skin aglow under a gaggle of stars. Her hands trail the tree, swiftly prancing around it. Her eyes are fixated on the blue bottles that swing and sway to their own rhythm. The light from the moon allows shapes to shine on her face.

"Technically, I'm not supposed to be off campus. Even before the lockdown, Chancellor wasn't too happy with me for catching eyes with that protest."

"Dang, that's wild the chancellor banned you from going off campus."

"Yeah, he'll get over it, though. Come fall semester, I'll be off 'punishment.'"

"Hey, one more question: *Yo ap vini*. You know what that means?"

Her face twists into confusion. "That's 'We're coming' in Kreyol. Where'd you hear that?"

I try to shrug it off. "It's just something I heard on the lil' field trip we took today." I pull out my phone and text Taye. "Before you go, I want you to meet Taye."

Speaking of, Taye is already at the door, giving Alexis that goofy smile.

"Wassup, Lik."

"Taye, I want you to meet somebody. This is Alexis. She left the orphanage a little bit before you came."

Clearly, she's a hugger, because she wraps Taye up in her arms. "It's nice to meet you, Taye. Malik told me so much about you."

"Nice to meet you too," Taye says, noticing me just grinning. "Wow. You got him smiling like that, then you must be special."

"Wow, why you puttin' me on blast?" I say to Taye.

"So, that means you have magic too?" he asks Alexis.

Alexis falls silent. I can tell in her eyes and her parted lips she was trying to figure out how to tell him.

"I promise, I ain't gonna tell nobody," he says, giggling.

"Good to know," Alexis says back, beaming. The way her lips curl, the small dimple in her cheek got me weak in the knees.

"Anyway, just wanted to come over here and say hey. . . . I know you two wanna talk by yourselves."

He bumps me with googly eyes.

"It's nice to meet you, Taye," Alexis tells him again.

Taye disappears back into the house. Alexis crosses over to the steps, almost giving way to the darkness of the yard. Just looking at her got me feeling safe and warm, just like the moments before she was taken away from me.

"You don't know how good it is to see you again, Malik."

The words that come out of her mouth are stronger than any magic I've seen today. To make sure I don't fall if my knees decide to give out, I lean coolly against the rail, catching the glint in her expectant eyes. "You too, Lex. Like, it's amazing how we've found each other after so many years."

I don't know much about fate and destiny, but maybe she's throwing a brotha a bone right now because just being able to look at her, to hear her voice after all these years, I high-key feel like the luckiest dude in the world.

When Alexis wraps her arms around me, she supplies that hit of drug of just being around her even more. I breathe her in. Her scent got me drunk off possibilities.

I'm slipping.

Falling into the void, hoping it's paradise, and she's there, waiting for me. I brush my hands on her back delicately, and this gesture of a hug lingers just a little bit longer.

A voice calls, "Malik, is that you, baybeh?"

Wow . . . really, Mama Aya?

The door cracks open. Me and Alexis quickly part. She laughs under her breath as Mama Aya sticks her head out. "Oh, you back?" Mama Aya gives us a side look. "I wanna hear all about it."

"Ms. Aya," Alexis says, all nervous like she's meeting Beyoncé or Oprah. "First, it's a pleasure meeting you, and I was just bringing your grandson home."

Mama Aya cracks a smile, letting her eyes shift between Alexis and me. "Nice to meet you, baybeh, and that's so nice of ya. You takin' care of my grandbaby at that school?"

"Yes, ma'am. I am." Alexis turns to me. "Well, looks like you're home safe, Malik. See you tomorrow at school?"

"Fa'sho."

Alexis turns to Mama Aya, blushing hella hard. "Good night, Ms. Aya."

"Night, baby."

Alexis mouths, *"Oh my God!"* and she uses her magic and disappears in a cloud of gold light.

I can't help but stare at her leaving.

A soft rumble of a laugh comes from Mama Aya as she makes her way to the rocking chair on the edge of the porch. "Looks like you had a good day."

"I'm not gonna lie, Caiman is pretty dope, and I even got to see this tree that's on campus." I pull out the picture of my mama right in front of the tree with that necklace dangling from her neck. I stare at it for a beat.

The silence is loud. Just the creaking of the rocking chair meeting the wood floor. We both look out to the yard, letting the coolness of the night hit our faces. "Taron treatin' you all right?"

I try hard not to roll my eyes. "He's whatever."

The front yard is lit by the circle of the moon, bathing the bayou in silver light. Everything else is blanketed in a sea of blackness. Endless. Knowing no bounds. "Everybody on campus says you are some type of legend around here. Say you beat some Bokors in the early 1900s?" I trip up on the word *Bokors*. "They got respect for you."

Mama Aya chuckles under her breath. "Chile, they still tellin' them stories?"

"Well, are they all true?"

The apprehensive tone in my voice makes her eyes peer over to me. Her lips curl to a grin, like she knows all the answers in the world. And since she's over a hundred years old, she probably does.

I grit my teeth, biting back a harsh truth. "Seems like everybody knows everything about you."

We both let that weighted statement sink in.

Mama Aya shifts in her rocking chair, making the porch sing under the tense quiet. I know how the words spilled out of my mouth. That's the problem with me—I wear my heart on the edge of my tone. But on the real, I'm feeling some way that they know all this stuff about my "grandma," and I barely know anything.

Mama Aya pulls her shawl over her shoulders to keep herself warm from the slight cool breeze. "When you live long as I do, folks make up all kinds of stuff. They revere ya as some sort of hero."

"Sounds like you really were one though. If those Bokors are as bad as they sound."

"That was all a long time ago, baby."

There's a sourness in her tone.

"I don't know about that. People at Caiman are saying the Bo-kors are back, maybe even behind these missing kids."

"You heard about that, huh? I promise, you don't need to worry about anything."

I suck my teeth, letting the suspicion sink deep into me. "It's not just that. I was learning about them in class, and . . . I think they might have been there the night my mama disappeared. She was into bane magic, just like them, right? That's what you two fought about when she left?"

"Malik, I'm sorry, but no good can come of talkin' like this. The Bokors were gone long before your mama made her choices. One day at that school an you're already talkin' about bane magic? I don't know; maybe this wasn't such a good idea. . . ."

"No! I wasn't—I'm sorry. I'm just trying to figure out what is what."

Mama Aya looks at me, and I scramble to return to safe ground.

"So, how old are you, really? 'Cause the way they were talking, they act like you're a thousand years old."

She lets out a really big laugh. One of them laughs like the old church ladies used to make while cutting you a piece of lemon pound cake. "Chile, they makin' me sound like I'm old as Methuselah." She laughs some more until it fades into something thoughtful. "Let's just say I was born from a slave woman in 1831."

My jaw about to hit the floor.

Damn, Savon, and 'em was right about that.

"So, that means you're almost two hundred years old? Dang, so you probably met, like, I don't know, Harriet Tubman?"

"She was a lil' older than I was, but we go way back." She winks.

And I'm gagged like hell because in my mind, I'm still trynna calculate how the hell that's possible. Then again, with this world, it seems everything is possible. "Do we *all* live a long time?" I ask.

"Not all of us. When you come into this world, you take on other folk's magic. You also take on their life force." She rocks in her chair. "My mama. Your great-grandmama."

"Miriam, the woman you told me about when I first got here?"

A weighted moment. "Yes. She gave me her power," she says, voice shivering. "Now, I won't live forever, but the natural way of things just . . . slows down." A heaviness falls on the yard. The crickets sing their nightly songs.

"I can still remember her singin'. It was magic in her voice." Then Mama Aya starts to sing:

> *Way down yonder in de middle of the fiel'*
> *Angel workin' at de chariot wheel*
> *Not so partic'lar about workin' at de wheel*
> *But I jes' wan-a see how de chariot feel*

When Mama Aya sings, it reminds me of a crisp Easter Sunday morning. Shoot, I remember those days, having to get up at what feels like the crack of dawn for the sunrise service. Yeah, it gives that. It seeps into me, planting something inside me that I refuse to let grow. Stirring and melting away any doubt that I let overcome my mind. Now, I'm not sure if this is magic or just pure coincidence, but whatever it is, I'm too tired to fight it.

My eyes flutter open to a woman standing in front of me. We're inside a small, crude shack. No bigger than an average bedroom. Moonlight sifts through the slats of a crooked door. Two chairs stationed carefully on either end of a small wooden table made just for two. Over in the corner is a pallet of straw and rolled-up cotton. With a broom in her hand, she sweeps and bustles around the room like she's at her own personal concert. Her own little corner, all alone. She stops. Thinks. Crosses over to the pit with a spitting fire and rubs her swollen belly like she's lost in her thoughts. A weary affirmation on her face is lit by the crackling fire as she secretly pulls out a cracked jar. In her hands is a small, crinkly paper.

Obviously, it's of importance to her, whatever she's reading.

A hooting sound and horses racing past the shack cause her to put the paper back in the jar and hide it under the floorboard nestled beneath the table. She rushes over to the door, opening the outside world of the 1800s to her sanctuary. It's as if the sun gave out because of the way the dark of the night shadows her worried face. A buncha rowdy white men gallop past her on horses with torches.

"Ephraim," she breathes to herself.

Mama Aya's voice thrashes through the vision from behind me. "Whew, baybeh, that song brings back a lot. That was your great-grandmama Miriam. She would sing the song 'round the shack."

Cresting on her majestic brown skin, the moonlight filters through the tall pines, evaporating everything I see into a cloud of mist. We're now back in Mama Aya's yard. "I remember you telling me when I first got here," I say.

"Yes, I feel her all through you, you know that. They used to say that she had magic that's older than God."

I turn to face her. "Who are 'they'?"

"The old folks, baybeh."

Her voice washes over me. I take that in, storing it in a place I'mma need it later. "What happened to her?"

Mama Aya's eyes glitter even more in the darkness. With a sharp breath, she points toward the tall, twisted web of trees. The wind bends, rustling leaves and the blue bottles. Like lightning licking the sky, her magic fills the darkness with bright sparks and a thick cloud. Shifting and moving, like it's drawing a picture. As it lifts, it finally shows her. My great-grandma Miriam appears through the puff of cloud. A river of sweat glistens on her forehead as she trudges through the woods with a purpose.

I stand up and walk over to the steps to get a better look. Goose bumps tickle the crawling skin of my forearm. A man steps forward under the moonlight. He's tall, with a thick neck, broad shoulders, and a heaviness in his eyes. He wears overalls and a straw hat on top of his head.

Another thick hum flutters through the trees, dancing on the soft wind. My eyes shift to the bottle tree, seeing the bottles move slightly.

Before I know it, I'm in the middle of the yard, edging closer to Miriam and the man. They can't see me. They shift to their left, hearing a hooting voice.

"Run nah!" he screams.

Miriam bolts toward me in a blur and as she passes me, she becomes like cool mist.

"That's my daddy, Ephraim. Your great-grandfather." Mama Aya's voice echoes. Miriam's singing rings in my ears like a soothing lullaby. Just as Mama Aya noted, there's magic in her voice.

It stirs something in me.

"What happened to them?"

In her own version of answering, Mama Aya waves her hands. Everything shifts. The memory drifts on the horizon, showing . . .

Miriam and Ephraim running through the woods, tired and scared. Ephraim holds a baby in his arms, and she has another one. Both of them rest against a tree. Torches of light slice through the darkness while wrangling voices are heard in the distance. Somebody is chasing them. Miriam quickly looks to Ephraim. Her eyes are full of fear and . . . courage. The baby in her arms starts to cry. Miriam holds her close to her chest, desperately trying to keep the baby quiet.

They dip left, deeper and deeper into the woods. Behind them, the sound of hound dogs closing in, barking in the night air. The whole yard in front of us becomes the woods, and Miriam and Ephraim continue to run, hiding behind a tree. Gunshots ring through the darkness, and bullets ricochet off the trees, cracking through the bark.

A scream rumbles in my throat. Because I'm panicked for all of them.

"You all right, chile?" Mama Aya asks in a calm manner.

My heart stutters in my chest. Just like that, everything is gone. The man, the cloud, Miriam, all of it. Gone.

CHAPTER ELEVEN

PUTTING TWO AND TWO TOGETHER ALL DAY GOT A BROTHA tired as hell.

For one, I stayed up late, studying my mama's silver box even more. I jot down my findings. My mama got mixed up in bane magic, maybe even got expelled for it. The same magic that these Bokors I saw in class are infamous for using. And it's looking more and more likely they were the ones who came to my house that night, even if Mama Aya doesn't want to believe it or even talk about it.

And lastly, the words *Yo ap vini,* which translate to *We're coming.* Now I just gotta connect the dots even more.

Cueing up my life soundtrack, J. Cole's "c l o s e" blasts in my ears as I rush to my Friday morning class: Intro to Black Magical Studies. Mama Aya hexes the bottle tree to help me teleport back to campus. She says that it acts as a conduit and it's ready to go. Gingerly, I touch it, feeling the rough bark under my fingertips.

From the porch, Mama Aya shouts, "Just think it, chile. Think of where you want to be, and ya magic'll take ya there."

Well, that's easier said than done.

I ain't trynna end up somewhere in the desert or land on something sharp.

Oooh shit. Just thinking about it got my stomach rumbling.

Okay, Malik.

Think with intention and don't crash.

As the hook of the song assaults my ears, my lungs fill up with air, and I close my eyes. With a slow exhale, I think it, and the entire yard and sugarcane field around me fold like origami paper.

Two seconds later, I'm back at Caiman University.

Wait—I'm really back at Caiman U.

But that wave of nausea comes. Instantly, I steady my breathing. It goes away.

Like Dorothy rolling through Oz, I speed walk through the sprawling campus, checking out the map on my Caiman U app. Apparently, my class is hosted in the humanities building. It's near the BCSU, right next to the T. Atwell Library.

Bursting through the door and catching my breath from the cool, humid morning air, I'm met with an empty regular classroom. Metal desks all lined up in sequential order.

I grab the one in the back.

A quick inspection of the digital roster and I can tell that the class isn't as full as I thought it would be. I'm sure everybody is ahead of the game because they've been here longer. After a few minutes of just sitting here awkwardly, muffled voices rise in the hallway. J. Cole in my headphones comes to a halt as people start to drag in with an air of exhaustion. After a few take their seats, one dude in sweats and a Caiman University T-shirt staggers in, gives a tap at the top of the door. Flip-flops, white socks, and a CAIMAN U key lanyard hanging outside his pocket.

He goes up to the girl sitting in the front, highlighting her paper, smacking on her fresh piece of gum.

She flips her braids and tries to ignore him.

I catch a snippet of their conversation.

"What's up with this party this weekend?" He licks his lips, trying to be all smooth.

"*Bwoy,* bye—I already heard you were taking Keosha to the party. Don't try to be slick—" Ole girl sounds like Rihanna. Her accent hella thick. "Got me looking mad dumb, cuz I'm hearin' through the grapevine on the CaimanTea app that JB takin' Keosha to the party."

She places the phone right in his face.

He reels back. Caught red-handed.

The dude clenches his jaw and continues with his lie. "Yo, why you buggin', ain't nobody takin' her—"

A lotta hurls of *be fuckin' for real*s and *get out my face*s makes me instantly bored.

More people drag in. Most of them give me a tight and wondering glare. Clearly, I'm the new kid.

A woman glides through the doorway like a shark in a tank, commanding the room. "Hello, class," she says without looking up. She's fine too. In a professional sense. Thick, wavy hair in a bun. Her heels click-clack against the floor, sending an intimidating echo all through the room.

With a methodical flick of the eyes, she looks at the girl in the front. "Natasha, the difference between Hoodoo and Voodoo, please?"

The dude leaves the Natasha girl alone and slides over to the seat next to her. Natasha, on guard, quickly answers. "Voodoo, which is from the original word *Vodun*, is a religious belief system originating in Africa. The motherland. Whereas Hoodoo is a derivative of the teachings of Vodun. *Enslaved* folks and their descendants took what they learned in their native ways and modernized it and mixed it with Christian ideology. The origins being from Kongo/Igbo."

"Correct, Ms. Hall. Thank you." This lady's gaze glides to me. A quick acknowledgment, and she paces back and forth. "For the new people in the class, my name is Dr. Akeylah Green, and I will be teaching Intro to Black Magical Studies."

Judging by the shared confused looks, that was obviously only for me.

She turns to write something on the whiteboard. We all crane, twisting our necks to see what she's writing. The letters start to jumble before she even put them in words.

WHAT IS MAGIC?

On command, folks write the words in their notebooks or type on their computers. I do the same. One girl catches my attention.

She blows on her pencil all seductively, and I swear to God, it writes the words without her even holding it.

That's dope.

Dr. Akeylah points to me, flashing the smallest hint of a grin. "May I have your name?"

"Malik," I answer, becoming intensely shy.

She stares at me square on. "Is that your whole name, *Malik*?"

I must be Tupac here because I notice that all eyes are on me.

"Baron," I finish. "Malik Baron."

Dr. Akeylah has this expression on her face as if she already knew that. "Can anyone tell me? What is magic?"

First-day jitters got me quiet and shifting nervously in my seat. I ain't gonna say nothing in fear of looking stupid in front of everybody. The dude JB who was trynna holla at Natasha shoots his hand up with eagerness. "The power of influencin' the course of events by using mysterious or supernatural forces."

A stone-cold expression shadows Dr. Akeylah's face. "Yes, that's the Google version." She paces again, sniffing out her next victim. "But what *is* magic?"

Another girl, with a shaved head and gold hoop earrings, stands and answers, "I believe that magic is a way of life. It gives us a connection to the unknown."

Dr. Akeylah absorbs her answers and then writes that on the board. We all follow suit. "Does anyone believe that magic is a choice?"

No one answers.

The sound of Dr. Akeylah's heels clicking against the tile floor makes my knee bounce up and down even faster.

"I mean, it's even survival and death sometimes when it comes to magic." Her eyes land back on me. Body temperature goes straight below zero. "Enslaved folks, carried here in chains, brought their spiritual practices, merging them with the land and changing the course of the action by mere words. An incantation. A spell." Dr. Akeylah leans against her desk, taking us in one by one with a sharp look. "There are two forms: ancestral, which we all tap into. It's a fact you all are here by some form of *ancestral magic,* drawing and channeling the energy and power from the ancestors to conjure a spell. Such as telekinesis—the art of mentally moving objects." She holds out her hand. Suddenly, a desk slides toward her with ease.

Everybody claps.

I'm still lost, trying to catch up.

"Boundary spells, hexing, which can be synonymous to conjuring, a layin' of hands, are all a part of ancestral magic." She stops, then carries on with caution. "Even weather manipulation. We as Black people, and our magic, have been influencing current events for hundreds, even thousands, of years."

Natasha raises her hand. "Just like the night the stars fell in 1833." She then turns to everybody like she's spilling tea. "When thousands upon thousands of meteor showers fell to the earth, scaring the enslaved's masters so bad, they freed hundreds of slaves—including my seven times great-grandmother, who started it when her magic manifested on that night."

A few murmurs of interest from the class.

Dr. Akeylah is back at the board, writing. **BANE.** Everybody in the class starts to write it down. I shift in my seat, on high alert. Because again, my mama's letter pops into my head.

"Bane magic—using your powers to tap into dark, sinister forces for your own will. Hexing someone just because. Taking life away, and in some cases, giving it back. With this dark magic, one key spell is using your precious memories to tap in and conjure dangerous and sometimes deadly hexes. You can alter people's perception, their whole lives, by tapping into their memories and channeling it. Tapping into their very souls. Bend the will of nature for evil. Even the ancestors themselves."

Slowly, I pull the letter out that was written to my mama.

Ma, what you was into?

Dr. Akeylah's voice disrupts my thoughts. "By being baptized in the ancestral magic, you have unlimited access to most of the abilities I just referred to above." She paces back and forth, constantly commanding the room. "What's the key motto here at Caiman University?"

When she asks that, I remember the banner that hung over the bridge when me and Chancellor Taron first showed up.

"Our roots are deep, numerous, and vivacious."

Dr. Akeylah stares holes into me. Softens. And then writes that on the board.

Another girl shoots her hand up.

"Yes, Oceanna?"

"They say magic is theirs. But nawl, magic has *always* been ours." The emphasis on the *always* makes me smirk. "It's *qwhite* interestin' that their great valued-ass magic is revered while ours is demonized."

Her and Natasha give each other a high five.

Another girl on the right of Natasha says, "Okaaaayyy, gurl. Hoodoo is not some chicken bones and tarot cards. It's a calling. It's a purpose. It's transforming."

Natasha continues in her thick island accent. "Them heffas in Salem was trynna bust it open, and in turn built their magic off the backs of our ancestors—and then blamed our Black queen *Tituba* for the mess. If that ain't America, I don't know what is."

She got the whole class on laugh mode.

Dr. Akeylah kinda smiles at that too. "Let me ask you all this: Is magic ethical or unethical?"

"Only unethical if you take away folks' free will," the JB dude answers. "Kinda like the Bokors and the Kwasan tribe."

A collective sound at whispers at the word *Bokor*.

Another student in the middle row raises his hand and asks, "But who can determine what's ethical or unethical? Like Dr. Akeylah said—magic can sometimes be used as a survival mechanism, and for people like us, it was all we had. And even that was taken from us. So, if conjurers have to do unethical things to protect themselves, then who are we to say if something is ethical or unethical?"

Another one of the students on my left raises her hand. "And who's to say that the Bokors are on the unethical side? I mean, my daddy said they weren't *all* bad."

Natasha throws in her two cents. "Well, your daddy is wrong."

"Ladies—" Dr. Akeylah warns.

The girl next to me continues, "Sorry, Dr. Akeylah. But we all know a few bad apples can spoil the bunch. Just mentioning the Bokors got parents of the incoming freshmen scared to even let their kids join here this fall."

"We all heard the stories of what happened before they were defeated. Innocent folks died just because they didn't wanna follow the Bokors and their way of doing things. Checks and balances. That's why the Kwasan tribe had to step in," Oceanna says.

Nothing but *amen*s and *period*s from the others. My eyes flick to Dr. Akeylah, clocking her studying the debate.

The girl next to me chimes in again. "All I'm saying is, who's to say what they did was bad? For our people, magic is all they had. Brought to this new land, stripped of their heritage and language— built this whole country on the bones of their children and children's children. I say *our* magic isn't either ethical or unethical."

JB says, "There is duality in things. Maybe that's why the Deyo tribe doin' they own thing now."

Natasha stands up. She's heated. "Hold up, hold up, can we be *freaking* for real? We can't honestly sit here and say kidnapping and killing folks in regard to magic is not ethical or unethical? That's what the Bokors did. And that's why the Kwasan tribe had to tap that ass and drive them out."

"Language, but your point is duly noted, Ms. Hall," Dr. Akeylah says.

All this stuff got me shifting in my seat, hoping and praying I don't look like a lost puppy.

"You're all absolutely right." Dr. Akeylah waves her hand, and suddenly, a projection appears. I guess this is her attempt to kinda change the subject and get us back on track. "That's why I posed the question. And in that, it shows that we all have our own versions and definitions of magic." The lights shift to dim, and the projector cuts on with a whirring sound, showing slides of people in church, enslaved folks chained like cattle.

"Ancient ways our ancestors brought over from the motherland were passed from generation to generation. It's in your blood."

Another slide, this time of people in white cloaks. I jump back in my seat. Even the chair makes a screeching noise against the tile floor. Everybody turns to look at me, hungry to laugh at the new kid.

"Is everything all right, Malik?"

I collect my breath and brush off the embarrassment. "Yeah, I'm cool. Sorry about that."

Dr. Akeylah presses on. "Our ancestors used nature herself to channel our *majik,* provide healing, medicine, and even had the power of divination and necromancy." She flips to another slide of people, gathering and falling down in church. "They channel the elements of the earth and technology. Most of our ancestors had to build anew. Start new traditions, while mixing with the old. With the slave masters forcing Christianity on them, they took the teachings of the Bible and their own and mixed it. Boom, Hoodoo."

Immediately, I think back to when Mama Aya cast that spell that showed me my younger self. Dr. Akeylah shows us more images of people. They're all in white, dancing around a fire pit. It's like they doing praise and worship, the way their faces look. Another student raise their hand. "That's the original *original* Divine Elam, right?"

"It is," Dr. Akeylah confirms.

Divine Elam—I'm pretty sure Alexis or one of her friends mentioned that name before. There's so much coming at me new every day, I don't know how to keep it all together.

"Dang, that's sad what happened to 'em," JB says. "I mean, it is dope that Africans came to America before it was 'America,' like, thousands of years ago, though."

I lean forward, itching to hear the response from Dr. Akeylah.

"All things happen for a reason. Because of the original Divine Elam's contribution. Without it, we wouldn't have this very university."

"Through their tragedy, they left a legacy of Caiman here for us."

"Caiman University has been here for hundreds of years. But some even believe, for almost a thousand years, founded by our ancestors from the continent. But we weren't officially a university until

1804, which makes us the oldest historically Black college in the nation," Natasha says.

Dr. Akeylah claps her hands. Outta nowhere, a white dove appears, flapping wildly across the room.

Everybody in class leans forward like they're real interested. Shit, my ass is too.

"They changed the course of action by taking their own magic into their hands and controlling their fate."

Everybody in class exchanges excited looks while Dr. Akeylah does this cool hand motion and the bird turns to dust.

"Pop quiz. A litmus test to showcase your abilities," Dr. Akeylah says, looking to the Natasha girl in the front. "Ms. Hall?" Natasha stands up, meets Dr. Akeylah in the middle. "Manifest your magic."

"No problem," she says confidently, raising her hands and chanting, *"Manifeste limyè ou."* A ball of light magically appears between her hands.

Dr. Akeylah addresses her while Natasha harnesses her magic. "The most important thing to conjuring is to have intention. We all have a go-to spell or conjuring moment. To ignite fire, *Ina*! Or harnessing our power to the center."

Natasha closes the palm of her hand, snuffing out the light.

"Thank you, Natasha." Dr. Akeylah's eyes scan the room for her next victim. "Mr. Baylor."

JB stands up and slides over to the middle of the room. He pulls out a thick book, places it on the floor. Does a weird hand motion. Like swirling vapor, the papers from the book flutter around the room. They swoop down like the bird Dr. Akeylah conjured up did, circling all around us.

"Watch this," JB says. He mumbles something inaudible under his breath. From his hands, bright reds and oranges crystallize the papers. They freeze in midair. JB looks over to Natasha. Winks. Then the papers slice the air with a whirl, spelling out her name.

Everybody hella impressed and stunned.

Even Dr. Akeylah.

"Mr. Baron, could you come down here, please?" Dr. Akeylah points to me.

Anxiously, I shuffle my way to the middle of the room. All expectant eyes are on me.

"Will you light this for me?" Dr. Akeylah asks.

She flicks her wrist, magically making a candle appear in my hand.

"A'ight. Bet."

Everybody watches me like I'm a hawk in the sky. My focus is on the candle, observing it closely. A rush of feelings, and the stub at the top smokes, but nothing ignites. So, I focus harder.

And again, nothing happens.

Damn . . .

My magic acting up in front of all these people.

Natasha and JB laugh under their breath. My focus is broken from the humiliation.

"Again." Dr. Akeylah's voice changes with a quickness. It makes me jump a bit. "No ego in this class. And as far as I'm concerned, you are *all* at the same level." Ole girl in the front got humbled real quick. Dr. Akeylah turns back to me and nods. "Mr. Baron, please. Draw from the candle."

My brain tries to focus.

Fuck!

Another snicker breaks my concentration. It's JB again. Now he got me fucked up.

I take a deep breath and think about my *intentions.*

And ohhhhh shit, a small flame flickers from the stem and burns around the candle.

"Hold it now," Dr. Akeylah warns me as the flame swirls around the candle. "Channel the flame, draw from its power."

The heat from the candle distorts the air.

As the lights above begin to flicker, I twist my wrist with some swag and continue to draw from the flame. I can literally feel the energy burn in me, like a thousand sparks setting off under my skin. But at the same time, pressure and heaviness push down on all my limbs. Steadying my breathing, I make the flame sorta take form, and the fire bends around the candlestick.

I'm concentrating so hard, I don't even hear Dr. Akeylah call my name. I'm stuck on the dancing flame like white on rice. My tongue meets the top of my mouth. I'm harnessing it. If I move, the flame moves.

The fire that stems from the candle turns blue.

Everything around me tilts like God himself broke the axle, and the flame abruptly turns supernova and spirals around the entire mightily impressed classroom.

Sa fiyah!

A word I never spoke before reverberates in the back of my mind as I curl my hand. The flame instantly spreads, locomoting around the room like it got some business to take care of.

The fire alarm goes off.

Dr. Akeylah steps forward, shoves the air in a quick hand motion. *"Etenn dife a!"*

A torrent of wind explodes from her hands, making the fire die out. Nothing but lingering smoke and burns on the walls. With a quick flick of the wrist, Dr. Akeylah whips her hand toward the walls, and the fire alarm stops.

"Well," Dr. Akeylah says, placing her hands on my shoulders. "You're shaking, Mr. Baron." I don't even respond. Just head to my seat and feel myself shrink into the smallest thing in the world. Because I could've made the same mistake I've been avoiding the past ten years.

"Job well done, everyone. I want to see your elemental abilities next class, no exceptions." Dr. Akeylah approaches her desk, organizing her bag. "Malik, may I speak with you for a moment?"

I pump the brakes. "Look, I'm sorry about that in class—"

"Malik, it's fine. Don't ever apologize for showing your gift. That's what this class is for, to learn and make mistakes." Part of me is still worried. Another part of me is like, *Whatever.*

"Look, you are very gifted. I can tell. I sense it in you, but your harnessing technique is off."

"So, I ain't expelled?"

"Of course not, Mr. Baron. If we expelled every student that almost burned down a building, we would no longer be an operating university."

Both of us chuckle.

"However, you seemed very afraid."

The tone in her voice is like she's really concerned. I try to play it off smoothly. "I just thought I was gonna get expelled my first week here. It seems like it's a lot of rules."

Her eyebrows knit. But I can tell she wants to change the subject. "I understand that Ms. Aya is your grandmother, correct?"

"Yeah, she is."

It still feels weird to even admit that.

"Wonderful woman." She leans against her desk, inviting her stern expression back onto her face. "So, you know there won't be any special treatment in my class?"

"I ain't looking for no handouts anyway. I'm just here to learn what I gotta learn and be out."

Her expression changes into a small, sympathetic smile. Prolly think that was gonna catch me off guard. "From what Professor Kumale tells me, Chancellor Bonclair has been giving you a hard time. Especially when you were out there." She nods toward the window. "I won't give you special treatment, but I won't make you feel like you don't belong, either. Never that. I will challenge you. Push you to your best to make you a better conjurer. Am I making myself understood?"

All I can do is nod. Because she seems like the type that doesn't play.

In her hands, a thick-ass workbook appears. She hands it to me. I look down and see *Introduction to Rootwork.* "Read it, study the spells. There are some nonverbal and verbal. But there is power in the tongue, so verbal spells are more powerful."

I flip through the spellcasting workbook. "Umm, yeah, thanks, Dr. Akeylah."

"Catch up. Sadly, people will expect you to fail." She crosses over to the whiteboard, staring at it, and the words there instantly disappear. "Good day, Mr. Baron."

"Yeah, umm, thanks, again. Seriously."

· · · ·

After hanging with Taye and helping Mama Aya around the house, I figured I'd get some studying in before my first full week of classes starts Monday. No lie, Hoodoo is hella cool. It's something that I've only kinda saw on TV or heard about, but I never dived into it like this. The more I research it, the more I feel connected to it. A connection that I never thought was there.

In my studying, I learn all things herbs, mojo bags, goofer and red brick dust for protection. The one really getting me is the vèvè symbols—which can be a magic point for a conjurer to use to cast very powerful spells. Whenever a conjurer draws these, it'd be good to place food or animal offerings on them. A geometrical symbol that, if channeled, can fuck shit up. Flipping a page, I even see Baron Samedi has a vèvè. According to this book, Unc is the guardian of the crossroads. He is the head of the Gede and the keeper of souls in the afterlife.

Dr. Akeylah's voice haunts me from a distance. *Bane magic— using your powers to tap into dark, sinister forces for your own will.*

I'm sorry. But something in me can't. Bane magic is tempting me. Please, I need your help.

Peeling the letter back, really studying the words, feeling the edge of the piece of paper.

Damn, something was clearly bothering my mama, but what?

Slowly, I feel myself drifting off. . . .

From behind me, I *sense* something. I turn, and suddenly, I'm no longer on my bed but standing in front of a candlelit hallway.

I slowly make my way forward as the walls shift and groan and then crack down the middle. The reflection from the candlelight makes my shadow appear on the floor. Everything around me separates into colors, like film being burned by the sun.

Magic is happening here. I can feel it.

The more I edge down the hall, the more my heart beats against my chest; beads of sweat pour down my face. Turning the corner, I see my mama on the floor.

She kneels as if she's praying around a circle of twelve candles. A ring of black dust is around her, and her hands move in a circular motion. Her jaw moves up and down.

Her magic is strong; it feels like it's festering around the room. The candles around her light up by themselves. The shadows of the flames dance across the wall as she draws from their power.

Under her breath, she continues to chant something.

"Mama," I say.

"*Sula, aka de re mo . . . ,*" she says aloud, then repeats, "*Sula, aka de re . . .*"

Mama continues to spread a handful of black salt in a circle while repeating the incantation. Since it's her, and I take what Dr. Akeylah said to heart, I verbalize it continuously. Maybe, with this vision, it can give some answers.

In unison we continue to repeat the spell, and my whole body starts to tingle like a thousand electric bolts. The more I say it, the more I feel the power.

Sula, aka de re mo . . .

The words are now inside my head, repeating over and over, growing louder to a roar as fire and smoke take over the scene. It's not just my mama's voice and me now—there's someone else chanting. . . .

Suddenly, I'm back in my room, hovering over my bed like I'm in the damn *Exorcist.*

I plop back down on the bed, and somehow I know this wasn't just a dream. What I saw was real. And it could be another clue.

CHAPTER TWELVE

NEW WORDS TO REMEMBER: *SULA, AKA DE RE MO.*

I'm gonna give myself an aneurysm trying to remember this stuff. Now hearing this, this one got me on my Nancy Drew shit. Flipping through the book Dr. Akeylah gave me, it doesn't have anything remotely close to those words. I jot them down and save the notes for later, along with my mama's stuff.

Right now, on this Saturday evening, I'm focused on being invited to my first college party. Alexis invited me, and so I figured I'll tell her the words I learned when I see her back on campus. Maybe she can help me interpret them. As I'm getting ready, I slowly realize it was the same party JB and Natasha was talking about in class yesterday.

Wear something cute.

I snatch my phone from the nightstand and strike up a text.

Bet. On my way.

With this trimmed yellow polo shirt and black pants, I'm *ret* to go.

This time I don't need Mama Aya standing on the porch, watching me do it. As I stare at the tree in the yard, I press my hand on the rugged edge of the bark. Suddenly, I'm back on campus.

The door to Alexis's residence hall opens, and she steps out. I swear to God, I'm like that cat from *Tom and Jerry,* because my jaw drops to the floor, and my eyes are obscured by big, pumping red hearts. Alexis comes out looking like a *whoooollle* brown-skinned Cinderella with her yellow see-through bikini dress that hugs every curve. Lawd *ham* mercy. When her full lips curl into that beautiful smile, it's making me clutch onto the art of being a gentleman for, like, five seconds.

"Daaaayyyum . . . ," I whisper, noticing her thigh slipping out.

Descending the stairs, she pats herself in a second-guessing gesture. "Do I look okay? I ordered this from this girl that set up shop in Congo Square. Cuz we support Black businesses around here."

"Lex, you fine as hell."

She cracks up, pushing the soft coils from her eyes. "It's a pool party, but I told Savon I am not getting into no water." I don't even have no more words. "Take a walk with me."

We start walking and approach the edge of this section of the campus where the bayou water shimmers under the sunlight. It looks like a painting literally come to life. We end up by a twisted tree trunk stretching inches above the murky water. She keeps staring out, as if she's lost in thought. It takes everything in me not to be a creep, because I just stare at her.

Finally, she turns and notices me getting lost in her beauty. "What?"

"Nothing, just . . . I just can't believe we're here."

"I still remember that day," she says, licking those lips. "The day I left you, and we drove off."

Silence. We're both rocked by the memory of her pulling off in that old blue car and me running into the middle of the street. It stings me all over. The pain feels just as fresh as it did ten years ago.

"Were they any good to you?"

Hope springs in her eyes. "They really were. The Williamses were a family of conjurers too. Powerful council people under the Kwasan tribe. They gave me a childhood, a life. They taught me so much.

Not only were they in our world but they were also fighting for civil rights in the regular world. They were activists."

"I mean, how they find you, though?"

"When they first came, they could sense my magic from a mile away."

That got me thinking. Did they sense me when they first came? I barely can remember, but I know I had some interaction with them when I first met them at the group home. Maybe if I wasn't so worried about keeping my magic hidden, they would have taken me too. My whole life could've been different. But then I'd never have met Taye.

We start to make our way around the edge of the bayou, watching the last rays of sunlight glint off the surface of the water.

"What happened to them?"

Her overwhelming smile evaporates into sadness. "They died." She then flicks her wrist, making the wind start up. "Not all magic is good, Malik."

"Don't I know it."

Part of me wants to ask how they died. Another part just wants to wrap my arms around her and pull her in and make us both just disappear from this world.

"How did you . . . how did you end up here?"

She twirls a curl of hair and gently tucks it behind her ear. Being hella cute. "When the Williamses adopted me, we moved around quite a bit, and finally, we settled in New Orleans. And I look up, and years pass by—and here we are."

Alexis looks back out to the bayou. It's something about her eyes—a low flame burning bright behind them, giving me a new-found strength. "I understand why you felt abandoned, and I thought—tell you the truth, I don't know what I thought. You sorta forget about those nights, you know. In the orphanage, crying and wondering why your parents don't want you. But since I started my activism, I went off the grid for a bit, cloaking magic to protect my-self and those around me. I'm a bit reckless," she continues.

Reckless. Chancellor Taron's voice pops up in my head. "Yeah, you're right about that."

Alexis lifts her finger in the air. The wind blows. The water from the bayou ripples, creating miniwaves, and the leaves assume their place on the ground. Alexis's magic feels light. Sweet and very familiar, like a cinnamon roll right out the oven on a Sunday morning. My chest rises, taking in the fresh air. The muted hum of the campus quiets.

"You still showin' off, huh?" I say to her, noticing the water slowly make its way back to the basin.

"Whatever. I'm dope, and I know it."

That's when I open the palm of my hand, harnessing the magical crystal blue light. It orbits around my hand. And I make it tattoo itself on the tree, crackling into the lining of the bark.

"Okayyyyy! Look at yoouuu."

"Like back then."

"Oh, wow, you remember?"

"Never forgot."

A wink. Hmmmph. There she goes, being competitive again. Right now a part of me wanna seize the moment and kiss her on the lips. Kiss her and tell her, *Let's run away and just be.*

But I can only offer a frozen look of contemplation.

Her eyes land on the campus. Shafts of light illuminate Caiman University, and the evening sky creeps behind the full moon on the horizon.

"This place is really amazing, huh?"

Somehow, my hand has guided itself to hers, sparking the magic between us that was once lost. And her soft, sweet laugh dances on the slow Southern breeze.

"Yeah, it is."

Alexis exhales a labored sigh. "It's our safe haven. Something like this, I would've never believed."

"Me either," I tell her. "This is a fairy tale. And I never believed fairy tales were made for me."

"Our magic . . . it's a gift." Alexis closes the palm of her hand. Her face sorrowful. "Too bad we can't share this gift with the world."

"Especially those missing people, right?"

Alexis thinks for a long beat.

"No matter how much this school tries to hide from it, trouble always have a way of finding the good in the world."

A chilling breeze starts, matching her cold tone.

"We should get going."

Her hands clap, and the world around us fades to black. . . .

• • • •

The moon looms in the lonely sky, raining down light on the yard of a frat house that sits on the edge of campus. It's right by Brimsfield Row, and the houses are lined up and down the street like glimmering minimansions. Privilege is evident here, because gahdayuuumm, this frat house big as hell. The fraternity's logo of a double-headed axe glows like Batman's signal. Cars pull up, people riding on the back of them, blasting that gutter rap from the speakers. Two bikers fly by, popping wheelies in the middle of the street. They race to the end of the street and back. One dude does a backflip and, I swear on everything I love, *transforms* into an eagle.

Whoa. Shit.

"Shape-shifters," Alexis say, like that shit is just normal.

Just taking in the party, I'm wondering about me and Alexis. Like . . . is this a date or something? Last party I've been to, we played games like seven minutes in heaven. And if that's the case tonight with Alexis, seven minutes won't be enough.

But until it comes out of her mouth, I'mma play it cool.

We step into the den of a liiiitttt-ass party. The bumping beat of Latto's "Bitch From Da Souf (Remix)" warbles from a DJ station. A girl with gold shades and long dark braids pushes headphones onto her right ear and speaks into the mic. "Wassup, y'all, it's ya gurl DJ Bawse Bish, and the Jakutas ain't playin' with this party!" Trina slides her verse on the track, and everybody in the house goes ham, throwing that ass with supernatural speed on the down beat. A couple of dudes straggle behind, being blessed by this one girl while she speed-twerks on them.

DJ Bawse Bish grabs the mic and says, "I see y'all in the middle, goin' innnnn."

A shaft of purple haze swirls, illuminating hungry shadows of people posted up, chilling and smoking. The whole living room is packed wall to wall while Latto continues to rattle the floor.

A group of scantily clad hotties flutter around the dance floor like moths under a streetlamp.

They twerk them goodies while the music pulsates. Dipping through the room is a dude with a red Solo cup in his hand, chasing after a baddie, serenading her with drunken compliments. A couch resting by the wall is decorated with bodies spilling their inhibited tales and exchanging kisses. Lights and smoke make love in this room. A big-ass brick fireplace is covered in orange snapping fire. People step out of it, completely unburned.

Fuck! I kinda jump back. Then I focus my vision, calming myself before Alexis notices.

"Oh, y'all *party* party," I say to Alexis, tracking everybody's eyes crawling to us.

I straggle behind her into the throng, where a group of girls with long, skinny legs descends from the mountain of stairs in gold dresses. They maneuver through the crowd like ebony goddesses coming to play with us mortals. They wink and hug Alexis. One of them pushes their faux locs to the side, revealing *pointy* ears like some *Lord of the Rings* shit, and investigates who is *who* at this party. A couple of "Guuuurllllll, come through, melanin" and "Them shoes and you is cuuuuuute" are exchanged, and then they go on about their way.

I shoot a double take to Alexis. "Wait—are they—?"

Alexis administers a wink that makes a brotha shudder. "Let's just say, a lot of the mythical creatures we read about growing up are not so *mythical*."

In the kitchen, Savon is spiking the punch bowl. Elijah is on the other side of a kitchen island full of chicken wings and celery with a big cup of ranch. Bottles of alcohol glitter with temptation under the kitchen light. Right by the sliding door, that D Low dude from history class loiters, hanging around the edge of a big-ass swimming pool that seems to stretch beyond oblivion. Black folks'll have a pool party but don't never actually be swimming.

"Well, if it isn't the *grandson* of Mama Aya," Elijah jokes, half-drunk.

"Wadup, y'all." We all dap.

"Thought I'd invite Malik, have him meet new people," Alexis tells them.

"Aye, yo, you trynna get some of this?" Savon grabs a ladle from the punch bowl. The liquid turns icy blue as they stir it. No lie, it looks like they're concocting a potion from *Hocus Pocus.*

"Yeah, I'll get some."

They pour me one. A dude stumbles into the kitchen right behind Savon. He leans down to kiss Savon on their neck. Savon giggles while dude's hand snakes up and down their backside.

"Uh, who is this?" Alexis asks, sipping her drink.

"This is Keevon, Hoodoo major." Savon motions their hands as if they're smoking. Out of nowhere, a blunt appears in Keevon's hand. "Keevon, this is Malik and Alexis."

We both give that *wadup* mutual nod.

"Keevon is one of the Jakutas." Savon clomps over to the island and grabs a drum wing with their talon of nails. "Thanks to him, our freshmen asses got an invitation."

Through the haze, Dominique from Professor Kumale's class walks up, smiling and wrapping her arms around Savon. She and Alexis ice-grill each other. It's cordial but forced.

"My name is Dominique," she says. "You?"

"Malik."

"You thinking about pledging, Malik?" Keevon asks me. He shows that blunt some TLC as swirls of smoke escape his lips.

"What? The Jakutas?" A quick glance to Alexis. "Maybe."

Keevon puffs on the blunt, chest heaving and *ish.* "Yeah—you should. We heard good things 'bout ya. We recruitin' for our fall semester, and I'm gonna be the new president. Shit, if there's anybody left."

City Girls and Usher's "Good Love" cuts through our tense silence. "Whatchu mean?"

His eyes shift to Alexis, and then to Elijah, and back to me. Finally, he answers, "Folks' parents trippin'. They wanna keep the incomin' freshmen and even upperclassmen home because people going missin'."

"That was a rumor." Dominique cuts in by reaching her hand over the platters of food. Her long braids swing like vines from a tree.

"No, it's a real issue. Not just magical folks but nonmagical folks as well." Alexis's voice rides on the beat. She sips down her shade, throwing Savon a *this bitch* look.

"Dr. Akim and the Deacons of the Crescent been holdin' meetings. So, you know what that means."

"Another Million Man March?" Savon jokes.

Keevon stubs his weed on the bottom of his lighter. "I'm just sayin', Caiman U incomin' class gon' look hella small."

A collective sip of the liquid courage.

"Anyway." Keevon motions to me. "You definitely should think about pledgin'."

I offer up a strained smile. "Yeah, I'll think about it."

"All I know is, I'm pledging the House of Transcendence," Savon says, throwing up a sign.

"That's the new Black Queer coed fraternity on campus."

"It's the Oyas fuhhh me," Dominique says.

Alexis raises a cup in the air. "Daughters of Oshunnnnnn!"

Keevon whisks Dominique behind the counter. "That's what's up. Y'all enjoy, a'ight?" Him and Dominique disappear back into the living room area.

Alexis throws her nothing but shade.

We make our way out to the pool area, where the smell of chlorine hits me, taking me back to them old days in Liberty Heights. But what I'm seeing here ain't got shit back in Bama. Strobe lights shine down, illuminating the swirling pool water. Out of nowhere, a dark-skinned baddie emerges from the deep end of the pool. She has long coiled locs and beautiful dark brown skin with a nose piercing. Water drips off her like diamonds. No lie, I catch myself kinda drooling, and my mind fogs when I take in her beauty, weaving through crowds of people. Savon's voice cuts through the buzz. "Lex, ya boy about to get lost at sea."

Alexis snaps, and I'm back to regular. *The hell?*

"Where the hell she come from?" I ask them.

"Let's just say, it wasn't too far-fetched seeing our *gworl* Halle Bailey as a mermaid."

Everybody starts cackling. It takes me a second to catch on.

"Fa'sho."

"Don't stare too hard," Alexis jokes. "Cuz them mermaids ain't nothing to play with."

"Oop!" Savon puts their cup to their lips, sipping like that Kermit the Frog meme.

The music from the DJ booth switches to Coco Jones's "ICU." "Ooooh, this my song!" Savon says, grabbing Keevon from inside, and they go off, dancing. Me and Alexis are left alone, just chilling by the pool lawn chairs.

I'm real nervous asking. Alexis laughs because she can tell. "Boy, let's dance."

We float over to the dance floor, under the iridescent purple lights—and we become shadows. My hand on her back, careful to not let it slide too far down. We sway back and forth, and I feel myself melting.

"I thought about you every day, Malik," she says in my ear. "But as the years went by, you started to become a faded memory. Was I that to you?"

Coco Jones sliding into the chorus gives me the strength to say, "Not at all, Lex. I never forgot about you. I wouldn't let my mind do it."

Her arms reach around my shoulders, bringing me into her gravitational pull. We end up in the middle of the dance floor while the world fades away to nothing. Images wrap me up, massaging every broken part of me. It's me and Lex at the state fair. The glittering lights rising to the dark sky. The Scrambler ride swishes back and forth, and we're laughing. It switches to us kissing under the flickering lights. Us at prom, where we're crowned king and queen.

This isn't a memory, but a dream, a want, a need.

I wish it was all real so bad, tears start to well in my eyes.

"Your magic, Malik, sensing it right now, I can smell the hot wet pavement from the summer rain. That last day . . ."

I breathe her in. "It was one of the worst days of my life, I ain't gon' hold you."

"I know," she says with a tinge of guilt in her voice. "I begged them for days to go back and get you. Maybe I should've fought harder. I'm sorry."

"No need to apologize," I tell her, drunk off the fading dream. The weight of reality gives my soul an unspoken ache.

"You've always been so smooth. I'm surprised a girl haven't snatched you up."

"There was only one girl for me."

My fingers instantly go to wipe the tear away from her cheek. This, right here, is the perfect moment to lean forward and kiss my first crush. The girl I can see my seventeen-year-old self spending the rest of his life with. Just one kiss . . .

And I lean in.

Elijah zips in between us. His face reads a *you already know* expression, making the world around us ramp in real time. "It's our boy, Donja."

We make our way toward the front door and onto the porch. In the middle of the front yard, a group is crowded around like a fight is about to go down. Shouts and yells cutting the night. One girl is between Donja and another dude, who looks heated. A fire pit lodged in the grass burns bright behind them.

"You a damn lie! You told me y'all wasn't fuckin' around," the dude says to Donja.

"Babe, you're drunk," the girl says to the dude yelling at Donja.

The way Donja looks, it's real calm. His lips curl into a smirk. "We're not exclusive. You knew that."

"Wow, really?" the dude says, and tries to push up on Donja. "You always put on for everybody, let's see how people would feel if they knew the *real* you."

"Chiiiiiile, a lover's quarrel," Savon says, sipping their drink. "A mess, just a mess . . ."

"Donja's . . ." I start to ask.

"Sexually fluid." Savon stops me from saying something whatever-phobic that was gonna spill from my mouth. "Ain't nobody tied down to one thing anymore, Malik."

Wallop! The dude socks the shit out of Donja right in the face. "That's what the hell you get for stringing me and her along."

Spitting blood from his mouth, Donja flicks his wrist and chants, *"Pou mande vyann."* Out of nowhere, the right side of the dude's face gets a big, gaping slash. Blood spills out, trickling down his cheek. It looks like something out of a scary movie.

Ooooh shit.

I even take a step back because the sight makes me queasy.

Like a record scratch, the music inside cuts off instantly. "Welp, it's time to go," Elijah says.

"Donja," Keevon says in a real low, intimidating voice. "What the hell you think you're doin'?"

Alexis storms up to them; I follow right behind her.

"Just showing your guest a good time, that's all," Donja answers Keevon.

They're face-to-face for a tense moment as if they are about to scrap right in this yard. The dude that was arguing now has blood gushing out of his face. Finally, somebody runs and gets him paper towels.

Alexis shouts, "Donja, you are gonna end up getting expelled. Why would you do that?! Chancellor Bonclair—"

"Mwen pa pran swen!" Donja yells back at Alexis in his Kreyol.

"You're disrespectin' our house," Keevon says, real calm. The girl that's helping ole boy mean-mugs Donja and Alexis. A bright light engulfs her hand, and the gash on the dude's face instantly closes.

A healer.

Which makes me think: What's gonna be my specialty?

"You obviously saw that he threw the first punch. I was merely defending myself," Donja says, trying to stifle a laugh. He stumbles a bit too. Hella drunk.

Like a cloud of ashy smoke, Keevon's crew appears behind him. About five or ten of them, rolling in deep. People bat their eyes with instigation, praying for some shit to go down.

"We got a problem here, Kee?" Donja says. His voice sounds like thunder, low-key.

"Nigga, you don't want none of this," Keevon warns.

Donja doesn't move, clenching his jaw. What the hell is up with this dude? For a moment, his eyes dance between all the crew, then back on Keevon. He's outnumbered. "My bad, your fiery prince." Donja bows obnoxiously. "I did not mean to ruin this lame-ass party."

Alexis steps in between them. "Donja, let's go. You are about to get your ass beat."

He snatches his arm away from her a little too hard and mutters something in Kreyol. Now that's when I step up to him.

"Aye, don't be snatching away from her like that, bruh," I tell him.

Laughing, he's now all up in my face. I can smell the liquor dancing on his breath.

He mutters something in that Kreyol accent.

I don't back down. I never back down. "You better go on. I ain't nothing to play with."

Everybody starts instigating, saying, "Ooh" and shit.

"Donja—" Alexis's voice gets deeper, warning him.

"Lex, you better get ya boy, 'cause this ain't some high school show where he thinks he can say anything and he won't get his teeth knocked out," I say.

"Fout ti gason," he grunts in Kreyol.

"Say that shit in English—"

I raise my hand, and my magic swirls in a small blue light, shivering up and down my arm.

"Malik, Donja, stop!" Alexis pulls Donja away. I don't know why, but his ass looks like he's sweating something black???? What the . . .

"I'm out," he tells her. He lifts his hands and disappears in a peppery red smoke.

The music cuts back on, and people start to go back into the house, partying.

My magic disappears back into my arm.

"You good?" I ask Lex.

She got a guilty look on her face. "Yeah, he's just drunk. I'm sorry; let me make sure he gets back to his dorm okay."

Low-key, I ain't want her to go. "Nah, do your thing."

She hugs me and disappears in a cloud of yellow light.

Feeling the weight of eyes on me, I avoid their gazes, feeling like a dumbass for letting Alexis go . . . again.

• • • •

Sunday morning's got me standing at the edge of the field, in the middle of all this greenery. Waist-high stalks shroud me as I continue my focus. Right behind me, Taye watches, intrigued as I practice my magic.

I'm thinking I need all the practice I can get so I can catch up with everybody else.

"Do it again," Taye says, holding up his phone.

"Shhh. I'm trynna focus."

With my eyes tightly shut, I inhale slowly. The wind begins to pick up, blowing around us. I can practically hear Taye's growing excitement. When I squeeze my hand, I feel the wind grow even stronger. Which is weird, because the harder it blows, the more I can feel its energy. It's pretty fucking dope.

"Whoa. Malik, you seeing this?" Taye screams.

My eyes pop open, and I turn so fast toward Taye, I 'bout break my damn neck.

Immediately, I notice the leaves from the trees peel themselves from the stems and circle all around us. They slice the air and move like they have a mind of their own.

Taye's ass hops up and down, trynna catch them.

I whirl my hand toward him, and the leaves suddenly turn into blue flames. Shit!

"Taye!"

But what's wild, Taye doesn't seem scared; he seems . . . all right. There's a light in his eyes.

All I can do is stare and feel my heart race, thumping against my chest.

Taye marvels at the blue flames spiraling around him.

"It's not hurting me, Malik."

My lips crack a smile. Then a soft laugh escapes. Middle finger to my thumb, I snap, and the fire dies out, and the *unburned* leaves fall to the ground.

Oh, I'm on my magical shit now.

"You really getting better," he says.

"Yeah. I thought this school was gonna be whatever, but—"

A grin from Taye stops me. "Oh, I know. That Alexis girl. Uh-oh, Malik in loooove."

I playfully hit him. "Chill, I'm—Alexis, yeah, she means a lot. But it's been so many years between us. Honestly, I got to get to know her again."

"You tell her that?"

I'm quiet. Taye smacks his lips and travels over to the porch to sit. "What?"

"I think you should tell her," he says. "Why not? Especially if you waited for her all this time. She ain't datin' nobody, is she?" I shake my head. "Good. Tell her."

I sit on the porch, chugging on this cold-ass sweet tea Mama Aya made for us and loll my head back, relaxing. "Since when you get so wise?"

"I've been wise," he jokes.

Both of us exhaling into the humid air.

"How've you been here?"

"Better. Auntie Brigitte got me a PS5, bruh! And I'm even decorating my room how *I* want. Dude, it's cooool living here."

"That's good, Taye. You deserve it."

"You too, Lik." He stands up and leans on the rail. "Besides, I think it's time for us to move on and make our own path. Here. You got that school, and you may not believe, but dude, you're happy there. I see it on your face. When you do your magic, you starting to not look afraid of it anymore. And if that school is doing that, I say stay there and learn all you can."

"I don't know. It's something about this place that don't sit right with me."

"What's happening?"

"It's, like, these rumors of kids going missing, and some people can't even come back to the school, apparently."

Taye's ears perk up. "I heard Mama Aya and Auntie Brigitte say something."

"Like what?"

"This lady came by to see Mama Aya. I don't think she had magic, but she seemed like she knew what was going on. Mama Aya did this kind of séance type of thing. Something you'd see on *The Conjuring*, and I think . . ." He trails off. Then swallows to continue. "Connecting with the dead. Apparently, her son was kidnapped and killed."

Everything in me feels cold.

"What else?"

Taye hangs his head. "She said they stole his magic."

"They? They who?"

He shrugs. "Whatever is out there. Maybe it's good that you're going to that school."

"But you—"

"I'm cool. Baron Samedi, Brigitte—dude, they're, like, ancient. Like, *ancient* ancient." A brief pause, and I can feel emotions bubbling up in Taye. "But I'm glad you're there, and I'm glad I'm here too. Because with all of this, Malik, we deserve happiness."

My arms instantly wrap around him, dissipating any growing fear from the new info he gave me. "Seriously, how the hell you get so damn wise? But you right, Taye. You so right."

. . . .

I wake up *hella* late.

My first week at Caiman U is gone, and I'm already messing up on the second one. I flick my wrist with some swag and whisper in Kreyol, *"Pou aparèy!"*

Alexis taught me that one.

The entire yard turns and shifts right back to campus, in the middle of the quad. There's a small wave of nausea, but it passes. Pulling out my phone, I see about five texts from Alexis, apologizing for leaving me at the party the other night.

With Taye's wise-ass advice, I muster up the courage to say what I feel.

It's cool. It's something I wanna tell you anyway.

Another text dings that makes my heart stop.

Where are you?!

Confused, I trek my way through the humanities building, and up ahead I see people huddled around in the hallway. They whisper to themselves and look at something I can't really see.

"Malik!" Alexis's voice rises from the huddled group.

I turn to find her slipping through concerned bodies.

"Wassup, Lex? I just got your texts."

Everybody moves to the side, and right in my line of sight is nothing but glass and red brick powder on the floor, making a geo-metrical emblem intricately drawn in a snakelike shape.

"Guuuurl, is that the symbol from them Bokors?" I hear some-body whisper.

"My mama said that's how you know they here," another voice states.

"Black Jesus, are they really back?" Someone else gasps and does the Hail Mary.

It takes a second for my mind to process everything as I ma-neuver closer, feeling the glittering pieces of glass crunch under my shoes. I kneel down and, with shaky hands, pick up a cracked frame, containing what looks like a school portrait of my mama. Her smile is covered by a jagged crack in the glass.

The voices go to a hush, and everybody looks at me—freaked out, curious. As if I'm an animal at the damn zoo.

Chancellor Taron pushes through and stops in his tracks when he sees me. "My office, Mr. Baron," he says.

CHAPTER THIRTEEN

A HIT DOG WILL HOLLA.

But in my case, I feel like that was a setup or maybe a clue, and I ain't trynna make myself look guilty on anything I haven't done.

We climb the spiraling marble stairs to the top, where the vast entry towers away into the shadows. I'm not gonna lie—my legs wobbly like Bambi taking his first steps. One wrong move, my ass can tumble all the way back to the bottom.

The roof itself curves and bends into an archway like an open, screaming mouth. Looking left and right, I detect writhing designs of stonework that resemble muscles and tendons bulging under skin. Up ahead, down the long hallway, we reach a set of gold double doors with gold-plated doorknobs.

Standing here, waiting for Chancellor Taron to open the doors. I'm trynna figure out why somebody did that to my mama's picture.

Chancellor Taron swiftly waves his hands over the door handle. His magic activates, and an array of metal clanks and shifts inside; bolts release and assemble themselves, making the door glide open.

No lie, his office seems like it's a world of its own. It looks more like a presidential suite. Looming shelves of books reach up toward eyelike glass windows. Rays of light filter through long red drapes that pool on the wood-paneled floor. A bay window curves outward with a large balcony to overlook the sprawling campus on the far right. You can see Caiman University stretch into the evergreen of the sugarcane fields. On the wall, placed real strategically, are framed awards. Photos. And more awards. But it's something weird how they're placed, though. Set like they're trying to hide something.

I know what that's like.

Hiding pain.

Hiding hurt.

Taron pulls his coat off, rolls up his cuffs, and walks behind a brown maple wood chair right in front of a mahogany-colored office desk. Papers are placed carefully on top, with a desktop on the right edge.

"Sit," Chancellor Taron commands.

"Yo, I ain't no damn dog—"

"Please sit, Mr. Baron." His tone a bit softer, reverberating against the paneled wood.

On my own accord, I sit down.

We linger in a tense silence for a minute as he reads the stack of papers. A quick lick of the fingertip and jets of air fan off them as he flips each page. This low-key really brings me back to the days of sitting in the principal's office, waiting for the punishments. Brushing down my waves with a stroke of my hand and sitting in the uncomfortable chair felt like a trial. Suspension or in-school detention would be my version of prison.

He signs on to his computer. Fingers rapidly click on the keyboard as if he's looking at my school record or shit. Again, I notice the fancy gold ring that he's wearing. He sees me looking at it, and like a smooth criminal, he quickly hides that hand under the table.

Behind him, I spot a picture of a Black woman and a young boy. Picture don't look that current, though. And the way it's placed . . . it's unlike the other photos, which are for obvious viewing. Nah, this one is special, and I can tell. His wife? His son? Gotta be his family.

Filtering in like the soft breeze is the sound of the drumline practicing their song. The tune kinda sounds like something from Earth, Wind & Fire. It takes everything in me not to bob my head and dance in my seat.

Seeing this, Chancellor Taron whips his hand forward, making the window close and seal shut. Now it's the rapid sound of typing as I continue to stare at his ring glinting under the light.

"I ain't had nothing to do with what happened," I say, hearing my tone sounding hella guilty. "Just savin' you the trouble of blamin' me."

"Yes, I'm aware," he answers back flatly. "And why would I blame you?"

A trick question, I'm sure. After a few seconds, he leans forward, arms on the desk, and his eyes feel like a sharp-edged machete, ready to cut my ass in half. "It is no secret that your mother was a student here." Chancellor Taron blinks. "I don't know what you've heard, but—"

"All I wanna know is if she's dead or not."

The bluntness of the question feels heavier in the bitter quiet. Chancellor Taron's eyes glaze with trepidation and recognition. But it's gone in a flash as his thoughts take new direction. "If she is, and y'all lying, trynna protect me, I'm a big boy. Just tell me the truth."

I wait for a second to see if he's gonna take the bait.

Mama Aya already confirmed she's alive; I'm just trynna fish for more info.

He pushes back from his desk. "I couldn't possibly know that. Your mother and I were classmates, but I haven't seen her in quite a long time."

I level him with a cold stare. "Maybe you know where she disappeared to?"

"No, I don't," he finally says.

He leans back in his chair, not saying anything else, back to his calculated demeanor.

Fuck this.

I slap the picture of my mama from the hallway, covered in red dust, on his desk.

"I'm just tryin' to get some answers. Now, do you know what it's like to go years without knowing?" The question itself makes me swallow the big lump that was forming in my throat, but I push it back down to the pits of brokenness.

"Where did you find this?" he finally asks after a minute of silence.

"It was next to that symbol thing. Why would someone put her picture there? Is someone trying to tell me something?"

I can't read his shadowed expression.

"What the hell do the Bokors want with my mama?" I ask. "That was their sign, right?"

"Mr. Baron, this incident has just transpired, and the Bokors have no connection," he assures me. "Probably just some silly prank."

"That doesn't answer my question," I snap. Deep in my thoughts, I let the words kinda just slip out. *"Sula, aka de re mo."*

Chancellor Taron places his hand under his chin. "Where did you hear that spell?"

"Around," I tell him.

His eyes narrow.

"So what the hell do they want? I mean, who are they?"

"Mr. Baron—"

"Somebody lyin'. Is that why parents pulling they kids out for next semester? Because the Bokors and them snatching kids and killing them?"

Time zaps back, and a succession of images—there's my seven-year-old self, surrounded by burned, crisp bodies. The night my mama disappeared, my magic manifested. Then it shifts back to Haiti, seeing that man, the leader, fucking stabbing that little boy.

Now I'm trynna connect all this shit.

"Enough. I've already mandated an off-campus restriction order for *all* students, given the ongoing investigation downtown. It's only fair that you follow suit. You will stay in Mancell Hall, the young men's apartments, for the time being. Your clothing will be delivered to you from Ms. Aya's home."

Oh, he's avoiding this shit.

"So they are back, huh? That's why we're on lockdown?"

"Mr. Baron, let me be perfectly clear. That scene with your mother's photo has nothing to do with my decision. Tensions have been high on campus, and some students were clearly looking for a chance to blow off steam. Likely, word of your arrival sparked talk of your mother's . . . history, and the unfortunate rumors about the Bokors resulted in this ill-fated stunt."

"But—"

He interrupts with a sharp tone. "I am upgrading you to a full-time student, and Caiman's policy is to have all full-time freshmen students live on campus."

I about jump from my chair. "I don't wanna stay on campus full-time. I ain't gonna have no time for Taye."

"No argument. I am also signing you up for another class with Dr. Akeylah and Professor Kumale for you to better learn your magic." Chancellor Taron types so fast, his hands move like a blur. "You'll be enrolled in Advanced Magical Defense Studies."

"Why would I have to learn that shit if you're saying the Bokors aren't out there? Why are we even on lockdown, then, huh?"

"This is all perfectly normal procedure," he says coolly. He magically pulls out a tablet, taps on it, and my phone instantly buzzes. It's a digital key to Mancell Hall downloaded as an app. "Your room is available now."

"What about Mama Aya—"

He interrupts me before I say anything else. "She already knows, and quite frankly, she agrees to this new and opportune situation."

"Ah, I get it. She don't want me at her house."

"It's not like that, Mr. Baron, and you know it."

I wanna argue. But then again, staying on campus would give me more leeway with finding out about my mama. Something Taron here clearly won't be helping me with. And I'm sure Taye would understand too. Besides, I can just sneak back off and visit him.

"Mr. Baron." I snap back to attention. "You are not to leave this campus; do you understand me?"

Grabbing my stuff, I whirl around, ready to go. His tapping on his desk stops me. "Just think about it," he says, smirking. "You'll get the full Caiman University experience."

I shoot him a respectful *fuck you* eye roll and walk out.

· · · ·

Outside, the clouds are scattered, inviting a strong light spilling onto the surface of this magical oasis. It's a good ten-minute walk from Chancellor Taron's office to the kingdom of residence halls. First one: Mancell Hall. I can tell it's one of those country club–looking apartment complexes. Crown moulding and picture windows are the first things I notice. The palmetto trees arch grandly over the entranceway. Mancell Hall is like a whole community.

Is this the mansion Jesus promised?

Through the courtyard, there's a boxed sand volleyball net, and a few state-of-the-art grills and lawn chairs. Crystal blue water pool. Grand marble fountain, spitting out water. It takes a good minute to get through the apartment's amenities and find the main lobby.

Gahhhhdamn, this ain't no apartment. This is a resort.

I use the app on my phone to scan the spinning key to the machine hooked on the door handle. When it opens, I step into the lobby. Couches splayed all over the place, a flat-screen TV mounted on the wall, and a little common area where folks can study or chill. Over on the right, a doorway leads to a small kitchenette. There's a couple in there cooking ramen noodles, laughing, and filming themselves doing dumb shit. The walls are decorated with flyers for kickbacks, prayer circles, and study group sessions.

My room key says ROOM 209. And I end up right around the corner, in front of the elevator. It takes me up to the second floor. The doors slide open, and I walk down this long, carpeted hallway with rooms on each side. A clutter of noises. Somebody bumping music, screaming, and more music. One dude has a broom in his hand, and he pours salt on it and then starts to sweep out of his dorm room with smoke swirling in his apartment.

Walking a few doors down, I notice the numbers: ROOM 209. As I open the solid oak entry door, a smell wafts out of the room, hitting my nose before I can step foot in it. It's sweet and sticky. Over on the corner, by the large picture windows, an incense burns. Smoke swirls in the air.

Shoes lie by the door on a rack. Nothing but Jordans and fresh

Dunks. The entrance to the half bath is open, lights on, and all kinds of jars full of essential oils are toppled over the counter.

This looks like a two-bedroom apartment, fully decked out. Tile floors. Nine-foot ceilings with another set of crown moulding. An *L*-shaped sofa is stationed right in the center of the living room. A flat-screen TV is mounted on the wall, showcasing a paused screen saver. On the coffee table, shavings of weed with a stubbed-out blunt sit next to a mountain of books.

"Aye, anybody in here?" I call out.

Music filters in from the room on the right, then a little bump. It becomes clear.

Somebody's in the room, getting their cheeks clapped.

A few minutes pass by. I'm standing in the middle of the living room, awkward as fuuuuuck, trying to figure out which door on the left is my bedroom. But on God, I ain't trynna walk into nobody's room.

The moaning instantly stops after a good minute and a half. I continue to wait, just for whoever to get themselves together. A dude stumbles out of the room, no shirt, just basketball shorts and flip-flops with socks on. He scratches the back of his neck as he crosses over to the kitchen. Some of that SZA spills from the dark while a shadowed figure shifts around, putting on their clothes.

I recognize him. It's the D Low dude from Professor Kumale's history class.

"Aye, wadup, bruh?"

"Hey, man, ummm, I guess I'm your new roommate for the time being. But it sounds like you was *busy,* so I ain't wanna bother you."

"Hold dat thought." He crosses over to the couch and reaches for the red sage smudge that's on the table. "I gotta make sure you good." He blows on the sage; it instantly lights up. The smoke swirls around me. He puts it in the air, above my head, my feet, all that. But no lie, I do feel my energy lift, and my mood boosts.

"Uh . . ."

D Low does another twirl of the sage over my head, all the way down to my feet. I catch a whiff of the earthy and peppery scent coming off it. "You goin' through some things. I can sense it all over you."

He blows the hungry flame out around the sage and throws it on the table and crosses over to the kitchen area. Reaches into the stainless steel refrigerator, grabs a carton of fruit punch, shakes it, and waterfalls that shit in one gulp.

"Look, I'm ya new roommate. Chancellor Taron sent me. I ain't trynna walk up in ya crib all unannounced."

"Naw, you good, fam. I just got the email." He looks back into his room. Claps. "Aye, yo, I'mma need you to roll on outta here." Whoever he is talking to moves about the room in a rush. Finally, he turns back to me, pushing a few strings of locs from his eyes. "Wadup, my dude, I'm D'Angelo. But people call me D Low."

"Malik."

"Oh shit, the new kid. You really Mama Aya's grandson and all that?"

A dude makes his way out of the room, tying his shoes. Welp—

"I'll see you later?" D Low says to ole boy. They kiss. Heavy. Basically sucking each other faces off.

Awk-MF-ward.

The dude winks at me and hustles out the door. D Low grabs a bowl, a jug of oat milk, and a box of Fruity Pebbles from the top of the fridge and eats that shit like he ain't just have a nigga come out his room.

"So . . . you and ole dude . . . ?" I ask, trying not to sound ignorant.

"I like what I like," D Low says back, defensive. "That ain't gonna be a problem, is it?"

"It ain't even like that, my guy. Plus, I'm just here temporary."

Chancellor got me bumped. I am not staying on this campus long-term.

D Low plops down on the couch, turns on the TV, and taps the Hulu button. "So, you a freshman, huh? Where you from?"

"Alabama. You?"

Instantly, he's surprised, almost jumping from the couch. "Get outta here? For real?! Aye, that's crazy . . . me too. Where 'bout you from?"

He throws back more cereal in his mouth.

"Helena. Right outside Birmingham. You?"

"I'm from Selma," he says, continuing to smack. "This my second year here at Caiman U."

"That's wassup."

Figured. Funny enough, folks from that small rural area, you just feel that sense of homeyness. He puts on an episode of *Living Single*. "Chancellor got you on straight lockdown, huh?"

"Yeah, I live with my grandmama on the bayou, and now he said I gotta stay on campus for the time being. 'Cause of the . . . Bokors?"

D Low pauses the episode and throws a look my way. "You won't catch Chancellor saying that, but yeah, them niggas ain't no joke. Fuck ya ass right up if they get close to you." He laughs out loud, mouth full and everything. "And that picture of Lorraine Baron and the Bokor vèvè mess in the lecture hall . . . I'm starting to believe they really might be back."

I blink, and that mental image pops in my head. "Yeah, that was my mama."

An awkward beat between us. "Ah, my bad, bruh. Wasn't thinkin' how she was Mama Aya's daughter, so that makes her your mama."

"All good."

"Aye, they said she was one of the best students here in Caiman U history. Everybody on campus be trying to get her study guides. Like, she's a legend, and apparently was a part of the Divine Elam."

I perk up. "Wait, what?"

I know I've been hearing that name a couple times now. But if my mama was in it, maybe it's going to the top of my list of what I need to learn more about.

Bet. Clue number four.

"Yeah—all the notes she took when she went here. Nobody ain't gonna be able to get it, though. It's in the library. Like a shrine or some shit. The secret society part, well, it ain't no secret no more, because of the war with them Bokors. The Divine Elam is what they called."

I mentally add getting my mama's study guides to my list. If anybody say something, I got an advantage. I'mma be like, *That's my mama, lemme have 'em.*

D Low takes out an ashtray and rolls a blunt real fast. He licks the outside of it, flips and folds, then lights it up. I sit down on the couch.

He puffs one more time and then hands it over to me. "You smoke?"

I pull my book bag off. "Not for real."

Honestly, I ain't had weed much. I smoke from time to time. Done a few edibles. Shit had me tripping last time, and I was out for three days. I take it and puff on it, letting the smoke fill my lungs. Then it all escapes out of my nostrils.

"The hell is that?" I say, tasting the bud and coughing my ass off. It got a kick to it and feels like sandpaper against my chest.

"Man, them Herbology majors, fam. This shit will faaaaawk you up for real." He puffs a ring of smoke into the air. "I'm pretty chill, though. Don't do shit but play basketball and go to class. And to wind down—what you just saw." He nods and then continues, "You can have whoever you want in here. I don't care." That's when he points to the kitchen. "In there, you eat it, you replace it. The same thing goes for me. Cool?"

"Cool, cool."

"Also, when in the house"—he inspects my shoes—"leave the shoes by the door."

Instantly, I pull my shoes off and place them by the door. "Oh, my fault."

He also studies my hair, which ain't been cut in a while. "And if you need a line-up, which you might, it's twenty-five dollars." Oh, this dude tried it. His shit looks a little crooked too, and he trynna come for me.

"Ummm, I'll keep that in mind." My fingers graze the dizzying waves on my head.

"Dope. Welcome to Caiman Uuuuuu." Awkward-ass moment. "My bad, it's a habit."

One more puff of that blunt, and I walk to the door that's right behind the couch. I guess this is my room.

Inside it is pretty standard. A bed, dresser, a computer desk, and a closet.

My phone buzzes. Alexis texts me.

> Meet me after dark. ASAP.
>
> It's important.

I text back.

> Okay. I'm staying on campus now. So, we can meet by the quad.

· · · ·

The sun gives way to the moon, giving the night her turn to fall with a quickness. A few folks linger by the quad, chilling and studying. Mostly on their phones. Me and Alexis meet around the Admissions building, away from everybody. She's standing at the edge by a gate, haloed like an angel, when I walk up to her. She's looking all tense.

"Aye, Lex, wassup? What's wrong?"

She wipes tears from her eyes. "They found her. Katia. She's dead."

Instantly, I wrap her in my arms. She's shaking uncontrollably. "I'm so sorry, Lex."

"We were too late. Her parents texted me the other day, but I just kept it in. Just processing." She shakes her head, composing herself. "She was sixteen years old, and if the police department would've listened . . . Hell, if the entire faculty listened. Her parents asked for our help, and we just left them in the dust off some politics of not revealing magic."

"Damn, that's fucked up."

"You're right. But fuck them. I'm taking matters into my own hands." She turns around and looks to see if the coast is clear. "Samedi wants me to meet him back at Mama Aya's house."

"Wait—?"

The expression on her face darkens. "I'll tell you when I get there."

Something tells me we finna break Chancellor Taron's lockdown rule.

She takes hold of my hand, and I feel her magic channel through me. There is a gust of wind, and my blue light orbits around my hand, and her bright yellow orbits around hers.

"The chancellor hexed the borders of the campus, but with magic and everything else, there's always a loophole."

She snatches the light that's in my hand and tosses it in the air. It sways back and forth like somebody let the air out of a balloon. It then travels and snuffs out like a puff of smoke.

"Just in case he'd want to sense you or me, our magic is here on the grounds of the campus. It'll be like we never left."

"Shit, remind me to let you tutor me."

She doesn't laugh back. *Really, Malik? Read the room.* She grabs my hand. In seconds, the entire campus vibrates around us like ripples in the water. In a swift movement, Mama Aya's yard is in our background.

The smell of cigar smoke makes my nostril flare up. In a shifting shadow, Samedi appears on the front porch, chest rising as he puffs. His crystal blue eyes flicker when he sees us.

Alexis carefully addresses Uncle Sam. "Forgive me, Baron Samedi. Chancellor Taron put a lockdown on campus. Everybody on the CaimanTea app saying they're back. The Bokors." A wispy cloud of smoke forms a ring in the air. I pull out my phone and go to the app for myself, and yup, folks all on this app, talking about it.

@ToriSwag: "Are these Bokors back or not? Cause I ain't trynna go to war."

"I heard," Baron Samedi says. "Them kids that was supposed to be comin' to y'all school been getting kidnapped. I've crossed a couple of 'em over to the land of the dead."

"Y'all known each other long?" I ask, suspicious.

"No, I summoned him for a bidding," Alexis replies.

Samedi nurses a mason jar full of brown liquor. I can smell the peppery scent of spiced rum from where I'm standing. "Before that girl died, a couple of her snatchers died too. A luck of the draw. One had an aneurysm, and the other done got himself shot up. They souls waitin' to be ferried." A stark curve of a smile forms a crease on the side of his mouth as he points to Alexis. "You really want justice for that girl?" he adds, sipping on that trapped brown liquor.

Alexis doesn't have to think twice about it. "I do."

"Let's get to diggin'." Samedi snaps his fingers. A thick black smoke swallows us up. As if the outside world tilting to the right, Mama Aya's yard instantly turns to open water. It takes me a quick second to realize that we're in a wooden rowboat that rocks from side to side.

Alexis is in front of me, perched on the edge of the rowboat. She whispers, "Seven nights, seven moons, seven gates, seven tombs." And she keeps repeating it over and over. Me, shit, I try to keep my balance. Up ahead, a wall of ghostly fog clears, and the half-moon shines down in a glow as if it's guiding us. It's cold and dark, and I'm shivering like I stole somethin'. Turning a bit, I notice that Downtown New Orleans fades in the distance the more we row and glide silently across the glassy water. It looks like moving tar, lapping lazily in one place.

"What the hell are we doing here?" I say to both of them as I freeze my ass off.

"Youngblood, you at the crossroads." Samedi pulls the boat to a stop. "It's best you have some reverence."

My teeth sink into the bottom of my lip as I peer into the black water, seeing my reflection staring back at me. First time I've seen my reflection in a bit. There's a new spark there, but that heaviness I carry still flickers in my eye.

Alexis hops out first on the edge of land, then me. I land hard on the mushy ground, almost slipping on the damp grass. One last glance and the black water disappears in the thick wall of fog.

I turn to Alexis and Samedi. "The crossroads, you say, huh?"

"In Haitian Voodoo legends, they say there's seven gates of Guinee located throughout the city," Alexis says. Suddenly I feel ice-cold, as if my whole body has been dipped in an ice bath.

With a leftover smile pulling the corners of his lips, Samedi travels over to one of the torches hanging on the side of a tall marble wall with scratches on it. Lying at his feet are several white candlesticks. Alexis kneels, presses her palms together in a praying position. All I can do is stare at her, puzzled.

She whispers an enchantment under her trembling breath. *"Ban nou limyè."*

The shaft of sparkling magic in her hand flutters all the way up the wall. The dancing flames snake around like dominoes falling, igniting each candlestick by Samedi's feet with purpose. My eyes shift from side to side, realizing something that's painfully obvious.

We're in a damn cemetery.

CHAPTER FOURTEEN

THE GATES OF GUINEE.

That's where we at, according to Baron Samedi. It's a murky place where spirits come before they go on to the land of the dead. He also says me and Alexis gotta be real careful 'bout what we do, because one wrong spell, we can open the floodgates of bad spirits entering the world. And he ain't trynna deal with that tonight.

An ominous feeling trickles down my arm in the form of goose bumps when he says this last bit. "Some say it's a land of torment and pain. I say it's nothing but deep waters for folks to pass on through to meet they ancestas."

From the shadowy corner, the moonlight leers on Alexis's focused face, temporarily tattooing illuminations on her skin. I'm so transfixed on her, I almost don't even notice Samedi leaning against a tall wrought-iron gate a few yards ahead, sparking up a cigar.

Around us are a constellation of white marble mausoleums lined up and down like a row of houses in a suburban neighborhood. Debris builds like mountains around the chipped tombstones. Rotting flowers and a dusty American flag lie limp over a grave that reads 1867. From there, dingy, tattered clothing is scattered like it's been left here for years. Crumbling rocks and shattered pieces of bottles all glitter in this land full of shattered dreams and lost hope.

Right in front of me, I notice two deep holes in the earth, with two shovels on the side. I look down and see the fresh, pristine white coffins.

A wall of white fog billows from the sides unexpectedly, clouding all around us. I blink several times, trying not to make myself disoriented.

When I look back at Samedi, he's right in front of my face . . . and I'm staring back at a white skull with a black top hat and sunshades with a missing lens. No skin. No flesh.

Baron Samedi is straight SKELETAL.

I back away, two seconds from shitting out my heart.

A raucous laugh escapes his exposed chest bone.

"Calm ya ass, youngblood," he says with a nasally Kreyol tone. He flicks ashes on the ground, and suddenly a wooden staff springs up like weeds. "You act like you seen't a ghost." His bony fingers wrap around the top of it, tapping the brim of his ornate top hat.

"What the hell, Uncle Sam?!" I scream at him, freaked the fuck out. Through the shaft of darkness, a slice of moonlight turns Samedi back to regular with all the flesh.

"Stop all that hollerin', you'll wake da dead." He laughs.

"Lex . . . ," I say, nervously making my way back over to her.

But she seems like she's in her own little world. Under her breath, she's saying an incantation.

"These muthafuckas gettin' stingy as heyell," Samedi grunts, kneeling to the ground, where broken bottles rest like shattered diamonds. "They gon' make me show my ass."

With a quick move of his hands, a translucent bottle appear in his hand, full of strong-smelling rum. He then lifts his arm and drinks straight from the bottle. The light from the moon hits it, and his skeletal body appears again. You could literally see it go down his throat, right through his rib cage. . . .

Alexis steps toward an unopened tomb. She takes a bit before she says anything. We both look at it, reading:

HUSBAND. FATHER. FRIEND.

WIFE. MOTHER. A TRUE LEADER.

My eyes scan to see the names etched into the stone. Effie Williams and Donell Williams.

She turns to me, her brown eyes full of tears. Then she wipes them away and takes a few Tupperware bowls from her bag, placing them on the side of the grave. "Brought your favorite, Mama. I didn't leave it in the oven too long, like you always told me." She takes out another plate wrapped in foil. It's a big-ass piece of lemon cake. "Daddy, I ain't forget about you. Extra icing, just how you like it."

"What she's doing?"

"Veneratin' her ancestors," Samedi answers. "Spirits like a lil' sumthin' sweet on the other side. It reminds them of they past lives."

Alexis saunters off, crossing back over to the two pristine white coffins. She looks down at the graves. Her eyes dance with rage like never before.

"Y'all, something doesn't feel right about this."

"Malik, please," Alexis begs. "These bastards deserve to go down."

I try and point out the obvious. "Go down? These muhfuckas already dead."

She doesn't respond, and she doesn't react. Just starts to whisper an incantation. I look over to Samedi with a pleading glare. He nods, letting me know to let her do her own thing. A snake slithers from the ground, tongue out, tasting the open air. Alexis picks it up. Pets it. Then out of nowhere, she stabs it in its abdomen, letting the blood trickle into the cold grass.

"Samedi—what the hell?"

"Youngblood, this is her biddin'. I'm just here to be a guide from the life of the livin' to the dead. That's what I do. Calm ya ass down." He offers me the bottle. "You wanna draaannk?"

His ass got jokes. But this shit is truly wild.

"You really are the Loa of the dead."

He chugs from the open bottle. "I guess that school's been teachin' you some thangs. . . ."

I look back at Alexis. "Apparently not enough."

Her bloody hands ball into a fist, and she whispers another incantation. A small gust of wind whips around us.

I back away, sick.

"Just trust me. Can you do that?" Her hands wrap around mine as she pulls me back closer to her.

With a whole lot of hesitation, I take in a sharp breath as a current of energy courses through my body.

As Alexis continues the chant, the ground beneath us shakes, and on everything I love, the spirits of two random dudes appear right before us! Skin falling off and everything. Like wax melting from the heat of a flame. One of them looks like their eyes is about to pop out of their sockets.

We all stand in tense silence as the dust settles.

"You two must be very confused right about now," Alexis says to them. "You assaulted, shot, and murdered an innocent Black girl, Katia Washington. Yeah, y'all remember her. She was only sixteen years old. A child. Just like me, with her whole life ahead of her. And what—you sold her to the highest bidder?"

Out of the clouds, she appears. Katia Washington. Unlike her murderers, she doesn't look like she's decaying like rotten fruit. She looks like her regular self. Beautiful. Long red braids down her back and scratches all up and down her arm. Her eyes flick back and forth between the dudes and Alexis.

"She was a daughter, a sister, a friend, and you sold her for money that you will NEVER be able to spend." Tears fall down her cheeks. But there's power in it. "When you bastards were done with her, you took her life."

"Lex—" I start, staring at the spirit of Katia Washington.

"Malik, please."

Alexis inches closer to the two men. In the angry sky, footage of Katia being slapped and thrown around in some random hotel room by a dude that's way older than her. She cries and yells for him to stop. It switches up, and it's her in the middle of the woods.

"Please—I ain't gon' tell nobody. Just let me go home! Please!"

Katia is thrown around in the room again. Blood spews from her swollen lip, and the door opens, inviting a darkness in the room as she slowly lies on the bed.

We all look to the spirits. One of them tries to talk; dirt and maggots spill out his mouth.

Shit, I think I'm gonna be sick.

"No, in this realm, you will not talk. You can't spread your lies. You won't win." Katia's spirit whirls around Alexis, staring dead in her murderers' eyes. "Black girls have a hard enough time in this world, and you killed her for a few measly dollars. Well, now it's time for y'all to pay."

Samedi steps up to them, pulling the cigar from his mouth. "You don't mind if I smoke, do ya? Course you don't. Ya dead." He blows smoke in their faces.

Alexis continues. "In this life, you would've gotten away with it."

Her hands glow gold and purple, magic summoning itself. On the ground, a vèvè is consecrated in cornmeal and a white candle.

A strange gust of wind blows a part of it away.

"But with what I can do, you'll spend eternity thinking about the pain you've caused."

The two murderers just give her a terrified look.

Another incantation spills from Alexis's lips. *"Mwen fè sèman pou m tòtire w pou tout tan. Ou p'ap konnen pa gen kè kontan oswa lapè pou tout tan!"*

The Kreyol she speaks translates in the front of my mind.

I swear to torture you forever. You will know no happiness or peace forever!

A loud boom explodes around us—and light burst from her fingers. Alexis's voice screaming, *"Seyè, Bondye, ki moun ki tire revanj; Mechan sa a pap triyonfe pou tout tan!"* rings in my ear.

Suddenly, the ground beneath us shakes so bad, I fall to the ground.

Samedi picks me up and pulls me back. Alexis lifts her hands; then she blows dirt in their faces.

"Fiyyyaaa es spira!" Alexis casts a spell with a thousand convictions.

Shooting from the crevice of the ground is a fire dragon, breathing and roaring. It twists and rumbles with life on some *Dragon Ball Z* shit. The fiery dragon swoops down, wrapping its body around the two dudes that killed Katia. Their entire bodies burst into fucking flames. They let out agonizing screams. I have to cover my ears. The fire dragon consumes them, dragging their souls literally to hell, and the ground closes up like nothing ever happened.

Then a soft breeze blows.

Baron Samedi, in his skeletal look, scoops up the dust, and places it in the pocket on his tux.

Alexis looks to Katia Washington's spirit, holding up her hand. *"Ale nan paradi."*

A bright, heavenly light wraps around Katia, and then her soul evaporates into floating embers, rising to the sky. Gone.

A quick breath. Everything is back to normal. Well, as normal as it's gonna get.

Alexis pulls out a case full of newly cut cigars and the fanciest bottle of rum. "As promised, Baron Samedi, for the ferry to the Guinee."

"Ahhhhh soookie sookie, this dat *guuuud* shit! Hmmm, me and da boys gon' tear this shit up!" He tips his hat to her with gratitude and moseys off, cracking jokes to himself.

Alexis then looks at me. Fire and pain in her eyes. "They will never know peace."

And from what I just saw, I don't know if I will, either.

• • • •

I'm trying to wrap my head around what just happened. I'm not sure if I wanna throw up or go curl in a bed and pray I don't ever have to see what I just saw.

Who am I kidding? That's something that probably gonna keep me up for the rest of the night.

Shit . . . maybe for the rest of my life.

Me and Alexis sit on Mama Aya's porch in complete silence. My lips part, but the words just tiptoe on the edge of my tongue.

"You gonna ask me or what?" I must've been quiet for a long time because she sounds hella annoyed.

It's like lava, the way the question just spills out. "How the hell you set them on fire?"

"I used a form of bane magic."

Bane.

I'm gripped with thoughts tangling in my head. "Lex, so, you playing God now?" She falls silent and gives me a *are you serious* look. "This . . . wow—so what now?"

"They got what they deserved. That's what." Her voice is laced with rage. "She was sixteen, Malik. Sixteen. And they sold her to a life of misery. It was only befitting that I repay it."

"You ain't God, Lex. You can't be judge and jury."

"Why not? We have the power, Malik. We have magic."

"Yeah, but isn't there a thing called 'return to sender' or some shit? This can blow back on you. Magic always comes with a price."

"Then I'll pay it all." She pauses, then holds out her hand, focusing. As the tears flow from her eyes, the wind starts up. "You feel that, Malik? You feel how just by me closing my eyes, I can conjure the wind? Just think about how we can help our community out there. On the outside! Instead of being in this bubble, living high on the hog, literally watching people like us get trampled down. We can provide medical aid. Black women can go to doctors without fearing death or medical malpractice. The elderly, we can provide medicinal herbs that can help ailments. . . . We can do it all with the snap of our fingers."

"To do alla that, Lex, you had to give up something, right? To conjure that spell. What did you give up? Yo, you sounding real Killmonger and shit."

That got her looking away as the hunger of guilt washes over her.

Alexis continues, warily. "We have abilities and talents that go beyond understanding. There's no reason we should just be standing by and doing nothing while our people suffer." She stands up to pace back and forth. "When you get deeper into Caiman, Malik, you will realize the technology, the knowledge that we have—we can change the entire trajectory of Black people."

"You can't save everybody, Lex," I tell her.

"I will help someone, Malik! Even if it's just one person, I am going to help them!" Another round of silence. Alexis then softens. "Look, I've gone to the Kwasan tribe and pleaded and pleaded for them to step in and help. But what do they do? They shut me out. Black girls are going missing; people are losing their homes. Malik, people are dying, and we have the power to help them."

We sit in silence for a minute. I can't help but stare at her. She's angry. I'm angry. And shit, all we can do right now is just get mad together.

"What? Why are you looking at me like that?"

The strained words struggle to leave my lips. "I ain't gonna tell you how to feel or what to feel. I'm just . . ."

"I'm getting really tired, Malik. Chancellor Bonclair will not be able to stop me for much longer. I'm fighting for my people. I'm not letting anything stop me. I can't just sit here and do nothing. They had nobody to help them or be there for them," she says; then her eyes flicker with tears. "You of all people should know how being abandoned feels."

Her words burn into me. "Yeah, but—what you did, that shit . . . It ain't gonna bring that girl back."

"It may not bring her back, but with our magic, we can prevent another Black woman or man from being murdered." She clocks me shaking my head. "I knew you wouldn't understand. The only person who understands me is Donja. . . ."

"Wow. So, you and the nigga definitely fucking."

"Good night, Malik." She crosses over by the tree.

"Yo, why did you even bring me tonight, Lex?!"

She stops and meets my gaze. "Because I—"

"Because what?"

Another long pause from Alexis makes my anger boil even more. Only because this girl who I'm looking at, I don't recognize.

"You help anchor me, Malik. I don't know, since you came to Caiman, it's like this feeling bubbles back up for me. A feeling how we were when we were little kids, and how we wanted to help folks with our magic. And maybe if you weren't there tonight, I probably would've lost myself even more.

"And you know what? Donja, he's been there, okay? He's been there for me in ways nobody has. And he would never question me or look at me how you are right now."

I'm on my savage shit and just shrug my shoulders. "Well, you should've brought him, then. If he makes you feel that way."

"Wow, I open up to you, and you make it about Donja," she says back. "Look, it's been ten years, Malik."

"You don't gotta keep reminding me."

"That I know. We all change, Malik!" she screams. "It's you who stayed the same."

Gut punched.

"See you back at school."

And she disappears.

Is this what they mean by *magic comes with a cost*? If so, Alexis paid a high price tonight. Maybe we all do when it comes to having this magic stuff.

And if Alexis going down the same path my mama did, then I'm thinking one thing and one thing only: Is having magic even worth it?

CHAPTER FIFTEEN

CHANCELLOR TARON REALLY GOT ME AT THIS MAGICAL-ASS HBCU, taking regular classes like algebra?

Man, he can go kick rocks for this bullshit.

Unlocking my phone, I land on the last text I sent to Alexis. It haunts me. The word *delivered* highlighted to remind me that I need to get over my ego and just apologize and move on. And I know I said some dumb shit about her and Donja.

But no lie, our fight kinda still got me feeling some type of way, and it takes everything in me not to text her a simple hey. Then I think, *Nah*. Because that might piss her off—the word *hey* is not a text saying sorry . . . or would she get even madder for the simple fact that I'm not texting her?

Man, girls are more stressful than this schoolwork.

It's more than just the fight that holds me back texting her, though. Maybe it's easier to think about that than to think about why we were fighting in the first place. I still can't believe everything I saw at that cemetery—we're all here taking classes, learning about magic like it's this regular thing when magic can do that kind of straight-up horror movie shit. It's so big I can't see how it's not what we're all talking about every minute. But I've got experience shoving things out of my head when I need to, and that's what I'm doing today.

Maybe this is how Mama Aya felt with my mama.

After study period, I sling my book bag over my shoulders and zoom out of the classroom with a quickness. Descending the mountain of a staircase, I get a text from Taye. We go back and forth on how him and a couple of friends been going to see this new movie, and he's seeking advice on asking out my cousin Sierra.

> I'mma ask her tonight. Hopefully she says yes, or it's gonna get real embarrassing here at Mama Aya's.

Right at the bottom of the stairs, by this bougie-looking coffee shop, is Professor Kumale. Me and him lock eyes. "Malik," he calls, stirring his coffee with a small stick. "Already got a college sweetheart?"

I smack my teeth. "Naw. It's just my little brother."

"Oh, you have a little brother. How old is he?"

My phone buzzes. It's Taye again, but I put my phone back in my pocket. "Twelve. He's going on his first lil' date."

He sips his coffee. "That's so cool, Malik. Hold on to him. Little brothers are always precious. Even if they may get on your nerves at times."

"Yeah, he's everything to me."

A brief pause. Professor Kumale sips on his coffee again. "So, you had Dr. Cherry?"

"Yeah—how are we at this dope magical school, and we still gotta take gen ed classes? What kinda mess is that?"

"Well, Caiman University wants you to get a well-*rounded* education. You have time to sit for a quick second?"

We both find a couple of chairs right outside in the courtyard.

"I see that you have Dr. Akeylah. Let me say this: she is tough, but she really cares for her students. Word of advice: speak up in her class. Dr. Akeylah really likes that, and have your spells already perfected before getting there, because having her breathe down your neck is nerve-wracking."

"Oh, you're speaking from experience?"

"Yes, I am. She was a TA when I was a student here. One of the best, might I add. I was a couple of years under her."

"She got us doing these book reports on how Hoodoo has affected Black history. So, I'm doing mine on George Washington Carver and his peanut invention. It's wild. That dude was a whole Hoodoo man, and nobody didn't really know it."

He raises his cup, smiling. "Our magic has been influencing the outside world for generations."

"Well, it's due by tomorrow. I'm half-done."

The stress of being a college kid got a brotha quiet right now. 'Cause even after something as messed up as last night, I'm still here writing book reports.

"Something on your mind?" he asks.

"Just thinkin' on a lot of things."

Which is true. But I know I can't tell him anything that Alexis was up to, and I'm not too sure if I can even trust this dude with my little mission on figuring out what the hell my mama got herself into. I don't know Professor Kumale like that.

"I know your first semester here can be quite overwhelming," he says, sipping on his coffee. "My first semester here was a disaster."

"Fuhh real?"

"I actually failed my first class. Potions. You think a stink bomb is bad . . . what I mixed up that day, it cleared out the entire science building."

We cut up, laughing.

"We alike then because I almost burned down Dr. Akeylah's class. Good thing I can't fail for doing that."

Which reminds me, I can't be playing when it comes to my own classes.

"Oh, don't be mistaken. They can and will fail you. Look, these professors here are tough. Some are old-school and feel that they have to give you that tough love to prepare you for the real world."

I think on that. I also question: Can this school, with all its resources, prepare everybody for the heartache the world got waiting for us?

"That is, until Professor Salim. He took this young Haitian kid under his wing and taught him everything he knew. Dr. Salim was the best mentor ever."

I scan what's in front of us, taking in the hustle and bustle of everybody rushing to their next class.

"Yeah, a mentor would be dope. Been learning this magic stuff all on my own. It's been like that since I was seven."

"I know you don't know me from a can of paint, but you seem like a really bright young kid, and I'd love to be your mentor. You know, help you around here, get acquainted."

My face tightens with hesitation.

"I don't know. . . ."

"Sensing your magic in this very moment, I know there's so much there. So much talent and potential just waiting to burst out."

"I'm all right," I say, feeling myself shrinking. "You filling my head."

"Don't do that."

I cock my head back, trying to play off the seriousness. "What?"

"Don't ever make yourself small. You are very gifted, and you belong here, Malik. No matter how much this world tries to make you feel that you don't."

Blindsided by that, my thoughts drift to a place. A cluttered place where I can't even remember ever being told that I belong somewhere. My whole life, nobody's ever told me I'm good at anything, and hearing it from this dude's mouth got me feeling . . . I don't know, seen. "Where'd you just go now?" he asks me.

"Huh?"

"When I said that to you, where did you go just now?"

I take in a sharp breath, leveling my voice with raw emotions. "I just . . . I never been told this before by a teacher, ya know? And my foster parents . . ."

I stop myself.

"I get it. We all got things; it's a part of life." I nod in agreement. "Look, the offer is on the table. Everything that you're going through, I went through it too. I might be able to help."

He makes valid points.

"Remember: set your intentions outright, Malik. With your magic, intention is important. It's the core of your power. Everything you want is literally in the palm of your hands."

A familiar voice slices the silence between us in half. It's Savon, with Elijah, and trailing right behind them is Alexis and Donja. Me and Alexis steal a glance at each other.

I don't know what I expected, but she looks the same as she did before she was out there in a cemetery raining down torture on dead men's souls. Seeing her now, I can't help flashing back to those sights, but whatever doing that bane magic took outta her, I don't see anything different today.

No cap, I wanna say something. And I'm sure she wants to too, but one thing hasn't changed: we're both stubborn.

Damn. Maybe I should've sent that text.

On the real, her words still bother me. *It's you who stayed the same.* But me being her anchor is something that I haven't grasped. Honestly, hearing that come from her beautiful lips kinda soften the blow of us not talking.

I hold on to that in case I need to be the bigger person.

"Wasssuuup, Professor Kumale?" Elijah says first. Then he throws a glance to me.

"How are y'all?" Professor Kumale answers back. "I'm looking forward to reading your history reports."

Elijah opens his mouth to say something, but Professor Kumale interrupts. "And no late assignments."

Elijah says, "I'm almost done. I just had to rearrange a few things."

"Told ya ass to focus on that," Savon says, walking up to Professor Kumale. "I already turned mine in. I'm ready to receive my A. I already manifested it." Savon squints at me, knowing wassup. I bet money they and Alexis talked about what happened between us.

"It's due. Twelve o'clock tonight. Not a minute later," Professor Kumale tells Elijah.

"Daaaang," Elijah says, chuckling. "No extensions?"

"I'mma catch y'all later," I tell them.

One soft glance to Alexis and I'm out of their vicinity in seconds.

T. Atwell Library sits right near the BCSU and the Langford Center. You gotta go through two sets of doors before you get to the main lobby. The library is big as hell. More books than I can imagine. D Low told me that there are ancient books going back almost a thousand years here. A melody of flipping pages and tapping on keyboards wafts all through this place.

Around a mountain of stacked books, I see a girl hunched over at a table, reading a thick volume of pages that would probably take me my whole life to read. Out of nowhere, she pulls the words from the actual page and puts them in her brain.

Okay. I'mma have to learn that, because that was hella dope.

There's an elderly lady behind a counter. Her frizzy brown hair wrapped in a tight bun. She's got thick reading glasses hanging from her neck by gold beads as she reads a Charlaine Harris book. When I squint, she kinda reminds me of Ms. Nell in my old neighborhood.

I decorate my face with a smile that makes old ladies feel good and pinch yo cheeks. "Umm, excuse me, ma'am, I was wondering if you have this book on George Washington Carver. Trynna get this one source out of it."

I hand her the book title on a piece of paper. She places her glasses on and reads it. Then types on the computer.

"We have it. It's, uh—Lemme show you."

Through the shelves, it's like we go into an abyss of books. The hissing sound of pages and soft whispers guides us to the back, where it seems more like Area 51. The librarian lady waves her hand, and the book slides magically forward.

She hands it to me. "There you go."

"Thank you, ma'am."

We make our way to the other side of the shelves, back to the checkout desk. "I also heard there are some notes from Lorraine Baron that's here, a book of hers. Can I check it out?" I ask, my voice jumping an octave higher.

"It's not available right now, hun," she says in a real country accent. "Chillun try ta take it out here, but they can't slip past me. I catch on to 'em."

One last attempt spills out of me. "Well, she's my mama."

This lady gives me the record scratch pause.

I hold my breath.

"You the son?" She doesn't give me time to even answer. But her whole demeanor changes. "Why you ain't say so, chiiiiile? Come on here, lemme show ya."

The old librarian lady hustles to the back, where shelves of books tower toward the ceiling. A group of students hush their giggles when they see me and the old lady. We turn a corner, away from the main area.

And there it is, right in front of me. Under a spotlight in a glass casing.

Mama's workbook.

"We still can't let you check it out," the old librarian reminds me. "It's a prized possession. Got all kindsa thangs in it, not all of them proper for students. No matter what folks say about her, Lorraine was sweet, real talented, and real respectful whenever she came in here. It's a shame that she just fell off the face of the earth."

I kinda brush it off with a cordial smile.

"Yes, ma'am," I say, keeping my voice soft. "Question: What happened to the original Divine Elam?"

Before she answers, she pulls off the glasses and wipes them with a small blue cloth. "Well, you know you was always taught that us folks, Black folks, came to this country four hunnit years ago?" I nod slowly. "Well, that is partly true."

She walks between the mountain of bookshelves, up to the glass casing slowly, letting the gold light hit it like a spotlight. "Our ancestors sailed the oceans, went to lands unknown."

She pulls a book from one of the shelves, waves her hand in a swift motion, and the pages hiss. A whirlwind of stenciled drawings of African people in long cloaks appear out of nowhere. She leans down, her eyes shifting left to right. Then she breathes on it, and I swear, it's like the air that left her lips colors their robes in decked-out colors. "A special tribe called the Divine Elam came to this land. Way before that Columbus 'claimed' he discovered it. They felt an

205

energy here. A new magic. Traded with the Native folks with gold-tipped spears, trading copper and gold. They built statues and stayed here peacefully for five hundred years." Like a 3-D rendering, a few tall stone statues with wide noses and thick lips appear. "Their very magic blessed the soil we all walk on today. They could even control the moon and the stars with the Scroll of Idan."

The library shifts, just like the classroom did with Professor Kumale. In the vision, I'm face-to-face with an African warrior. He stares blankly past me. As I get a good look at him, he's dripped in the finest golds and lavish robes that trails a few feet behind him. He kneels, grabs a fistful of dirt, blows into it, and the vision in front of me changes to nothing but bare feet slamming into the mushy soil. Screams . . . but no, it's not out of fear, but out of joy.

A group of kids, probably around my age, wrestling. The dirt rolls off their skin like they're made of it. One of them lifts their hands, shooting a jet of brown light toward the other.

Behind them, I see six tall figures in white robes. One of them steps forward, with a long, thick rolled-up paper in his hands.

It glows like the sun.

The Divine Elam.

"And then what happened?" I ask the nice librarian.

A dark expression crosses her face.

"The Idan Ọlọrun Eclipse."

The entire vision in front of us fades away and we're back in the library. The librarian shakes off whatever is giving her the chills and closes the book. "Listen, if ya need anythin' else, lemme know."

"Wait—what happened after that Idan whatever-you-call-it Eclipse?"

She exhales, riddled with heavy memories. "When that eclipse happened, it sorta cut off their connection to their homeland. It was the end of a golden age. Their power has been fading out from this world ever since. You don't hear about many folks with that kind of magic anymore."

Another vision pops up.

It's a big-ass, weird-looking eclipse happening in the sky. It's like God himself is covering the sun with his whole hand. The same kids from before are now screaming out of terror. They rush to the water.

I stand in the middle of it all, confused and dazed.

The scroll that was in ole dude's hand from before, it dims and then starts to turn to ash, except one part of it. It all kinda collides with the librarian's worried face.

"They were stuck here, cut off from their homeland, waiting to go back."

The leader cries uncontrollably as his magic blasts from him. It seeps into the earth below him, and suddenly the ocean is clouded with a mountain of smoke.

In this moment, I can just remember what Dr. Akeylah said back in class. *Through their tragedy, they left a legacy of Caiman here for us.*

"It's even believed they created this university, and of course, in 1804, it was renamed Caiman University. And to honor the Divine Elam, a group of special conjurers was created here on campus to carry out their ways."

"And my mama, she was a part of it?"

Her eyes shift from me to the studying students. "Hmm. They say she was messin' with some things she wasn't s'posed to."

I press for more. "What things?"

"The Scroll of Idan." She replies like one of them old church ladies gossiping in church. "It's a piece of paper—and it's ancient. I believe it came from the land of Kemet, where it gives you powers just like the gods of ancestas. She knew that and wanted to find it for herself. That temptation got to her."

I just know this info will help me understand my mama a lot more. One more question . . .

"Like, what did they do? The Divine Elam? The ones at Caiman, I mean."

"Whew, chile. I'm not sure—it's all real secretive, you know. The elders only allow the strongest students to be initiated. Every generation it be about three to four students are called, and even a seer."

"Seer?"

"A person who ain't got the root magic in 'em, but they are tied to our world with one foot in and one foot out. They record stories, spells, but they so few and far between, chile. The last one I came to know was Mama Moses."

"Mama Moses?" I ask.

The librarian leans in, smiling. "Harriet Tubman. She had the gift of seeing things happenin' before they even happened."

Again, I absorb all of this.

"And who was in it with my mama?" Maybe that's the next person I gotta find.

"Last time I believe it was Chancellor Bonclair, Lorraine, and one other— Lawd, what was that child's name? Oh, Antwan Bivins. Yeah, that's it."

"Wait—Chancellor Bonclair was in it too?"

She nods.

I knew his ass was hiding some shit. A'ight. Bet.

The corners of the librarian's lips turn up, revealing pearly white teeth and deep lines in her wrinkled honey-brown skin. "Lemme know if ya need anything, hear?"

"Yes, ma'am."

"Call me Ms. Faye," she says, pinching the hell out of my cheeks. "You so handsome. Love to see you young, beautiful Black men in here readin'. You enjoy." Ms. Faye slowly walks away. I continue to look at the glass casing, waiting for her to fully be gone. Yup, it's Mama's handwriting for sure. She had the most perfect cursive writing I had ever seen. It's straight across like it's printed on the page to be sold in bookstores. Me, I could never get it right because I'm left-handed. Straight chicken scratch. My shit used to be slanted when my teachers called me to write on the board. Had me hella embarrassed.

Wow.

As I stare at it, I realize that there's a piece of my mama I never even knew existed. Her thoughts and secrets are shaded in ole pieces of paper. But trapped by a glass casing.

Something has to be in there to give me more clues about that night.

Yeah, I gotta steal this.

It belongs to me, not some magical school trying to keep it as a relic.

Before I try anything, I lean all the way back to make sure nobody coming down this aisle. Ms. Faye is typing slower than a snail at the front desk. She's looking up a book for another student.

A'ight. I'm in the clear.

I place my hand on the glass, and it starts to splinter. Shit! Never mind about that.

My fingers press on the glass, and I can feel a protective spell emanating from it.

How the hell am I gonna do this?

A'ight.

I press my palm fully to the glass, closing my eyes to focus. Whatever spell I gotta make up swells my lungs with air.

More pressure from my fingers meeting the glass, and it starts to splinter even more. Cracked lining snakes down the casing like veins. I'm about to shit a brick because I am not trynna get caught.

I take a deep breath and focus my wants for this book real hard. The incantation pools inside of me like it's a natural thing. It rolls from my mind, lingers at the tip of my tongue in a soft whisper, and out of nowhere, a slight gust of wind.

One by one, the books from the shelves start to fall. My ass is causing hella commotion. When I lean back, I see that Ms. Faye is looking my way with a rise of suspicion. She steps from behind the counter and starts to march my way.

I'm starting to sweat bullets.

My eyes dance to the ceiling, where a fire alarm rests in the corner. I flick my wrist, and like I'm directing a church choir, the fire alarm lets it rip. Bending back, the old lady stops, looks around. Students gather their belongings, filtering out.

Back to the workbook. I recalibrate myself with focus. I quickly exhale, and a book falls right on top of my head.

I move my right hand, and the glass completely shatters.

And I don't have time to think. I just grab the notebook and try to teleport—but I end up crashing inside a storage room.

Taking in a deep, calm breath, I feel my whole body lift off the ground and out of the library. I crash right in the middle of my bed, and my ass hit the floor.

Thank God it's carpet.

"Aye, yo! You good?" D Low calls from the other room.

Rubbing the pain from my backside, I manage a "Yup!"

Back to the mission. The study guide lies flat on my bed, peering up at my wondering eyes.

The words come to life. From love spells to healing and cleansings. Santeria. Lukumi. Ifa. Some I cast; some I try but fail—shit is hard. My mama was, like, a genius when it came to this stuff.

Honestly, reading all of this is like peeking into her brain, into her life. Some of her writings suggest that something personal is needed to cast a very powerful spell. Something like hair, blood, semen (we ain't doing that), or a personal item from a loved one.

So, I figure I'll lay down the picture and the mysterious note.

Through all of this, I take a moment. Just relishing the fact that this is a piece of my mama I never knew I needed. Her class schedule and notes from her research. I trace the edges of the paper, silently praying for an image of her writing it.

*The Divine Elam and the allegory
to the Black American experience
Written by Lorraine Baron*

Continuing to flip through, I see spells from justice magick. Roots. Her little note at the top: *Spellwork must be justified.* Then a passage from Exodus 21:24–25: *"Eye for eye, tooth for tooth, hand for hand, foot for foot, burning for burning, wound for wound, stripe for stripe."*

Flipping another page, I see the familiar words that been haunting me since the other night.

Gula, aka de re mo . . .

With a sad attempt, I channel my magic and make the six-point candles that are on my dresser light up. I'm getting better at that for sure. The energy from the flames feels as though it's igniting my insides. Then I kneel on the floor, just like my mama did that night.

With closed eyes and bated breath, I silently pray those words.

Sula, aka de re mo . . .

Nothing.

Maybe I really do need a mentor.

CHAPTER SIXTEEN

"WHAT'S GOING ON, MALIK?" PROFESSOR KUMALE ASKS, clocking me leaning against the doorway.

I step farther into the classroom with a look of exhaustion. "If I let you be my mentor, can I ask you questions you may deem dumb?"

He puts on one of those teachery scoffs. "No such thing as a stupid question, only stupid people, or something like that—"

I give him that *bruh, you hella corny* look.

He laughs and props himself against his desk, twirling the dry erase marker between his fingers. "Of course, what's on your mind?"

Welp, here comes the scary part, and that's actually trusting somebody that I don't know. But Professor Kumale honestly seems like the coolest guy here. And the fact he offered to be some sort of mentor is kinda dope. I reach into the pits of my book bag to pull out my mama's workbook. His expression shifts as he reads the words.

Sula, aka de re mo . . .

"What does this mean?" I ask him.

Pushing his glasses to the bridge of his nose, he says, "Do I wanna know how you got this workbook?"

"Not if you wanna be an accessory to thievery."

"Ah. Well, this spell is a transference-of-power spell. One of the oldest, actually, and the most forbidden."

"Forbidden?"

"It gives a conjurer an immense amount of power. Essentially stripping the god they summoned with this spell of their powers."

I already knew it was bad, but wow, my mama was really into some shit that she ain't had no business in.

Professor Kumale continues. "It's so forbidden that when the Bokors used it to win the war, they were punished by the gods."

A mental image of the night of the Haitian Revolution. The group of men dancing and shouting in Kreyol pops back in my head. But more importantly, the human sacrifice.

"Yeah, Alexis and her friends told me about a lil' bit."

"The gods turned on them and cursed them for trying to take too much power, upsetting the natural balance. The original spell is said to be derived from the Scroll of Idan, an ancient text containing some of the most powerful hexes."

Another mental image: dude from the Divine Elam crying. And that Idan scroll that Ms. Faye, the librarian, talked about.

"The Scroll of Idan, yeah, that was, like, a Divine Elam thing, right?"

"Someone's been studying. Yes, the Bokors drew a lot of inspiration from the original Divine Elam, hoping to claim the same kind of godly powers. But when the spell went wrong for them and they were punished . . . Well, legend says they sought the original Scroll of Idan, hoping it could reverse the curse and bring them the true power they sought."

"And did they find it?" I ask intently.

Kumale laughs darkly. "If they had, history might look very different. No—in fact, Caiman's own Divine Elam was founded to protect the scroll from those like the Bokors who desire its power. Would you like to see?"

He holds out his hand with a smirk. Getting the idea, I wrap my hand around his, feeling the buzzing of his magic.

"Damn, you really are the Black Ms. Frizzle."

He forces a laugh while snapping his middle finger to his thumb. Just like before, the paneled walls fold, and the entire classroom dissipates in a speeding blur.

Suddenly, we materialize in a small, dark room. A few feet ahead of us, a black podium rises from the ground. A roar of rushing flames covers us, licking the walls. When I blink, the Divine Elam appear in white cloaks.

Professor Kumale points to them. "Each generation, the elders choose new members of the Divine Elam. Think of it as the Freemasons . . . but with magic. A society that gains knowledge of the Scroll of Idan and protects the idea of its knowledge and whereabouts. Oungans, which are priests, and Mambos, which are priestesses."

"Can anybody join?"

"No, you must be called to join. The elders, the first ones, made it like that for a reason."

"Well, how you get in?"

"You have to be initiated," Professor Kumale replies. "They go through a process called lave tet." He clocks the confused look on my face. "It means head washin'."

We see it play out.

Another elder with hard, intense eyes pull out a long stick with a ball-shaped thing at the end. He shakes it.

"Then they go through what we call the ason."

A long blade is pulled from a pocket somewhere in his cloak. He jabs each person on the palm of their hand. Blood pools. I step forward, catching the group of conjurers bend back, eyes clouded in a grayish-white color. And then they start to dance around a crackling fire, shouting and vocalizing some weird sounds.

With their magic riling up, a mist of a hurricane blows into the room. "Last but not least, they have to be open to be possessed by the spirits."

One woman bends back so far, you'd think her whole spine would break.

The vision changes. From there, they hover their hands over a thick, old-looking book. Their magic manifests, and droplets of blood drip onto the pages and move, creating a vèvè symbol.

A person who I can't sense any magic from records it. His hand moves in a blur.

"They call him the seer. He doesn't have magic but has a closeness to the supernatural, records it all."

Wind. A flickering of lights as a golden thread encircles us like the rings of Jupiter. This magic is hella powerful. Beads of light bubble to the surface of the thread.

"And are they always students?"

"They usually are," he answers. "Only the most special of the upperclassmen. When it's time for the graduating students to leave, they typically pass the mantle down to the new generation that comes behind them."

Everything in front of us shifts like time going forward. We witness generations and generations of folks coming in, protecting, learning the secrets. "For generations, each year a few selected students guard those secrets. Protect it. Honor it. That is, if you believe the scroll is really out there. Many think it was lost for good in the eclipse."

The entire vision whooshes in front of us, and we land in a room with three students. It's more modern this time. Like early 2000s. All three of them stand in a circle, holding hands and chanting.

One, my mama. Two, Chancellor Taron. The librarian already mentioned him, but it's still crazy to me.

"Mama," I whisper, feeling the tears well up in my eyes.

I walk up to her. She doesn't see me. But I see her, in her element. Her magic manifests in bright, brilliant gold. It soars to the ceiling, creating a sheet of rain.

As my hand reaches out to grab hers, everything switches.

She's gone.

From above, the vèvè hovers in midair just under the lamplight. Professor Kumale causes this.

"Not only does our magic come from nature, Malik. It's directly connected to our ancestors. And if it's corrupted . . ."

A pang of resistance churns in me because I know what's about to come next.

"That's why the transference spell will require the lex talionis hex."

"What's that?"

His magic forms into a shape with a quick swirl. Moving like moths to a flame, I can feel its coolness, like a chilling breeze whipping across my cheek. "The law of retribution," Professor Kumale says.

"You know a lot about all of this?"

"Listen, the more you excel, the more you'll learn the good parts, but also the dark parts. Malik, there's duality in everything. I know, because I witnessed a lot of it."

And like a cloud, the vèvè turns into a fiery ash.

He levels me with a cold stare. "This is why we say that 'magic always comes with a price,' Malik. For the Bokors, the price was their humanity, their ability to produce their own magic. Power, the kind of power found in the scroll—there will always be those who seek it."

CHAPTER SEVENTEEN

A HARD HEAD MAKES A SOFT ASS.

Another sharp shrill from the dramatic-ass phone alarm reminds me that it's the crack of dawn. Which means I didn't get absolutely no sleep.

Climbing to the edge of the bed, I'm met with the gray morning sky trying to peek through the blinds. Rubbing the kinks out my neck, I let my mind swim until the next set of alarms assaults my ears.

After a quick brush to the waves and teeth and putting on my Aaliyah T-shirt, I go over it all before Dr. Akeylah's defense class: First, the Bokors and them sacrificing that kid—using the spell I heard before, *Oya—Ban mwen pouvwa lavi ak lanmò.* And the spell I heard my mama practicing. Second, the Divine Elam and this Scroll of Idan— which my mama knew about, and the Bokors were looking for too.

My mama done got herself into some dark *ish,* and it probably cost her more than she bargained for. But I still don't know how any of it adds up to where she's been all these years.

When I walk into the lecture hall, the advanced class is full of people. Savon is the first to say something to me when I make it to one of the empty seats in front of them. I can feel Donja's stare, but I'mma chill today. Don't feel like getting into a fight.

Elijah steps up to me. We give each other a dap of the hands. "Oh, so they just transferrin' people in here now."

"Talk to ya boy Chancellor Taron," I tell him, laughing.

Alexis looks forward and writes whatever is on the board in her notebook. Me and Elijah whisper to each other, chopping it up.

I catch the edge of another conversation. It's a girl with short hair that sits in front of me.

"Damn, another person went missing. And this time, it's somebody that just graduated last year."

The girl beside her replies, "I know, and my daddy said this keeps happenin', I ain't gonna be able to come back here."

Another student says to them, "Me either. And the Kwasan tribe is still silent on this issue, chile."

My phone buzzes. It's the CaimanTea app. It's a whole buncha statuses being uploaded.

> @TeeTeebaby: Y'all! Please spread the word! Brian Minor has been missing since last week. Last seen in the Quarters. We can't let this keep happening to our people.

> @HoochieVoodooDoll: These Bokors got me bummmmped! I am not dealing with this. I'm trynna get snatched for fall semester!

My phone buzzes again. It's another status and a selfie of a girl outside her dorm, looking upset.

> @Treslay114: Buddy system intact. Dorms may go on curfew. Effective this weekend. Let's get this last-minute party on.

So more people are going missing? I wonder, *Does Chancellor Taron know about this?*

"Good morning, class," Dr. Akeylah says, addressing all of us.

Everybody chants back the simultaneous greeting: "Good morning, Dr. Akeylah."

Not her pointing right at me. "First, I would like to introduce our new student, Malik Baron. So, let's give him a warm welcome."

A few claps here. A few chuckles there.

Professor Kumale stands beside her.

"Hold up, we get to fight both of y'all?" Elijah asks, getting the whole class rumbling with laughter.

"Gentlemen," Dr. Akeylah warns. "We left off with defense mechanism, I believe. Next up is"—she reads from a clipboard—"Donja Devereaux."

Donja hops up and makes his way to the middle of the floor. Dr. Akeylah steps forward. *"Zansèt, telepòte nou!"* Her spell crackles around the room, turning the whole lecture hall into an outside field. I look down, and we're all sitting on bleachers.

"With this class, we have to have the tough conversation: defending yourself. With everything going on in the world, not all of us with these special abilities are good. There are always bad apples in the bunch." Dr. Akeylah stands before Donja. "And to combat that, you will have to know how to hex."

She and Donja stand about ten feet apart.

"Donja, please, can you use your magnificent speed and charge at me?"

Like lightning, Donja charges for her. And even faster, Dr. Akeylah uses her magic to throw him across the field like a rag doll.

Everybody on our side claps.

"Oh shit. That was dope," I say.

"Donja's pretty fast, but Dr. Akeylah? That sista is nothing to play with," Savon replies.

We all see Donja shaking it off. "Okay, now you can try something on me. But take it slow now," Dr. Akeylah tells him.

"I got you, Professor." Donja whips his hands forward, letting the Haitian Kreyol spill from his mouth. *"Mare . . ."*

I think I read about this spell. Something like *I bind you* in Kreyol?

A small gust of wind whirls around us, and, right in midair, a ripple of waves. The boundary spell coming in hot. When I squint my eyes, I clock the force field manifesting around Dr. Akeylah. The invisible barrier.

"The binding spell. Impressive." Dr. Akeylah nods. On the real, she doesn't look that impressed.

"But not too impressive." Dr. Akeylah holds out her hand, and the small ripples all get sucked back into her hand as if she was siphoning gas outta a car.

What . . . ?

Dr. Akeylah's magic manifests in a plume of black-and-silver dust swirling in the palm of her hand. She sends it to Donja, wrapping him, keeping his arms bound to his sides.

Donja spins around, breaking free of the barrier, and sends the cyclone of dust right back at her. The way Dr. Akeylah moves, though, it's like she's dancing when she casts an incantation.

Her hands go up, and she blocks it.

"Told you this sista don't play," Savon comments.

No cap, I simmer with some hateration. Because I can't do that. Me and Alexis catch a glance at each other.

"Very good, Donja," Dr. Akeylah says, catching her breath and having him bound up at the end. "Your force field is stronger, much more durable." Professor Kumale locks eyes with him.

Donja comes back to his seat, muttering something under his breath.

"Alexis," Dr. Akeylah calls. "Come on down." And then she turns to all of us. "Again, class, you want to best your enemy any way you know how. Surprise them. But never, never turn your back or let your guard down."

Dr. Akeylah steps aside, leaving Alexis alone on the field. Sprouting from the ground are three tall-ass shadows running toward Alexis. This shit looks like a live video game where you fight the computer instead of a second player.

Alexis grabs the dirt from the ground and throws it into one of their faces. She sharply spins. Her magic comes out strong in a whitish-gray light. The wind tousles her beautiful braided hair. Trying to catch it all, my eyes switch back to Dr. Akeylah, then Alexis. Long, sharp black shapes wrap around the three dudes, making them fall to the ground. Alexis crouches almost to the ground as if she's a feline.

"*Teruh!*" she yells, and the figures explode right before her.

The last shadow grabs her from behind.

Like the sun, the light sparkles between her fingers on a thousand, shining all around the field. Alexis channels it and blasts the dude. She makes this weird hand gesture, and suddenly the dark shadow disintegrates into a million pieces.

Dr. Akeylah steps back onto the field. "Channeling kinetic energy as a defense mechanism is the sanest thing. Only use deadly force when it's necessary. Nicely done, Ms. Williams."

The whole class erupts in applause as Alexis returns to the bleachers.

"Can Malik have a try?" Professor Kumale steps up, asking Dr. Akeylah. Bruh, why is he putting me on the spot like this?

"I'm not sure if that's a good idea; he's still new—" Feeling the eyes on her, she glances to me and then back to Professor Kumale, caving. "Malik, can you come down here, please?"

A bundle of nerves jumble up at the pit of my stomach as I make my way to the middle of the field. Professor Kumale steps on the grass, meeting me right in the middle. "Do whatever you can," he says. "Don't hold back."

I can feel the eyes of the whole class on me. Man, I hate being put on the spot. And the way these people in this class been casting spells . . .

"*Mare!*" he shouts in Kreyol.

My throat closes, and I can barely breathe.

Professor Kumale's palms open a little bit more, and boom, I can breathe again.

Everybody starts to clown me. Laughing. Even Alexis.

And I can't even lie. It stings.

"No," Professor Kumale says, and then winks. "You can do this; you just need a little practice."

All I do is take a deep breath, channeling the energy from my magic. It rings in the palm of my hand.

I manifest blue fire.

A binding hex ripples toward me. My right leg feels like it's glued to the ground. Damn, I'm stuck.

"Don't anticipate it, Malik," Dr. Akeylah says to me. "Channel the magic."

Sweat drips down my face, and I throw my hand forward, sending whatever I can toward Professor Kumale. But he teleports, moving so fast that I don't see him appearing behind me.

He whips his hand toward me, and my whole body goes flying.

Shit. All eyes were on me. More laughter. Alexis, Savon, Elijah, even Donja. His ass is trying not to laugh. Dr. Akeylah turns to them, administering a cold stare. They shut up.

Then I turn around and manifest a barrier spell around me, blocking his magical blows.

"*Kase!*" He shouts a spell in Kreyol.

And instantly, my whole barrier wall shatters to pieces, imploding.

"That's all right, Mr. Baron." Dr. Akeylah tries to cheer me on.

Now I'm frustrated as hell. This shit makes me look bad in front of everybody. In front of Lex.

A'ight. I gotta try something else.

My hands curl by my sides, and from what I remember from my mama's workbook, from that moment with the ancestors and Mama Aya, I think bigger and brighter. I think about the bullshit I've been through. The laughs, the cries, the pain. I think about when Taye was taken from me. When Alexis was taken from me. Hell, when even my mama was taken from me.

All I can do is kneel down to the ground. People look at me real weird.

Between my fingers, I feel the softness of the grass. A deep inhale rises in my throat as I pull the energy from the earth. My eyes close as I channel nature herself. Pressure building. The hot, soggy air brushes across my skin. Clouds roll in like they're here to see what will happen. And I can literally feel my magic course through my veins. It feels like ice.

A quick exhale, and I manifest a strong torrent of wind. Colored lightning stretches itself across the sky like long tentacles reaching for something to grab.

With some swag, my magic manifests into a ribbon of bluish-white light, creating a raging flame, snaking toward Professor Kumale in slow motion. The storm above shifts into a hurricane, and we're in the eye.

Whoa. My body levitates.

Spinning and hovering in midair, I can see people's surprised expressions. Even Professor Kumale looks shocked.

For the first time in a long time, I feel like I'm . . . in control. A cold determination rushes through me, and the blue fire spreads so far, it almost reaches the school.

"Malik!" I hear voices scream. But I don't stop. I continue to focus. When I look down at my arms, my blue magic courses under my skin in ridges. Dr. Akeylah steps forward, her hands toward the sky. A glitter of light spreads from her fingertips. *"Tunu!"*

It's like everything gets sucked back up, and the weight of the spell lifts off me. The sky goes back to normal, the fire goes out, leaving nothing but burned grass.

And I drop toward the ground.

CHAPTER EIGHTEEN

FALLING . . .

My body flails through the pitch black.

As I hover over the ground, the fading blue light flickers, turning into memories of Mama and me sitting on the porch, laughing and eating ice cream. Then the Fourth of July.

Firecrackers popping in the night air. I can still smell the spent gunpowder.

Mama sitting on the floor, screaming as the blinding burst of green light implodes the entire room.

Everything goes to black. In that darkness, there are voices at the edge of hearing. It's Chancellor Taron, mad as all get-out. *"He is not that advanced! You should have had him watch. Not participate on the first day! You two know better."*

Professor Kumale's voice argues back. *"What if this is what the ancient Divine Elam spoke about?"*

Chancellor Taron says back, *"Impossible. He's just a kid."*

"He's not, and you know it," Professor Kumale argues.

"If he gets hurt, it's on us."

I hear shifting around the room. Then Professor Kumale says, *"Don't pretend you care for him."*

"Gentlemen!" Dr. Akeylah's voice comes through.

A slam of a door causes my body to bolt upright from a couch stationed in a small office. Professor Kumale and Dr. Akeylah are at the foot of the small couch with a world of worry on their faces.

"How long have I been out?" I ask them groggily.

They both look amazed and scared at the same time. "An hour at most," Dr. Akeylah answers. "You used a lot of energy, and it depleted you."

I sit up, still a bit delirious from passing out. "Am I in trouble or something?"

"No, of course not," Dr. Akeylah answers, kinda stressed.

"Malik, that was amazing." Professor Kumale looks to Dr. Akeylah like he's a proud dad at a football game. "You summoned a powerful storm just by thought alone? Just out of nowhere and contained it? It was like the orisha Oya herself granted him the ability." I thought he would be mad, considering his ass almost got struck by lightning. But no, he's jumping around like he just won the lottery.

Dr. Akeylah applies a cold, damp towel to my forehead. "You were mumbling in your sleep, Malik."

My body is grateful for the cold touch. "For real? Hmmm."

"Yeah, you were having a bad dream."

I try to remember, but it won't come to me. My head pounds. "Yeah, I tend to have those a lot. Especially since I've been coming here."

Dr. Akeylah and Professor Kumale trade a *WTF* look.

I swing my legs over and plant them on the floor. My hands tremble, feeling weak. Dr. Akeylah crosses over behind her desk and brings a bowl full of blood-red watermelon chunks. "Here," she says, handing them to me. "It'll boost your energy and help with the dizziness."

"Watermelon? Really?" I groan, trying not to laugh. "This is kinda cliché, don't you think?"

Dr. Akeylah puts on her *stern professor mode* voice. "Okay, so I see I have to give you a quick history lesson. Black folks and watermelon actually have a positive relationship. Back in the Reconstruction era, Black farmers sold watermelon as a means of income. Profited greatly because of it. Some even became millionaires. White people grew jealous of this self-sufficiency, Malik, and deemed watermelon as this stereotypical and uncouth thing that Black people eat. But in the magical community, watermelon is beneficial for our magic. It's an elixir. The real natural fruit sustains life and has all the nutrients we need. It's been that way for our ancestors for thousands of years."

A tinge of guilt and ignorance makes me clamp my mouth shut.

"The power of influence," Professor Kumale says mockingly. "A bastardized version of *our* magic. The watermelon in its purest form has all that you need to sustain life. It's indigenous to our motherland and can replenish our magic, just as it replenishes life."

Hearing all that, I bite into the chunks of the watermelon, and gaaahdayum, it's something I never tasted before. Sweet. Juicy. And Dr. Akeylah is right; I feel my energy boost all the way up.

Dr. Akeylah sits in front of me. "Malik, your untapped power is quite astonishing, but you use a lot of energy, and that energy—"

I fuck up the rest of the watermelon chunks. "Is that bad?"

"No, you're not used to expending that much power. It takes a lot out of you." Dr. Akeylah makes her way toward the desk. "It's impressive what you've done, but also dangerous. Our magic is a lot, and you just gotta learn how to sustain it."

I glance to Professor Kumale, who has the biggest smile on his face. This mentorship finna be interesting.

"You've done good work out there today," Professor Kumale reminds me. "The way you commanded that storm. Your mom would be proud."

· · · ·

Professor Akeylah's crystals definition homework got me pacing around my room. It's a big part of our grade for the intro class, and I am not trynna fail so Chancellor Taron can kick me out of school. My phone buzzes on my dresser. A notification from the CaimanTea app. By way of the caption, I know Savon wrote it.

@ZeeNola: #StudyGroup Summer midterms is gon' take us out.

Jealousy seeps in and makes a home. I miss Alexis like my lungs miss air. Us being mad at each other means her friends ain't gonna talk to me, and that got me feeling some kinda way. I wanna reach out.

Everything in my body wants to too.

However, stubbornness wins again.

Turning off the lights, I'm just gonna go to sleep. Drifting off, I start to dream. Eyes popping open, I see my mama's bedroom door. The smell of her meat loaf and cabbage. My mouth waters as I hear her cooking in the kitchen. I sneak into her room and look at her desk covered in stacks of paper, even though I know I'm not supposed to snoop.

"What you doin' in here?" My mama's voice rings clear in my head. I turn, and she stands at the door, washcloth in her hand. Her eyes narrow with suspicion.

I look to my left, staring at my reflection. And it's me. How I look now at seventeen. My mama waltzes into the room and sits on the bed. That look. It's a look I know all too well. My mama was so pretty. Real dark skin. Just like mine. She said I'm like midnight black and that our skin is nothing but royalty. Made from the stars. Her luscious, thick hair is wrapped in a small bun.

"I just wanted to read it." I try to make my voice sound as innocent as possible because I ain't trying to get no whooping. Mama didn't like me going through her things. She said that all I do is ramble through her stuff, and things get lost.

Her honey eyes land on me. We flip through the pages together, seeing notes and drawings of places.

"You know what this is?" she asks me.

"Yes, Mama," I answer back innocently.

"It's a map, baby boy. Well, pieces of a map. It's what we have so far."

She smiles while flipping through more pages. Mama always had a smile that could brighten the world if the sun gave out. She sits on the edge of the bed, wrapping me with her arms, and I get a whiff of her perfume. I look right into the mirror, expecting to see me . . . but it's my younger self.

It's low-key, high-key an out-of-body experience.

"This map, it can help us find the Scroll of Idan," she says.

I'm tripping out, because all of this seem so familiar, but then again, it doesn't. How can I remember this?

"What's that?" The word *Idan* throws my seven-year-old ears off.

"A piece of paper of spells." Her hand graces my chin. "A powerful one at that. They say when you hold the scroll in your hand, you can control time and create other worlds."

I can feel my eyes light up. Mama always could make anything sound so interesting. Just by the way she told stories.

"But lemme let you in on a little secret," she continues. "We gotta wait on this eclipse."

"What's that?" my younger self asks innocently.

"It's when the sun and the moon cover each other, and according to Mama's research, this *real* special one only supposed to happen three times. Two already passed, and the other one, it's coming."

Her hand lands on my cheek. The warmth I feel from it. Feels like magic.

"One day you gonna be able to do great things. There's a power in you so big, you're gonna change the world."

I smile at her. Her hands then grasp mine.

"My beautiful baby boy. What you have inside ya, they gonna try to take it away, because they scared."

"Who is they, Ma?" I ask, tears falling from my eyes.

Her lips part a bit, and she looks like she's trying to think of the best answer possible. A real fear set in her eyes.

"I'm going to find this one day."

"What's gonna happen when you find it, Ma?"

Without a word, she gets up and looks at herself in the mirror. From the drawer, she pulls out the same necklace from before.

Finally, she turns to face my younger self.

"I'm gonna make things better, baby."

I nod. "Yes, Mama."

My younger eyes are fixated on the necklace that glows black against her brown skin.

The entire vision warps like smoke clearing.

And I'm back in my dorm room, wondering once again just what the hell my mama was really up to.

CHAPTER NINETEEN

GOING TO THE DINING HALL WITHOUT YA ROOMMATE CAN BE
considered the eighth deadly sin in college.

And here at Caiman University, they take this shit seriously.

Between studying and rushing to my next class, I promised D
Low we'd go and grab lunch on our break. *Roommate bonding,* as
he calls it. Outside of Taye, I ain't really do too much bonding with
other people. Plus, my social battery can drain really quick. But I
guess I'm excited to get to be a college kid and just chill and hang out
and not worry about what my mama had got herself into.

With everything that's going on, that's the hardest to do.

After passing through the quad between the moving marching
band practice, we end up in the dining hall and on our third plate
before I know it.

"Man, it's gon' be fun," D Low says, dipping his pepperoni pizza
in a bowl full of ranch. He's been begging for me to join the team for
this Dorm Wars thing for a couple of days now. The way everybody
talking about it, it's a big deal on this campus.

I stuff a few Tater Tots in my mouth. "Magical dodgeball? I ain't
gon' hold you—that shit sound fire!"

"See! That's what I'm talm 'bout. We a man out, and Khalil said
you can join. Bruh, it's a sure way to get in with the Jakutas, I'm
tellin' you. I'm trynna pledge this fall semester."

I scoop up some more Tots. "Shiiiid. Sign me up."

No lie, it does feel good to have that other set of familiarity in this world. We crack up at the same shows. We talk about the way of life back in Alabama. How sports is basically God in our hometowns, Roll Tide Roll versus War Eagle, and our experiences in the Alabama school system.

"The way you've been going at it, I ain't think you wanted to do it."

"Nah, dude, I'm just trynna catch up. Y'all mofos waaaay ahead of me."

"Yeah, but bruh, look . . . I ain't trynna come at you," he says. "But it's been real depressin' watchin' you just come back to the dorm from classes and then be locked in your room."

I don't say nothing. Only because I'm a lil' embarrassed.

"You're at one of the dopest schools in the world. Where you can study magic and shit."

"I know, it's just—I ain't grow up like most people here. It's been pretty much me, alone and learning and not learning with my magic. At least y'all had somebody to teach you about this magic stuff."

"I feel you." D Low drums his fingers on the table. "I kinda feel, like, you know, you bein' from Bama, and I'm from there too, we automatically friends." He pulls out his phone, types. Then holds it up. "Smile for the Tea."

"Nigga, chill."

"C'mon. Do a pose. Let these mofos know we out, being friends and shit."

Cracking a smile, I do my lil' pose I always do for pictures. Throwing up that deuce sign and squinting my eyes, trynna be a Insta model.

His phone snaps.

"Yeah . . . boooy. That's the first time seein' you smile. Ever. I'mma upload this to the Tea. Getchuuu a whole buncha followers. Done."

My phone buzzes. It's D Low's tagging of me on the CaimanTea app. Already at, like, three hundred likes.

"Thanks, D," I say back. "And I'm definitely down for this dodgeball—gon' be lit, thoooough."

"Oh, you ain't said nothin' but a word."

A group of baddies strut by. "Hey, Maliiiik . . . Hey, D Low . . ."

Me and D Low do that Craig and Smokey thing: "Heeeyyy."

D Low turns to me. "See—that's what you need to be focusin' on."

"Damn, nigga, you don't play!"

"Shiiiid, when you've been locked in a closet that was made to trap you, you go wild when you get that lil' taste of freedom."

"Hey, you out that biiihhh now."

He chugs on the last of his sweet tea. "Damn right."

His eyes cut over to a group of bougie-ass-looking dudes. One of them I recognize—it's the dude that was in our dorm room when I first got there. D Low's whole demeanor changes when they lock eyes.

I catch it.

"Damn, now are *you* good?"

"Man, yeah, I cool. They think they all that. We trynna beat the House of Devereaux this year."

"They really that bad?"

"Bruh, hell yeaaaah. You ain't know this, but it's a *hierarchy* here at Caiman. A'ight. Look. There's the House of *Devereaux,* which Donja's family owns, and they are the bougie dorm on campus."

He points to a few people filtering in through the door and those posted up at different tables. "Then there's Awon dorm. They apparently can't participate in the Dorm Wars competition because they got caught using divination to get ahead."

And right by the back of the café, it's like a whole buncha dudes in tuxes, sitting and reading from their books. They look like they work for Malcolm X, low-key. "House of Devereaux's a beast at dodgeball. Mostly they do the drumline, but they always like to play. And then there's us, Mancell Hall. Which is led by the Jakutas. So, they take this shit real serious."

"Damn, it's a whole world, I see."

"Fuh real," D Low says, eyeing me with playful suspicion. "Yeah, I heard what happened at the party. I was a lil' *preoccupied.*"

"He on one for real."

Speaking of the devil, Donja strolls past us, meeting Chancellor Taron at the entrance. They walk back, talking.

"Hold up, is they close?"

D Low narrows his eyes with a glare. "I guess they is."

We both clocking the two making their way to the salad bar. Shit, this is the first time I see Chancellor Taron smile. The hell they got to talk about? Whatever it is, it got my suspicion on haywire.

"I heard Chancellor Bonclair trynna get dude ready to be initiated in the Divine Elam. Since they've been disbanded for ten years."

"Damn, how can he get in it?"

"His parents was in it, so I guess he's trynna prep him to take the mantle. Lucky ass."

Donja strolls away, wrapping his arm around ole dude that he gashed up at the party.

"Them niggas hella toxic," D Low says.

Me and Donja lock eyes, and he goes to sit at a table with ole boy.

Talking about the Divine Elam, I can't help thinking of my mama, and the Bokors, and all this shit. So much for a chill roommate lunch, I guess.

"So, you think the folks with magic going missing a coincidence?" I ask.

"You know what, I don't know what to think. But it got folks talking about it, though." His eyes shift around, making sure nobody is in earshot. "And those they are kidnapping, they're stripping those kids of their magic." He throws up his hand. "At least that's what *I* heard."

Sounds pretty much like what Taye overheard at Mama Aya's house.

D Low shakes his cup full of ice. "Yeah, they gon' have to do somethin' soon, because if people keep dropping out like flies, Caiman—"

He stops midsentence. I lean in. "What?"

"Dude, Caiman U is built off magic. It is sustained by our energy and magic; if people keep dropping out, Caiman U can literally dry up and wither away."

A grim beat.

"So, they really gotta find out who's behind this, if it's really the Bokors or what, and stop it. Fast."

"Damn skippy," he says.

And with that, we rush to finish our lunch before the next class.

• • • •

Another week of classes passes by, and the whole campus is on a hundred because Dorm Wars is tonight. On campus, it's really a big deal. I mean, it ain't like fall semester, as I hear some upperclassmen say, but Dorm Wars is bigger than the damn BET Awards. Walking through the door, I pull out my phone to FaceTime Taye and eat me a quick bowl of cereal.

"Sup, Lik?" He dances and bounce around the kitchen.

"Aye, did you ask Sierra out?"

"Yup."

"How'd you do it?"

He puts his phone on a tripod and maneuvers to the stove, stirring something in a pot. "I did exactly what you said. If that's what you're axin'."

He's on his Gordon Ramsay *ish,* throwing some seasoning into a sizzling pan. Mama Aya passes by the camera. She waves. Damn, I wish I could be there with them.

"I saw you and Brigitte's video," I tell him. "Y'all be dancin'."

"Yup. I'm trynna get Samedi to do one next. He said he got to sing one of his songs," Taye says back, shaking his head. "But I'm like, Unc—don't noooobody know them old-people songs. He even got a playlist from, like . . . 2005."

I cut up. "Aye, so, when y'all going out?"

He grins hella hard. "Tonight—"

"Hmmmm, that's his *lil' girlfriend* now," Mama Aya shouts from the back of the kitchen. "They 'bout to go to the movies."

Taye grabs a towel from the handle of the oven door, trying hard not to blush.

"Okay, bruh, I see you!"

His face is all in the camera, trying to whisper. "I ain't supposed to say nothin', but, dude, Sierra . . . she's like somethin' you'd read out of a book."

I drank the rest of the milk at the bottom of the bowl. "Whatchu talking about, Taye?"

"She said she's a . . . um . . . Aziza or somethin'."

"Azi— What the hell is that?"

"Maaaan, she's, like, a fairy."

I pause, trying my hardest not to bust out laughing. "Like Tinker Bell? You cappin'."

"In the words of Uncle Samedi, if I'm lyin', I'm flyin'."

Flushed, I can't help but crack a smile. Taye is really out here, having a normal-ass childhood. Well, as normal as you can get if your first girlfriend is a fucking fairy. He looks into the camera, basically telling me to chill out. We both bust out laughing.

"Y'all have fun? You need some money?"

"If you trynna give a brotha some, sure."

I click on my phone and go to my Caiman U app and transfer some money to him. He looks at the screen, cheesing hard when the coins sound effect vibrates his phone.

"Thanks, Lik," he says, tapping on his phone. "Here's Mama Aya. I'm finna go get ready."

"How's school, baybeh?" Mama Aya's voice comes through the video.

"It's good, Mama Aya. We are learning a lot of spells and stuff. I wish Taron would lift this ban of not being able to go off campus. I wanna come home." That last part slips. Mama Aya even notices. "You know, see y'all," I say, correcting myself.

"I know, baybeh, but he feels like you should be there. And you gettin' that full college experience."

Of all this new info I got 'bout the Bokors and the scroll and shit, I wanna tell her. But I'mma hold on until I get the facts straight, so she doesn't freak out again.

"Yeah, Lik," Taye says, throwing his amens in from the other side of the room.

Mama Aya holds the phone all awkward, just like how old people do, showing herself from the bottom. "Chile, go get ready. Brigitte gon' take you into town. And don't put no more cologne on."

Me and Mama Aya both crack up.

"Yes, ma'am," he says, and throws up a *let's get it* hand sign before disappearing off.

"You sure you all right?" Mama Aya asks.

"Oh yeah. I'm good. We got this game tonight, and I'm doing real good in my classes." To be honest, I ain't trynna tell her my mission on finding more things out about my mama and this workbook. "But I was just checking in. I'll talk to y'all later."

"A'ight, baybeh," she says. "Taye, come show me how to turn this thing off."

We hang up.

Another notification pops up on my CaimanTea app. I'm getting hella followers since D Low posted me. And . . . even though these are followers from a distance, it feels good.

Alexis, Savon, and Elijah all follow me simultaneously. With my eyes stuck on Alexis's account, I inch my finger toward the follow-back button.

I do it.

Maybe this is a start to getting back to . . . us.

CHAPTER TWENTY

NIGHT FALLS, AND IT'S FINALLY TIME FOR DORM WARS.

A week of straight practicing late nights in the gym finally about to come down to this. I meet the team behind the rec center, right by the outside tennis courts, next to the basketball courts. Keevon and the other Jakutas are practicing, while D Low is off on the side, checking his phone every five minutes.

Going to pee real quick, I overhear a gaggle of voices arguing in a small corner. One of them is Chancellor Taron. He's in a heated debate with this one professor I haven't seen around campus. Mediating between the two is Dr. Akeylah.

I hide behind a wall, catching the professor whispering through gritted teeth, "You and your mother need to get on this, Chancellor. If not, there will be dire consequences if this gets out!"

"I'm well aware, Dr. Akim," Chancellor Taron tells him, sounding hella annoyed. I crane over just enough to see him pressing down on his tie and clenching his jaw. "What do you think I've been doing?"

"Gentlemen, if I may," Dr. Akeylah chimes in. Hell, she can't even get a word in edgewise. "We can have this discussion at the next meeting."

"No, the Kwasan tribe has been letting this go on way too long. Students are dropping out or not coming back. That is very detrimental to our institution, Chancellor. People in the community are getting antsy. The Deacons of the Crescent, the Deyo tribe—we are not going to let this happen again. We will stand up to the Kwasan if need be. That young lady, Alexis, maybe she's right, and we're not doing enough. We cannot and should not be standing by idly while people on the outside run amok."

Alexis . . .

"Ms. Williams is lucky she wasn't expelled; she put herself and others in danger."

I suck in breath through my teeth. Of course Chancellor Taron thinks that.

This Dr. Akim says, "We have to give it to them, the younger generation are far more . . . How can I put this? More unorthodox in their approach when it comes to activism. Maybe we should enlist her and her friends."

Chancellor Taron interjects. "No, absolutely not. We are not notifying any students of this until we get clarity."

"What is it that we should do, then, huh? Your mother, with all due respect, should not sweep this under the rug. The Deacons of the Crescent have been talking, and we want to implement security patrol in the neighboring parishes."

"It doesn't have to come to that, Dr. Akim," Chancellor says. I crane a little bit farther, watching Dr. Akim pace back and forth. "I have things under control."

He doesn't.

"Do you?" Dr. Akim asks in an irritated tone. "I say if this spreads through this campus, Chancellor, I will resign immediately. You need to step up and protect this community."

"I am!" Chancellor Taron yells, then quietly continues. "These students and their safety are my *top* priority."

All three of them stand at an impasse. The yelling from the gym grows, beckoning them to wrap up their conversation.

"How many?" Dr. Akeylah asks Dr. Akim. He doesn't answer quick enough. "How many more people are missing?"

"One of the Fentons. Their twenty-year-old son. Their youngest was supposed to start here in the fall, but they pulled him out of the school. If it is true, and if they are back, Caiman University will be no more. And it will be your fault, Chancellor."

Dr. Akim storms off toward where I'm standing. With a quickness, I slip into the bathroom, cracking the door open just a little. Dr. Akim walks past it and back into the gym.

Dr. Akeylah whispers to Chancellor Taron, "What if he's right? Bodies are piling up in the Ninth. Magic folk and nonmagic folk. We need to get ahead of this before this spreads across the campus."

"They're not back," Chancellor says back. His voice sounds more strained under the whispering. "The Bokors . . . they can't be."

"Are we willing to wager on that, Taron? We have students and faculty to think about. The war with the Bokors, we had a lot of bloodshed. And I fear it may come to that again. But Caiman University will be completely eradicated if it does."

Their silence lingers as I grapple with the fucking inevitable.

We're all fucked.

• • • •

Our RA, Khalil, is giving us the lowdown before we do our march in. The banging music from inside the gym rattles the walls.

"Now, don't make no mistake." Khalil walks back and forth like we're in the army. He's tall. Long locs raining down his back, he looks like a warrior ready for blood. "They win this round every year for the past ten years."

I turn to the right, seeing everybody pile into the gym.

Khalil continues by saying, "A'ight. 'Mancell Hall' on three. One . . . two . . . three."

"MANCELL HALL!!!" we all scream. Well, they do. I kinda just say it a bit loud, because honestly, they doing *thee* most right about now.

Upon entering the student rec center, I see that there's Caiman University memorabilia everywhere. An upstairs workout area. Saunas. And right by the door is a small area for massage chairs.

One thing for certain: Caiman University got *money* money.

In the center, under the flight of stairs, is the main gym. It's packed. Like if-Beyoncé-had-a-free-concert packed. In the quick few days of practices, I learned there's a hidden rule on campus on Dorm Wars Day: Only upper-level students are allowed to get the good seats right by the court like they are about to see LeBron play, and we don't have to have classes because the event on campus is more important than a Lakers game.

All the others are cramped like sardines in the bleacher section, screaming and cheering for their respective dorms. My eyes trail curiously straight ahead. Gold lettering that reads DORM WARS races along the wall. It sparks into a buzzing scoreboard.

Being in front of the entire university got a brotha nervous.

On the court are long blue mats that cover the entire wooden floor. The band is clustered up in a group, right under the basketball goal, playing . . . oh shit. They're playing "Knuck If You Buck."

An announcer comes on the microphone, hyping up the crowd. "Ahhhhhhhhh, it's about to goooo downnnnnn." The whole stadium quakes with applause. "Really 'bouta show out on ya ass. Give it up for the Caiman University Marching Baaaaand."

A roar of applause rises in the gym. Caiman U's band and the majorettes take their place in the middle of the floor. Instruments are raised in the air. With one quick signal from the band leader, they roll into their personal cadences. Getting hella hyped.

The crowd goes apeshit.

The band continues playing their drums.

Off to the side, that Dr. Akim guy who was arguing with Chancellor Taron stands beside Professor Kumale. He holds a microphone in his hand.

"Well, I see it's that time of the year where it's the annual Caiman University Dorm WAAAAARRRRRRSSS."

The whole crowd goes buck wild.

"As most of you know, I am Dr. Akim, head of the student body. And like every year, Dorm Wars is one of the most exciting campus-wide events in Caiman University history!"

One dude off on the side snaps, and he appears right behind a table, deejaying. Everybody gets hype, doing the New Orleans bounce.

We put on these black shirts with gold lettering on the front that says CAIMAN UNIVERSITY with a periwinkle flower right in the middle of the words EST. 1804.

"Get ready, y'all," Khalil says to all of us.

"Shiiiiid, this got me hyped. I'm definitely ready."

All the Jakutas crowd around, doing the bounce. This ain't a thing back in Bama, but I catch on quick.

All the Jakutas hype me up, circling me. "Dayyyyummm, Malik! Fuck that shiiiiiit up!"

And that's exactly what I do. I fuck that shit like it ain't nobody's business. Even some girl comes up to me and starts twerking on me. Her booty going berserk, causing my world to go upside down. Even my teammates hold me back while homegirl go ham on me.

The color hovering over the crowd changes from burgundy to gold and brown.

"Who that freshman getting blessed?" the DJ announces. "Getting that Holy Confirmation before they go out on that cooooooourrrtt."

A mountain of applause.

Nerves tangle themselves in my throat.

Dr. Akim continues on the microphone. "And we got something special for y'all. As always, it's the exciting, the jaw-dropping segment of Dorm Wars: dodgeball.

"We have Mancell Hall versus the House of Devereaux."

The building rocks with stomps and yells.

"Let's get this Dorm Wars started!"

Dr. Akim whips his hand, and the auditorium lights go straight dark except for the court area. The dudes from the Devereaux dorm are on the other side, ready. Damn, D Low wasn't playing. They all look like they were born with silver spoons in their mouths and brooms up their asses.

"You all know the rules. The balls are hexed, so they won't cause any physical harm. So, keep it clean, fellas," Dr. Akim tells us.

Me and Donja lock eyes.

He's coming for me. But he just doesn't know, I'm ready.

Dr. Akim steps off to the side. Right in the middle of the court, in a straight line, are balls of orange fire. From where I'm standing, I can hear them crackling. The warmth from them makes the adrenaline pump through me even more.

"ARE WE READY?!" Dr. Akim asks the crowd. His voice booms all around me.

The crowd cheers, and then everybody starts to count down. The band starts to play "Flight of the Bumblebee."

"*Ten!*"

Me and D Low give each other our signal. We got each other's back as the side guards.

"*Nine!*"

Khalil kneels, ready to meet the other RA in the middle.

"*Eight!*"

Me and Donja study each other's hand movements. His hands ball into fists, his magic riling up. Our eyes burn with rage.

"*Seven!*"

"*Six!*"

"*Five!*"

I give a quick glance to Alexis in the crowd.

"*Four!*"

My knees bend, getting into position.

"*Three!*"

I stare at one fireball. Right smack in the middle. Then back on Donja. He's quick. So are the twins, Savon and Elijah.

"*Two!*"

Shit! Think of another plan, Malik.

"*ONE!!!!*"

Too late. The whistle blooooows.

Both teams speed toward the middle, with our sneakers pounding against the wooden floor, grabbing balls. I use the telekinetic spell, swoop two balls into my hands, and throw one to D Low. Balls of fire whip right past me, missing my face by an inch. The dude in

Room 103 in my dorm hall is hit hard with one, sending him back. He has to go out-of-bounds. The floor rumbles with footsteps as the other team makes their way back to their side.

D Low twists around, and soon as the ball of fire comes at him, he catches it. Sending one of the dudes next to Savon out. He then uses his magic and spreads the ball into two, throws one, directing it right for one of their guys.

Plop. He hit that dude right in the chest.

Soon enough, the out-of-bounds is full of both our teams.

The crowd goes wild, chanting the names of both our dorms. Even the drum line and majorettes start to play and dance along with them.

Then the roaring quickly changes to another chant: "CUUUUU!!! YOOOOU KNOW!!!"

My gaze is fixated on Donja, clocking his every move. He's good, and he never misses. And I just know he's saving me for last.

Adrenaline shoots through me like ice as one ball almost hits me. I sling it back, zeroing in, knocking two dudes out-of-bounds, and crashing to the floor. The sound coming from the fireballs is like firecrackers.

My right ear chimes like a warning.

My left hand shoots forward, making a ball rocket across the gym. Elijah's out.

"Okayyyy, freshman," he shouts from the opposite end of the court.

Another of our teammates, Travis, teleports back on the court, shooting fire dodgeballs left and right. Donja speeds like lightning and catches one, sending Travis back out-of-bounds. He slams his hand against the floor, mad as hell.

The ref blows a whistle. Evidently, D Low got put out-of-bounds by getting hit in the leg.

That's when I look over, seeing Donja smirking.

This dude . . .

"Get his ass," D Low says to me just before going to the sidelines. Somehow, it's just me, Donja, and another dude. They try to gang up on me, throwing balls right at me. I collect them and plan to shoot about five of them right at Donja and his teammate.

"Lehggoooo, Malik!" several people in the crowd scream. Everybody else chants for Donja. Alexis, off on the side, looking worried. Her doubt in me is gonna cost me the game, because that's all that's on my mind right now.

The crowd screams, "LET'S GO!!! DEVEREAUX!!!"

Donja grins and clutches a few balls in his hands. Again, I gotta be strategic in how I do this. One: conserve my energy and don't tire out. Two: I can't be too predictable. But my mind wraps around another possibility: he could catch it, costing us the game. Or he can send—*Whoosh!*

One passes me, almost hitting me in the leg.

"That was a close one," the announcer says the obvious.

With an unrelenting force, I send a fireball of energy right at Donja's teammate, hitting him on the left foot. The crowd goes wild as he stomps to the out-of-bounds section, probably cussing me out under his breath.

"It's now between Donja Devereaux and first semester Malik Baron!" Dr. Akim says to the crowd. "WHO WILL WIN?!"

A bang of drum sends me back to the Haitian Revolution. Boom. Boom. Boom.

Coming back to reality, my eyes scan up for a quick second, seeing the Jumbotron, showing the both of us and our dorm names. When I look back down, Donja's fingers twist, and the balls lift in the air. He moves his hand to the right, palms facing me. My eyes squint, seeing that his lips move, trembling.

I remember that move Professor Kumale did in that class, so I try to copy it. Then I throw one right back, but Donja's too fast, making the ball bounce off the wall. Just a few more inches, and that shit would've smacked him right upside his head.

Damn.

The entire crowd cheers both of our names. Then, just like that, they're screaming for me.

"MA-LIK!!! MA-LIK!!!"

And it all happens so slow—Donja's eyes narrow, and he manifests a bright orange light. He throws it, making it rocket right past me. I step to the right like a gazelle dodging the jaws of a lion.

"You missed!" I tell him.

"Did I?" He gives another smirk and points behind me.

When I turn around, the ball crackles and explodes right in front of me, and the impact knocks me straight to the ground. Instantly, I feel a burning sensation on my side. My skin sizzles like bacon grease.

This nigga using *real* magic!

Ah, hell naw!!!

The whole crowd goes quiet.

I struggle to get up and use a spell. All I can do is grunt in pain. I muster up enough strength and clap my hands, sending a big sonic wave of magic raging toward Donja. He goes flying through the wall. The side of my stomach continues to burn like a muhfucka! Ah!!!

I can feel it swelling up.

"Boys, stop!" Dr. Akim says.

Donja comes out from the crushed and falling wall. He looks to the crowd and uses his magic to create a powerful force field.

All of them are blocked in.

He then flicks his wrist, and a tall cloud of smoke sprouts from his hands, forming itself into a dragon-like creature. *The* same *gahdamn* one from when Alexis conjured it up. Wait a minute? It rushes toward me, and I dodge it, making it crash against the wall behind me. My hand shoots forward, and my magic whips out of me like long spirals of energy, and lightning strikes around Donja.

The dude uses the momentum of my magic and twirls all around like he is in ballet—360 degrees. The whole building starts to shake as our magic collides.

Donja's hands slide across the floor, sending the entire foundation raging toward me. I put up a blocking spell, letting the wood crash around me. Pain and adrenaline shoot through me like a drug, weakening me and giving me strength at the same time. He rotates his arm, making the lights above us flicker, raining down sparks.

My palms face out, and wind comes into the gym, swirling

around us. Mustering up whatever energy, I send it back. A *return to sender* type of hex.

Donja's quick with it and holds a diamond shape across his chest, counterattacking the blast.

The force field is broken, raining down in sheets of energy. That's when both teams crowd the floor, fighting. I make my way through the crowd, heading straight to Donja.

He comes closer, and just as we're about to throw them hands—

Professor Kumale steps in and snuffs out our magic.

"What are you two doing?!" he yells.

Royal purple smoke swirls between us. Chancellor Taron storms on the gym floor, a whole world of mad written across his face.

The whole auditorium goes to a hush.

Dr. Akim's cold brown eyes land on me, and he shakes his head.

"My office. NOW!!!" Chancellor Taron turns to the crowd. "You all go back to your dorms. Dorm Wars is now over."

Everybody just sits there, too stunned to move. "NOW!!!" Chancellor Taron's booming voice echoes across the entire gym.

People start to run out like it's a free night at the club.

My hand goes to my side, feeling the burn.

"Both of you in my office." Chancellor Taron's voice sounds like thunder.

Forget finding more shit about my mama's disappearance or worrying about the Bokors, because it looks like my time here at Caiman University is over.

CHAPTER TWENTY-ONE

PROFESSOR KUMALE AND CHANCELLOR TARON RIP INTO THE both of us for a good fifteen minutes before me and Donja can get a word in.

"Aye, that shit wasn't my fault!" I argue back.

"Quiet, Malik!" Chancellor Taron yells.

"Nah. Fuck that! Like I said, that shit wasn't my fault. Everything was going good until his bitch ass started using real magic." I rub my side, *pssssss.*

Donja stands up, getting buck. "Who you calling a bitch ass?"

"You, you fake Drake-ass nigga. Yo, you got the wrong one, bruh—"

We get in each other faces. Chancellor Taron slams his fist on the table, sending energy through both of us. Every part of me sits in the chair, trapped. Donja seems affected too.

"This is unacceptable!" Professor Kumale's voice goes deep. Real deep. He looks at me, disappointed. "You two turned an innocent game into something petty and dangerous."

"I don't know why y'all looking at me like I'm the problem," Donja snarls.

Professor Kumale leans against the chancellor's desk. "You both knew the rules. I don't know what you two got going on, but you need to fix it now."

Chancellor Taron has his hand on his chin. "Right now, or—"

Donja leans forward. "Or what?"

"I told you I was doing good, and then this muthafucka threw a ball of real-ass fire at me." I point to my burned side to prove it.

Chancellor Taron's pointed gaze cuts into Donja. "Did he throw the first punch, Professor?"

Professor Kumale looks at Donja and shakes his head like a disappointed dad. "He did, Chancellor. And he knows better than to do that."

Donja tenses up at the sound of Professor Kumale's voice.

Chancellor Taron goes up to Donja. "You're right about that. Donja, you're suspended from all activities and classes for a week."

"But Chancellor—" Donja starts to argue.

"You want to make it two?"

Donja shuts his mouth. "No, sir, Chancellor Bonclair." Then he storms out of the office.

Bitch-ass nigga.

"Mr. Baron," Chancellor Taron says, snapping me back to attention. "You are walking on thin ice as well. Because of recent events, I will not expel you. But just know I do not offer second chances."

"Yeah, whatever. Can I go now?" I wince from the pain.

He twists the ring on his finger. "Yes, the medic in the Hoodoo building is all ready for you."

• • • •

The medic gave me some healing properties that made the fresh burn go away in an instant. Got me feeling like brand-new and everything. It was actually kinda cool, because all she did was read some passages from the Book of Psalms, and *boom*—I was all healed. The walk-through back to my dorm, I already know it's about to be some shit because I can hear Savon and them yelling from outside my door. Key slides into the doorknob, and the door opens, and I see everybody waiting in the living room. Savon, Elijah, and Alexis, right along with D Low. Even that Dominique girl is here.

"Y'all need to keep your boy on a leash!" D Low screams at Savon and Elijah. They all turn to me when I step into the living room.

"Yo—" D Low is the first to stand and come up to me. "You good?"

"Yeah, they had to send me to the medic," I tell all of them.

"Can I see?" Dominique says, coming over to me. She lifts my shirt a bit where the burn was. Her fingers feel like ice, rubbing a cool relief against my skin. "Yeah, my homegirl Shayla did a fyeeee-ass job. Fixed you right up."

Alexis's eyes narrow, burning with jealousy. I even swear she mumbles something under her breath.

I'm about five seconds away from being on my petty shit, because we ain't talked since that night with her doing bane magic.

"That was foul what your boy did, y'all. For real," D Low turns and says to Alexis.

Alexis just sits there, acting like she ain't got nothing to say.

Savon stands, crosses between me and D Low. "We ain't even know it was gonna go down like that. C'mon, we are not about that life."

"Nigga is wild," D Low continues. He turns to me, kinda smiling. "Keevon and 'em definitely want you to pledge this fall."

"You ain't gon' say nothing?" I ask Alexis.

Everybody falls silent. She looks up like she's been put on the spot. "What do you want me to say, Malik? Y'all cannot be fighting like that."

"Like I told our uptight-ass chancellor, that nigga started it first. Then he used real magic on me and burned the fuck outta me. What the hell was I supposed to do?"

"You thought it was best to retaliate? Malik, we're not kids anymore. You can't throw temper tantrums."

"Are you kidding me right now, Lex? Fuck that nigga!"

She shakes her head. "You're doing the most right now."

"I'm doin' the most right now? Really? Well, ain't that the pot calling the kettle black. You know what, how you gon' take up for him, knowing what he did? I'm your friend way before you known that nigga. What, y'all smashing or something?"

"And if we were, which we're not, it isn't any of your business."

"Bet. That's all I need to know," I say back.

"I know we haven't seen each other for quite some time, Malik. But there's something you need to know about me, okay? I am NOT your girlfriend. I'm not anybody's. This is not some damsel-in-distress, weird love triangle, okay? Get over yourself!"

A tense silence falls onto the room. Dominique curves her head, mumbling a "chile" under her breath. Savon and Elijah look away, and D Low shakes his head. After Alexis says what she got to say, we all stay like that for a minute.

Anger bubbles inside me, but you know what, I just let it go. She's right; she ain't my girlfriend, and judging from my time being here and how we ain't really get to know each other for real, why would I expect us to still be in that puppy-dog-love stage?

We was kids.

"Malik, this is—"

"Get the hell out."

Alexis looks real taken aback. "Are you serious?"

"As a heart attack, get the fuck out. And you right, Alexis, we have changed. So you better tell ya boy I ain't nothing to fuck with."

A look of a thousand knives, and then she storms outta the apartment. Savon and Elijah give a lingering nod, then they walk out too. Dominique turns to me before she leaves.

"You did your thing out there," she says. "Devereaux needed them hands. Good job, freshman."

" 'Preciate it, Dominique," I say back.

She's gone. D Low goes to shut the door behind them. "He was really foul for that shit, for real. We were gonna retaliate."

I sit down on the couch, trying to rest. "Then you got the professors thinking I'm in the wrong. For real, that nigga got me messed up."

This ain't some teen movie where Donja thinks he's gonna just bully somebody. He got another thing coming.

"What the chancellor say?"

"Nothing but bullshit, but Professor Kumale had my back. He said that Donja started it first, and Chancellor suspended Donja for a whole week."

"That's good for his ass," D Low says. I take a swig of the water he brings me from the fridge.

"Aye, yo," I say, still wincing from the pain. "I heard Dr. Akim and Chancellor Taron go at it before the game started."

"About what?"

"With that Fenton kid going missing on the outside, and from the way Dr. Akim is talking, he and the Deacons of the Crescent ain't too happy how the Kwasan handling it. He even said something about employing some of them to set up shop and be security."

"Because they all for show," D Low says back, plopping back down on the couch. "Man, it's finna be another civil war."

"You really think so?"

"Man, yeah. If these people who have magic going missing like that, once that shit really goes over to the communities, folks gonna start axin' questions. And magick folk and the nonmagick folk, they already don't get along."

Something else I learned in the books—just the way Black folks, especially Christian Black folks in the South, be reacting to magic like it's demonic and shit. This will give them hella ammunition.

"Deacons of the Crescent don't play. They're like they own little military. And if they talkin' about settin' up shop, shit finna hit the fan fuhh real."

Maybe he's right. And maybe that's what Chancellor Taron been so stressed out about.

"Man, I'm going to bed. All this magic shit got me hella tired."

"I feel you. Aye, you won, though."

We shake hands, and then I head back to my room.

My phone vibrates. A text from Taye comes through in all caps that makes my heart drop:

> YO, SOMETHING HAPPENED. YOU NEED TO COME TO MAMA AYA'S HOUSE. NOW!

CHAPTER TWENTY-TWO

SIX WHITE CANDLES SIT ALL AROUND MY ROOM.

It's just a few items to break the chancellor's boundary spell and get back to Mama Aya's house. I pace around the room, and it takes me a whole minute to remember it. My mind better work fast, because I gotta get back to Taye.

My mama's book got something in it about breaking boundary spells, and the six white candles and a personal item are all I need to draw from.

With Taye's picture in my phone, I flip open my book that talks about using objects as a conduit and draw from the energy of the picture. My eyes close, and the mental image of Taye in his room chillin' pops up into my head. As I repeat the incantation in the back of my mind, everything around me melts, slowly changing into white walls and a screen door. I open my eyes and look down, seeing my carpet transform into creaky wooden floors.

Everything around me spins.

I'm back in my room at Mama Aya's. Downstairs, I hear an unfamiliar voice. My heart drops when I look out the window and see a police cruiser in the front yard.

Taye . . .

Slowly opening the door, I make my way out into the hallway. The voices drift up from the living room. Static from a radio echo throughout the house. Oh shit. I pull out my phone to text Taye.

> Don't make no noise. I'm in the hallway.

> It's a cop! He's here to take me away.

His nervousness comes through the phone, seeping into me. Shit! The voices soon become clear. "These are children, Mama Aya! They're missing!" the cop shouts. "The tribes are trying to find out who did it. This can't be no coincidence. The signs are all there, Mama Aya." They all shift their movement downstairs. "Stealin' these young kids' magic and using bane spells. The Fentons are requesting the Kwasan to step in, or they will have to go rogue."

"I'mma talk to Alma. She's a good friend; I'm sure she's in need."

"What she needs or want, Ms. Aya, is vengeance. She's the one who found him."

Nothing but silence on both ends.

"I got a weird feelin' . . . ," the officer continues to tell Mama Aya. "They may really be here this time, Ms. Aya. Someone may have reanimated them."

My hands tingle, and I massage the feeling out. His magic feels familiar. I harp on his energy. He feels sorta *conflicted.* The front door burst open, and Samedi glides through the living room so fast, you don't even see him for real. The smell of a cigar hits my nose before he even says a word. "What weird feelin', Antwan?" Samedi asks the dude. "You tellin' me you're sensin' somethin'? Thought you gave up majik to become a normal person and whatnot."

Antwan?

The vision of my mama, Chancellor Taron, and Antwan staring right back at me pops up in my head.

Samedi's footsteps are louder than his rumbling laughter that bellows in his chest. The Antwan dude sounds irritated when he answers. "I covered every inch. And there's talks the Deacons of the Crescent may get involved."

Damn. Dr. Akim is working fast, I see.

"I'mma still keep an eye out. But if they're back, then God help us all," Antwan says.

"God ain't got nothin' to do with it," Samedi says, a bit harsh.

The door creeps open, then slams shut. A few seconds later, the sound of an engine sparking to life and wheels meeting the dirt, driving off. I slip into Taye's room, and he's on the bed, frozen. "We good," I say, and a sense of relief pools through the both of us.

Taye peers up like a spooked horse. Tears fall out of his eyes as he starts to pace the room. "I thought he was gonna take me away, Lik. I thought he was gonna take me back to the Hudsons."

Without any words, I just wrap my arms around him, pulling him in so tight, he ain't got no choice but to calm down. A beat. He's still shaking, but his heavy breathing subsides.

Damn. My heart sinks to the pits of my personal dark place seeing him like this.

"I can't go back, Lik. I can't, and I won't."

"Shh. I got you, Taye. I got you."

• • • •

After settling Taye down for the past hour, I make my way down the stairs. Mama Aya is the first to notice that I broke ole dude's rule. "That boy must've been eavesdroppin'."

"Yeah. All he saw was a cop car."

"Everythin' is fine," Mama Aya says, hoarse.

Back to business. "My lil' brother ain't fine. He's shaken up. What is going on? Kids with magic out there dyin'?"

Brigitte's eyes fall to the floor, and Samedi leans against the wall, toothpick swiveling from the corner of his mouth. I don't even have to ask the question out loud, because Mama Aya nods her head and crosses to the rocking chair.

"They really back, ain't they?" I ask anyway, looking to Mama Aya. "The Bokors . . . the ones that you defeated."

Her eyes flicker.

"And if y'all got police comin' around here . . ."

Mama Aya clears her throat. "Antwan is an old family friend. He ain't gon' bother you or Taye."

"He sho'll ain't," Samedi says, adding his two cents. "That's my patna, my nibi up there, and he ain't gon' bother him."

Mama Aya turns to me. "Baybeh, it's probably best for you to go back to the campus fore ya get in trouble."

"I heard Chancellor Taron talking with Dr. Akim. Dude seems real worried that they are back."

"It might be some folks in the city, Mama," Baron Samedi says, swinging his cane. "You know they been feelin' some way since everythin' went wrong. Especially with dat damn Kwasan tribe."

"That can be a thing too. They lookin' and waitin' for somethin'. Empress already callin' a meetin' tomorrow," Mama Aya says. "They want me to attend."

Connecting all the dots that I discovered, I realize she's talking about the Kwasan tribe. The ones that went to war with the Bokors. It crosses my mind to tell her what I saw in the memory with my mama, but I'll save that for later.

"I wanna come," I tell Mama Aya. She looks hesitant. "They did somethin' to my mama's picture, Mama Aya." Dead silence fills the living room. "It's obvious that my mama was involved somehow."

She takes in a breath and then looks to Samedi. He throws up his hands.

"He's ya grandchild. He's gon' meet them one day or the other," Samedi says.

Another beat. I can tell Mama Aya is contemplating.

Mama Aya then relents. "All right, nah. We leave tomorrow."

CHAPTER TWENTY-THREE

THE KWASAN TRIBE REMINDS ME OF THE PEOPLE IN THAT MOVIE *Eve's Bayou.* Hella bougie and Black.

The movie is old, but I remember the Markhams watched it that one time, and I couldn't forget about it since. A literal case of Black excellence wafts through this entire compound. That type of excellence that'll make you exaggerate a *daaaaayyyyyum.* We teleport right in the middle of the compound. Expensive cars line the driveway like an auto show. Sensing the vibe, I see that some folks dress like they don't even live in this time. Some come in like they're leaving a church revival. Pulling up in clouds of bougie, swirling smoke, and cars. . . . Shit, you'd think it's a weekend getaway at the Hamptons.

But nah. This is their tribe meeting.

A grand mansion stands before us like the Taj Mahal. This gotta be, like, ten thousand square feet of house that stretches to oblivion. Ornate ironwork, tall white pillars, and hedges trimmed up like a nigga at a barbershop on a Saturday. *Rich Black people* vibes with a hint of *Southern hospitality.* Some yardmen remove tarps from luxury cars, clean pools, and scatter around this beautiful but restrained driveway. The *help* stand motionless on top of the mountain of steps that leads to the grand mansion, with white linens and trays of food perched in their hands. The way this is set up, I would've guessed I stepped into Emerald City. But I'm sure there's a curtain that's gonna reveal the fake wizard somewhere, and all of this is just a façade.

"Damn, is Jay and Bey gonna be here too?" I jokingly ask Mama Aya. She lets out a chuckle, and we carry on until we reach the mountaintop. On the door is wrought ironwork featuring a golden family crest and swirling letters spelling 𝕭𝖔𝖓𝖈𝖑𝖆𝖎𝖗.

Wait—Bonclair?

Is this where Taron grew up?

Ah. This must be Mrs. Empress Bonclair's house.

And that it is, because a sea of *uptight* people stands by a long, outstretched table full of bougie-ass food and champagne. Others meander and drift by a pristine white baby grand. I catch a glance as the piano player plays some classical music, rising through the air. Is this a party or a meeting? Rich and *magical* Black folks gather around, talking, stuffing their faces, hugging the air out of one another, and living without a care in the world. The sun shines down from a skylight, illuminating grand family portraits lining the wall next to the twisting white-and-tan staircase. An army of staff hustles in and out, refilling trays of food and people's champagne.

"This is real fancy for just a meeting," I tell Mama Aya. She then points to a big poster of a bald Black man with enticing eyes that says, VOTE FOR AIDEN DUPONT FOR MAYORAL ELECT! THE FUTURE OF THE CRESCENT CITY IS BRIGHT!

Oh, right. That's the same one that's littered all over campus.

This place is buzzing with the magic of the elite.

A gavel slams down, and the grand room goes straight to a hush.

Before we got in, Mama Aya told me to stay near the back, so I do. Everybody watches her every move when she glides to the front. A few warm hugs and hellos. Me, I'm on the receiving end of cold stares and looks of suspicion.

"The meeting has started," a lady at the podium at the front says. She's something, I say. Almost regal, as if she's a queen.

"Empress Bonclair, thank you for callin' this meetin'," Mama Aya says to the lady.

Savon wasn't lying; she does kinda favor Lynn Whitfield a bit.

Her brown oval eyes cut over to Mama Aya, and she forces a smile so tight, it could break her face in half.

"Now I know you all been hearin' 'bout the Bokors and their return," Mama Aya says to her.

Everybody in the room starts to mumble under their breath as they trek back to their seats to stare and gossip.

"Yes, and I find the rumor quite preposterous, don't you think, Ms. Aya?" Empress speaks through gritted teeth. "Surely, this is a mistake."

Another echo of sighs.

"It ain't no rumors," one man stands up and says. "My brother, who is in the Deacons of the Crescent, has belief that they are back."

His voice sounds like it's dipped in honey.

"And then all these missing kids. Some of them Bokors took them?"

"Again, let us not jump to conclusions. We have our best folks on the job to bring these children home," Mrs. Empress Bonclair says, trying her best to reassure him.

But if they've met Baron Samedi already, they're sure as hell not coming home.

All eyes on Mrs. Empress Bonclair. Her expression is very calculated and methodical. Like she has twenty responses already lined up in her head. Oh yeah, that's Chancellor Taron's mama, all right.

One woman stands up with an intense expression. "Now what about the school?"

Mrs. Empress Bonclair seems like she's already ahead of it. "My son, Taron, has implemented a campus lockdown for the time being, and he assures the Kwasan tribe that Caiman University is perfectly safe. There's a protection spell around the campus."

"Well, I ain't comfortable sending my baby girl there this fall. It's too much goin' on out here, and I want her close to me. Chillun is goin' missin', and whatever it is out there is strippin' our babies of they magick."

A frail-looking man stands up. "What about the folks in the Ninth? Now that them rowdy kids went and stirred up trouble at that police station 'cause of the Katia Washington girl. It's a shame what happened to her, but now they comin' into our neighborhoods heavy, patrollin'."

Another man springs up. It's the Aiden Dupont guy. "I have been in conversations with the police commissioner about that. To tell you folks the truth, those students from Caiman U showing up to the police station didn't do anyone good. My team is working tirelessly to clean up and make the conversations heard on both sides."

Another woman stands up. She got salt-and-pepper hair and pearls running down her neck. She really gives off that church revival lady who thinks everything under the sun is a sin.

"You all promised our folks that we ain't gonna have no trouble. Now my ward, we ain't got no magic, but y'all promised us protection. Doncha try to renig on it now."

Wait, no magic? I thought folks who don't have magic ain't supposed to know. See—Chancellor Taron ass be lyin'. . . .

"We hear you, Mr. Ducchanes and Mrs. Giselle." Empress gives that tight-lipped smile again. "It's unfortunate that some folks in the tribes wield their magic so recklessly. We must continue to keep our existence unknown. Let tourists believe they are getting the real 'Voodoo' experience down there in the French Quarter, with their cheap parlor tricks." Mrs. Empress Bonclair rolls her eyes at the last part. "However, our beautiful mayoral candidate Aiden Dupont will steer us in the right direction, and the rumor of the Bokors tribe is merely just that: a rumor."

"Thanks, Madame Bonclair." Aiden Dupont exchanges a few handshakes and smiles with folks around him. "The conversation at large is also about uniting all of us and making better changes for our city as well."

The frail man offers his two cents. "The tribes, all of them, are not to meddle in the affairs of nonmagic folk. It's been that way for over three hundred years. There are rules set in place for a reason."

The door flies open, and four people—two men and two women—stroll in. Their eyes are pure white. No irises. One dude has a black top hat with a feather, and long, sharp black nails that can go for talons extending from his fingers. He low-key looks like a younger Samedi with real dark skin.

Their footsteps cause the whole room to go quiet.

"Mr. Damone Cartier. Nice of you to join us," Mrs. Empress Bonclair announces with a strained smile. "You're late."

"You know we have to make an entrance," the head guy says. His voice is deeper than I thought it would be. He crosses to one of the chairs to sit.

That tingling feeling got me rubbing my fingers together, because it's a bit overwhelming now. I try to remember back to our conversations about the tribes. A girl that's a few feet behind the crew that just walked in rudely scours the whole room. Her long braids touch the floor. Her face is caked in dark makeup, giving off goth vibes.

"What have we missed?" Damone asks.

They all start to sit, and Mama Aya comes to sit next to me.

I turn to Mama Aya. She answers before I can ask. "They the Deyo tribe, chile. They practice duality."

It's the bitter tone for me.

Mrs. Empress Bonclair continues. "The missing children. You wouldn't know what happened to them, would you?"

"Of course we do," Damone says. "The rumors are true. The Bokors back, and somebody in this community raised them back up."

Murmurings spread throughout the entire room. I clock folk's mixed emotions—fear. Disbelief. Anger.

"We saw this." He holds up his hand, manifesting a video circulating around it. Four bodies laid out on the ground. Like they're desecrated or something. "Their vèvè symbol carved on their chests. They're channeling their magic, growing and regaining their power."

Shit. That's the same symbol that was at school with my mama's picture.

Another round of murmurs. Mrs. Empress Bonclair slams her gavel. "No need to panic. We will investigate and keep this under wraps until further notice."

"Why?" The word slips out of my mouth, causing everybody to

turn around and look at me. "People deserve to know what the hell is going on."

Mrs. Empress Bonclair looks at me with the most annoyed look. She recovers, though. "Malik, is it? Everyone, this is the gifted young grandson of Ms. Aya. Whom she just plucked from . . . Alabama, is it?"

It's the way she says *Alabama* with disgust for me.

Folks pivot to stare. The air in my lungs seize up just by all the stares I'm getting. A fish definitely out of water. Damone's eyes change from white back to regular brown, and his lips curl to a half smile.

"Young man, we go through the proper channels—"

"The proper channels ain't doing shit."

Mrs. Empress Bonclair slams the gavel with an even tighter smile. "You will not use such language in my home. I'm sure your grand-mère has taught you some semblance of being a good houseguest."

Mama Aya's eyes land on me, signaling me to be quiet.

But I ain't care. I keep talking. "My friend Alexis is helping the people. Isn't that what we should be doing too?"

Here I am judging her, and I'm sounding like these bougie up-tight folks with all the magic in the world, and they ain't doing shit about it. Damn, that girl know she's always right. That's the one thing I know for a fact that hasn't changed.

"That girl—"

I interrupt Mrs. Empress Bonclair. "That girl's name is Alexis."

"Do not interrupt me again, Mr. Baron." Her voice sends a shiver up my spine. "Surely, your grand-mère has taught you to respect your elders."

The room whispers like a sinner walked in the church house.

I find Mama Aya's brown eyes scolding me. It definitely feels like those *old ladies in the church* stares to shut you up during the sermon.

"She could have revealed magic, causing serious implications for us all. We do not want that, now, do we? That's why we do *not* get in the middle." Mrs. Empress Bonclair goes back to her regular smile. "The Kwasan tribe will continue to respond to any and all threats to our community. Rest assured, justice will be served." And with that, she bangs the gavel again, cutting the meeting short.

People go up to her like she's some local celebrity. Damone Cartier walks up to me. "She's an interestin' woman, ain't she?"

"I guess if you say so," I reply.

Damone grabs a kebab, peels the meat and vegetables off with his tongue. "So, you're Malik Baron."

I nod.

"Hmmmph. I've heard a great deal about you. Will you do me a favor?"

My eyes shift to him; I'm on the verge of cussing this dude out. "Tell Alexis, whenever she's ready, she has a place with us. She will never have to feel like she's fighting two battles again." His gaze is riveted on one of the girls in his crew; she does a hand signal. "I'm sure we'll be meeting again, Malik *Baron*."

He whisks away.

Somewhere in the foyer, I drift between talking folks, sensing their magic. It's so overwhelming, I start to have a headache. Somehow, I end up in this one windowless, over-the-top room. It reminds me of Chancellor Taron's office or something you'd see in a magazine made only for architects. But this one has a little bit of a personal touch.

Right on the wall—a portrait of Mrs. Empress Bonclair and a man, sitting in a chair. Scaling the wall are photos, some happy, some serious—and others I know for a fact are from a time where cameras was new.

One catches my eye. It's Chancellor Taron and his wife with a newborn baby in his arms.

The moment is curbed when I hear a voice from behind.

"That is my grandson, Ade Bonclair."

Mrs. Empress Bonclair walks in, nursing a fancy-looking glass of champagne along with that synthetic and unwelcoming smile. "He was such a gift," she says.

There is a pause between us. Then I go on to say, "Was?"

She nimbly sips on her wine. "You don't know the story? Hmmmph. Of course, you don't."

"What happened to him?"

"He was murdered. Along with my daughter-in-law, Celeste." A wary beat, then she continues with a small sip. "Ten years ago."

My eyes land back on the picture of Chancellor Taron and his wife and son. Suddenly, I feel a sense of empathy creeping through me. "I'm sorry about that, Mrs. Bonclair."

"Yes, you are." That iciness in her voice makes me stop, because I realize she's hexing me with that guilt feeling.

"Did I do something wrong?"

Suspicion rises in her eyes, and she circles me like a hyena with fresh meat. "I've heard quite a bit about you, Mr. Baron, and the trouble you've caused."

"I don't know what you talkin' about."

Mrs. Empress cocks her head back, laughing. "You are a clever young conjurer, aren't you? Most of your generation are so fascinated with being on the front lines. You raise your bullhorns and shout into the ether and cause chaos without so much as a thought."

I swallow back a few cuss words.

"But you all lack tact. That young woman—Alexis Williams— you so bravely stood up for today does not know how to approach any measure with humility."

"And y'all just sit here and don't do nothing, don't you?" Mrs. Empress Bonclair takes in my sarcastic tone. Sips on her wine. "Folks out there dying, getting kidnapped, and y'all sittin' here having a fancy-ass party. Maybe Alexis is right. Maybe y'all don't really care about the 'community.' "

A tense beat between us.

She travels over to the window, looking down like she's the Queen of Sheba. "You see them?" she says, pointing at a young-looking Black couple admiring the sculptures. They're dressed to a T. "The Du Lacs. They are two of the leading heart surgeons in the entire world. Their family has led the School of Medicine at Caiman for over three generations. With their magic, they have saved hundreds of thousands of lives out in the real world." She then points to an older man walking by the pool. "Mr. Thomas Banks. One of the most successful Black lawyers in Mississippi. Even repped a few civil rights leaders from there. He also comes from a long line of witch doctors who have been practicing law in this country for over two hundred years. He represented a young woman who was trying to save one of the first Black neighborhoods because the city was trying to build a prison on it. She even set up a land ownership defense fund to help local citizens avoid being forced out."

A guy meanders over to the Du Lacs; they chop it up.

"Oh, just one more." Mrs. Empress points to an older woman stationed at a table, picking at a piece of cake. "Mrs. Efe Matterson, with her brilliant talent and knowledge of mathematics and elemental magic—she was the one who helped Katherine Johnson with her orbital mechanics. All very influential people. All helped the entire Black community."

I turn to her. "Is there a point to all of this?"

Mrs. Empress turns to me; her cold eyes constrict every breath in my body. "Actually, yes. You and that woefully ambitious young lady Alexis open your mouths and make claims as you are doing. I need you two to do your research and stop catastrophizing. No, they don't actively go around showing their magic to whoever they please. We must be strategic. We don't want to end up like certain people that can be reckless with their magic."

Tsk. That damn word. Ooh, it burns a hole in my chest.

"Maybe that's what gets things done. Instead of sitting around here, eating fancy food and sipping on overpriced wine. Y'all livin' large around here."

She steps up to me, face-to-face. "You know how you asked me just a few moments ago if you've done anything wrong?" I don't answer. "Mr. Baron, you have *no* idea the extent of the things you've done wrong."

"You don't know me—"

"I *know* that you are treading on some dangerous grounds, young man. Dangerous grounds."

Mama Aya peeks her head in. "What's going on in here?"

A beat of us staring holes into each other. Mrs. Empress turns away, code-switches with a smile like she didn't just threaten the hell outta me. "Oh, I was just telling your *very* handsome grandson how wonderful it is to finally meet him."

Out of nowhere, she grabs my hands like how one of them old church ladies do. I sense her magic. It's powerful. And feels cold, like stepping on the tile floor early in the morning back in Alabama.

Somebody knocks on the door. It's a man, one of the butlers I saw from outside. "Mrs. Bonclair, Kemyondo from the Mojani tribe would like to speak with you."

"I'll be there in a moment," Mrs. Empress replies, turning back to Mama Aya. "Given the new facts we received, we must be careful not to alert folks. Track them down and nip this in the bud before chaos begins."

"So, they are back?" I ask. "And those kids, we need to be out there, looking for 'em. That's the first sign of the Bokors—and that's why y'all rose up against them all those years ago, right?"

That fake smile Mrs. Empress does comes back around. "I see those stories are still spreading around on that campus. Remember the last time there was a war, and our own blood was shed? We cannot let it get that far again. We are still rebuilding our community."

"I hear ya, Empress," Mama Aya says back to her as if she was trying to keep her cool. "If it comes to it, I will know what I have to do." Mama Aya's voice goes cold. So cold, it takes me back a bit.

"Of course," Mrs. Empress replies. Her gaze drifts back to me. A faint, displeased smile tugs her lips. "Malik, it has been a pleasure. Good luck with your studies."

And with that, she gives Mama Aya a formal nod and drifts out of the room.

"Don't worry about her none," Mama Aya says to me. "She's all bark and no bite."

"Well, she must be Cujo, because that was *all* bite."

Mama Aya wraps her arms around me with a chuckle, and we walk out. "C'mon, chile."

CHAPTER TWENTY-FOUR

SCRATCH A LIAR, FIND A THIEF.

Because with all this that's going on, something in the water ain't clean. Everybody around here seems like they love to suck on a lie, and it's obviously getting people killed.

Mrs. Bonclair saying Chancellor Taron's wife and kid got murdered ten years ago. Same as when my mama went missing. I already concluded that the men that attacked me and Mama that night were Bokors, back somehow. If she was looking for the scroll too, it makes sense they'd be after her.

It's all kinda starting to click. With that Antwan cop guy saying more kids are going missing, this can't be no coincidence. The shattering beats got me concentrating even more as I click through Google pages. There's not much on them. But given the kids went missing in the Lower Ninth Ward, it's bringing me back to Professor Kumale's class.

I pull my phone out to sign in to the CaimanTea app. Damn, more statuses and memes of Blue Ivy dancing being uploaded.

> *@TristanTrudaux: Chancellor needs to issue a statement or something. What's going on? We know the Bokors are back.*

> *@ChristyDeVoe: Lemme head to the Magnificence building and get this training in. Because the Bokors got me fucked up.*

@SalimOk: IDK. The Bokor tribe got shit done, though.
I feel like it was a conspiracy theory on how they were
overthrown. Stay woke, my beautiful Black people.

A whole buncha tea floods the timeline, which makes my heart drop. No lie, seeing all this and seeing that lil' kid get sacrificed like that still got me messed up.

J. Cole becomes background noise as I dive deeper down the rabbit hole. Some legend says the Bokors defied the gods that night, and in return, they were cursed to forever roam the earth.

The way Professor Kumale told it, they lost their magic because of it. Maybe that's why they gotta steal it from others.

Crossing through the campus, I end up seeing Professor Kumale in a tutoring session with somebody. We lock eyes. I wave at him, but he kinda gives me the cold shoulder with a half smile and a nod. Damn, I guess he's still upset with me after that whole Dorm Wars thing go down. I just keep walking until I end up by the BCSU. Inside, I order one of these peanut-butter-and-chocolate smoothies called Bear Claws before my next class.

"Hey," Alexis says from behind me. Her eyes . . . man, they do something to me. But I'm petty, so I still act like I'm mad at her.

"What you want, Lex?"

"Can we talk?"

Dude at the cash register hands me my smoothie.

"Now you wanna talk?"

Damn, this finna be harder than I expect, because she's looking fine as all get-out with her purple eyeshadow and real pretty dress. "I haven't heard from you," I tell her.

"So, I heard through the grapevine you took up for me at the Bonclair meeting," she says as she stands next to me in line. The cashier is looking at us real awkward.

I try to keep my guard up. "Yeah, so?"

We come together by a table. Her brown eyes almost make me melt right here and now. "Look, I wanna say how sorry I am for blowing up on you like that. What Donja did was very wrong, and thank you for having my back."

Tsk. "Look, we may have grown up and changed and all, but I'll always have your back, Lex. No matter what. And I know I said some messed-up things. But what you said was some foul shit too, Lex."

Alexis nods and looks at me the way I remember, like it's just us two. "I know. Look, I just wanted to say I'm sorry. You didn't deserve that."

I immediately soften. "You sure nothing is going on with you two?"

"This is my last time even giving attention to this, okay? So, here it goes. No, we are not. We've been friends for a long time. Basically, we grew up together. Our families were close and have been joined at the hip ever since. He made me feel welcomed when no one else did."

It takes everything in me to put the green-eyed monster away. But Alexis was right. Damn, she's always right. All this is way bigger than her and Donja, and maybe I made it about that because the rest of it was too hard to think about.

"Donja just had it hard. Whether y'all like to admit it or not, you two are a lot alike."

"That's cap."

We both walk out of the student union, back on the sidewalk, walking toward class. "His parents were tragically killed."

Dead silence.

"How?"

It takes a minute for Alexis to answer. So much so, we end up by the quad. "It's not my business to tell. But he was taken care of by his uncle, but he's since abandoned Donja, and then the Williamses took him in. Took us in."

Empathy trying to rear its annoying head in the corner of my mind. "It's whatever. I don't even care about him. I just wanna make sure we cool. You feel me?"

Our eyes lock. That feeling creeps back up again. Got my hands sweating like when I first see her pretty face and my heart beating against my chest like it's about to run out of time. But this time, I just wanna kiss her. I want her and all of her.

"Yes, we'll always be. You're—I care about you, Malik. And you know what, we gotta get to know each other again."

"I got class in thirty."

"It won't take long."

My guard coming down faster than the London Bridge falling. I suck on the rest of the smoothie. "How you propose we do that?"

She smirks. Then claps her hands. Wind whips around us, and the ground lifts. We end up on a rooftop overlooking the campus, blessed by the golden sun in a matter of seconds.

"Ahhh, it's hella public, but it's freaky."

She playfully swats me on the shoulder. "Boy, stop. . . ."

"We used to sneak up to the roof at that group home, remember? Watch the stars."

"Yeah, we did. I remember we'd try to dream our way out of that place."

Her beautiful brown eyes meet mine. She holds her hand up. "I'm Alexis; it's nice to meet you. . . ."

I place my hand right in hers. In the tangling of our fingers, silver and blue spark from the palms of our hands like we're holding stars. The way she breathes, the way she slightly smirks and her lips curl. Her magic and mine colliding—it's like whoever is up there in the sky cut off the gravity.

"I'm sorry, Lex. You know, for tripping on you and stuff."

We're inches away from each other. "It's okay, Malik."

In this moment, I may be the biggest simp, but I'on even care. Because in this lingering moment with Alexis, she got me falling in love.

* * * *

After all this studying, I know if I go to sleep, I'll maybe get another dream. Soon as I hit the bed, I feel the mattress sink in. Somewhere in the corner of my unconsciousness, my eyes pop open, and I float effortlessly toward blackness. Slowly I come to the realization that I'm surrounded by twisting trees. Moonlight filters through the branches, evaporating the shrouding darkness. In front of me is a small cabin, where a dim light filters through the window. When I come upon the door, I hear her. I hear Miriam singing.

Way down yonder in de middle of the fiel'
Angel workin' at de chariot wheel
Not so partic'lar about workin' at de wheel
But I jes' wan-a see how de chariot feel
Now let me fly
To Mount Zion, Lord, Lord . . .

Her eyes scan over to me, and just like how if you flip a channel on a screen, things change and dissipate into another scene. I've been transported to the middle of the woods again. It's hella cold. Dark. And I hear footsteps up ahead. After a ring of silence, there are the sounds of dogs howling.

"They went thataway!" somebody says through the dark trees.

Through the moonlight and the blanketed marsh, shrouded figures emerge. It's Miriam, along with enslaved men, women, and children. They all dart through the trees, running in a zigzag. I focus on Miriam; her babies are strapped and swaddled on her back. They start to cry. The others break left, hiding.

A group of white men patrollers emerge from the woods with guns pointed at her.

"Y'all go on 'bout ya business nah." Miriam struggles under her breath. The babies let out a piercing cry that echoes through the trees.

One of the white men spews venom. "You don't tell us what to do, nigger bitch."

"I done warned ya!" Miriam reaches into a small mojo bag and blows some dust into the air. It falls, making a circle around her.

There's a terrorizing fear plaguing the air.

Time slows like molasses as I run toward Miriam and her babies. Suddenly, gunshots ring through the night.

"No!" I scream.

In an instant—the bullets swivel, splitting the air with a vengeance. On the other end, Miriam stands firmly planted. The bullets miss her completely.

Miriam's weary eyes flicker with a gold ring of light. She kneels, hands stabbing through the mushy soil. She mumbles a spell. *"Pe'n sasa tutnaka mjobo!"*

The earth rumbles violently with the magic, and the enslaved men appear through the trees, staring at the slave catchers like mindless zombies. The light from the full moon shifts through the whistling trees, and the slaves' bodies twist and convulse beyond belief.

Bones crackling. Guttural growls vibrate in their throats as the enslaved men are TRANSFORMING. Their Black skin ripping and turning into brindled stripes, like gigantic werecats. Miriam looks at the white slave catchers, retribution set in her eyes. *"Ikolu."*

The now-transformed men move with speed faster than a blink of an eye, and as they surge past me, the scene shifts in a swirl of screams and blood and terror. The next thing I see is Ephraim and Miriam embracing, safe with their babies at last.

As he kisses her, she pulls out a long, wrinkled parchment paper, burned at the edges. It glitters in the darkness.

From where I'm standing, I can't read it. But I do notice the words seem to rise from the crinkling paper and then fall right back on the page.

My eyes go buck because . . . there's no way that's what I think it is. . . .

Miriam twirls her fingers around the paper, and the wind whips all around her. Miriam takes a pocketknife from Ephraim's pocket. Slices her hand, and her blood drops onto the paper.

"They can never find it," Miriam tells Ephraim.

"We gon' make sho they don't," Ephraim says. "We'll keep it safe and hidden until it's needed." The two babies coo in their arms. Miriam uses her magic to make the page burst into ancestral blue flames. From her hands, they spread, licking the dark soil, and nip right at the bottom of my feet.

I wake up with a sharp breath and a head full of questions. This Scroll of Idan, the one everyone seems to want to get their hands on. The one that grants its owner godlike powers—like maybe the power to summon your own shape-shifter army—did I just see what happened to that scroll?

CHAPTER TWENTY-FIVE

LIKE A RAG DOLL, MY WHOLE BODY IS FLUNG IN MIDAIR IN slow motion.

With a hard thud, I crash against the mushy soil. In an instant, I spring up, facing the person who had me thrown on my ass.

"Again!" Professor Kumale is on his drill sergeant vibes. It's hard, but I try to catch my breath before an animation of a student appears in front of me. "Stay focused, Malik!"

I am focused! Low-key, high-key, I wanna cuss him the fuck out because I'm not really that focused. The dream of seeing Miriam got me off my game. Plus, I'm itching to get past this sparring session. The student speeds, and I teleport around him, doing a dropkick move that sends his animated ass into a puff of cloud.

I wipe my forehead on my forearm, trying to catch my breath. "Damn, I ain't think we was gonna be out training like we in the Avengers."

Professor Kumale meets my gaze, still in that blank drill sergeant–like stare. "A conjurer mustn't rely solely on his magical ability. Because there will be times where you'll have to rely on your physical strength as well."

A sharp shrill of his whistle.

My chest burns from the lack of oxygen. In a virtual blur, an animation of a girl appears and blitzes down the field toward me. She throws magical firebombs like her life depends on it. I dodge them mofos with a cocky grin splitting my face.

I'm flung again across the field from a vicious blow.

"Never remove your eyes from the enemy. I keep telling you that, Malik." A brief pause as he helps me up. "Take a water break."

I stumble over to the bleachers to take a sip of cold water and chow down on some watermelon chunks. He saunters over to me.

A loaded silence between the both of us.

"Good job out there today," he tells me.

I ignore him.

"Is there a problem, Malik?"

Flicking the sweat from my face, I whip around. "I don't know, is there? You've been riding me hard these past couple of days in class. I mean, I appreciate you for staying after class, but I feel like you're still mad at me after Dorm Wars."

"I'm not mad—"

I spring up, slamming the bottle of water into a trash can next to us. "I apologized to you like a thousand times. You got me doing this and a whole oral report on the Louisiana Purchase. I just don't understand why *I'm* being punished for defending myself!"

Again, nothing.

"Come," he says, motioning for me to sit beside him on the bleachers. We sit in silence for a quick second, and I swallow my irritation. "Malik, I'm not out to punish or embarrass you. I'm doing my job and my duty to you as my student: I'm calling you to excellence. You're good. Damn good. Magnifik, even. Your technique is off, but that comes with learning. However, your impulse is what will get you into trouble."

He's right. But I'm too hardheaded to let him know that in this moment.

"You belong here, Malik," he tells me. "You just have to act like it."

"I guess when you get told all your life that you don't belong anywhere, that's why I am the way I am. I mean, all I had was me. And this." I manifest a blue spark around my hand.

"I understand, Malik, truly, I do." Professor Kumale places his hands on my shoulders. "You're so like my little brother. I swear, it's scary at times."

"Really? How?"

He chuckles at my disbelief. "He was seven years old when his magic manifested. I was well into my training, but my little brother was a hothead. So strong. So powerful. I didn't feel my magic until I was nine. Different ages for different people," he says. "The memory is still fresh in my mind. I was in the middle of the woods back in Haiti. People in my village thought I was a *dyab pitit*." Professor Kumale laughs harder. "My mother was a mambo. A priestess. She was powerful, my mother. And she and my father loved me something serious." A heavy pause. "My father, he was a strong man. Proud and prideful. He used to say to me, '*Se apre batay la nou konte blese.*'"

He pauses with mixed emotions. In this moment, my brain doesn't catch up to the Kreyol, even though I've been studying.

"What that mean?"

He clears his throat, pushing down emotions. "It is after the battle that we count the wounded."

We both ruminate in the growing silence.

"No lie, Professor. I think the scariest part for me is not even that night anymore. It's me forgetting her. Memories really do fade over time. It's me actually . . . moving on."

Whoa. I don't think I ever said that out loud.

"Losing a mother, it's one of the most painful things in the world," he admits. "It is not something I wish on my worst enemy."

I grit my teeth. "Yeah. I just wish I really knew what happened to her. I've been thinking . . ."

Am I really gonna tell him all this? After that talk with Alexis, maybe letting someone else in isn't the worst thing in the world.

"Okay, I have this theory. I think whatever happened to her had something to do with the Bokors. Like, if it turns out they're back somehow, and if she was really into bane magic and the Scroll of Idan and all that . . ."

His eyes shift. I really hope I don't regret this.

"Ya know, the Bokors are misunderstood in stories, Malik. Once upon a time, they were healers and mathematicians; they helped their community."

"They killed kids, though, Professor Kumale," I say back. "Stealin' their magic and alla that."

"I completely understand, Malik. I'm not excusing what they did, but I will say, some folks can chalk it up to the art of war."

"You said it ya self. 'Magic always comes at a price.'"

"Magic will make you act out of character," he says. "Trust."

"I know that all too well, believe me." A moment between the both of us. "Before I came here, I almost killed my old foster parent. I could literally feel my magic wrap around his throat, and I—" I stop myself from admitting the bitter truth. "Part of me didn't wanna stop."

Professor Kumale's gaze falls to the floor. I'm not sure if it's in a judging manner or if he's just letting me vent.

"He was putting hands on my foster brother, Taye, and I told him if he ever do that again—" I feel my whole arm becoming hot as I abruptly stand up. When I look down, the swirling blue pulsates with my anger.

With a deep breath, I calm myself down. The blue light goes away. Now I'm looking at Professor Kumale, all apologetic.

"Have you always been able to do that?" Professor Kumale asks.

"Nah," I say, "it just started. It's weird, though; every time I use it, it's like . . . it's like I feel different."

"Different how?" he asks.

"I don't know. I can't explain it. It's like I feel connected to something that I've never felt connected to before."

Professor Kumale goes quiet for what seems like a full minute. He then places his hands on my shoulders, looking at me square on. "You had to do what you had to do." The night pops up in my head, but Professor Kumale's voice fights through. "You were just surviving a horrible situation. I commend you for that."

He pats some encouragement into my shoulders with his hands.

"No judgment here."

"Thanks, Professor," I say, voice cracking with emotion.

He holds out his hand. I shake it. "Just know I always got your back."

We start to pack our stuff.

My mind seizes up, thinking about my dream and Miriam. About power, and what it can do to those who possess it. "Professor Kumale? Can I ask you something?"

"Yeah, sure."

"If you could find the Scroll of Idan . . . if you knew where it was, would you take it?"

He looks at me with curiosity.

"Hypothetically, of course."

"That much power could do a lot of good. But it's dangerous—to use it, yes, but even to possess it. It would make you a target."

His look of concern got me pivoting back to my mama.

"My mama, she was onto something. She was tryin' to find it. I think that's what got her in trouble."

"If that's true, then all the more reason to be cautious. I can't and won't allow anything to happen to you."

A dark uncertainty in his eyes sends a chill up and down my spine.

. . . .

Friday night.

We're breaking down the tables for Savon's Black Quitches event. It was pretty dope hearing D Low tell everybody his story. Being a Black man and his journey of bisexuality.

I ain't never thought about anything like this before. Guess I'm privileged in that way as a straight dude. "Black men don't get to be bisexual," D Low said, addressing the audience. "We gotta be either gay or straight. It took me a long time to break that stigma over my own life."

"That was dope, man," I tell D Low. "Your story."

We hug. "I appreciate that, roomie."

I grab the fold-up table, heading toward the door.

"Where this goes?" I ask Savon. They come up to us, smiling like they got no sense when looking at D Low.

"Oh, um, in Room 102," they say, and then go back to cheesing at D Low. Apparently, they already started the *talking* phase.

The hallway is empty. Room 102 is just up ahead on the left. I turn in, put the table down in the back closet, and try to head back to the door. It instantly shuts on me like it has a mind of its own. My hands tingle . . . but it's a different feeling. Fight or flight activating as goose bumps appear up and down my arm.

Sensing . . .

And then my stomach turns into knots. Something moves in the darkness, sounding like a creak or shift.

I look around, thinking maybe somebody followed me into the room to put the remaining tables up. But I've seen enough scary movies to know I shouldn't say no damn hello or believe any of that is true.

The palms of my hands ignite with a bright blue orb of light dancing between my fingers. Ready to blast on anybody that comes my way. The room is completely silent and dark. At first, nothing. Searching the dark room, I don't see—

Just like that. Something or someone grabs me by my neck and slings my ass across the room. I crash against all the stacked chairs. Pain shoots up my back, and in a flash, whatever is attacking me waves its hand, and my whole body instantly smashes against the wall.

Everything in my mind freezes. But I hear it stomping around in the darkness. Feet heavy as hell, like it's wearing boots. A tall, dark shadow rushes at me, and I put up a block with my magic—creating a torrent of rippling vibrations. My magic manipulates itself into a powerful quake, and everything goes in slow motion as the power extends from the palm of my hand. The shadowed figure flies back and crashes through the window. Then the whole room, the walls cave in, tumbling down until I can see the outside.

Savon, D Low, Elijah, and Alexis come rushing in. "Malik, is—"

They turn on the lights, seeing all the glass and the ruined wall. I pick myself up off the floor.

"Somebody was in here," I say, my voice going out.

They all run over to me, helping me get up. "Who?!" Alexis says. I try to catch my breath.

D Low crosses to the pile of bricks and sees half the trees are falling down outside. He turns to me, looking all kinds of surprised.

"I don't know, but it flung my ass across the room; I know that."

Savon speeds toward the window. From their hand, it's like crackling embers, and they close their eyes and whisper something in Yoruba.

Their magic flutters around the room, bathing the wall. From there, we all notice blotches of twisting shadows climbing. "He's right," Savon tells Alexis. "Something was here."

"You didn't get a sense of who they were?"

"Nah," I say back, trying to remember, but it all happened so fast. "I didn't."

Savon picks up a piece of glass stained with blood, and then right next to it, I see a pile of black dust.

D Low guides me to a chair. "Was it Donja? Or them House of Devereaux niggas?"

"No, we're texting now. He's been in his dorm all night." Alexis pulls out her phone and starts to tap on it. Probably sending Donja a message.

"Was it a Bokor?" D Low asks.

The whole room goes cold at how everybody falls quiet.

"Didn't the chancellor put a boundary spell around the whole school? So, nothing evil can get in."

"Malik," I hear Alexis say. She stares with wide eyes at my arm. "What is that?"

I look down at my wrist, feeling a burning sensation. A mark on my arm starts to illuminate and burn deeper into my skin. My mind swims. Everything in front of me spins.

"Ah!!!" I bend over, putting my other hand on my wrist.

"Malik, what's wrong?!" Alexis says. Panic surges through all of us as the mark on my wrist glows even brighter.

Energy crackling around the room.

My body falls off the chair and hits the floor.

ACT III

CHAPTER TWENTY-SIX

THEIR SKIN IS BLACK AS MIDNIGHT.

All of them. Beautiful Black skin wrapped in glory and frustration like stars in the inky, dark sky. Welts and bruises decorate their faces like war paint.

It's their story. Their history.

Through the boscage and mist, they all stand idly in the middle of the sugarcane field like they're waiting for something.

The ancestors.

Waist-high stalks of pure emerald green shroud them and sway from the calming wind. The moon in the sky washes over the land and bayous in shades of glittering silver, kissing their raised foreheads. From the look of things, it's like they're watching God.

It's the most beautiful thing I've ever seen.

Thunder rolls in. Under the low hums of the cicadas, I hear a woman sing the same song as before with panted breath. Her voice is riffing and running so hard, it'll make you do that stank face.

"You got a right to the tree of life. . . . Ups and downs, but you got a right to the tree of life. . . ."

Behind her, streaking across the sky, is lightning, stretching its tentacles on for miles. From their magic, a pillar of light and clouds blanket their feet. Their faces, still as statues, illuminated by chromes of magical silver light. On the right, the cypress trees pierce the murky swamp water. The ripples grow as I find myself stepping into the water. I stretch out my arms like I'm receiving a layin' on of hands.

My magic blossoms, causing the breeze to billow around me. Soft, melodic sounds of the bottles hanging from the tree sing to me. Through the tangled bodies of tree branches, *Miriam* appears from the swirling fog.

Her dark mahogany skin has a sheen of sweat, and her shoulders rise in syncopation with her steady breathing. This woman keeps singing, and something in me tells me that I should kneel and grab a pile of the cold dirt. Miriam does the same movement, kneeling and grabbing the dirt. The dust sprinkles from her grasp.

Magic has always *been ours.*

From there, she begins to sing:

> *Way down yonder in de middle of the fiel'*
> *Angel workin' at de chariot wheel*
> *Not so partic'lar about workin' at de wheel*
> *But I jes' wan-a see how de chariot feel*
> *Now let me fly*
> *To Mount Zion, Lord, Lord . . ."*

A swelling wave of motion swishing inside, nestling deep into my bones. The ancestors hum the rest of the song while my magic buzzes under my skin like wings on a honeybee. With each building breath, I feel my chest rise and my blood sing right along with her. When I exhale, my magic manifests into a circle of ancestral blue fire, globing around my whole body. Me and Miriam lift into the air, flying through the vast clouds.

On everything I love, we are literally flying.

From the ground below, I see my ancestors running with supernatural speed through the clammy woods. Most of them, swallowed by the darkness, run so fast, they become like a blur. I shift my head to the right, seeing some of the ancestors shift into birds, others into jackals.

Shape-shifters.

The singing from Miriam soothes my ear. It's like a lullaby, a spell. My eyes are getting heavier the more she sings.

Now let me fly
To Mount Zion, Lord . . .

I can literally feel a faltering rhythm beat in my chest, witnessing Black folks doing the impossible. A collection of emotions warms the pit of my stomach. In the corner, by the bottle tree, one of the ancestors lift their hands in a praise motion, and the bottles light up like a million stars.

Glittering golds and blues illuminate around the bodies of my ancestors as they inch closer to the sea. Where they are standing, it kinda reminds me of the Gulf Shores back in Alabama. Small waves move like the water is longing to make its way back to the shore. Up ahead, miles away, I see a cyclone of grayish-white clouds form in the sky.

Hanging on the hinges of the horizon is the same eclipse that I somehow know cut off the original Divine Elam. Something tells me to step into the water. With the voices of the ancestors rising and blessing my ears and tunneling through every fiber of my being, I hover my hand over the calm water. At first, ripples. Then they grow and grow to small waves that seem to separate. No lie, it's kinda like that epic scene in *The Prince of Egypt.*

The ancestors move like paper in the wind, floating and effortless. Their beautiful Black skin glistening from the ocean spray as they edge the shore, waiting for their bare feet to touch the cold water.

The wind around us picks up like it's about to carry me someplace.

And one by one, they start to move into the water.

After they all disappear, I end up right back at the tree in Mama Aya's front yard. The bottles swaying, and the root of it bleeds with crimson blood. My breathing picks up as I see the blood gush from the open tree bark.

In a blink of an eye, it all changes. I am in a small cabin, somewhere where the sun shines brightly inside. The door bursts open—a little girl in tattered clothes rushes in, being chased by a little boy.

Great-grandma Miriam appears from the corner of the room. The rocking chair she leaves behind still rocks back and forth.

"Aya Mae."

Oh shit. This is Mama Aya, but as a young girl.

"Yes, Mawma," she answers back obediently.

"Time fuh ya lesson. Come, sit wit me."

Mama—I mean, Aya—steps forward to a kneeling Miriam, who holds out her hand to her daughter with a smile. Aya's brother, who she ain't really mentioned, stands by the door, looking away.

"Remember what I taught ya."

Aya shakes her head. Lifts her hands, manifesting little butterflies from her fingers. Slowly, the younger version of Mama Aya whispers, *"Awlotae."*

Awlotae.

"Das guuuud, bayby gurl. Real guuud. You's keep practisin', cuz wun day, you gon' have to pass down this power."

Like a spiraling tornado, the flapping butterflies swirl up to the ceiling. They disappear through the wood.

When they clear, it's Mama Aya, only a bit older, standing bedside by an older Miriam. Tufts of gray hair stick out from her head wrap. Unspoken words brew between the two.

Miriam hands Mama Aya the same paper I saw her hide with Ephraim.

Could it be . . .

"The Scroll of Idan is yours to protect now. It shall be done," Miriam says.

Holy shit.

Mama Aya takes the scroll and wipes her tears in one motion. Miriam nods, ready.

Struggling, a young Mama Aya hovers her hand over a weak Miriam and whispers, "To be absent from the body is to be present with the Lord. *Àṣẹ.*"

Miriam suddenly turns into a bed of ash.

I jump out of my sleep with a fit of coughs, the images from my dream chased out with a dull ache invading my head. Mouth feeling all paper dry, and my chest feels like it's being incinerated.

My eyes drift around, clocking something moving in the dark. I quickly hold up my sweaty hand, ready to throw a hex.

A shift in the light: it's Mama Aya.

"It's all right, baybeh. You just havin' a bad dream." Mama Aya cups my face in her cool hands.

Struggling to catch my breath, I feel something hanging from my wrist. A wrapped silver chain with a half-sun shape dangling at the end. Instantly, I'm all confused. But the magic that radiates from it calms my anxiety.

Mama Aya lights a candle, inviting a warm glow into my mama's old room. She pulls something that hangs around her neck: a small purple flannel pouch with a gold string tied around it. A *mojo bag*.

"What happened?"

Mama Aya doesn't answer. She just pulls out a brown rock that looks like a big herb. Something you'd find at the bottom of a tree.

I ask another question. "What's that?"

"High John the Conqueror root. It's for a hedge of protectin' ya. Sit up and face thataway fuh me." She points to the left side of the wall while rubbing the root with her thumb and index finger. "'So shall my word be that goes out from my mouth; it shall not return to me empty, but it shall accomplish that which I purpose, and shall succeed in the thing for which I sent it.' Bless him, John the Conqueror. Bless him, John the Conqueror. Bless him, John the Conqueror."

Her eyes shut, and she mumbles something that I can't pick up on. The effect of her magic makes my skin crawl with goose bumps. It feels like that cool blast of fresh air when you walk inside a house from playing outside in the summer heat all day.

It's lemon pound cake. It's home.

Mama Aya grabs a small jar and pours some kinda oil in her hand. One more mumbling whisper, and she applies it on my forehead and all over my face. Honestly, I feel a thousand times stronger.

I tuck my sleeve over the bracelet. "What happened, Mama Aya?"

"You're just tired, is all. You need to rest," she says. Right then and there, she starts to place the contents back into the mojo bag. "You got a lot on ya mind and ya spirit."

Mama Aya turns on the lamp, letting the light fill the whole room in an amber color. When she sits on the edge of the bed, I notice her brow creasing, creating little wrinkles in her face.

"Them chirren downstairs say somethin' done attacked you."

It takes a second for my foggy mind to clear. *Is that what happened?* "Yeah, I guess. It's probably nothin', right? Chancellor Taron said there's no way Bokors could get on campus."

"Well, somebody definitely tried to hex ya."

She points to my arm, where long blue streaks are traced out like snake prints. A branded reminder that I was almost killed.

"Who was it?"

Her shaky fingers wrap around my forearm. With a luminescent vapor, her spell makes the mark on my arm go away on its own.

Man, magic comes so easy to her.

"Ain't no tellin'," Mama Aya replies, breathing heavy. "Somebody was tryin' to tap into ya. It's an old trick, tryin' to steal ya magic. But ya memories—"

I grit my teeth just thinking about it. "The dream."

"—they protectin' ya."

I absorb that. My feet meet the floor to climb outta the bed, and I stagger over to the closet. I put on another shirt because I was sweating through the one I had on in my sleep. "I saw her again."

"Who, baybeh?" she asks, a bit out of breath.

"Miriam," I say, turning to face her. "It was a wild dream. Like, we was flying, and then it all switched up. It was you and her on her deathbed."

A wave of stillness brews between us. Mama Aya looks up, eyes and face flickering with concern.

"I feel like she's trynna talk to me or somethin'. I don't know." Our eyes lock. "She gave you the scroll, didn't she?"

Her expression changes. Then she lets out a quick sigh.

"Do you have it? If you do, then we can't let them Bokors know nothin'. They can come here—"

"Malik, about the—"

The door bursts open. It's Alexis. "Oh my God. I'm so sorry, Ms. Aya, I—"

"It's a'right, honey. I'm sho everybody wanna know he all right," Mama Aya whispers, offering her a simple hug. That's when I notice Mama Aya has a heavy walk as she meanders to the bedroom door.

"You good, Mama Aya?"

"I'm just fine. Old as I am, ya bones just gets a bit tired."

She hobbles out of the room.

Alexis slowly makes her way over to me and wraps her arms around me like I'm breakable. I squeeze her, letting her know it's okay. No words exchanged. I hold her for a moment, wishing that it can last forever.

"I'm just glad you're not hurt," she says, sniffing. "I couldn't live with myself if anything ever happened to you."

I crack a grin. "Nothing can't get Lik Lik down."

She musters up a small giggle, but then her brown eyes glisten, threatening tears.

"Hey, I'm good," I tell her. I gently grab her chin, staring deep in her glossy brown eyes. "I promise."

Alexis places her head on my shoulder, listening to my heartbeat. The air buckles between us something serious. We both lie flat on the bed, just staring up at the ceiling. Her index and thumb are at her temple, pulling a gold thread from her head. She then tosses it up like a feather. It floats all the way up, making the ceiling ripple like a watery mirage. It instantly turns into the night sky. Vast stars lined in shimmering dots, placed innocently in a twisting and familiar shape of towering gods.

"For old times' sake," she breathes, wrapping one arm around me. An anticipation builds between our warm bodies.

"The Anunnaki . . ." Each inhale is a battle. Laced in the memory of our time back in the group home. Us sneaking on the roof to watch the night stars. "Just like how I remembered."

She whimpers something between a laugh and a cry. "We always prayed that they'd come and take us away from that group home."

"They probably still out there, looking for us, watching over us."

"Yeah, maybe."

Our magic surfaces like a cool breeze. The stars swirl into place, showcasing a drawing of two gods holding hands. Like how we did when we were little.

Her hand lands on my rising chest with tenderness. "Just lie here with me for a second."

She ain't gotta say nothin' but a word. This time I pull her deeper into my orbit. I know I should be puzzling through that vision, finding Mama Aya and demanding the truth. But all I can think about is Alexis's intoxicating smell. Our own little cocoon, and Alexis is my butterfly. My breathing steadies, keeping me from drowning.

A good hour passes by, and me and Alexis both make our way down the steps to meet familiar concerned faces of our friends. D Low is the first to come up to me, hugging me.

"You good, bruh?"

I shake it off. "Yeah, I'm cool. Just tired."

"You don't want me to step on that campus? I'll shut the shit down." Samedi's voice is like thunder, yelling at Chancellor Taron from outside on the porch.

"That's not necessary," Chancellor Taron tells him.

Auntie Brigitte shuts the screen door, shaking her head and rolling her eyes.

"Malik, you didn't get a good look at him?" Eljah asks.

"Nah. I didn't. The room was so dark, I couldn't see anything."

Taye lays his head on my shoulder. It took him the longest out of everybody to calm down. I had to remind him I'm fine like fifty-lem times.

"We swept through the room and can't tell who it was," D Low says.

It takes a good bit of energy for me to remember. "Word? Whoever it was, they had some heavy-ass feet. Sounded like they were wearing boots."

The commotion on the porch instantly stops. Mama Aya makes her way to the front door, peeking her head outside, whispering something to Samedi and Chancellor Taron.

When she comes back into the living room, Chancellor Taron follows. There's a look on his face that I ain't never seen before. Sadness. Worry. When he sees me, he clears his throat and averts his gaze.

"Bruh, I am hungry as hell," Elijah says, sniffing the air. Whatever Brigitte is cooking up, it's got my stomach touching the back of my spine.

Savon playfully nudges him. "Damn, you are always hungry."

"Uhh, shut yo ass up. It's the metabolism." Savon and Elijah continue to joke with each other.

I look to Chancellor Taron again. He leans by the door, fixing his tie.

"Y'all stop all that cussin' in my house." Mama Aya's voice drops an octave lower.

"Sorry, Ms. Aya." Savon and Elijah do that twin thing, both speaking at the same time.

She gives them that grandmama type of smile. "Go on in that kitchen and get y'all somethin' to eat."

Elijah, Savon, and D Low move toward the kitchen area like a stampede. Alexis and Taye slowly follow them. Samedi hustles in through the front door, toting a shot glass in his hand and staring holes into Chancellor Taron.

Chancellor Taron's steps to me, a worried expression flickering across his face. High-key, it throws me off a bit, but I know it's a façade because I can feel his wrath from a mile away.

"Malik, you have no idea what the person looked like?" His investigative tone catches me off guard.

My brain is a little fuzzy trying to retrace everything. I go to sit on the armrest on the small chair by the TV. "Nah. Like I was telling everybody earlier, it was so dark in the room, I couldn't see."

"Could this be somebody on campus trying to prank him?" Samedi asks. Liquor blows heavy on his breath.

"It's possible." Chancellor Taron answers as if he has razors on the edge of his tongue. Yup. Back to regular programming. He looks down at my arm, where the hex once was. "I'm not sure who would hex a freshman in this way."

Samedi steps up to Chancellor Taron, accusatory. "I keep tellin' you, you don't want me to step on that campus."

"Yes, you've reiterated that several times," Chancellor Taron says, annoyed. The way these two mean-mug the hell outta each other, you'd think it'll be World War III in this living room. "But I can assure everyone the protection spell around the school is impossible to penetrate. Some of the most powerful conjurers protect the school. So, no outside evil force can get in. Including the Bokors. Trust us; we would know."

I can't help but laugh. "You won't even admit to your students that the Bokors are back, but now we're supposed to believe you can keep us safe from them?"

Chancellor Taron ignores me, buttoning up his coat with a bougie flair, moving toward the kitchen. "We should get back to campus." Everybody groans. Elijah and D Low pack even more food onto their plates with superspeed.

"Nah. I'm not leaving," I tell the chancellor, following him to join the others by the table.

"Baybeh, it's fine." Mama Aya's arms wrap around me. "Go on back to school. You can't let this mess with ya schoolin'."

"Nah. I'm not leaving Taye. And I got some questions for you—"

"Malik." Taye crosses over to us. "Just do what they say. I'm good here."

"Oh, the Bokors ain't gonna bother him. We gon' make 'sho of that." Brigitte wraps her arms around him.

I feel a twinge of guilt and relief sloshing in my head. Taye's good. He's been good. And in this clear situation, I'm not.

I hug him real tight.

"Get ya studies in. Learn all you can," Mama Aya tells me. "We'll talk soon, once you've recovered. I promise you that."

Me and Chancellor Taron make our way to the yard. D Low, Elijah, Savon, and Alexis teleport back to campus.

"You cannot keep going on and off campus like that, Malik. It is obviously too dangerous."

"I was attacked there," I remind him. He gives me a weighted look. Ain't had nothing to say after that. "I'm fine."

"You're not—"

"I am. Look." I hold up my arm, showing him the healed spot.

There's a brief pause between us as we walk toward the tree in the front yard.

"What did I tell you before? You can't just go off gallivanting, showing off your magic. It is very apparent that these are trying times, and until we get to the bottom of this . . ."

"So, you sayin' this is *my* fault?"

He softens. "No, of course not. You were just attacked."

"You think I'd forget?"

His hand goes to his pocket, fiddling around with something. Mama Aya's yard suddenly turns into Caiman University. I'm in front of my dorm.

"This is drastic what I'm about to do." He snaps his fingers, and it's like a whole bunch of weights are tied around my ankles. "You are completely barred from stepping off campus."

"Yo, you can't do that!"

"I can, and it's already done." He flails his hand in the air in a very showy way. A big bright light slaps itself into a force field, surrounding the campus. It rings with energy. "Go to your dorm, Malik. Focus on your classes. I hear you're excelling."

Let me bargain with this dude. "I want my brother, Taye, here with me, then. It'll help me stay focused on my studies without worrying if he's okay or not."

"Nonmagical people are not allowed on campus. That is the rule. He has some of the most powerful people surrounding him. He will be fine."

"This is bullshit! Just because you ain't got nobody doesn't mean—"

Chancellor Taron gets in my face. "Do not test me, Mr. Baron. This is for your own good. Whatever attacked you is not done with you." My heart drops when he says that. "You need to be on safe grounds. Not out there."

Before I can argue, he says, "Mama Aya and I amped up the protection spell around you." He points to the bracelet on my arm. It's searing in gold colors from Mama Aya's magic. "You can thank her for that."

And he disappears in that stupid-ass royal purple cloud.

CHAPTER TWENTY-SEVEN

OLD EPISODES OF *LIVING SINGLE*, STUDYING, AND WEED SMOKE got us all straight vibing.

Since I got attacked, everybody been posted up at me and D Low's apartment, chillin' and studying for our summer midterms. Also, here to "protect" me too. They ain't slick. But I won't lie, it's nice to feel like I have folks looking after me. Having everyone around like this, I'm not even thinking about all this scroll shit so much.

"Don't be pushing my shit back," I tell D Low. One of the clippers in his hand sparks to life, and he works his magic on my sideburns and neckline. I don't really trust people to cut my hair, but the way my shit is looking hella rough, I ain't had no choice in the matter. Plus, D Low be on this whole "holistic self-care" when it comes to his barbering skills.

"Keep talkin', I'll have yo ass lookin' like George from *The Jeffersons.*"

"This stupid portal is down! I swear, if the class is full, I'm gonna be soooo mad." Alexis grunts, tapping on her tablet. "I'm trying to sign up for memory spellcasting class in the fall."

"Good luck with that," Savon tells her, lounging on the couch and filing their nails. "You know that class is hella selective. Try the botany one."

Alexis sucks her teeth and tosses her tablet to the side. "The website keeps crashing. Everybody would choose today to try to last-minute pick their fall classes."

"Wheeeew, chile, I'm so ready for the semester to be over!" Savon says. "Because all these professors got me bumped. I'm ready to be on my droppin'-it-like-a-thottie vibes." They start to twerk, making us all cut up, laughing.

"I wish I could get into the memory class. But you gotta be an upperclassman, or so good that they'll bypass all the rules," Elijah says.

"Who teaches that?"

They all throw a look my way.

"Your favorite person on this whole campus," Savon jokes. "Chancellor Bonclair."

"He only allows a few selected people in that class," D Low adds, putting the brush to the side of my temple. "He got that shit locked the hell down."

"Facts," Elijah comments. "But on the real, we all got, like, close to 5.0 GPAs, and we still can't get in."

"Then how the hell Donja get in?" I ask Alexis.

"Chile, I don't know. I guess he done met his ancestor. You know he all Kreyol and shit. He tapped in early, and Chancellor thought he'd be good in the class. The only freshman to do so."

Me and D Low glance at each other.

"Shit, what I'm really ready for next semester"—he starts to stomp and clap like he's in the fraternity—"I'mma pledge the Jakutas."

"House of Transcendence for me, dahling," Savon says, then goes to their phone to strike up a status on the CaimanTea app. They show Alexis, and they start kiki-ing.

"If there be a next semester. Since homeboy almost got clutched by the Bokors, y'all think they gonna make it back on the campus?" Elijah up and asks. He's on his phone, scrolling. D Low leans down. Getting eye-level to give my top some TLC from his sharp clippers.

"Nope. We'd know if they was. Y'all heard the stories."

A collective stillness.

Elijah grabs a bag of Garden Salsa SunChips. "People died . . . a lot of them. Plus, there're still some that follow them and believed in what they were doing. You know Professor Slaten caught ole boy Dante drawing their vèvè, right?"

Savon looks at him, wide-eyed. "You lyin'?"

Alexis throws her two cents in. "With this school, you never know."

"Some girl on the CaimanTea app says it was one of her lil' cousins that got snatched up, and they found her a day later. Her magic stripped from her."

"Like, what the hell do they want? Y'all lost the first time, you wanna lose again?"

I take in their conversation, still feeling the burn of my attack. Savon's eyes drift to me real subtle-like, then back to their phone.

"I ain't gon' hold you, this shit kinda nerve-wracking."

Alexis jumps in. "Don't worry, y'all. We're protected here."

"Wish there was something we can do on the outside world, thooough," D Low says. He hands me a mirror to check out his masterpiece. No lie, shit is tight.

"Well, Chancellor Bonclair already shot me down." Alexis grabs her tablet, attempting the portal once again. "I'm tired of asking him for us with magic to actually go out into the community and help these people."

Her phone dings. She checks it, rolling her eyes.

"Who's that?" I ask.

Savon quickly grab it. "I knooooow Damone Cartier is not callin' you still."

His face flashes in my brain. The way he stalked off after asking me that favor. *Tell Alexis, whenever she's ready, she has a place with us. She will never have to feel like she's fighting two battles again.*

"He just wants me to think about—"

Savon interrupts her. "Absolutely not. He was already trending on social media because he got into it with that pastor online."

"You talkin' about Pastor Prentis, the woman who has been on one talking about magic and witchcraft is a part of white supremacy?"

"That's her. Gworl—she's doing the most. Right along with that Aiden Dupont too."

I grab a broom, sweeping the hair off the floor. Everybody cutting up, laughing, when Savon screams, "Yes! I got the classes I want. These muhfuckas ain't stoppin' me!"

The doorbell rings.

"You a fool, Savon," I say, traveling over to the door.

When I answer it, everything in me tenses.

Alexis and everybody quiets down as we see that there's a police officer at our front door.

"You must be Malik Baron," he says, taking off his sunshades. "I'm Antwan Bivins."

I turn back to everybody. They on guard. "How did you—?"

"I used to be a student at this school. Let's say I have alumni rights. Can we go somewhere and talk?"

CHAPTER TWENTY-EIGHT

THE POLICE SHOWING UP AT YOUR DOOR CAN'T BE A GOOD sign. Especially the one who has magical powers.

We're deep off by the quad. This Antwan dude sits down on one of the benches, pulling off his dark shades. "I'm not here for no trouble. I just . . . can't believe they found you. Mama Aya talked about you a lot. For years she was trying to come up with a hex to locate you." He pauses, then turns off his radio static. "There's been some more activity going on in town. Dark, baneful magic."

I don't know why he's telling me this.

"I came to warn you, Malik." His voice stoops low, real low, into a whisper. "The Bokors are clearly here for something, and I just want you to know that you can't trust everybody."

"Okay . . . well, that won't be a problem anyway, because I don't trust nobody. And I think we *all* know what they're here for: the Scroll of Idan."

"You're right about that. They've been looking for that to fully make themselves whole again ever since the war over a hundred and twenty years ago." A pause. "How are you doing here at Caiman?"

I lie. "Uhhh. Everything's cool. I'm about to be on my way to class."

"I know what it's like to be plucked out of somewhere and

dropped into a world you don't know. Or that you didn't know existed. They make you feel some type of special. But it's no different here than outside in the real world."

"I was dropped in this world. But it's cool."

He scoffs. "This world may look cool and magical, but I wouldn't trust it if I were you."

Tsk. "This comin' from a cop?"

His expression changes. "Look, we're not all the same."

"Yeah, that's what they all say. Until they're throwing ya ass against a car. Trust. I had my run-ins with them."

"That's why I became a cop, Malik, to change the way things are."

"Can't change something that's been built off the backs of niggas. You a part of the system."

"I get it. The system's broken—"

"Nah. You don't get it; this system is doin' exactly what it was designed to do."

I grab my shit and start to walk off.

"My mama didn't have any magic, but my daddy did."

I pause, wondering for a second about my own dad, if he had magic too. I'm used to not really thinking about that man, since it's not like thinking about him would change that he's got zero to do with my life. I turn around to hear what else Antwan has to say. "And here they want you to be full, or they will treat you different. Let me guess, Taron treats you like an outsider?"

That question feels like a knife in my back. Because Chancellor Taron's been on one since the day I met him. But I won't let this Antwan dude see it.

"Everybody treated me different except for your mama."

Everything in me stops.

"She was a good friend, your mama. A very good friend. Hell, me, her, Taron used to be friends. We were the clique."

"You talkin' about the Divine Elam?"

His face flushes.

"Look, man, you don't know me. I don't know you, but I'm trynna figure out what happened with my mama."

He looks around, then steps up closer, whispering, "Well, you definitely came to the right place for that."

"What do you mean by that?"

He sucks his teeth. "Your mother and Taron—there are secrets you should know. Secrets about them and what happened here when we were all in school. I just want you to be careful, Malik."

"That's what everybody telling me, but ain't shooting it straight with me. I know to be careful, but what I need to know is the truth."

Antwan looks down like he's gathering his thoughts, but before he says anything, royal purple clouds spring from the ground. Chancellor Taron steps out of it like he's on a mission.

"What are you doing here?" he asks Antwan.

"I just came to talk and meet the infamous Malik Baron."

The tension between them is hella thick.

"How did you even get through the barrier?" Chancellor Taron pulls him to the side and whispers. Both of them start arguing under their breath.

"Despite what you and everybody else believe, magic *still* runs through my veins, Taron," Antwan hisses.

"Well, you certainly don't act like it."

Antwan steps to him. Both of them size each other up with chins raised and locked eyes. "Wow. You think you're really all that since they made you chancellor, huh?"

"I earned it."

Another scoff from Antwan. "You ain't earned shit, Taron. That privilege you were born into bought you a lot more than this damn title."

"Okay, that's enough. Malik, get to class—"

"He needs to know to protect himself," Antwan throws out.

"I need to know what?" I ask, stepping up to them. "Tell me!"

"Antwan." The chancellor's voice gets hella deep. "I'm warning you."

"Nah. I wanna know. Ever since I got here, y'all been talking in riddles, and I'm tired of this shit! Where the hell is my mama?! Antwan, you know . . ."

Antwan throws a hard look to Chancellor Taron, then to me. Wanting to say something so bad. "Malik, there's been some killings in Alabama. We've been getting calls, and they're getting closer."

I'm sure a look of shock washes over my face. "Killings in Alabama? Where?"

A conflicting moment. Antwan looks like he's struggling to say it. "Your old neighborhood. The Hudson family and—"

For some reason, my heart drops. Carlwell . . . Sonya . . . dead?

"Thank you for the message. We'll send our condolences," Chancellor Taron says.

"This seems targeted, Taron. The Bokors—" Antwan says.

"It's being handled," Chancellor Taron interrupts.

"You can't ignore this, even if your mother wants to save face with all the tribes."

Chancellor Taron turns from him, grabbing me. "Mr. Baron, get to class—"

"Nah, you know where my mama is at?"

I say that all loud. Everybody in the quad stops and looks at us.

"He deserves the truth, Taron!" Antwan shouts.

Chancellor Taron whips his hand forward, making Antwan disappear outside the wall of the campus boundary spell.

"Everyone, back to class. NOW!" Chancellor Taron barks.

People scurry off like roaches. Chancellor Taron gives me a real mean mug before walking off. "Go back to your dorm, Mr. Baron."

"Fuck you!"

He gets into my face. "Go back to your dorm, now!"

My breathing and heartbeat elevate, and above in the sky, a rumbling sounds. Thunder. I feel the blue swirl run up and down my arm. Even the wind picks up around us, howling.

Suddenly, the sky clears, and the blue magic around my hands ceases like fire from the rain.

And I do the unthinkable. I just walk off.

• • • •

Back in my dorm room, I slam shit around and pace back and forth, thinking of a way to find a loophole in Chancellor Taron's hex.

Think, Malik.

An idea pops into my head. I'm not sure this gon' work, but I'm finna get creative. My fingers tap rapidly on my phone. The Face-Time screen chimes that special noise.

Taye's face pops up on the screen. "Waaaduuup!"

"Taye, do me a favor."

"Whatchu trynna do?"

"Just do it."

"What I need to do?"

I love how he's on my bullshit. "A'ight. Put your phone on the ground and take a step back."

His video shakes, indicating that he has put the phone on the ground. Shout-out to Professor Kumale for teaching a brotha some new dope matter configuration theory. With my eyes closed, I just imagine myself getting sucked into the phone, tying myself to the image on Taye's screen. This spell, I don't say words; I just think it.

This time I'm on my Afrofuturist *ish.*

My entire essence becomes pixelated, sucking every part of me into the phone. I feel my body stretch apart and rejoin in one swift blur. Taron can stop me from teleporting, but he can't stop me from traveling via good ole wireless data.

"Whoa!" Taye screams, jumping back. "How the hell you do that?"

I notice that I'm standing in front of him. "I just thought of it."

"You gotta do that again."

"Later," I tell him.

We both run down the stairs to find Mama Aya sitting on the couch in the living room. Her eyes are closed. But when I turn the corner, she wakes up.

"Chile, what is you doin' here?"

"Antwan came by the school. Telling me about my old neighborhood."

Her eyes shift, internally wishing I didn't know that. "Does Taron know you here? Now, Malik, baby, you don't want to get in—"

"Is it true? Carlwell and Sonya dead?"

She slowly peels back from the chair. A slow, grim beat grows between us before she says anything. "Yes, baybeh. They are."

Me and Taye clock each other.

"Taye—"

He recoils and crosses to the bottom of the stairs. *Fuck . . .*

Carlwell was low-down as hell, but a part of me feels bad he had to go out like that. And Sonya too. And Taye doesn't deserve to know death. I never wanted him to be exposed to something like that.

"The Bokors ain't playing no games," I tell her, having to sit down from the weight of the news.

"Whoever did bring them back, they playin' with real dark majik."

The tone in her voice sends a chill up my spine. She wraps her shawl tighter around her whole body.

"Mama Aya—they've gotta be after the scroll. If you know where it is, you could be in danger."

She sighs. "You let me worry about all that, okay? You'll be safe at school."

"Nah, I gotta go back to the Hudsons'. Then back to my old neighborhood. I gotta see what's going on."

"No, baby, we don't know what's out there. . . ."

"I need to go back," I argue. "I need answers. My mama could be out there. And maybe we can find clues to where she's at."

After a beat, Mama Aya stands up and crosses over to the screen door and out on the porch.

She gives me the palm of her hand. "We gon' go together."

I grab hold of it, feeling the gust of wind. "Together."

CHAPTER TWENTY-NINE

GOD BLESS THE BROKEN ROAD THAT KEEPS ON LEADING ME back home.

Because after me and Taye left for our new life, I never thought I'd be back here. But being at Caiman U, I realized that Alabama is a part of me, and I'm a part of it.

Me and Mama Aya materialize right outside the Hudsons' house. The entire neighborhood looks as if it was drowned in sadness. No badass kids. No nosey neighbors. Just a haunting wind breezing.

The house looks even shittier, and Simmsville is all drained of color and life. Caution tape decorates the entire yard, warding off any trespassers. I rub my fingers against the side of my jeans.

Death was here to collect.

"That Antwan dude wasn't lying," I tell Mama Aya.

She goes to touch the caution tape with her eyes closed. Her expression hardens as the thick ripple of energy appears around her hands. "Dark bane magic is all around here."

The fact that she's shuddering right now, some shit about to go down.

Both of us step up to the house, looking back.

"We can't just walk in," Mama Aya says.

"You right."

She does this little hand gesture. Simple and elegant. Suddenly, time slows. A grayish-white cloud makes us invisible to the outside world in case anybody shows up or rides by.

I look to Mama Aya, impressed.

"You gotta teach me that."

"C'mon," she says, chuckling to herself. "We ain't got much time."

Inside the Hudsons' house, it's ransacked. Chairs turned over. Glass all over the place. Busted TV and fresh dents in the walls. The feeling of dread is even stronger in here. A ghostly memory of me choking the hell out of Carlwell right before me and Taye arrived in Louisiana plays out in front of me.

"They were here, huh?"

Mama Aya doesn't answer; she just paces back and forth, mumbling something under her breath. Her hands release waves of dark energy.

In my own investigation, I flip through the same pile of bills. A cigarette, barely smoked, is lazily placed on the table.

Carlwell's dusty ass is in his chair, flicking through the sports channel, when there's a knock at the door. With a slight grumble, Carlwell calls for Sonya.

"Answer the dayyum door!" he says through a fit of coughs.

Sonya crosses into the living room through a cloud of smoke, rolling her eyes at Carlwell. *"You sittin' right there; you could've answered it."*

Carlwell cusses her out in a mumbling breath.

As soon as she opens the door, *BLAM!* Sonya's whole body flies from the impact of an explosive telekinetic force. She crashes against the wall, bleeding out, dead. Carlwell ducks out of his chair and dives, scrambling to get away. Then he turns to look who's coming in, probably thinking it's a robber—but no, it's a dark entity entering the room. It floats a few feet from the ground in a long, tattered cloak.

"What the hell you want?!" Carlwell shouts at the Bokor.

At the head—he pulls his cloak, revealing that twisted face with red eyes. The same one from the Haitian Revolution.

The leader.

A decrepit hand reaches toward a terrified Carlwell.

"Please don't do this! Don't do this!!!"

Snap! Carlwell's neck is broken from an invisible force. Instant death.

The leader motions for the rest of the Bokors to enter, and they ransack the entire place, looking for something. Then a blast of green light sends me out of the memory and right back in the living room, breathing hard. Mama Aya's eyes drift to me, and her soft hands meet my cheeks.

"Baybeh, you all right?"

My focus lands on the spot where dried blood stains the carpet. "I saw his death. I saw both of their deaths."

"This was where you was at too?"

Just a nod.

Her hands land on my shoulders, giving me a gentle brush. "Show me where you grew up. I got a good mind on somethin'."

I shoot her a worried look. "Okay."

• • • •

Liberty Heights looks even more in disarray.

Most of the houses are abandoned. Rusty old cars lie dormant across the yards like they're open graveyards. Especially Ms. Doll's house. This is kinda weird, having just been here a month ago, when it didn't look like this. When I step back to look at the whole neighborhood, the houses lined up on either side of the street, it seems like a whole tornado ransacked its way through here.

"This where y'all was? This whole time?" Mama Aya asks me, confused. She looks around as if she's in a different world. Even her hand hovers in midair.

"You feeling something?"

"Not ya mama's majik, that's for sure. But I feel somethin' familiar, yes."

Mama Aya's eyes are still closed, and she hums to herself.

"Whatever majik was cast here ten years ago, it was some real strong stuff."

She drifts over to the built-up gate that leads to my old house and goes still as the memory clouds over her. It's a funny thing about memory. For me, every little thing can trigger it. Smells. The way certain things look. Things just flood in my mind, things from my childhood.

At first, it's the smell of the fresh-cut grass, then the ringing of the ice cream truck. Mama leaning on the porch, cackling with some other aunties from backstreet. Instinctively, I walk to the spot where the same blue blow-up pool would be. The memory echoes, and I hear laughter. I hear songs riding on the wind. Looking down at my hands, I see the calluses from holding on to my bike's handlebars for too long.

The sun, high in the sky, shines bright until . . .

It all fades into the burned, crisp bodies.

"Malik," Mama Aya says. "Baybeh, come back to me."

I'm outside my childhood home, holding on to the gate. I ain't realize it, but my body does before my mind does. My magic chokes the air, and the gate in front of us dissolves.

Using my magic, the door swings right open. Dust swirls, and light filters into the living room. Everything is still here. Our couches, lamps, everything beyond the blast zone. I didn't expect this stuff to be here after nearly ten years. Abandoned. Just like how I felt for all these years.

Touching the walls, feeling the rugged edges of it, I think that it doesn't seem like how it would look on the outside.

"I remember I used to run around here, getting on my mama's nerves all the time."

Mama Aya's concerned eyes drift from me back to the entire living room.

"I guess after that went down, nobody wanted to live here no more. With the dead bodies."

As soon as my hand touches the wall again, the memory comes

to life right in front of me. The chipped walls become like new, and the room slowly rewinds to a night when I was seven years old. I'm running all through the house. Being bad as hell. Mama is in the kitchen, frying golden-brown chicken, talking on the phone to Auntie Coretta while the TV plays reruns of *Family Guy*.

My energetic younger self sits on the floor, playing with my toys: Spider-Man and Superman. I remember those. I would make them fight.

"You can't win!" My younger self crashes the two toys together. Then everything goes quiet.

Mama is still in the kitchen on the phone.

My younger self makes the toys float in midair in that same blue cloud as the way my magic manifests.

Just like magic . . .

Wait . . .

Both the toys disintegrate into nothing but ash. Here I thought my power manifested that night on the Fourth of July.

I've *always* had magic.

How did I forget this?

Soon as my mama rips into the living room, the toys become whole again, and the memory fades back into the fucked-up reality of chipped walls. Ripped-up carpet, busted-out windows, mountains of dust, and my mama gone.

Pain sears all through me as I trek through this brokenhearted museum.

"You showed it at a young age," Mama Aya says to me. She walks around the living room, looking. Studying everything. Touching the walls. "The Kaave."

I turn to her, eyes welling up. "You could see that?"

"Memory is a powerful thing. Those early flickers of yours didn't reach me, but as you got older, it just got stronger. I see why that led me to finally finding you. The ancestas blessed you with Kaave."

She points to my hands, the blue vapor swirling around them.

I close my fists, making it disappear.

Something in the air changes. Mama Aya cocks her head, alert. She walks over to the wall, where a large crack snakes down to the floor.

I bend down to where the crack meets the floor and remove the singed rug. It's a cutout on the floor that outlines a trapdoor. Me and Mama Aya hover our hands in midair, her eyes rolling to the back of her head.

Finally, she whispers, "Let it be revealed. . . ."

Her magic and mine pulsates around the room, and just like that, the floor disappears, revealing a hidden compartment underneath the house. It's full of stuff. Mojo bags. Books. Letters.

"Chile, that's my grimoire." She grabs it and dusts it off. "I knew she done stole this."

Something else catches my attention. A piece of paper with a drawing of a tree that's reminiscent of Mama Aya's yard, and a long gold necklace on top of the paper. The same necklace from my dreams. Soon as I touch it, energy buzzes around the room, and a gust of wind whips around us.

"Mama's pendant and—"

Mama Aya takes the piece of paper. Shakes her head. "She was tryin' to make a map to the scroll." She smacks her lips. "She knew I was never gonna tell her, so she stole my grimoire and tried to track it down. That girl, always meddling in things she ain't had no business in."

Both of us, drowning in the moment, just sit in stillness at the revelation.

Crack! We both turn, seeing the walls line with cracks, raining down plaster. Spewing through the crooked lines are a river of blood. It spits out like a running faucet. Then, out of nowhere, white flowers bloom. Small. Milky-looking.

"What's happenin'?"

Mama Aya edges away from the wall. "The datura flowers. Very poisonous. They can subdue our magic, renderin' us powerless."

Fuck . . .

Small vines push out the walls and ceiling. They inch toward us in hunger. Mama Aya waves her hands toward them; a bright light emits between her fingers.

Instantly, the flowers wither away.

"We need to go now," she warns.

We hear a commotion outside.

I grab the necklace and map as we rush out of the room and back outside to see folks running all kinda wild. A cardinal rule in the hood: when Black folks start running, you drop whatever the fuck you are doing and dip out that bitch without question. Because they are either running from the po-po, or some shit about to go down.

Either way, just fucking run.

The sounds of chaos—rumbling wind, yelling, screaming—swirl in the distance. A kid on a bike pedals so fast, it's like he's moving at the speed of light. Behind him, turning the corner of the street, is a figure in a dark cloak.

My focus back on the little boy. He looks so scared. The riotous energy in the air is mirrored in his eyes. Of course, the kid can't be no more than seven.

Another set of cloaked figures appears from a cloud of smoke. Blinding green light orbs around their crinkly fingers.

The Bokors.

"Malik—" Mama Aya warns me. "We gotta save that chile!"

"Right, we can't leave him." Maybe Alexis is right. What's the point of having these abilities if we can't help our own? This is the time right here. Right now. I curl my hand into a fist, feeling the electrical current of my magic orbit my fingers.

The rest of the Bokors part, and the leader makes his way to the front. And something in me clicks.

In the middle of all of this, I finally feel it. The boy's magic, manifesting. It's crazy because I never knew anybody else in Helena, Alabama, that had magic. And here I am, right now, seeing this little boy's magic manifest right before my eyes, and the Bokors sense it, too. And they're here to steal it.

I turn to Mama Aya. "They trynna steal his magic, Mama Aya. I can feel it."

Obscured by hooded black cloaks that drag along the concrete ground, the Bokors advance on the boy. The more they walk, the more I can hear a drum bang with rhythm, just like in Haiti. Everything around them dies. The flowers. The grass.

The kid yells, tears streaming down his face. "Mama!"

It takes a moment for my brain to realize. I was led here for a reason. I was led here to help this little boy. Help him in a way that nobody helped me when my magic first manifested.

This little Black boy deserves better. He don't deserve to have this stolen from him.

We've had too much stolen from us already.

Sweat and fear decorate his brown face. His chest moves up and down with a quickness. I know he's trying his hardest not to make no sudden moves, doing everything in his natural power not to become another whisper in our magical world.

He don't deserve to be another casualty that the Kwasan tribe just sweeps under the rug.

The boy's deep brown eyes grow wide when I step in front of him like a shield. A protection hex spills from my mouth in a soft whisper. My magic vibrates against my bones. It radiates from my pores.

Like a robot, the leader of the Bokors stares down at me. I don't even move. I continue to stand as a shield in front of the boy. Hands balling up, feeling the Kaave swell between my palms.

"I knew you'd come back," the leader finally says. His voice is gruff, kind of like Carlwell's, but with a slight Kreyol accent.

Around us there is a gust of unnatural wind. All too quick, my hands twist, feeling the magic activate all over my body. Every muscle relaxes, and vibrations stream all over my arm. I flick my wrist on instinct, and the leader screams. Bones breaking. Hands reel back, pained.

The streetlights flicker and strobe, adding to the confusion. *What. The. Hell—* My hands tingle as dark magic sweeps over Liberty Heights.

Every house I bobbed and weaved through, or had secret laughs

310

in with the other kids in the neighborhood, starts to crumble and disintegrate. I hear folks scream inside, dying.

Oh shit! I glance to Mama Aya. Her eyes widen with surprise as we watch the Bokors get in formation for an attack.

"Malik, the more folks they kill, the stronger they get," Mama Aya says beside me.

The realization dawns on me. "First the Hudsons. And now this. It's a trap. They knew I would come. They think we can lead them to the scroll."

A violent wind erupts. The houses around us continue to crumble.

I look down at the boy, his eyes fixated on us like we're heroes in his favorite Marvel movie.

I finish the last part of the protection spell. Sparkles of purple particles surround him. "Run!" I tell him.

The boy darts off on his bike without question, and he's gone in the blink of an eye. Mama Aya turns back to me, probably about to tell me the same thing. "No, Mama Aya. I'm not running."

Back on the leader—he narrows his scary bloody eyes and cracks a grin. Like he's a man possessed.

Mama Aya stands her ground. "You ain't got business here."

"Nou fè sa, prèt yo."

His voice is deep, raspy, and demonic-sounding.

"I can drive you back to where you came from; you know I can."

The leader looks shook as hell. *"Nou sèlman vle yon sèl bagay, ak yon sèl bagay sèlman."*

My index finger taps the tip of my tongue, using a small hex to understand him.

His voice echoes in my head in English. *We only want one thing, and one thing only.*

"And what is that?" Mama Aya asks.

His eyes drift over to me, and he points, just like back at the Haitian Revolution. *"Pitit pitit ou a."*

Your grandson.

My heart stammers in my chest, feeling his dark magic shrouding me.

Mama Aya chuckles. "If you think you gon' touch my grand-baybeh, you got another thang comin'."

In a speed of light, one of the Bokors flicks his wrist toward me and Mama Aya. Long, sharp black tendrils burst out of his hand.

I get in my fighting stance, just like in Dr. Akeylah's and Professor Kumale's defense class. With a flick, I make the metal on the cars bend and twist. Glass shatters into a million pieces.

Between all of us, magic rips the concrete in half.

The leader of the Bokors looks right to me. His thumb and middle finger snap. With the telekinesis spell, a whole car is thrown toward Mama Aya and me. She blinks us away, and we crash against the side of the house.

Mama Aya utters a spell, and the folks that's standing outside all freeze up with a grayish color in their eyes. "That takes care of the regular folks."

With a casual menace, the Bokors march toward us.

Mama Aya moves with a majestic stride right to the middle of the street, creating a standoff between her and the Bokors. Combat hexes bounce off the cars, homes, sounding like bombs dropping.

Her magic flows from her like an explosion. The cars lurch forward, the trees bend, and I now know Mama Aya ain't nothing to play with.

She sends some of the Bokors in the air, making them crash against the trees. Orbs of greenish-black magic are thrown at her like firebombs. Just like at the dodgeball game, my hands instantly go up, and they all slow down; I block them from hitting her.

I whip the orbs around, sending that shit right back to the Bokors. They all dodge them. Together, me and Mama Aya are like the Avengers. Going to war. The Bokors try to get us down, but they ain't got shit on us. They all form a circle around the leader, trying to outnumber us.

Nobody makes the first move. Then, the sound of buzzing. In

the distance, a swarm of buzzing locusts comes out of nowhere. They stop in midair.

Everything quiets down.

When I look at the leader, I see his hand twirl.

"Oh hell naw!"

The evening sky instantly becomes dark, like a blanket been put over the setting sun. Thousands of locusts come swooping down, and me and Mama Aya lift our hands. Using our magic to block them from swarming around us.

She whips her hand back, sending the army of locusts back toward the leader, who, in turn, makes them disappear. One of the Bokors sends a line of flames toward me and Mama Aya. But in defense, Mama Aya claps her hands so hard, the wind from her fingers puts the fire out instantly.

She and the leader start to go at it.

The leader sends another spell block toward Mama Aya. His magic manifests in a ribbon of reddish-black color. All the glass from the houses explodes with magic. She's too quick, though. He tries again, but she just continues to block it.

Mama Aya's arms rise like she's preaching to a spirit-filled congregation. Her magic ripples under her Black skin like a mighty wave and stretches forth from her fingertips as if it were branches on a tree. From the torrent of wind, her dress billows, and a jet of light explodes from both Mama Aya and the leader of the Bokors. Her eyes are determined, and her jaw tenses as she clenches her hands into fists, making the air buckle and swell with energy.

Because of Mama Aya, I just knew that magic has always been ours.

Sparks of her magic blaze through the gray skies and drop down with one twisting motion of her hands. I focus on one of the Bokors on the ground. He siphons Mama Aya's invisible spell.

"*Parun!*"

One of the Bokors speeds to me. I twist around, dodging his stretched-out hands, and use my magic to make his whole body burst into little pieces.

As Mama Aya uses more of her magic, a ribbon of light bursts off the houses, and the splintered glass that rests on the ground rises like it has a mind of its own.

It rockets toward us. I blink fast, and the glass turns into sheets of rain. Suddenly, the ground beneath us shakes.

With Mama Aya, she doesn't have to say no spells. It just comes to her like breathing. From the ground, little black shapes come out. They circle and assemble into a tall figure, shifting and then turning into three werecats, same as my vision of Miriam.

The werecat things let out a sharp shriek.

And all three of them go straight for the Bokors. Snapping at them with their razor-sharp teeth, hoping to rip their flesh.

The leader and the Bokors move the hell outta the way, running wildly from the werecats.

My hands slam into the soil of Helena, Alabama, sucking the energy into me. Feeling the epic charge, I give off a supernova blast, like the Roman candles from my childhood. Like a bomb that went off, my magic sprouts out like stars of fire. Ricocheting and swirling around the Bokors, hindering them all from fighting back. A tall werecat rips into them like Thanksgiving dinner.

The leader shifts, snapping his fingers. Then, suddenly, he disappears in a cloud of inky-black smoke. Mama Aya whips her hand in the air, and the cats also disappear in a wall of mist.

CHAPTER THIRTY

THE CHAIN FROM MAMA'S PENDANT WRAPS AROUND MY fingers.

Ever since I found it, it has a hold on me like nothing else in this world. It's the only piece of her that reminds me of what was and what wasn't. But I will say, for the first time in the ten years of her being missing, this piece of jewelry makes me feel closer to my mama than anything.

Dread claws at me when I plant myself in the rocking chair on Mama Aya's porch.

The thought behind my mama being dead or alive starts to blur for me, no lie.

I push that to the back of my mind as I rock in this chair. It's something peaceful about sitting on the porch. The way the reflection of the evening sky meets the bayou waters, painting them in pink and oranges. Even the humid wind blows about the whole yard, whistling through the bottle tree.

A cough comes from the inside of the house.

Mama Aya walks out with a long and old-looking bedsheet with an array of patterns stitched on it. She doesn't have on her head wrap this time. Just beautiful, long luscious hair raining down past her shoulders.

I stand up to let her sit down. "You feeling all right?"

"I'm feeling just fine," she answers, rocking back and forth. Her voice cracks a bit, and her eyelids seem even heavier after the intense battle we just came back from in Bama. Really studying her now, I notice that a few wrinkles fold her skin in dark mahogany creases. "I wanna finish this quilt before the day's out."

There's a comb sticking from her hair. I grab it and part her hair, massaging her scalp.

"Thank you, baybeh," she says as I start to comb through her hair. "That's mighty fine indeed."

"What you got there?" I ask.

She continues to put the thread to the needle, finishing up an X-looking shape, reminiscent of the crossroads that I read about in my books from school. There are other shapes on there too. Some ovals, squares, and a bear claw. And then a bird. So much history embedded in this fabric.

Mama Aya inhales and points to the pink-and-orange swirl hanging in the sky. "Ever since I was a little girl, I'd watch my mama make these. She'd spend the rest of the night, when she wusn't workin' in da house with Massa and the Missus Johnson, threading this quilt. She say these patterns tells stories."

I point to a perfect sphere shape. "What's that bird-lookin' shape?"

Her eyes drift to me, and her lips crack a smile. "We call that Sankofa," she answers. "It means to the Akan tribe, 'Go back and get it,' or 'To retrieve what's been left in the past.' It's our memories, baybeh. Slave folk only had their memories to keep them going. They had memory of songs, of legends, that helped them to freedom. And it's the memory of folks who didn't make it across the ocean."

There's another shape that catches my attention. It's the shape of a boat riding along waves. "These are messages, aren't they?"

"You see them clouds there?" she asks, shifting her light brown eyes to the glitter of gold dancing across the bayou water. "That's God's work. You see, God got magic too. He sho'll do."

A simple yet tired chuckle escapes her pursed lips. Her laugh feels like a soft hum along my skin. And her shaky hand softly pats my hand with an unspoken confirmation.

"He shows us every day. He shows us the beauty by paintin' the sky. Lettin' the moon and the sun take turns to bless the darkness. Most folks don't even pay attention to his work of art. They try ta denounce, sayin' that it's galaxies or all this stuff creatin' it. But they just don't know everythin' that's created has to have a creator. Even magic. Magic is all around us, baybeh. Even when we don't wanna believe."

Growing up the way I did, I'm not so sure I even believe that there is a God. If he did exist, he wouldn't let a little boy like me cry himself to sleep, thinking he was alone in this world when he wasn't.

"Life is somethin', baybeh. It gives ya lemons, and ya got to make lemonade. I watched my mama, a beautiful Black woman with glory and frustration in her dark skin, spin gold from her fingers." From the side of Mama Aya's face, I see a tear fall. "She useta say, 'We as a people always had to make a kingdom out of nothing.' A kingdom built on the bones and the river of blood from those who came before us, and those who comes after.'"

A mental image of Miriam running through the woods pops into my head.

Her intense expression warms my bones.

"She healed the sick, she brought life into this world, and she helped usher folks to the next life. She had somethin' down inside her nobody could take away. She believed in the water. She believed in the land too. She always say, 'Both the land and the water got they secrets that they hide from the world.' She say, 'I believe in the water because that's where our freedom is. Cuz our enemies, whoever they may be, will try to build everythin' they have on the bones of those less fortunate. For a time, they cup will runneth over with the river of blood. Though it may linger, the bones will turn to ash, just to salt the ground they'll walk on. And the blood, it'll turn bitterness from vengeance. Their kingdom will fall. Yes, Lawd.'"

Through the stretch of silence, I just continue to comb through her hair, choking back the gravity of it all. "I ain't got a lot of regrets in my life. Cuz I sho'll lived a long time. Not getting to watch my grandbaby grow up into this *beautiful* young Black man I'm seein' right now is somethin' I ain't gon' never forgive myself for."

With tears falling out of her eyes like diamonds, she grabs my hand and kisses it softly.

Hearing her talk like this got me floored. Got me in my feelings.

"*Baybeh,* sometimes you got to get to the root of things. Find out what's planted deep inside ya that's rottin', and you pluck it. Only then can you fill it with good things that'll spring forth everythin' you need in this life. The world may be fallin' down round us, but best believe we gon' laugh, we gon' dance, and we gon' be family. That's how we've been for generations. No matter how much hate, how much pain they throw at us, we always gon' rise. Resilience is a form of magic . . . that's in our blood, chile, and that's somethin' they ain't gon' neva take away. Ya hear me?"

"Yes, ma'am. I hear you." I just keep combing her hair and allow her words to haunt me from every turn. I place my hand on her shoulders. A warm feeling swells inside me. "Mama Aya—"

"When yo mama left and snatched you outta my arms, chile, I had so much turmoil inside me. I held on to it until I had to let it go. I can't bring back the time we lost, but I'm grateful that the Lawd gave me a second chance." Shit. Tears fall out of my eyes now. "I love you, baybeh. . . ."

I wanna say it back. It's there. It's on the tip of my tongue, waiting to leave my mouth. But I just can't.

"Now get on back to this kitchen, chile. It's still a lil' tight," she says, laughing and continuing to thread the quilt.

And I start to comb the back of her head again as a million thoughts race across my mind.

"So, what we gon' do about the Bokors?"

She hums something under her breath. "In due time."

"And my mama? I know you two disagreed on a lot, but if she was looking for the scroll, they might have kidnapped her and forced her to help them or somethin'. It doesn't matter what she did back then; if she's out there, we have to help her."

Before Mama Aya can answer, purple smoke swirls in the yard. Chancellor Taron appears right along with Dr. Akeylah and Professor Kumale. The chancellor looks soooo pissed at me. His eyes grow tight with resolve as he steps onto the porch.

"I will deal with you later," he mumbles before going inside the house. Dr. Akeylah softly pats me on the shoulder and then follows him.

Ah, shit. My ass is definitely in trouble.

"Lemme go talk to him," Mama Aya says, and makes her way inside.

"Heard you had a run-in with the Bokors?" Professor Kumale asks, smiling from the corner of the porch.

Hmmph. "Yeah, I guess . . . if that's what you call it. It's crazy how they found us. I just went to my old neighborhood, and they showed up out of nowhere."

"Well, it's a lot of magic there. Memories are energy, and when you tap into it, it can become quite powerful to deal with."

The door bursts open, and Chancellor Taron glides out the door, huffing and puffing. "Mr. Baron, back to campus now!"

I know better than to try to argue.

I go to hug Mama Aya. "Think about wha' I said. And hey. We did the thing, huh?"

"We did, baby. Of course we did," she says, laughing. We even try a handshake.

"Uhhh . . . you'll get it."

She hugs me again, and I feel her hands shake against my back.

• • • •

Something on me burns, and it wakes me out of my sleep. It's the necklace. It's brimming with energy. I peel it from my neck and throw it on the bed. After studying talismans, I know that sometimes they have lingering power from the conjurer themselves stuck inside of them.

So, maybe my mama's magic still has an effect on it.

Like glowing embers, the necklace vibrates with a green-to-black light.

When I go to touch it again, it feels like my whole body got hit by a train. I'm sucked into some kind of vision, and everything around me is cold and dark.

A buzzing noise. Up ahead, a long hallway stretches before me, lost in the shadows. Rows of doors on each side, with cracked and peeled-off paint, stand in deadening silence. Something about this whole place got me feeling some type of way. The light flickers.

With hesitation, I approach a white door and look through the small window showcasing darkness on the other side. A tall shape jumps right at me! Oh shit! I stumble back, falling on the floor, hitting my head. Everything goes blurry. A sharp, shrill ringing pierces the inside of my ears.

A loud banging reverberates when I look to the door.

I back up at the sound, feeling a cold chill up my spine.

"Malik!" A voice rangs in my ear.

My whole body whirls around, trying to find the source of the sound.

"Malik!" the voice screams again.

Instantly, my eyes well up with tears. "Mama!"

I'm looking all around me. Everywhere. The walls. The doors. The flickering light that's about to give out. Her voice rings through again, sounding off everywhere. Reaching me from the dark corners of the hall. "Malik!!! Baby, I'm here!"

My eyes land on the door right in front of me. Something on the other side bangs so loud, it doesn't seem natural.

It stops.

"Mama?" I say aloud.

A quick pause. Then a psychic blast throws my whole body against the wall. Pain sears through every part of me. Shaking it off, my body tingles on a thousand as everything goes back to blurry.

This time it's heavy energy. Dark. Twisted.

Just like how I felt with the Bokors.

"Malik, baby!" Mama's voice continues to ring through the empty hall.

My eyes land back on the door, seeing a hand slap against the window, then snatched away back into the room's darkness.

"Ma!!!"

And I wake up with a start in my room the next day. It takes a minute for my beating heart to calm down. In my hand is the necklace, and for the life of me, I got this gut feeling. Like one hundred percent assurance that what I'm feeling is real. I know one thing for certain.

I just connected with my mama!

I connected with my mothafuckin' mama!

• • • •

"I know what the hell I heard, a'ight!" I yell at Chancellor Taron. We teleport from campus back into Mama Aya's front yard through the bottle tree.

"Malik—"

I'm feeling all the feelings, while he's all cool, calm, and collected. Which is pissing me the hell off. "Mr. Baron, please calm down," he says, rubbing his eyes. "It was a dream, obviously."

"It was her. I know it. I felt it, and I connected to her. She's out there, alive, and trying to get back to me." My voice cracks as a lump forms in my throat, and I can feel my face flush with anger. Why doesn't he believe me?

He and Mama Aya stand on the porch, looking at me like I'm all kinds of crazy. But I'm not. I know what the hell I heard. And I know what the hell I saw. The distorted image pops back up in my head repeatedly.

And then her voice. Her sweet, sweet voice rings in my ears like bells.

"Maybe the Bokors have her."

"Baybeh," Mama Aya says weakly in her accent. "It was a dream."

"No, no, no, it didn't feel like it, Mama Aya. It didn't feel like a dream. It was her, her magic talking to me, traces connected to the necklace we found." Pacing around, I travel up to Chancellor Taron. "Maybe we can cast a locator spell or keep asking around." Then I take out the necklace to showcase it. "This. This is what brought me to her."

"Mr. Baron—"

I hop off the porch, into the yard. "My mama is alive, and the Bokors have her. I'm about to go fuck them up—"

"STOP THIS!" Chancellor Taron screams. "STOP!"

It feels like everything around us goes quiet. Chancellor Taron steps off the porch and comes closer. The expression on his face is something I've never seen before.

"You have been through something so traumatic. At such a young age." I want to argue, but his look is catching me way off guard. "You deserve more and better, and I know you have a hard time, but listen to me when I tell you this—your mother, she's gone. She's dead. Okay, and those Bokors . . . will do any and everything to trick you."

Everything in me explodes. "Don't fucking say that!"

"She's dead, Malik! She's gone, and you just have to let her go! You have to move on, because this will consume every part of you and leave nothing else!"

"Fuck you!" My voice cracks. "My mama ain't dead! And you don't give a damn about me, and you may have been friends with my mama, but you don't give a damn about her, either!"

"Mr. Baron, she died that night. She did. It was very traumatic for you, and I'm sorry, but you must let her go."

"Tell him, Mama Aya. She's not dead."

Her screams. Those muhfuckas that came in and attacked her.

It all crashes into me.

"Malik, baybeh." Mama Aya's voice cuts through the grief. "I saw how much it hurt you, thinking she was gone. And I couldn't help but ease that pain. But maybe I was wrong. I know you want to find her, but if your mama is really out there somewhere . . . well, she's been deep in this darkness for a long time now, and I—I don't know what you're going to find if you keep looking. Alive or dead, my daughter chose her path. If I had accepted that, stopped fighting it, maybe you and I wouldn't have lost all that time together. I just hope you can accept it too."

I stare at them, distraught. Maybe it's time to let go of this heaviness that I've been carrying for the past ten years. Because I am tired. I am tired of the dead ends. The secrets. The lies.

Hell, I am tired of holding on to the simple fact that, in the coldness of that dream, maybe she's dead. The Bokors killed her, and now they're out there, trying to kill me too.

Just like that moment, seeing her disappear in that blinding green light, she was gone. And like Professor Kumale said, if she was into something that she ain't had no business in—maybe she had to pay the price.

Magic always comes with a price.

And I can't spend whatever time I have left on what-ifs.

I have to move on.

But fuck this. I can't. And I won't. I'm gonna try to find that scroll for her, and bring her back, and get to destroy these Bokors for good.

If magic really comes with a price, I'm ready to pay it all.

CHAPTER THIRTY-ONE

WITH MAGIC, THERE'S A LOT OF THINGS YOU CAN DO. THINGS that you can't even dream of.

But magic can't give back the time I lost.

Or what's been stolen from me.

Black kids like me ain't afforded a childhood where you can just . . . be a kid. You gotta grow up early and deal with it the only way you know how: by sweeping that shit under the rug.

For the past two weeks, me and the crew been hanging out. Or, in my secret mission, upping my practice on defense. Savon leads the charge with teleporting to the right spot. Elijah and them show us their skills on ending up at the right spot to disengage our attackers.

Me and D Low practice hand-to-hand combat. He moves in a blur, but I'm faster. My body feels like it's ripped in a thousand ways as I body-slam him on the floor, pinning him down. Since we not trynna solely rely on our magic. Ass-whipping can come in all forms.

Chancellor Taron and the entire faculty has been on edge about the missing kids from the Ninth, but you can tell during Dr. Akeylah's class, she's trying to keep a straight face. Through the app, we all find out another person went missing, and then two more bodies of conjurers was found. And through the statuses of multiple people, Caiman U incoming class for the fall semester is looking real light next month.

With all of this and practicing with Professor Kumale, I'll be good when the Bokors come for us again. And with everything that's going on, I'm a hundred percent sure they will. Maybe I'm even wanting it a little, to finally get some of these answers to the questions tearing me apart. But I can't lie, that fire I had after my last talk with Taron to keep trying to find my mama at all costs doesn't always burn so hot, when I really think about what those costs could be. And what I've got in my life now too.

We have our finals, since it's almost the end of the summer semester. After that, we won't have to be back until the fall semester. We have a few weeks of freedom at the end of August to do whatever. Pool parties. Theme parks. Some of the crew said they wanna go to Georgia and go to Six Flags. Which I'll be down for, and I'm sure Taye would love to go too. Especially with his lil' girlfriend. He deserves to have fun, to relax. I don't know—maybe I do too. Especially after all this studying.

Dr. Akeylah gave our exam early for Intro to Black Magical Studies, where I had to jot down different incantations and then perform them, and we had to know fifty herbs and their purposes.

For Professor Kumale's class, we had to write a book report. I decided to write about the similarities between Christianity and Hoodoo in America. Zora Neale Hurston's *Mules and Men* was a great resource.

After class, me and Professor Kumale grab a quick bite to eat and sit outside in the courtyard. He seems a little quiet this time.

"You doing okay, Professor?"

He shakes a cup full of ice, mind clearly elsewhere. "Yeah. Today is hard. Sorry, I don't mean to be a drag."

"Nah. You good. I can go back to the dorm and leave you. You wanna be alone?"

"No, no. You're fine. It's just . . . it's my brother's death anniversary."

A long pause. I slink back in my chair, shaking my head.

"I'm sorry about your loss. You mentioned him before, but I didn't know he died."

"You really do remind me so much of him," he says, swallowing the pain. "He always had this smile—I mean, it could brighten the darkest days."

I think of Taye.

"What was his name?"

He clears his throat. "Kenson."

"What happened to him?"

The question spills out of me before I can catch it. Professor Kumale tries to compose himself, but his sadness is like a faucet.

"Born at the wrong place and the wrong time." His voice cracks. "People are often scared of what they don't understand. Or they take something that's extraordinary, and they try to snatch any and everything good about it."

I can only imagine if Taye was put in a situation where my magic couldn't save him.

"Magic always comes with a price . . . ," Professor Kumale whispers. "Just didn't know my brother would be the one to pay for it."

The truth penetrates the both of us.

I wouldn't do anything to put Taye in jeopardy or trade him to get more power. I rather give my magic away than to do that.

The question I've been plagued with: Why did my mama want power? I know she wanted to know about the forbidden spells, and betrayed the secrets of the Divine Elam. That map I still have up in my room is proof of that. Self-doubt of who she really was is strong today.

"Thanks again," I tell Professor Kumale.

He looks up, tears welling in his eyes. "For what?"

"For being a friend. A mentor. I'm not gonna lie to ya. I don't trust too many people. Growing up the way I did, you had no choice. But you were the first to be really nice to me when I got here."

"Malik, in my experience, it's not the actual hurt that is the most painful. It's the letting go. And you are not as broken as you think you are. You are talented, good, and one of the brightest young men I know. I truly mean that."

"That's the lesson I'm still trynna figure out." I give a resigned

326

nod. "Is the letting go. My mama been gone for a while, and some people think I should stop trying to figure out that night. But I'm not sure I can give up."

"Can I ask you a question?"

I nod.

"If you had one chance, would you bring her back? Even if it meant you had to do some unforgivable things."

I think on it for a second.

"If you'd asked me this a year ago, a hundred percent, yeah. And depends what day you catch me on, still could be yeah. But right now, to tell you the truth, I just don't know."

For me, it's hard to not see the brokenness. That little boy from Helena, Alabama, who had been broken and is still attempting to put back the broken pieces.

"Malik," he says. "That necklace was your mom's?"

"Yeah, it's kinda the only thing I have of her left. And a map."

His eyebrows crease. "Map?"

"Yeah, just studying it, it don't make a lot of sense. Bunch of scribbles and drawings. Seems like a certain part of it is missing. Like, she's gotten close, but . . ."

Kumale stares off into the distance. He seems so inside his head, I grab my phone. "Look, I'll give you your space."

"Yeah, sorry, I'm all over the place today. I'll see you in class."

"A'ight. Bet. Later, Professor."

CHAPTER THIRTY-TWO

ALL IS FAIR IN LOVE AND MAGIC.

Me and Alexis sit on the balcony, overlooking the campus that's bathed in orange-and-gold light from the setting sun. Alexis, with hair that defies gravity, looks to me with her deep brown eyes, causing my heart to pump blood everywhere. It takes me a minute, but I just stare at her. Clearly, there's a God, because I'm here. With her. Something that I've been dreaming of for ten years.

That lil' puppy-dog childhood crush is turning into something different the more we spend time together.

"It's beautiful," she says, noticing my mama's pendant around my neck. "It's like you have a piece of her right close to your heart."

"Yeah, still can't believe I found it."

A long pause between us.

"Shoot, I have to finish this speech."

"Read to me what you got," I tell her.

"You know I'm not a writer, but this just been heavy on my heart today," she says, sheepishly changing the subject. She holds a piece of paper in her hand like it's made of gold.

"I ain't gon' laugh. I promise."

A quick exhale, then she starts to read. "Dear Black girl, you are wrapped in gold. Your hair twists down your head like roots from a tree—you are wonderfully and fearfully made. You are the living image of God herself. Dipped in honey and mahogany. The standard, even when they try to tell you you're not. Black girl, you are the foundation. The lineage that holds a million generations."

While she reads, I just lose myself in her soft voice.

"Black girl magic is not just a hashtag. It's a spell conjured up from the mouths of our ancestors. Black girl, you are God herself. Queen mother. Sister. Cinnamon princess. The healer of wounds. The giver of life. You are. I am. We are. Infinite. The head and the tail. Your body is made like mountains for them to build themselves upon. You are wonderfully and—now I know—not fearfully made. Because their fear is not your fault. It's steeped in ignorance. And with that, they teach us to shrink ourselves. To disappear and not matter. They don't know we are the foundation that they try so hard to mutilate and even kill themselves to be like a . . . Black girl."

Her voice trails. Her face is frozen in contemplation as the words hang in the soft breeze.

"That's beautiful, Lex." My fingers lightly tapping on hers, tracing the lines in her hands.

She turns to me, inches away from my face, and twirls my mama's pendant between her fingers. All the sound drowned out by the sweet hum of our breathing. Something between us is mounting.

"Malik," she says. My name feels like a blessed assurance coming from her mouth. Between the stretch of silence, her face clouds with some hesitation.

"What's goin' on?"

A meeting of the eyes, and a couple of nods without moving. Her expression changes.

Thoughts assembling . . . "I—"

Suddenly, her lips meet mine. This kiss, hungry from years of separation. Deep as the ocean floor. My fingers touch her softly, feeling and exploring every curve.

She pulls back, contemplating what to say next. "I love you, Malik. Do you love me?"

My heart stammers, ready to break from the prison that is my chest.

"Lex, I loved you from the first time I saw you. Even though we got on each other's nerves lot."

She laughs softly and suddenly gives me a very quiet look. "There are things about me—"

Our lips press against each other. Slow and deliberate. An ocean of feelings between us. Blood pumping. The thudding of my pulse makes my head spin in a thousand different directions. "Look, that whole graveyard thing, I don't care," I say, kissing the nape of her neck. "We all got shit we gotta deal with, and you do that, you was helping your people. I mean, Lex, when I was in that gas station before I even came to Louisiana, I thought I saw you on that TV screen, fighting for Katia. But something in me knew. I took that shit as a sign. No lie. I love you."

Tears fall down her cheeks. "Malik—you—"

Before she can get the next word out, she's in my arms, and I kiss her with everything I got.

· · · ·

My hands tangle with hers as we make our way into my room. No evidence if our feet even touched the carpet. Moving slowly to the center of my bedroom while clothes start to come off, our exposed brown bodies are illuminated by the spilling orange light through the blinds on the window. More kissing, more touching, as our tense breathing slice through the sweet pause of the end of my playlist. With a lil' bit of swag, I wave my hand in midair, and the Bluetooth speaker cuts on, warbling out one of my favorite indie artists. Aunasti's "Brown Eyes."

Alexis meets my eyes, smiling. Butterflies flutter in my stomach, and a nervous sigh escapes my lips.

In between kissing, there's a cadence to us, our hands searching, finding, and squeezing each other all over. Before I know it, we've drifted over to my bed, letting the mattress sink in with our bodies.

It feels like we're floating on air. My lips travel from her temple down to the base of her throat. With a deliberate slowness, my lips find hers again, and I take all of her in.

"Have you done this before?" she asks breathlessly.

I can't even lie as my lips hover over hers. "Yeah, once."

Her hands slowly make their way up and down my chest. Small movements with feeling, with thoughtfulness. Both of us, lost in the moment.

"Malik," Alexis sighs, closing her eyes. "There's something I really need to tell you."

I wrap us in my bedsheets. "I really do love you, Lex."

She answers, "I love you too."

And that's enough for me to dive in.

So many unspoken wants and needs edging at the tip of her tongue. But she pulls me back in, kissing. Breaths and pants from somewhere deep. My lips find her neck. She shudders. I shudder too. Everything pushed to its limits. Her face drifts to the side, inviting me to land a soft kiss on her chin. With a culmination of feelings, I melt into Alexis, falling deeply and more in love with her as I support my weight on top of her. The spray of the setting sun filters through the blinds, just enough to make our shadows appear on the wall. Our bodies move beneath the sheets to a rhythm that took ten years to build.

A collective gasp falling in the air like rain.

The beginning of something new.

A thirst for air as our bodies meet in the darkness.

And I drown in her ocean.

CHAPTER THIRTY-THREE

AS I COME UP FOR AIR, I NOTICE ALEXIS IS GONE.

It isn't until I search through the piles of clothes scattered all over the floor that I find my phone and see a message from her.

> Had a beautiful night.

> Get some rest. Talk to you soon.

In the middle of the kitchen, Savon occupies the stove, cooking breakfast with an episode of *That's So Raven* playing in the background. The smell of sausage, scrambled eggs, and bacon hits my nose before I even make it to the fridge.

"Good *mornting*." Savon winks, scooping the perfectly scrambled eggs onto a paper plate.

It's obvious Savon and D Low was kicking it last night too.

The cold fruit punch juice hits the back of my throat, waking me up instantly. "Wadup?"

"Mhmm. I see you and Alexis had a good night. She thought she was slick, trying to slip out of here early this morning. Not her trynna do the walk of shame across campus, chile."

"Ain't nothing shameful about last night," I say, grinning and blushing like a kid.

Savon cocks their head back, flicking their wrist, pouring seasoning over the next batch of scrambled eggs. "Awwwlllright. We love to see Black love."

"It can seem sudden. Hell, it is. But I feel like I came to Caiman for a lot of reasons, one of them being to reunite with her. Yo, I love that girl with everything."

"Not you gonna make me cry this early in the day!"

I laugh. "When you know, you know. Alexis has been a part of my life ever since I can remember, and I thank whoever is up there lookin' out for ya boy that we're reunited."

Savon clicks their nails. "Yup, a good cry it is. Go 'head, Black boy. You deserve."

Savon slides the sizzling bacon onto a plate.

"You know, you always hear that we accept the love we think we deserve, and I know I kid around a lot, but love is something I don't wanna play around with. Because we may have magic, Malik, but my dad taught Elijah and me that there are some things that is more powerful than magic, and that's love. It's like what we learned in science class when it comes to matter: Love ain't created nor destroyed. It just is."

"Dang, nigga, you in yo feelings." I laugh.

"Nah, I'm being serious, though. No matter how hard the world tries to convince us, when it comes to us and this here, there is always something left to love."

That shuts me up real quick.

Because it's true.

D Low stumbles out of his room, rubbing the sleep from his face. He goes straight to the fridge, downs the last swallow of apple juice left.

I throw a grin back to Savon. "Even that?"

"Yeah," Savon answers, reaching for more seasoning. "Even that." D Low hugs Savon from behind.

Now they being all lovey-dovey and shit.

"Wadup, bruh? Where Alexis at?" He wraps one arm around Savon, the other grabbing the plate full of food.

"She slipped out this morning."

Him and Savon exchange a glance with each other.

"Y'all smashed last night, huh?" D Low asks.

I feel my cheeks get hella hot. "Bruh—"

"D Low, don't act so uncouth," Savon says, snatching a golden bagel from the toaster. "They shared something special. And don't kiss and tell." They playfully swat him.

D Low presses even more. "Did y'all?"

"Y'all wild," I tell the both of them.

Savon hands me a plate full of eggs and sausage. "Awww, that puppy-dog love."

"Whatever." I sit at the table, downing the food. Shit is good as hell.

"You must be special, because Alexis doesn't date nobody. She's all about her activism. Shit, we don't call her the Hextivist on campus for no reason."

"You in love, bruh?" D Low asks, mouth full of food. "Ain't nothin' wrong with that."

All of our phones ring. A campus-wide video message from the CaimanTea app, citing dark magic happening in the Ninth Ward. Somebody turns the camera, recording something that snatches every inch of joy away.

Flipping my phone around, I see it's the same figures from my old neighborhood, trailing down the cracked concrete road. People are running and screaming. One of the figures whirls his hand toward somebody, magically throwing them against a tree.

The Bokors . . .

"Well, there goes our morning," Savon says with a little tremble in their voice.

• • • •

I rush over to Chancellor Taron's office. He's sitting at his desk, on his phone too. He looks up when I come in.

"How can—"

I barely let him get a word in. "Did you see?"

"Of course, Mr. Baron." He sounds annoyed but worried at the same time. "We are handling it."

"How?"

"It doesn't concern you," he replies, putting down his phone. "You have class."

"Damn that, they're out there, getting people hurt. Do we even know what they want?"

"The Kwasan tribe has already mended the situation and offered the memory loss hex. Seriously, don't you have class?"

"I have my brother out there, Mama Aya—"

"Ms. Aya is almost two hundred years old. She can handle herself and protect young Taye. You just worry about yourself, and it's my job to keep you . . . all of you safe here at Caiman U."

"You seriously just sitting there? We should be out there, helping."

He stands, buttoning up his coat. "I'm not going to risk any more lives. The situation has been handled."

Chancellor Taron grabs his briefcase, and something falls out of it. We both go to pick it up. I touch the hand with the gold signet ring—a bright light blinds me as I get a warped vision of a young Taron and my mama, running around Mama Aya's yard. With a whoosh, the vision switches to them, on campus and attending classes. Another switch, and it's them, laughing and kissing. . . . He puts the same necklace that I found at our old house around her neck. She uses her magic to forge a gold signet ring.

And the vision shifts to Chancellor Taron, a bit older. Like college age. They exchange notes, scribbling the same words I've read a million times by now.

You're gonna get in trouble.

I need your help.

Then it switches real quick to him kissing another girl, the same woman that's gonna become his wife. . . . My mama storms up, hitting him in a fit of rage. A whole fight breaks out, and Mama whips her hand, and the other woman goes flying.

"Lolo! Stop!" Chancellor Taron shouts.

"Go to hell, Taron Bonclair!" she screams back.

"I'm sorry," Chancellor Taron tells my mama. *"You did this to us! I told you not to dive into that forbidden magic."* They really go at it. *"I love her! I'm sorry, but I can't do this anymore."*

"You gon' regret this!" Mama's sharp, shrill voice pierces us both. *"You promised!"*

Mama storms off, coming toward me. The vision ripples like little waves.

With a psychic blast, Chancellor Taron yells, thrusting me back into the moment my seven-year-old self is standing in the hallway. He stares at me as if he's lost. I stare right back. Running footsteps come from behind me, and I pivot my whole body.

Through the haze, I see my younger self run toward my mama's room and stand right there by the door.

There she is. On the floor, crying and screaming while the men in cloaks cast a hexing spell. Ribbons of green light burst from their fingertips, keeping her pinned on the floor. The energy of their spell ripples through the air, cracking the walls, shattering the mirror, and rumbling the ground below us. It vibrates the entire house. The light from the magic wraps around Mama like a tight belt, squeezing the life out of her. She cries even louder as the magic burns around her.

"Stop!" my present self yells at them.

Through the light, Chancellor Taron's face appears. The Bokors repeat the incantation, voices rising louder and louder. *"Lex talionis."*

One final guttural scream from me before the explosion part, and my mama disappears in the blinding green light. I'm sucked right back into Chancellor Taron's office. The shock of it all got me stumbling back, tripping over the chair in front of his desk.

"Is something wrong?" he asks stupidly.

I jerk away from him. "Get away from me!"

"What is the matter with you?"

The words are caught up in my chest. I'm shaking so bad, I'm afraid to even move. He inches closer with concern.

"You . . . it was you that attacked my mama, you the reason she's missing! What did you do to her?!"

It all makes sense. Why he didn't want me here. The lies. That gnawing feeling, shredding every part of me. The vision of him and her haunting me at every turn.

"Malik, wait—"

Chancellor Taron edges close to me, and I pull away from him again. "Fuck you! You probably killed her!"

I teleport out of his office and back to my dorm, where I shut the door behind me. Breathing hard and heavy, I feel my knees give out on me. The utter devastating truth hits me from every angle.

If my mama is really dead, he's the reason why.

. . . .

To calm myself down, I go to look for my mama's necklace that's in the drawer on my nightstand.

WTF? It's gone. And I'm just now noticing?

Mama Aya's bracelet is there, but the necklace has been stolen.

My heart drops as my hands search around my neck and inside my shirt. Anxiety now on a thousand as I go berserk. Tearing my room from corner to corner, looking for it. Clothes fly. Books tumble to the floor. Even flipping my mattress. I'm tearing my shit up.

Shit! It's gone. Her necklace, and the map to the scroll.

I text Alexis.

> Aye. Meet me at my dorm.

> Wassup?

> It's important.

Dropping the phone on the bed and pacing around my room, I wrack my brain, trying to put the pieces back together. That word *reckless* stings the back of my mind. And now Chancellor Taron stole my mama's necklace. But why?

There's a knock at the door. Alexis steps in. She looks around, seeing the mess. "Malik, what's going on?"

I finally stop my nervous pacing. "Alexis, what I'm about to say, it's gonna sound kinda wild."

"Okay . . . ," she trails off. We both sit on the bed. "What's going on, Malik?"

"I don't know why, but when my hand touched Chancellor Taron's, I got all these visions . . . more like memories of him and Mama, and that night ten years ago. The night my mama disappeared."

"Malik, what is it? You're scaring me."

"I think he had something to do with it," I tell her.

She's quiet. Too quiet. Which makes me even more nervous and mad as hell that I let him play in my face like that. "That's a big accusation, Malik."

"In my dream, I saw him with the Bokors, casting some spell," I tell her. "Lex talionis."

"Retribution-and-exile spell," she says.

Everything in me tenses up. "You know it?"

"Exile spell, so she's . . ."

Alexis turns to me, snatching my trembling hand. Her mind churning just as fast as mine. "If that's the spell you heard, Malik, then your mother is alive. She has just been exiled."

I stumble back, thrown.

"Malik," Alexis says, worried.

"So, Taron knew this whole time. . . ." My breath gets caught up in my chest.

Her soft hands wrap around my face. "What exactly did you see?"

"I saw Taron. As one of the Bokors. He's gotta be the one who brought them back."

She stands up. "Wait—what?"

"Alexis, I'm not playing. He was there."

The expression on her face shifts. "This doesn't make any sense. Why would Taron wanna be a part of the Bokors?"

"I don't know. And when me and Mama Aya went to my old childhood house, I found my mama's necklace. And now it's gone. My mama's pendant is gone. And her map. I think he got it."

"Malik—"

I just continue, ignoring her. "That's why he's been acting real shady, and now he's keeping us bound here to the campus. He wants to lead the Bokors right to the scroll."

A moment of hesitation. "What do we do?"

"We gotta get into his office."

CHAPTER THIRTY-FOUR

RECKLESS. THAT'S THE STAMP CHANCELLOR TARON HAS PUT on me. A hex, a curse. That's what he's been thinking of me this whole time.

But this muthafucka was the one that's been reckless. Reckless with my mama's feelings. Probably with his family, and he was reckless that night when it all went down. The night my mama disappeared, the night that I had three dead bodies on my conscience. He wasn't one of the bodies, but who was? Thinking about that as I trek across campus got my brain all scrambled.

Ten years. Ten whole fuckin' years, and after all this time, he had something to do with my mama's disappearance. He wanted me to hit these constant dead ends, he wanted me to forget the entire thing, he wanted me to believe she was dead.

My heart thuds in my chest with a rhythm of rage. But what keeps me going is Alexis telling me I need to play this smart. She's right. Even though everything in me wants to go up to Taron and confront him right now.

I can barely keep it together by the time Alexis and I meet up outside Taron's office while his bitch-ass is teaching a seminar. All according to plan.

With a swift motion of her left hand, Alexis chants, *"Pou antre!"*

No lie, that was sexy as hell.

But focus, Malik.

Suddenly, the doors to the upstairs unlock. Me and Alexis storm into Taron's office, getting right to it.

"We don't have that much time," Alexis reminds me. She peers out the balcony window. "His class should be letting out soon."

Like spies, we cover the entire office, searching. Alexis crosses over to his desk and sifts through papers. I'm rambling through closets, through books and jackets. Hoping and praying I find my mama's necklace.

Alexis stops, then turns to me. "Malik, I don't think it's in here."

"It's gotta be," I argue, not daring to give up. "And my dumb ass had to tell him about it."

I dig through the books and clothing in the closet, stopping midtrack. Mama's screaming voice shrills in my ear. Everything comes at me real fast. Fragmented images are yanked from the back of my mind.

Malik!!! Baby, I'm here!

"Wait!"

The memory fades, and I'm back in Taron's office. Something tells me that I knew it all along. The picture that's behind Taron's desk. When I first saw that picture, there was something I felt about it. I break the picture frame, and there it is, behind the picture of his family. This time it's a picture of Taron standing by the tree on campus. On God, it looks like it's missing the other half.

"Pictures," I tell her. "They can be used as a conduit, right?"

"Yeah, Malik, they can," Alexis answers. "Something like a picture of the one you love is one of the most powerful conduits a conjurer can use."

I pull mine out and put them together. Closing my eyes, I let out a cool breath on them. Out of nowhere, the pictures melt together as if they are one. Oh shit. It's the same photo! They were just torn apart. It's them, my mama and Taron, under the tree. She's all smiling and giggling.

"They knew each other?" Alexis asks me.

The shock of it all got me looking wide-eyed. "Yeah, they were together while here at Caiman."

"Malik, do you remember what activated the vision this morning?"

"Yeah, it was the ring he wears."

"So, you touched his ring, and you tapped into Taron's energy?"

"I ain't do anything. Our hands touched and boom. Hella visions of him and my mama."

Alexis looks confused as hell. She paces back and forth. "Nah. That can't be possible."

Realizing that touch is the important factor here, I zero in on my focus, staring at the photo.

"Say this," Alexis instructs. *"Iranti vula bukum . . ."*

The hex hisses from the back of my mind.

"Iranti vula bukum . . ."

Out of nowhere, a gust of wind and a coil of purple light create a little wave of watery ripples in thin air. A portal.

Oh shit. The ring and this photo are both conduits to Taron's magic.

"Malik, y-you j-just—" Alexis stutters in disbelief. "You just tapped into Chancellor Taron's memory."

I glance at her, confused.

"You can't just tap into other people's memory. It's . . . magically impossible unless you have a deep connection to them."

The ripple of magic pulsates even more. The pull of it makes me edge closer to it, and I slowly enter the portal, feeling the cool mist clash against my skin. Taron's memories flash in front of me like a jumbotron that be in the big city skylines.

This time it's Taron and . . .

Baron Samedi?!

Baron Samedi enters Taron's office with a long purple-and-black cane and a top hat. Taron is on the balcony, overlooking the campus.

"We had a deal, you and I."

That familiar chuckle and singsongy voice. *"Things changed."*

Like a quick shadow, Samedi steps into the shining moonlight, blossoming as his skeletal self.

Taron turns around, eyes shifting away from Baron Samedi. *"If he finds out what happened that night, we'll all be in danger."*

Baron Samedi puffs on a cigar. *"I got thaaangs under control. But he's bound to find out about you and his mama. Ain't no sense on lyin' to the boy."*

"He can't find out."

Like a wave of smoke, the memory switches. This time it's Taron and my mama. Right by the tree in front of the BCSU. Seeing her makes my breath catch in my throat. In the golden connecting light, they exchange the necklace and ring, followed by a passionate kiss.

Like film being burned by the sun, it all switches, showcasing my mama and Taron, sitting by the bayou, practicing their magic as kids. He kisses her. She kisses him back.

A thousand emotions sear through me, punching a hole in my soul.

First Taron.

Then Baron Samedi.

"Malik!" I hear Lex scream from the top of the portal, snatching me out of the memory. Alexis calls again, "Malik!"

Collecting my breath, I teleport back to the top, through the portal, to see Alexis's eyes bulge, scared. Her lips tremble as she stares at the door.

He stands there. Brown eyes narrowed, sending a cold chill up my spine.

Taron.

CHAPTER THIRTY-FIVE

THE BOGEYMAN AIN'T NEVER SCARED ME.

Because I knew that story was only used to frighten kids in the neighborhood, to get us to act right. I ain't believe in none of that shit until that night ten years ago.

After all this time, Taron is the bogeyman in my story.

He's the reason why my life is so fucked up now. He's the reason why my mama is out there, suffering. Seeing him stand here with that stupid look on his face got my blood boiling. I wanna kill him right here and now.

"What are you two doing in my office?" he finally asks. His beady brown eyes masked in disappointment. The nerve.

A deafening silence lingers among the three of us. I hold my hand out, and Alexis comes and stands by me.

Just like with Carlwell, one swift move, and it's over.

"Where is my mama?" I ask Taron.

He looks confused. "What are you talking about?"

"Where the fuck is she, Taron?!"

His eyes go cold. "You need to calm down, Mr. B—"

I yell over his bullshit. "You're one of them, ain't you? The Bokors."

His face twists even more. "The Bokors? No, Malik—"

"Don't lie to me!" The glass from the window instantly shatters.

"Your suspicion is misplaced." He exhales with frustration. "I knew this was a bad idea. . . ."

"You were there that night." My voice shakes. Which makes me even madder. "I saw you; this morning in your office, I saw everything. What you do to my mama?"

"You tapped into my memories. You are really a gifted young conjurer who just doesn't know it yet. Who's—"

"Reckless?"

The hurt on his face is evident. That's how it feels, though. To have something thrown back in your face. He did that when he first met me. Judging me without even knowing me.

"You've made my life shit. It's all your fucking fault!"

His hands reach out for me. I back away. "Malik, you have to listen to me. . . . The things that you *think* you remember are not what they seem. Your mother was too far gone. She was dabbling in dark, baneful magic. She went too far. There was no hope for her." He stops, letting tensity grow. "She put you in terrible danger."

A record scratch moment. My mama ain't never laid a finger on me.

"Malik, I'm telling you the truth." He groans, desperation and sadness trying to break through in his voice. He continues, taking a step forward. "That night. Ten years ago. She had already done unfathomable harm. And she was building up to more. We had to put a stop to it."

"You're lying!" I tell him, and the outside rumbles with a quake. "You and the Bokors just wanted her to find you that scroll!"

"We were there to protect you. *I* was there to protect you."

Instantly, I sense his magic.

The vision pops back in my head: Taron, reaching out to me surrounded by the green light I had thought belonged to the Bokors. Moments before the room erupts in blue flame. And this time I finally notice it glint in the darkness. That gold signet ring. My doe eyes, longing, trying to reach back. The memory is snatched from me just like everything else in my life.

"Shut the hell up!"

"Malik, she's a danger to you. Your mother is a danger to—"

With the blue swirl vaporing around me, my hands whirl toward him. Taron's body soars in the air, crashing against the bookshelf with a loud thud. He falls to the floor as wind whips into the office like a tornado, causing all the books to rain down on us. Alexis ducks, screaming. My magic going haywire like somebody threw a fiery Molotov in Taron's office.

Papers fly. Just like he did at Mama Aya's, I move my hand, making the broken glass from the balcony window magnetize.

"Where is my mama?!"

Taron struggles to get up from the floor. "Malik, please, listen—"

"Tell me where she at!!!"

His hand reaches for his throat as he struggles to speak. "Malik . . ."

Just like Carlwell, only this time I don't plan on stopping.

My hands curl, forcing the blue magic to close his throat even more.

Alexis screams my name, but I ignore her. His body starts to lift from the floor, levitating. I want him to feel what I've felt. The loneliness. The heartache, the fucking pain. But that ain't enough. Physically, no.

Fuck. I can't do it. But I know what I will do. I take the picture of him and my mama and throw it in the air. In slow motion it twists with a vengeance right by the bay window, leading to the balcony.

He scrambles back on his feet. "Please, Malik, don't . . ."

"You're gonna tell me where my mama is. Or at least, your memories will."

The bright royal purple portal swells around the room. Without a word, I snatch Alexis's hand, and we dive headfirst.

Swooping down, the cold air invades my lungs as we spiral down the portal. Images pop up on the side like we're in a *Tron* video game. The memories is a swirling vortex shape. The ground comes at us fast. Shit! We're about to crash through it.

But we don't. We drop right into a living room I have never seen before. It's night.

Everything around us looks like a typical suburban home. Pictures, Caiman U diplomas, and mirrors all grace the walls. A TV displays the nightly news on mute.

This ain't my house. Or the Hudsons'.

This is somewhere new.

From outside, we hear a loud popping noise. It's a powerful gust of wind howling. I go to look out the blinds, seeing Taron fighting somebody. He moves like a blur in the darkness. A bolt of light rockets around him.

"This is his memory, Malik." The fear in Alexis's voice dampens my rage. "I still can't . . ."

Through the curtains, a younger-looking Taron whirls around in a royal purple cloud. He sends a telekinetic blast so big, it rumbles the house.

"Celeste, go inside!" he tells a woman who stands on the porch. She rushes back into the house, slamming the door behind her.

She's a real pretty lady under the flickering fear in her eyes. The same lady from the picture in his office. The same lady that Mrs. Empress Bonclair told me about. Her eyes scan the entire living room, clocking every light in the house starting to bob, shorting out.

"Dad!" Taron's son runs down the stairs. Celeste grabs him, holding him back.

"Ade, no! You have to stay in the house!" she tells him.

It sounds like World War III outside, the way spouts of magic bounce off the concrete.

"Ade, go upstairs, please!" Celeste screams.

Seeing his family up close and live . . . it makes me clutch every emotion I have welled up in me. This is the night of their murder.

"Oh my God. It's his last memory of them," Alexis says, reminding me. "This isn't possible."

We position ourselves right in the middle of the living room, watching it all go down. There's translucent ripples on the side of the wall, the same few ripples I've seen in other memories. They lick the wall up and down, like heat waves rising above the asphalt.

"No, Ma, I can help. I've been practicing." His magic manifests in the form of maroon-colored sparkles. Celeste looks at her baby boy with a thousand smiles in her eyes. She believes him. But hell, he's too young. A sharp, shrill sound snatches their attention to the front door.

All the windows shatter, raining shards of glass inside. A jet of light come through the house like bullets from a drive-by. We all duck, trying not to get hit. The back door flies open with a crash. Celeste and Ade pivot with speed, clocking three people in dark cloaks charging in.

Celeste grabs a satin cloth bag, shakes it. The dust falls into the palm of her hand.

She whispers a spell with conviction. *"Khusela olu sapho."* She then blows the dust, making the particles swirl in the air in slow motion. The Bokor is hella confused and still like stone. Ade uses his lithe frame to his advantage like he's in a game of *Mortal Kombat.* He epically twists his hand with flair, sending a spell whizzing past me and Alexis.

The three Bokors are vaporized.

"Get out of our house," Celeste hisses at another Bokor with black boots stepping into the kitchen. She fires a stunning hex, blasting whoever is in the cloak against the wall. The cloaked figure recovers fast, and in one swift motion of the Bokor's hands, Ade's knees buckle, and he crashes to the floor, screaming.

Me and Alexis can't do shit but watch.

"Ade!!!" Celeste screams. "Stop it!"

The cloaked figure lifts their hand toward Celeste, magically dragging her across the room.

Celeste looks at whoever is under the hood. Her eyes go buck wide, recognizing the person.

The betrayal dawns in her eyes. "You!"

Crack! With a simple snap of the neck, Celeste's body drops to the floor. Fuck! Her dead eyes peer right up to us, full of betrayal.

"MAMA!!!!!" Ade's screams cut through me like a knife. So young. The trauma of heartbreak and death clutching him.

He lifts his hands, and a string of light explodes from them, but the dark figure with the black boots blocks it instantly. Taron comes back inside, eyes full of shock. Sweat beads on his brow, and his lips quiver at the sight of his wife's body lying limp on the ground.

"Iku lori re," the person with the black boots grunts in Yoruba. And just like that, Ade's young heart is ripped from his open chest.

A matter of flesh and blood soaks the carpet.

"NOOOOO!!!!!" Taron yells. The house fills itself with his screams as he crawls to his family's dead bodies. In the long, dark cloak, the Bokor disappears in a cloud of smoke. Watching Taron cradle his son to his chest is a horrifying sight.

A voice comes in like it's speaking into a thousand microphones. *"Yiza apha!"*

Taron's memory suddenly fades fast, and the ground beneath our feet lurches, the entire living room spinning and separating. A wind rises, and everything becomes a blur until . . .

We land heavily back in a front yard that looks awfully familiar.

A presence is felt behind us. She's standing there on the porch, hands on her hips, raining down a look that could make God himself shiver.

Mama Aya.

Instantly, we step into the living room.

"What was you thinkin'?!" Her look makes me wanna go get a switch.

"Problem is, they were not thinking at all." Taron appears out of nowhere. He steps on the front porch and through the front door in one stride. "How did you conclude that *I* was a Bokor?"

I step in between him and Mama Aya. "Mama Aya, he's lyin'. Been lyin' to all of us. I saw it in my memory. And he was there that night. That night that it all happened."

Her eyes dart over to him. "Taron, what's he talkin' 'bout?"

"He stole my mama's necklace and the map, and he knew about my mama this entire time! And now he's trynna get to the scroll."

Guilt blazes in his expression. "I was—"

I spin to him. "Tell her! Tell her about that night, my mama— you were there. It's that damn ring that's on his finger. He and the

Bokors cast some kind of banishment spell, and now they're hiding her away somewhere!"

"Taron," Mama Aya says, slowly walking up to him. "You knew what happened to my Lorraine this whole time?" He doesn't even have the balls to answer her. "Don't lie to me. I sacrificed and cast a hex to break that protection on him to find him."

"Ms. Aya, please, let me explain—"

Mama Aya slaps him powerfully across the face. "You and that daughter of mine. I know y'all was in love. I know she dabbled in things she ain't had no business doin'. But . . . it was you." Her voice slices through the tense silence. "You knew all this time—"

"If you just let me explain, I—"

"Uh-uh. I walk in through this house, hearing the memory of laughter. I hear all the screams and the cries come from the walls. The ghosts of my shame hauntin' me, day in and day out! Ten years ago, I lost my daughter, I lost everythin'!"

Taron crumples down on the floor, begging, "I'm sorry, Ms. Aya. I'm so sorry. . . ."

"AND YOU KNEW WHAT HAPPENED THIS WHOLE TIME?!" Mama Aya goes into a fit of rage, crying in her Yoruba tongue. *"Fi agbara han mi!"*

"She wasn't going to stop, Ms. Aya. You know it. Her obsession, it was worse than you thought. She wasn't just looking for the scroll. She performed the transference spell, brought the Bokors back. Ten years ago, they started taking kids again, and I had to do something. You knew what she was capable of, and I put a stop to it. I put a stop to her hurting you, hurting everyone in this community. Hurting those kids. Mama Aya, it had to be done."

Her face darkens. Stained with betrayal. She ignores him and travels to the couch, leaning on it and getting herself together.

"Why was I not let in on that moment? You was at her house when this child was seven years old. You did that!"

Taron continues to plead his case. "You know that I had no other choice. He was safer not knowing."

I step up to him. "Safe?! Why the hell y'all was in cloaks that night?!"

"We weren't. Malik, your memory is not all what it seems. It wasn't the Bokors that were there in your house that night; it was the Divine Elam. A few of us, at least. After your mother started working with the Bokors, trying to find that scroll and bring them back to their full power—I knew she had to be stopped. She *killed* my family."

Mama Aya stumbles with a half step back. A world of hurt written across her face. But not as much as me.

"You're lying! My mama wouldn't do any of that!"

"*Ti bray,* everythin' ain't what it seems." Samedi appears in a cloud of smoke. "You gots to trust us on that."

"Trust y'all? All y'all been doing is lying!" I turn back to Taron. "You summoned Baron Samedi to do your dirty work, didn't you?" I hate to add fuel to the fire, but she needs to know too. "Mama Aya, Baron Samedi and him was workin' together. Hiding and keepin' secrets and shit. He knew I was out there, alone, scared, all these years."

Nothing but quiet among all these supposed adults. Alexis makes her way over to me and grabs my hands.

"It's true, ain't it?" Mama Aya asks Baron Samedi.

Baron Samedi just looks at her with a hint of guilt in his eyes. Brigitte and Taye materialize by the bottom of the stairs. Tears in their eyes.

"Mama Aya, there are things even bigger than you and me here. And you've always known that." Baron Samedi looks to me and then back to Mama Aya, guilty. "It's true, Mama Aya," Baron Samedi finally admits. "I was summoned to work for him too, and I knew youngblood was out there on his own, and I helped keep that hidden."

Gutted by the admission, Mama Aya slowly walks up to him. She doesn't yell, she doesn't scream, she just says, *"Mwen pa bezwen sèvis ou ankò. Apre sa, mwen reprann envitasyon w lan."*

I no longer need your services. After that, I take back your invitation.

"Mama Aya," Baron Samedi says, voice cracking.

Suddenly, the front door flies open, and Baron Samedi's body is pulled back to the front porch. Mama Aya does this cool hand-whip move, and the door shuts right in his face. The whole living room is heavy with silence as she makes her way to the steps. She climbs them as if all her limbs are in pure agony.

"Ms. Aya," Taron calls for her. But she doesn't stop until she reaches the top of the stairs.

"If you not gonna tell me where my mama is, then I'm gonna go out there and find her myself. Taye, go pack your shit." I turn to Mama Aya, seeing her frozen stare. "You're not gonna do anything? You have info about your daughter, my mama, and you're just gonna stand there?"

"Malik, wait a minute, nah—"

"Or maybe you knew the entire time? You knew, and you didn't say nothing?"

"Malik, just listen to meh—"

I back away. "Nah. Don't bother. We're leavin'."

Taye has tears in his eyes. "Malik, no, please—"

"TAYE! Go, like I said." Taye stomps upstairs, huffing and puffing. It takes everything in me not to look at Taron and bust him all in his shit. "We never should've come here."

"You don't have to go," Auntie Brigitte tells me. "Taye was doin' real good here."

"I can't have y'all around him. If you'll lie to me, you'll lie to him too. And he doesn't need that."

"He needs a home. He needs family."

"What he *needs* is somebody that's gonna protect and not lie to him. That's what he needs."

I have Taye pack all his shit in under five minutes, and before I know it, we're outside, in the yard, storming toward the same car that stalled when we first arrived. I wave my hand in the air, unlocking it and cranking it up. Alexis follows me.

"Malik, where you gonna go?" she asks me.

"I'm gonna go find my mama."

She starts to cry. "Malik, don't go."

I turn to face her. "Lex, you said you would rather be out there with your activism, helping those who can't help themselves. Come with us. All of this, that school, it's a joke. Come with us and do yo own thing."

Taye hops in the back seat, slamming the door, with tears running down his face. Everybody comes out on the porch, looking like distant shadows from when me and Taye first got here.

"Lex, please, I love you. What's keeping you here? You'd rather be out there, fighting for the community."

"I know—"

"Then come with me," I beg her. "Please."

She thinks about it. Then she looks at me and kisses me like never before. I can't tell whether it's a good-bye kiss or a *she's coming with us* kiss.

"Let's go."

Before getting in the car, I look to Mama Aya's house, the yard, all of it.

Fuck it.

I peel out this bitch like no tomorrow.

"So, where to?" Alexis asks, eyes still peeled on the road ahead of us.

"Wherever. Back to my old neighborhood. Maybe we can start there. Start from the beginning."

Twenty minutes down the road, I'm speeding. The speedometer on the car rises unusually fast. I try to press the brake to slow down, but it's not working.

"You're going too fast!" Alexis yells.

"Yo, I can't— What the hell?"

"Malik!" Taye screams.

Up ahead, somebody steps out in the middle of the road. And the car is not slowing down. We are about to pummel his ass if he don't move.

"Watch out!" Taye yells.

Just as we are about to hit the man, he lifts his hands toward us, and the car jerks to a stop so hard, windows bust from the impact, splitting the air. Everything crunches up around us. We float in mid-air in slow motion. Alexis holds on to me for dear life, face frozen with fear.

Everything comes to a sharp standstill.

The external force causes the car to plop down on the ground.

Through the windshield, he pulls his hood off.

And it's that nigga Donja.

CHAPTER THIRTY-SIX

IF I DIE BEFORE I WAKE, I PRAY THE LORD MY MAGIC TO TAKE.
My mind drifts through the surge of pain as a loud ring goes off in my head. It grows and grows until my eyes flutter open to billowing smoke and faint light coiling through the leaves of trees.

Pangs churn in me, and I suddenly taste something weird— metallic-like. Fuck. It's blood.

A few blinks gives me a foggy clarity, clocking that the front of the car is crunched up. Shrapnel of metal are scattered all over the ground, and glass glitters against the dark pavement like diamonds.

Coming into full consciousness, I struggle to move in my seat, and a swell of pain aches on my left side. My eyes shift, seeing the smoke from the engine rise up to the sky. *Ahhhhhhhhh! Sssssss.* The seat belt slices into my chest. I shift my body, trying to look over to Taye. He seems all right, just a bit banged and shaken up. Alexis holds her palm to a gash on her forehead.

"Malik, what's—" She struggles to move, blood staining her brown skin.

A heavy-accented voice echoes in the darkness. "Get the fuck outta the car!"

Donja's shadow shifts to the front of the car in a flash. The doors are ripped off the hinges. He then hisses a spell, and I'm dragged out of the car by an invisible force.

Tiny footsteps crunch on the rocks. I pull all my energy to try to regain my strength, but I'm failing like hell.

"You're pathetic," Donja says.

"Donja, what the hell are you doing?" I hear Alexis say to him.

"Taye!" I call out, my whole body flinching as I spit out blood.

I try to make my way back to the car, to Taye, but a piercing ache shoots down my side, and my legs give out. Every muscle in my body convulses, tightens up, and spasms outta nowhere.

"Stop, Donja, you're hurting him!" Alexis screams.

Ah! I struggle to swallow. Muscles moving and constricting with agony. Donja's magic burns into me like a hot iron.

"Donja!" Alexis screams again.

Finally, it stops. A sudden charge of relief, like I just dipped into the pool after being in the sun all day.

Alexis's magic.

She's simultaneously healing me while arguing with Donja.

"Donja, you don't have to do this!" Alexis says.

He whips his hand to shut Alexis's mouth. She can't get a word out. That just pissed me the fuck off, giving me enough strength to teleport. It happens so quick. I can feel my hands delivering blows in the face and stomach. Donja's body disappears right from under me.

AHHH!!! The pain rings down my back. My breath is caught up in my throat, and my body goes limp.

"I've been waiting ten years for this." Donja stands up in front of me, dusting himself off.

Ten years, my dude?

I knew Donja had a problem with me, but this attack—it's bigger, it's something deep and dark. "What . . . are you talking about?"

No answer. He just flings his hand toward me, and my entire body flies, landing against the cold ground. As he speeds up to me, I gain enough strength to punch his ass right in his stomach.

Fiiiiyaaahh.

The boundary spell spits from my hand like venom from a cobra, creating a circle of flames around Donja. With one flick of the wrist,

I add an extra layer so he can't break through it. I look over, spotting a woozy Taye standing next to the destroyed car. "Taye!"

He nods, giving me the sign that he's okay.

"Take Taye!" I tell Alexis as I whip my right hand to keep Donja bound. Taye and Alexis start to run.

I pivot toward a tree with my right hand, but Donja is gone. He moves faster than lightning, and a wall of fire comes crashing down on me. The flames roar toward me, heat biting at my skin. I whip my hand forward, and the fire bends around me, turning to blue and orange.

A look of surprise splits Donja's face.

The flames give me energy as I channel the energy from them. A deep breath. Focused. And the blue from my magic crackles around my fingers.

I use the *return to sender* hex.

Donja goes flying, crashing against the tree.

"Get yo bitch ass up!!" I scream.

The telekinesis hex hisses from the back of my mind. His body slams against the crunched-up car, then back to the ground. The ground beneath us ruptures, causing the dust around us to flutter as the wind swoops us up. Donja speeds toward me, but a knife appears in his hand this time. He slams it down, inches away from my face.

"Enough!" a voice shouts from behind the trees. A sonic wave of magic throws us both to the ground. When I turn, Alexis and Taye are in midair, and appearing from a cloud of swirly gray smoke is . . .

Professor Kumale???

I feel a rush of relief. Professor Kumale will protect them.

"Taye . . . ," I breathe. "Alexis."

"That is enough," Professor Kumale commands.

I look at Donja, waiting for him to back down. But something's off about his face—he doesn't look scared to see Kumale here. Or surprised. He looks smug as fuck. Confusion sweeps over me like a storm cloud.

"What are you doing here?" I ask Professor Kumale.

He laughs. "Donja." He shakes his head. "Self-control is not your friend."

Professor Kumale waves his hand, and Taye and Alexis drop to the ground right next to me.

A sick feeling starts to rise in my gut.

"You're . . . you're . . ." I can't get the words out. The betrayal stings too much. Because from behind him, dark figures illuminate through the darkness. The howling air sizzles with the snap of cloaks.

The Bokors.

No . . .

A tense silence hangs in the air.

"Yes, this may come as a surprise to you," Professor Kumale says a bit guiltily. "But it had to be done."

I strain, trying to gain the understanding of what the hell is going on. "Whatchu mean, it had to be done?"

I look at Taye, trying to figure out a way to safely get him back to Mama Aya's. I just know with one wrong move, Alexis and Taye are dead.

"Malik, what's goin' on?" Taye asks innocently. "Ain't this your professor?"

His question feels like a thousand pounds sitting on my chest. Even Professor Kumale has a conflicted look while silently answering the question.

I'm broken. "Let him go."

His eyes shift back to me. "You are a gift, Malik Baron. Do you even know what your name entails?"

"Why the fuck does that matter?"

"Oh, it matters. A lot," he answers, clicking his tongue and circling Taye. Professor Kumale's eyes eerily dance between all of us. He then looks to one of the hooded figures, who pulls the covering down, revealing himself to be the leader.

Shit.

"You are a descendant of some of the most powerful conjurers in our history. The Kaave runs through your blood. Malik. Malik, king."

"I'on care about that!" I yell back. "Just let them fuckin' go!"

This is the dude that I've been training with. That I trusted. That felt like an older brother.

Hell, even at times like a father.

"Betrayal is painful, I know, *zami*."

The agony and rage burn in me. I try to suppress the rising panic, but I'm failing like hell. "So, what? After all of this, you're gonna kill me now?"

Him and the leader laugh.

"Now why would I do that?" Professor Kumale asks, eyes glittering with fascination. "You're too *valuable*. Your magic is ancient. I knew it the day I met you. I felt it. And when you found your mother's map . . . I knew you were something special. As a conjurer, you just needed that extra push. The access you have has been more beneficial to me than anything."

His words hit me hard. To him, I was basically a pig fattened up to be taken to the slaughterhouse. A piece in his game of chess.

Damn. I should've known not to trust folks.

"Your mother—"

Just him mentioning my mama makes me shuffle forward, trying to get my hands around him. With a quick movement of Donja's hand, my body goes airborne and crashes against a tree. Soon as I hit the ground, every fiber in my being feels like stone and razor blades grinding against my bones.

"What are you doing to him?! Yo, stop!" Taye yells at Professor Kumale. The fear in his voice keeps me fighting through the pain.

I don't scream. I don't cry.

I won't give Professor Kumale's ass the satisfaction as I fight through my spinning mind.

Taye's piercing cries break me even more. "Malik!!!!"

Stillness.

"Why y'all doing this?" I manage.

"Because I want my brother back!!!" And there it is. The pain and hurt that'll make you go crazy. The price you'll pay that comes with magic. "I want him back. And my folks couldn't do nothing for him.

Sayin' it's the way of the ancestors. No, I don't buy that. My brother deserved to live! And I'll sacrifice any and everything for that."

A vision comes to life. Professor Kumale's mother and father, both scared. I see in their eyes Professor Kumale standing over them, jabbing two blades into their hearts. Magic bursts from them like a prism of light. Then it's sucked back up, pulling me back to another memory. Now it's Professor Kumale standing on the edge of a cliff with his hands raised, shouting an incantation. *"Rèy ou a pre. Leve kanpe avè m!"*

The clashing of thunder, howling wind, and cracks of lightning stretch out in the dark sky. Professor Kumale snaps, and the Bokors all shift right like they're being controlled.

The vision fades.

"So, you the one who brought back the Bokors, huh? You're the one who kidnapped and sacrificed those kids for their magic?!"

"Not originally," Professor Kumale says. "That was all your mother's doing. I thought you might follow in her footsteps, be sympathetic to their noble sacrifice; that's why I showed you the history of the Bokors that first day in class, when the other students were watching the battle. A history lesson *within the lesson.*"

My memory slaps on the side of my head, remembering how Alexis and her crew disappeared off to the sides, leaving me alone.

"I needed you to see a different POV, Malik." He steps forward. I raise my hand, ready. He puts his up in a surrendering motion. "You led yourself to believe that she was attacked by them." He points to the Bokors. "It wasn't the Bokors who attacked your mother ten years ago."

"But they kill innocent folks, Professor Kumale."

"But have you ever wondered why?"

"I don't give a fuck why!" I scream. "They are kidnapping and stealing folks' magic."

He rubs his temples, acting like he's frustrated. "You are so smart, but you haven't looked at the full picture, Malik. Do you or anybody else ask themselves why they did this in the first place? They did it to win the war."

"Don't justify shit," I tell him.

"You remember how I told you that magic comes with a price? The Bokors used up their magic and made the ultimate sacrifice to help their villages, to save them from their captors' hands. To give their people a true taste of freedom. A trade for trade."

"But Oya or whoever punished them, right? Obviously, they weren't thinking about no damn village or winning the war."

"Your mother understood them. She understood more than you can possibly imagine, Malik." A brief pause as the wind picks up around us. "It wasn't no secret that your mother was heavy into bane magic. She was drawn to things she couldn't quite understand. But only because one side of the picture was told to her. Until she went to find the true answers."

Through all of this, I finally notice the leader start his stroll of a slow arc, circling me like I'm his prey.

My brain tries hard to process everything.

"We want the same thing, Malik. You and I. Vengeance," Professor Kumale says.

"Nah. That ain't the same," I tell him. "You on some Killmonger shit, and you see where that got him?"

"A silly movie does not compare."

He shows us through magic. It's like a screen appearing in the air. It's Taron and my mama, kissing in the middle of Mama Aya's yard. It switches too quick for my mind to process it. Now it's my Mama in the middle of a room, slicing her palm, letting blood drip into a gold cup. She mumbles a spell.

Once again, it switches. It's my mama and Mama Aya, arguing with me on my mama's hip. Nothing but screaming is thrown between them while I burst into tears, clutching onto my mama's arms.

"Leave that chile, Raine! I ain't gon' tell you again."

"Stop—" I say.

"He's my child, Mama! Not yours! You can't control me no more! If you won't tell me where the scroll is, I'll find it myself."

"They never should have let you into that damn Divine Elam! You made ya mess," Mama Aya says. They're both on the edge of the porch. *"You lay in it!"*

The memory fades.

"That anger, that righteous rage—it is fuel, Malik Baron. To get what *we* want. Same for your mother. Quite honestly, she took it a little too far . . . but it was Taron. It was that damn Divine Elam who banished her to God knows where. Not us. We are not your enemy." He points behind us, where the air ripples, showcasing Mama Aya's house through a portal. "They are."

I'm defeated. I can't even say anything else.

"You saw it for yourself," he says, reminding me of the image of the creepy hall. The lights flickering and her screaming. The clouds in front of me begin to spread, showing me the hallway, going up to the wall and seeing the door. And on the other side is . . . my mama.

"This is where they keep her, Malik. Locked her here for the past ten years. Your mother dipped into forbidden magic, and she owes a very powerful entity a soul. She completed the transference spell, used the power to bring the Bokors back, and Taron punished her for it."

So everything Taron said . . . it can't be true.

"Ten years ago, when your powers fully manifested, you subconsciously used a certain spell as a trade to try to save your mother from the Divine Elam, but you did something extraordinary at your deepest pain." A conflicted pause between all of us rips me from every direction. "You erased that evil, sadistic version of your mother and replaced those memories with false ones. Your own personal ghost kingdom. It's Childhood Trauma 101."

Mama Aya's voice comes to me. *We as a people always had to make a kingdom out of nothing.*

He waves his hand over me, and it floods back to me now. The memories of my childhood change like a montage in a movie. Mama is in the kitchen, marching around like she's nervous. Pulling her hair, banging pots. Breaking glass. Yelling at a seven-year-old me. Then I remember that one time she slapped me. My mother. The truth of who she was begins to overwhelm me.

The memories flash; Helena starts to disappear like a mirage, replaced by what was really there. That night where it all began. Then my mama screaming, trying to reach for me. The cloaked figures—only this time not cloaked. It's Taron and three other people, chanting. Taron reaches for me, and all I can focus on is his gold signet ring.

My seven-year-old self inches back toward the wall, yelling. And that's when the boom happens, and the entire house implodes.

Kumale's voice draws me back. "But she didn't crack the code; she couldn't find the location of the scroll, and she gave everything she had to find it. Once I stole the map from you, I realized how close she truly came before Taron and the Divine Elam banished her."

With this news, I fight to steady myself. But everything I wanna fight for snuffs out of me.

I'm tired. And I don't have nothing left.

I look to Taye. I look to Alexis. And all I can do is pray they'll make it out alive. Even if it's me that dies today.

"The bridge between us and the ancestors. You are the root, Malik Baron. You are past the point of potential. You are it; you are the key, and your mother, your grandmother, Taron—they all knew that." Professor Kumale throws me a conflicted look.

I don't move.

I'm numb. Numb to it all.

"It's not personal, Malik," he says. "I have to resurrect my brother. I really didn't want to hurt you, but my brother means much more."

He snaps his fingers, and they all disappear, leaving Taye, Alexis, and me in the middle of the dirt path.

Alone.

All three of us teleport back to Mama Aya's house. The pain is so much, I fall to the ground.

"MAMA AYA!!!! HELP!!!" Taye screams and cries. "Malik, get up, man. Get up!"

They all appear on the front porch, haloed by the dim lights from the inside, except for Mama Aya.

"Where is Mama Aya?" Taye asks, out of breath.

"She hasn't come out of her room," Auntie Brigitte tells us.

Taron steps forward. "What happened?"

"It's that Kumale dude. He's behind everything. He's the leader of them Bokors things," Taye tells him for me. Which I wish he didn't do. But fuck it.

"He's behind all of this," Taron says, as more of an admission than a question.

"Yeah, he's the one that fuckin' kidnapped all those kids for the Bokors too," I say.

Before I know it, we're inside the house, and I'm lying down on the couch. My side hurts like a bitch. *Sssss.* Ahh. My hands shoot to the source of the pain. When I lift up my shirt, my whole left side is black and blue from my fight with Donja.

Taron leans over, touching me. I recoil. "Don't fuckin' touch me."

"Malik," he says, voice full with guilt. "Let me heal you."

My voice cracks. "Get the hell away from me. Don't you ever touch me."

"Malik, I am sorry you had to find out this way."

I wince from the pain, holding back a river of tears. But I rather deal with that than have him heal me. "Man, whatever. Professor Kumale was the one who stole the map, and I bet the necklace too, for whatever reason, and Donja is working with him. They talk about getting vengeance."

As Taron closes his eyes and whispers a healing hex, my eyes shift over to the stairwell, hoping and praying Mama Aya will come down. When he's done, I instantly feel better, and I spring up from the couch.

Chancellor Taron crosses over to the door, stepping out on the porch.

He gives that look. The same look he had when his family was murdered. I shake my head.

"Aye, wait up." I follow him. "I know where she is now."

He stops in the middle of the yard. "Malik, believe me when I say, it's for your own good. It's too dangerous. That place she's in has very, very dark magic."

And then I step off the porch up to him with that man-to-man stare.

"Everything you know, it's not what it seems, Malik," he whispers. "But just know Mama Aya didn't have anything to do with it. I should've known she was going to find some way to break the spell."

I don't even look at him. I can't. "And how she do that?"

"She made a sacrifice to find you," he replies, looking up at the dim light coming from Mama Aya's room. "A great one at that. I didn't know what she was planning until it was done. Too late for it to change anything if I told the truth of what I knew. And even then, searching with all her strength, it took her years. As soon as she felt your magic, she sent for you."

"Everybody lies. . . . My whole life is nothing but one big lie."

"Don't say that, Malik."

"It's true. My mama was behind all this." Chancellor Taron just stares at me with pity. "Maybe she should stay where the fuck she's at. Because I'm done!"

CHAPTER THIRTY-SEVEN

I GET HELLA TEXTS FROM D LOW, SAVON, AND ELIJAH IN OUR group chat. Now I'mma have to explain all that went down.

> ELIJAH: What the hell is going on?

> SAVON: Where are you guys?

Savon sends an angry emoji.

> D LOW: Malik, bruh, when you coming back to the dorm?

> D LOW: I heard what happened. What the fuck!!!

Each ding from the texts hits me like a bullet in the chest. It's tiring as hell reliving the past twenty-four hours. The betrayal, all of it, hits me like a freight train. Sitting here, I feel so damn stupid for opening up to somebody. For trusting folks I don't even know. That's my fault, and I'll take that.

I can promise that it won't happen again.

It's too much to text back, so I just ignore them all by turning my phone off. The silence consumes the room, leaving me to battle with my thoughts. When all this hit you at once, you ain't got time to be sad.

"Malik," Alexis whispers from under the covers. I pull her closer to me and kiss her like it's our last.

With everything that's going on, it may be.

"Everything just got me fucked up," I tell her. "Like, Professor Kumale, I thought I could trust him. I mean, Donja, that nigga, I already knew something was off with him."

"And your mother?" she asks. "You haven't talked much about what happened."

"Because I don't want to."

"Malik—"

"Lex," I snap. "Please."

She's quiet for a second, and then she leans her head on my stomach.

"You ain't had no idea what Donja was into?"

"No," she replies with a shaky voice. "This is all new to me too."

Nothing but tears falling from her face. I give her an apologetic kiss on the forehead and slip out of the bed to put some basketball shorts on. She rises up, covering herself with my bedsheets.

"Where are you going?"

"Downstairs. I gotta check on Mama Aya and Taye."

"Maybe we should head back to campus. . . . We don't want to miss our classes."

"I don't give a fuck about that school right now."

A mixture of emotions competes on Alexis's face.

"I'm sorry; that wasn't toward you, I promise," I tell her. "But I can't leave. Kumale and the Bokors might come back. They're still looking for that scroll, and they might try to get to Mama Aya to find it."

She starts to put clothes on. "Everybody back at school is really confused about what's going on. I'mma head there and tell them. Savon and Elijah are gonna be devastated about what went down."

I feel her soft hands wrap around me, and her head rests on my back. My steel emotions are cracking under pressure, and I can't contain it anymore. "I'm sorry for everything that happened."

I turn around and plant a kiss on her lips. "Long as I got you,

I'm all good. I shouldn't have let my guard down when it came to Professor Kumale."

She kisses me again, hard. "I love you, Malik."

"I love you too, Alexis."

After Alexis leaves, I finally manage to get out of my room and cross down the hall where Mama Aya's room is. I knock.

But I don't say a word at first.

I knock again, and then I press my ear to her door. A muted hum on the other side. My eyes shift to the bottom, seeing the light from the sun shift a bit.

Stillness.

The shadow that's on the floor moves again.

My hand presses on the door, sensing the weight of exhaustion through my fingertips. The feeling of magic is different this time. "Mama Aya, you all right?"

"I'm all right, baybeh." Her voice sounds weak. "I'm just a lil' tired."

Something tells me don't press further. Mama Aya's dealing with some shit that I won't understand right now. And truth to be told, I just don't have the energy to understand it.

• • • •

The next evening, I find myself in the front yard, staring up at the bottle tree as it whistles, singing into the night. Mama Aya told me the tree powers a protection spell that surrounds her house, pulsating with heavy energy. The crew is laughing from inside the house, and I'm still trying to make sense of things.

I pull out my phone and text Alexis because I ain't heard from her all day.

> Wya?

> Been calling. Hit me back.

I continue to just chill outside, feeling the cool breeze on my skin. The front yard looks ominously dark this time. Like everything is swallowed up in nothingness.

"Wassup, Lik?" Taye appears right beside me. I ain't even hear him walk out the door.

"What you doin' out here?"

He detects the seriousness in my tone. "I'm just checkin' in on you, dude. Dang."

"I'm sorry, Taye. I ain't mean—"

His long arms is around me before I can get it out. "It's cool, bruh." He falls silent, taking in the vast world in front of us. "I'm sorry that all this happened."

I can't answer. The wound is too fresh.

"You know, I never thought we would be here. Dealing with all of this."

I continue to look up at the stars. "Me neither. Now I'm sitting here thinking, 'What would've happened if we kept driving?'"

"Probably be in Cali, living hella good," he says, cracking up. "Shit, I might be in some TV show or something. I always wanted to do that."

"Really?"

"Yeah, why not? Maybe the youngest chef. Like, being here, I really love cooking. I wanna be like Tabitha Brown. Have my own restaurant for folks like me with diabetes."

Even in the dark, I can see Taye smile. So innocent.

"I'm glad we came here, though. I really am. I mean, you reunited with Alexis, so even though some shit went down with your professor, at least you got her."

"And you," I remind him.

I'm not sure if I can say the same, to be honest. You live the kind of life I live, and you can't help but wonder. And then when good things do happen, you kind of expect the worst.

"I want you to be happy, Malik," Taye blurts out. Which is random as hell.

"As long as you're here, I am. Nothing is ever gonna change that. What did I tell you when we first got here? It's you and me. Nothing else."

He gets up and hugs me.

"Thanks for that," I say to him.

"A'ight, enough of that mushy shit," he jokes.

His phone buzzes. Whatever he's looking at got him smiling hella hard. "Whatchu smilin' at?"

He doesn't even answer back, just keeps on texting. He hops off the porch. His lil' girlfriend, Sierra, appears in the yard. They talk. I'm about to go in the house when I notice that they're edging out of sight.

"Taye? Sierra?"

She looks at me, her face . . . *rippling*.

Wayment—that ain't no damn Sierra. It's a trick!

"TAYE!!!!!!!" I scream for him.

I'm too late, because Taye's whole body is suddenly snatched and dragged across the yard by Sierra. Sprinting off the porch, I hex myself to teleport across the yard with speed, just over the edge of the protection spell.

"Malik!"

"I got you. I got you!"

Sierra—or what seems like her—disappears in a black plume of smoke. Dust swirls around us. Silence. Trees bend from the gust of wind, and that feeling of a thousand needles pricking my fingertips is back on a thousand.

Bane magic.

"Taye, you good?" I look at him. He's a bit bruised up.

"Yeah. . . . What the hell?" he says.

We both look around and see cloaked men stepping into the moonlight. The Bokors. Taye instantly starts screaming and grabbing his stomach.

"What's wrong?!"

He folds over from pain, yelling.

"You better help him, or he's gonna die," I hear a voice say.

Professor Kumale steps out from the dark woods and into the moonlight. He has his hands up, casting a hex on Taye.

"What the hell is you doing to him?"

His index finger curls, and Taye crumples over, gagging. "Malik, help me!"

"We had to get you out here somehow," Kumale hisses. His fingers wave in the darkness, and behind him, Alexis and Donja appear. "And since you were kind enough to let your *girlfriend* past the boundary, she helped lure you out."

"Malik," Alexis says, her voice trembling.

"Lex, what you doin' here?"

That's when I notice it dangling from her hand.

My mama's necklace.

Kumale holds out his hand. But from the look of things, Alexis seems hesitant. "Hand it to me, Alexis," Kumale warns.

Finally, Alexis tosses it, and it gleams in the dark air before it lands in Kumale's hand. The betrayal of it all sets in.

"Alexis . . . ," I breathe.

"I did my part," she tells Kumale. She then puts her head down in shame.

Not Lex.

Tears well up in her eyes. "I'm so sorry, Malik."

And that *sorry* shatters my heart into a million pieces.

"If only everybody agreed on our politics. You see, Alexis here, she needed the help of the Bokors. To help her with her magic and gain justice against an unjust system. She wants to break it, but I find that it was never broken." He glares at her, then circles around me. "They don't call her the *Hextivist* for no reason. A trade for trade."

I feel so sick, my knees about to give out. "Wait—"

"She was the closest to you; it only made sense."

The flickering eyes from Donja bring back that heat of rage.

A fragmented image pops in my head of her and Donja. *"You can't fuck this up! Stick to the plan!"* The vision changes again. Our sweet reunion when I first get to Caiman, and Donja on the side of her, watching with a close eye. It shifts again. This time it's her using her magic to make the picture of my mama fall on the floor in the middle of the humanities building after the party.

The final vision gets me.

It's her, taking my mama's pendant. She slips out of my bed in the darkness, looks back at me, sleeping, with hella guilt in her eyes, and sneaks out of my room.

All of this. It was fucking her.

The leader steps forward. *"Pa gen plis jwèt. Mennen nou nan woulo Idan. Koulye a!"*

Take me to the scroll.

Mean-mugging him, I stand my ground, ready.

His hand whips to Taye, hexing him. "MALIK!!!"

Taye falls to the ground, writhing in pain.

"Stop!!! Fuckin' stop!"

Professor Kumale's eyes shift to me, and a twisted grin decorates his face. "If you do not want him to kill Taye, take me to the Scroll of Idan."

"I don't know where that shit is!" Taye falls to the ground, writhing in pain. "Fuckin' stop!"

"Lorraine's map was clear enough about one thing. Your grandmother knows where the scroll is, even if you don't."

"Malik, just let them through," Alexis pleads.

All I can do right now is give a simple nod.

"San sou tè a, kraze."

Out of nowhere, my blue flame sparks around my arm, swirling around my hand. A gust of wind starts, and thunder rolls in. I whip my hand forward, making the protection spell around Mama Aya's yard burst into flames.

The Bokors slowly raise their hands, pulling on the protection hex. *"Pyebwa lavi a,"* the leader breathes in Kreyol. "We must do it there. The full moon is high, and our magic is at its apex."

Hesitantly, the Bokor leader takes a step forward, reaching out into the open air. He walks closer to where Mama Aya's protection spell would have begun. He gives a quick look back to Kumale, nodding a confirmation as nothing happens.

They all teleport toward Mama Aya's house. I instantly grab Taye, and we speed to the front yard. When we get there, it's Chancellor Taron and Dr. Akeylah, ready for war on the front porch. Their magic manifests in silver light, protecting the house.

As soon as the Bokors reach the middle of the yard, the leader realizes he can't move closer to the house.

Ah shit, chaos breaks out.

"Taye!" we hear Brigitte scream, teleporting over to us. "Malik, I got him."

"Protect my brotha," I tell her, eyes full of tears. "Protect Taye!"

She nods. Taye screams my name in the night air as they disappear in a cloud of purple-and-green smoke.

Instinctively, I kneel to the ground, feeling the cold, damp soil between my fingers. The vision in front of me slows, and my heart thuds in my ears. A harsh wind kicks up in response as I mumble a binding spell. Magic rips from me like a string of lights, jetting forward around the Bokors breaching Mama Aya's yard.

A surreal moment as a blurred battle ensues.

The Bokors come in hot, with inhuman speed and a jet of that same green light. The first to attack is the one on the right side of the leader—fist first. Dr. Akeylah disarms him with a hex. He explodes in a cloud of ash.

On my left, I clock one coming for me. I whip my hand forward, manifesting my magic in a twisting blue light. It snatches his ass up in midair. *Poof!* His ass turns to dust.

Back in the front yard, Samedi appears out of a thick cloud of ashy smoke with a cane, top hat, and dark sunshades.

"Mhmm, y'all done messed up now," Samedi says, taking off his sunglasses. His eyes glowing like ocean blue.

Out of fight mode, I survey the scene with a lot of clarity: First Samedi instantly transforms into a walking skeleton and shouts so loud, we are all thrown back. Then he turns into a tornado of ash and goes ham on the Bokors. He slams his cane into the chest of one of them. Then whips around with style, like he's dancing. Twists his cane up in the air, knocking Bokors out left and right.

Brigitte comes through the screen door and jumps so high in the air, she lands with an epic thud. She fights just like how they did back in the Haitian Revolution. But with some magical flair. A Bokor tries her life, but she spins around in a blur—knocking his ass back all the way to the edge of the yard.

Whizzing past me, a Bokor shouts, *"Pou lanmò!"*

Spreading from his entire body is a black vapor, snaking around him. I hold up my hand, making everything around me go into slow motion. I exhale a pain-inducing hex. The Bokor's body tenses up with a slight seizure.

My magical blue light and his dark magic collide, causing a chemical reaction blast.

Both of us are thrown to the ground.

My eyes drift over to Chancellor Taron and Professor Kumale. They go at it, hissing Kreyol spells at each other. Chancellor Taron is just like how I imagined he would be in combat. He's very calculated when he throws out his magic. Like he's working math problems in his head.

They exchange blows. Professor Kumale getting the better of Chancellor Taron. It's just like when I first got to Caiman, when he showed me those magical combats.

Glittering in the dark are red and blue lights from a police cruiser. Antwan steps out, pulling off his shades. From the back seats, Savon, D Low, and Elijah step out too.

What the fuck . . .

Antwan motions to all three of them. Savon and Elijah speed over to us like lightning. D Low—his ass charges, delivering deadly magical blows.

Antwan moves with icy calm. He tosses his sunshades in the air, and they slowly whirl past me and explode, the glass shards ripping a couple of Bokors to shreds.

Antwan glides over to me, helping me up off the ground.

"We don't have much time!" he warns.

Two Bokors appear in front of us. Antwan rams right into one, sending him back. The other tries to throw a lick my way. I sock his ass in the face and use the same move I did training with Professor Kumale.

Dr. Akeylah is really dope when she's in battle. Just like in class, she spins and blows—one of the Bokors disintegrates and turns to dust. Another one, she moves like she got precognition.

She jumps high off the ground, landing with a harsh thud.

Savon and Elijah fight side by side. They sweep a couple of Bokors off their feet.

To the blind eye, it may seem like we're all winning, but the Bokors are holding their own too. They're vicious, deadly, and strategic.

The leader glides through a few of us, knocking us on our asses. Him and Antwan go at it. Back on Professor Kumale, he appears in a plume of gray smoke. Hatred flashing in his eyes as he shouts in Kreyol, *"Sipriz!"*

His magic descends, snaking through the grass.

"Yọọ Kuro!" Chancellor Taron spits a disarming hex in Yoruba, cracking Kumale's hand.

"You on the wrong side of history, Taron! You are always the one to be in the wrong!" Kumale says as he holds his hand in pain.

Chancellor Taron drop-kicks Kumale to the ground. Kumale whips his hand forward, sending Antwan's police cruiser toward him. "Chancellor Taron, watch out!!!" I yell.

He reacts in the nick of time by clapping his hands. A ripple of royal purple magic bursts from him, choking the airborne cruiser into pure hypnotizing dust.

"Kumale, give this up!" Chancellor Taron says weakly. "This is not you!"

Even through all of this, I still see my mentor. My friend. My professor. He's hurting, and so he's administering that hurt to everybody.

"Pa janm. I got tired of waiting, tired of feeling the guilt. I want my brother back just as much as you want your family back," Professor Kumale hisses.

His hands twist around in a circular motion. Black smoke twists from him like coiling snakes—sharp-edged black tendrils ready to stab through skin and bone. It shoots out, and I teleport right toward Chancellor Taron, crashing into him. We roll onto the ground, recovering. Standing side by side, me and Chancellor Taron are ready. Professor Kumale whips his hands forward, disappearing.

My eyes lock on the leader. He runs toward us but then stops abruptly, and his bones start to break in several places. Twisting up like a pretzel.

Elijah moves in, confident as fuck. He uses his telekinesis hex, sending ole leader dude across the yard.

"Ah!!!" the leader shouts, recovering. "*Sòsyè!*"

A sharp pain shoots up my arm, and I reel back. Donja appears out of nowhere with his hands motioned toward me. With one glare, he yeets Dr. Akeylah all the way across the yard.

"Bet you didn't think I learned that in class, huh?"

Donja then grabs me by the neck, yanking me. I try to use my magic, but we both teleport all the way to the bayou, crashing into the swampy water. The thick water sloshes in and out of my mouth like I drank a barrel full of tar.

Nothing but eerie silence as I flail my arms to reach the surface. My lungs putting in overtime as my weight slowly pulls me down. Deeper and deeper, I can feel myself slipping.

Eyes losing focus and going blank. Sinking deeper to the bottom. Voices.

That's all I hear as my body crashes to the bottom of the bayou. Voices that my brain instantly recognizes.

"*Ija . . .*"

Fight.

Weakly, my hand points as I hear the word *ija* hiss one more time. With a boost of my blue light swirling around my hand, I shoot straight to the top. I scramble to reach the surface and then climb to the wet, clammy grass, coughing as the dense, humid air rips into my throat.

I lie on my back, catching my breath.

The air prickles with energy.

"I guess I underestimated you," Donja says, rising from the bayou water like a light-skinned Superman. "The great Malik Baron . . ."

His magic manifests in a scarlet color, drifting around his body like smoke.

"Donja, stop!" Alexis appears from a wall of cloud. "Don't do this!"

He whips his hand forward. Alexis is instantly out of sight. He turns back to me, eyes swollen with rage. "Everybody fawning after you, it's quite pathetic. You and me, we always gon' have problems."

I try to lift my hand, but he kicks me so hard that I go crashing against the rotted wood by a shack. The same slew of shacks I saw when I first got to Mama Aya's.

"You don't even realize what you did that night," he says. "Ten years ago. I'm sure history will repeat itself."

"Donja, it doesn't gotta be like this." Wallop! Donja kicks me in the stomach. The pain shoots through me like fire in my veins as I go flying fully inside the shack, crashing against old sheets and thankfully padding. My lungs constrict around my stomach so much, my body scream for air.

"Your bitch of a mother was doing dark magic. Had to get the elders from the Kwasan tribe all in it, because she couldn't keep that shit to herself."

That's when I manage a jab in his face for talking shit about my mama. He reels back, laughing. He bitch-slaps me. I go flying, crashing into the wooden wall. "The Divine Elam and Kwasan tribe initiated a banishment. How do I know that, you might wonder? Because before your mama was in the Divine Elam, my parents were. The generation before. They were Chancellor Taron's backup. But something went wrong. A ghetto kid's magic manifests, and an explosion. You even killed Dr. Alistair McMillan, one of Caiman's top professors. Damn."

His finger taps me on the forehead, and the memory slaps itself into my consciousness. It's from that night. The dead bodies with burned skin. Me, in the middle of it all. Finally, I notice their faces in the jet of green-and-blue light.

"My mother and father died that night. Died because of you." He finishes my thought. He kneels so we're face-to-face. "And you're gonna be dead right along with them."

The nausea and dizziness make everything in front of me spin on an axis. My hands try to find a sturdy wall to keep my balance.

"Koulye a, ou pral soufri," he shouts in Kreyol.

Now you will suffer.

In a sweeping motion, my body lifts in the air from the pile of rotting wood, pain ripping through me. I catch a glimpse in his eyes. His mama and daddy, killed by a seven-year-old boy. The agony of their screams as my magic incinerates the skin off their bodies. The deafening sounds of my childhood home imploding, raining wood and glass on them.

I feel it.

I feel their pain as I struggle to scramble to my feet.

"I was a kid, dude! I didn't mean—I didn't mean to kill them."

"Bullshit!" Donja screams and twists his bloody hand in midair. Somehow, a sharp knife blazing with fire appears between his fingers. "I'mma do you just like how you did my parents in that house of yours."

Just as he's inches from stabbing me in the stomach—

They start up again. The whispering voices, bleeding from the walls, filling my ringing ears. They echo and hum around the entire shack. Their voices low. Hungry. Rising in the silence between us. Getting the idea, I scratch along the rough edges of the fireplace brick, hexing it to make fire snake through the cracks, licking the walls up and down.

"Ina baba . . ."

Ancestral fire.

We both look around. The voices become more and more apparent. More haunting. Twisted shadows sift into the room like a cloud of ash. They swirl up and down, drifting aimlessly around us.

From the bayou water to now here.

It's her voice . . . Miriam.

Their energy surges around me. A summoning of spells. Debris goes flying, and Donja is tossed back.

"What the fuck is this?" Donja asks.

The whispers grow like a chorus, singing into our ears. My eyes land on Donja, seeing pieces of his face start to crumble. The ancestors' energy quivers around my hand.

Like energy being sucked back into me, I feel a surge of magic. That's when I speak the Kaave like a thousand voices coming from me. *"Tutwow oh fufaycuce."*

Two faces become one.

It's a time-stop moment. Everything slows. . . .

My spell hits Donja. His skin wrinkles, falling off the bone, and from his mouth, gooey black blood bleeds out. The flickering smoke swirls around us, creating a gust of wind.

"What are you doing to me?!"

I swear to God, it's like somebody took over my body. From my hands, the crackling blue light brims to full. Donja looks *soooo* scared. He yells and then speeds away. I drop to the ground.

Alexis stumbles into the shack, beaten. I go up to her, tangling my fingers around hers. Her eyes are apologetic.

When I start to exit the cabin, Alexis grabs my arm, twirling her hand into mine, and she stares deep in my eyes. "Malik . . ."

"I ain't got time for this shit," I tell her.

In the distance, we hear screams.

With a quick whoosh, we teleport out of the shack.

CHAPTER THIRTY-EIGHT

OUR MAGIC IS HIGH AS THE LISTENIN' SKIES.

And like a mighty wave, me and Alexis teleport right into the yard, seeing the magical combat that is our friends and fam, fighting in a ring around Mama Aya's tree. It's less Bokors, but no casualties on our end. With a sigh of relief, I count Chancellor Taron and Kumale still fighting. Dr. Akeylah and Brigitte man the fort, holding their own.

The leader runs up to me, jabbing his whole fist into my chest.

I'm airborne. My ass goes flying across the yard.

And all is gonna be fucking lost if we don't do something.

The screen door finally opens. Just like before, Mama Aya, even more tired and worn down, limps out on the porch with a stride that's deadlier than any baneful magic. The big dog. Ah, shit. "Now I know y'all ain't fightin' in my yard!" She lifts her outstretched hands. A powerful psychic blast covers the yard.

My eyes catch the leader speeding toward her. But she's too quick. *"Dide, Nunda!"* The Yoruba spits powerfully from her mouth, summoning a deadly quake from the ground. Like wisps of ghostly light, the spirits of the werecats, what Mama Aya calls Nundas, rise up. They roar so loud, they break the windows. Just like they're marching off to war, the Nundas go berserk, chomping on Bokors, whipping them around like rag dolls. The Bokors' howls split the night air as they're mauled one by one.

But the leader, he dodges one, twisting sharply in the air, landing with a thud. He rises with his hand. From there, long black tendrils spread from him. They shoot out, threatening to pierce flesh. Mama Aya rotates into a flock of birds. Coming back together, she appears behind the leader and shouts, *"Ukufa nphan!"*

Like Dippin' Dots, the Bokor leader disintegrates.

Mama Aya becomes a shadowed blur, fighting alongside these supernatural werecats. As she reaches Kumale, backed up against the tree, he holds the necklace chain between his fingers, conjuring up a pain hex. Mama Aya backs away, screaming. Ah hell naw!

I zip to her with superspeed and gently carry her to the porch. "I got you, Mama Aya."

After making sure she's all right, I teleport back to the front yard, and my fists pound the ground, sending a ripple of energy through everybody, pushing them back a few feet. Every muscle in my body tenses as my magic rumbles. Then a blinding blast of lightning strikes down around the yard, and a cyclone of a portal opens out of nowhere. The power from the swirling portal starts to pull the Bokors in one by one.

My magic is deadlier and I can feel it.

A prism of light bursts from me as Kumale and I meet eyes. He looks just as surprised as he did in class. With a quick move, I try to use a hex on Kumale, but of course, he's strong and knows every move I can make, and maneuvers around me. Without hesitation or remorse, he slashes something real sharp across my forearm, making me reel back into the tree. "Malik!" Mama Aya yells weakly from the porch.

The world spins, and my body goes in shock as I look down, seeing my mama's locket wedged in a gash between branches. A gush of my blood rains down from my fresh cut, milking the tree's bark in crimson. All my willpower snuffed out, replaced with fresh weakness.

He hisses a spell in Kreyol. *"Lè m' te san san nou, m'ap lage nou . . ."*

The ground beneath us begins to tilt and shake violently from the volatile wind. Kumale's magic feels like a thousand hands pulling me back. The tree begins to groan and shift, and the bottles sway, creating a swirling portal.

"*Malik . . .*"

That voice. That familiarity of its tone sends a shock down my back.

Mama . . .

Out of the portal and shifting clouds, she finally materializes. She steps into the blinding light like an archangel coming to bring in a fiery judgment. The woman I've been dreaming and searching for. Her beautiful brown skin. Thick, swooping curls. Her amber eyes light up like Christmas when she gets a good look at me. "Malik!"

Instinctively, I move to her.

Before I know it, I collapse into my mama's arms, hugging her. I hold her. Squeezing her till there's nothing left.

"It's really you?" I ask in disbelief. Touching her. Embracing her. Her warmth against my skin feels like home. "It's—"

She cries too. Tears fall down her cheeks. "Yes, baby, it is!"

Her warm arms wrap around me. All doubts, all fears erased the moment I feel her embrace.

"I missed you so much, baby. They can never take you away from me. Never. You hear me? Baby, I don't have much time." She nods at a confused-looking Kumale. "I knew you couldn't keep with it."

"I've done my part," Kumale growls. "I brought your locket here, where your ancestral magic is strongest, and activated it with your son's blood. You're free now."

She turns back to me, eyes shaken. "Baby, you gotta tell me where the Scroll of Idan is at. I know you know."

I'm thrown. Caught off guard. "I don't—"

"I know Mama Aya told ya, baby," she hisses. "They got me locked up. They took me away from you. With that scroll, baby, you can save me. Remember when I told you, 'They gon' take it away from you'? I was talkin' about the scroll. I was talkin—"

Mama Aya finally steps forward. "Raaaaine . . . baybeh."

My mama flicks a hard look at Mama Aya. Conflicted emotions rolling through Mama. But they quickly turn into bitterness.

This sweet reunion turning into rotten fruit.

Mama Aya spits with fury, "You get away from that chile!"

"Why?! 'Cause you don't want him to know the truth?!" My mama's convicting eyes land back on me, making me feel like that little boy from Helena, Alabama, again. "Malik, baby, they took me away from you," she says, pointing to Chancellor Taron and Mama Aya. "They put you through so much pain." Her hands cup my chin.

A tangle of thoughts squeezes every ounce of discernment out of me. "Wait, what? Mama Aya didn't know."

"That's a lie. They took me away from you. I ain't messed with no Bokors. They banished me because they didn't want the truth out."

Mama hugs me one more time, causing the anguished memories to play over and over like a fever-induced dream. Mine and hers all wrap into one. It's my mama, walking back and forth, screeching at herself in the kitchen. Me in the room, trying to make sense of her scattered notes, and she storms in and slaps me to the ground. Yelling at me. My younger self cries.

From the darkness of the hallway, I appear. Eyes from my younger self linger on the door closing. I hear nothing but silence and distant yells. The walls begin to crack, and lights bob. The sparkling blue light licks the walls, repairing the cracks, fixing the ghost kingdom.

The dark magic shifts to Chancellor Taron's house. His young son's heart ripped from his chest. I'm suddenly looking through his eyes as darkness floods in, and I see that it's my mama.

Her maniacal laugh makes me shudder as a black vapor covers my mama's mouth. She kneels to a crying Chancellor Taron.

"You hurt me, I hurt back."

I notice the black boots. The same ones from the memory of Chancellor Taron's family's death. Everything goes back to normal.

"What is it, baby?" Mama asks with a dead-eye glint.

"So, it *was* you." My voice cracks under the knowledge of betrayal. "It really was you this whole time."

The treachery of it grows, gnawing and tugging at me. Knowing she was behind all of the killings, all of this pain, and all this hurt I've been carrying around.

Now it all makes sense. Chancellor Taron was protecting me from her.

"Malik," Mama says, her voice changing a bit. Kinda demonic, the way it sounds. "I need that damn scroll, boy!!!"

Her face is twisted and contorted, with blood-red eyes. The real her.

"WHERE IS THE SCROLL?!" She lets out a shriek so loud, it almost bursts my eardrums.

"Malik!" Chancellor Taron rushes for me.

Mama reaches for me, trying her hardest to snatch me up. Her hands shape-shift into long, sharp talons.

"WHERE IS IT?!" Mama bellows in rage. She lifts her hand into the sky, and a bright burst of light spirals up, shattering the blue bottles in the trees. Shards of glass rain down like missiles.

The intensity of her magic feels so evil, so twisted. Corrupted. I can't even form the words.

"Lolo!" Chancellor Taron steps in and shouts. "Stop this! You don't have to do this!"

Everything stops at his voice.

Mama pauses with a look at Chancellor Taron. Confused. She notices his trembling hand with the gold ring. There's a tenderness there. Tears mist their eyes. He cautiously goes up to her; his hand meets her cheek.

"Don't do this, Lolo," Chancellor Taron pleads, looking at her with a look of a thousand wants. "Please."

A moment. Everything around us quiets. Slows.

These two, for a moment, hold each other. Her eyes drift to me and then back to Chancellor Taron. So many unspoken words between the two. Just like me and Alexis.

"Oh, now you care for him?" Mama says.

Her meaningful look turns into rage, and then she flicks her wrist with force, making Chancellor Taron collide against the porch steps. "You broke my heart, Taron Bonclair." She turns to all of us, a world of wickedness set in her eyes. "So, I'm gon' break all of you."

Mama spins and transforms into a swirling black vapor of flapping moths. As it reaches its apex, the shaft of darkness that my mama controls explodes outward, and the Bokors and Kumale disappear in the cyclone.

An imploding blast sends us to the ground as they dissipate.

The stillness of the night falls on Mama Aya's yard.

I walk up to Mama Aya, holding my gashed-up arm. "Wow. You, like, the dopest grandma I've ever seen. You're my *grandmama*. . . ."

The word surprises both of us.

"My grandson . . ." She hugs me so tight, it feels like home. But just as quick as her arms wrap around my shoulder, Mama Aya spins me around. Her eyes widen, and her body tenses up. It all happens so quick, my mind can't process it. Blood pools around her stomach area as Donja appears behind her. She falls to the ground. Everything in me screams.

"NOOOO!!!"

"DONJA!!!" Alexis screams.

Chancellor Taron and Dr. Akeylah speed over and grab him.

His twisted smile causes me to get out of character. Or maybe in character, because all I see is red, and all I can feel is rage.

A vengeful rage.

"Malik," Chancellor Taron says with fear in his voice.

When I look down, I notice my magic orbiting around my hand in dark blue. I twist my hand toward Donja and scream.

Donja's body falls to the ground, bones cracking.

Chancellor Taron's voice cuts through the chaos. "Malik, don't! You're better than this!"

With a quick move, I pin everybody to the ground. They all plead my name in the thick air.

"Malik!" Dr. Akeylah screams.

I move to Donja with a silent fury.

His whole body contorts as I shoot the pain hex through his body.

"Kill me. . . . Kill me like you did my parents."

The memory flashes in my head: the Divine Elam and Donja's

parents surround my mama as she screams at them. The explosion, then their dead, burned bodies staring lifelessly at me.

"FUCKING KILL ME!"

"No," I say slowly. I lean down to eye level. "Because I know if I kill you, you'll find peace. You'll find your parents again, and you don't deserve that. You deserve what I've been battling with all this time. I'mma send you back to the last night you spoke with yo folks, and you'll know it's the last time you'll ever see them. And it'll replay over and over and fuckin' over. Your very own ghost kingdom."

"Malik," I hear Mama Aya call. She's weak. "Baybeh . . ."

But I ignore her in my fit of rage while looking at Donja. "You hurt the ones I love, so I'll hurt you back."

Donja, grim-faced, starts to speak.

I interrupt him. "Eye for an eye, tooth for a tooth." I breathe the next hex. *"Lex . . . talionis."*

Suddenly, blood spews from his mouth. Then clicking on the ground are all his teeth. They fall out of his mouth one by one until he becomes a bald-mouthed mothafucka.

With a snap of my finger, my blue magic wraps around his body like an anaconda, and Donja just goes . . . *poof!* The same as my mama ten years ago.

"Baybeh," Mama Aya breathes.

I rush back over to her.

I cradle Mama Aya in my arms. "You gonna be all right. Mama Aya, you gonna be all right!!!"

I try to heal her with my magic. "Baby, it's all right," she keeps saying.

"Don't you die on me! No! Y'all heal her."

Mama Aya's trying to get my attention.

"Heal her!"

"Malik," Baron Samedi says, looking up to the moonlight. As the light shines on his face, he instantly turns skeletal. "This is what she wanted."

Finally, it all dawns on me.

This is something they don't tell you in church or school: when you're at the end of your life, everything that happened to you while you're on earth, you see your entire life flash before your eyes.

Only it's not my life.

But Mama Aya's.

I'm just tapping into her memories.

"Malik," Chancellor Taron says to me. In his eyes, I know. I finally know what Mama Aya sacrificed to find me. It was always gonna end this way.

I wrap her tighter in my arms, whispering the spell to heal her. But it ain't working. It ain't fucking working! The ground shudders. Thunder booms in the distance. My magic feels as though it's ripping through my body.

"Baby, remember who you are." Her hands grace my face. Her eyes glisten. "Say the words, baybeh."

She whispers a *please,* and finally I say, "To be absent from the body is to be present with the Lord."

Her eyes flutter closed, and then her whole body turns into a cloud of reanimated black butterflies, flapping their wings up to the full moon.

CHAPTER THIRTY-NINE

OUT OF THE ABUNDANCE OF HEART, THE MOUTH SPEAKS.
But right now, I ain't got shit to say. No spells to cast. Nothing.
My eyes are heavy and my throat is raw from crying. I just lie here,
stretched out on the bed, under the sullen light of gloom. My arms
under my head as I stare up at the ceiling. Time doesn't seem like
it's waiting on nobody to settle, because it looks like the day came
and went, and now it's night. Mama Aya is dead, and the couple of
people I trusted . . .

It's too fucking hard to even think about it.

There's movement downstairs. Then voices. I hear Brigitte and
Taye. Footsteps slowly fading . . . then back to silence. Grief taking the
form of a friend. It's in us. It might as well move on in at this point.

After a couple of days resting, I peel myself out of the bed and sit
back on the porch. The horizon of the sky is blue, mismatching with
what I'm feeling right about now. Every second that passes by, I try
with all my might to make sense of some things.

I sit on the porch until the sky turns pink and orange, just like
Mama Aya used to.

Samedi appears by the steps. "You mind if I sit with ya a bit?"

All I offer him is a shrug of a shoulder.

He sits anyway, whipping out a fresh cigar. An apologetic look
rides on his shoulders.

"I'mma do somethin' I ain't done in over two thousand damn years," he says, lighting and puffing on his cigar, letting the smoke escape his nostrils. "That's apologize. You and Brigitte the only ones I've done it to."

If I wasn't so mad at him, I'd laugh.

He continues, "You ain't deserve none of that. Youngblood, I am truly sorry. I promise that I'll never lie to you again."

Finally, I look at him. "And how you gon' do that?"

Another puff in the form of a false cheerfulness. "Shiiiid, name ya price."

Right next to him, I see a bottle of his favorite Cognac. His eyes meet my gaze. An idea percolating. Then he bursts out laughing. "That's cold, youngblood."

"Magic always comes with a price."

He looks out absently. "Yeah, well, secrets gotta be paid in blood somehow."

Mama Aya dying and turning into black butterflies pops into my head. It stings. And I need a drink. So, bottoms up.

"I wish I can say some cookie-cutta shit to make you feel betta, like it gets better, ya know?"

I take another long swig. It burns in the back of my throat and filters down my chest, temporarily helping me forget the bullshit the world got to offer.

"Yeah, it just hurts, is all."

Another puff. His crystal blue eyes land on the yard in front of us. "Pain is life. And life is hell. It's funny thing 'bout death, nephew. In this life, y'all consider it the end, but y'all just don't know. Death is ya friend, nephew. It guides you to places that's far better than here. Shit, death is only the beginnin'."

That's that Loa speaking.

I mean, he *is* the Loa of Death.

"How is it the beginning?"

I hand him back the bottle. He downs it.

"Well, this"—he points to my body—"it's nothin' but a shell. But the soul—the soul ain't bound to nothin'. It's free. It's boundless. What they teach y'all in school, youngblood? Uh, that matter is neither created nor destroyed. Just transferred. The *majik* in ya blood flowin' to keep ya alive. But dere's gon' come a point in time where you have ta lay all ya bones at the crossroads and choose a path that's going to change ya life forever."

Lay my bones at the crossroads . . .

Something about that part stings me to my core.

Suddenly, he starts to sing like he in a suga shack. "But ya gotta let the good times roll, nephew. *Laissez les bons temps rouler.*"

We both chuckle and start to choke on the cigar smoke.

"I hear that," I say back, still staring at the sky.

He looks over at me. "Malik, there's somethin' Brigitte and me been wantin' to talk to you about."

"Wassup?"

"Taye."

My eyebrows crease at the mentioning of his name. "What about him?"

He puffs. He drinks. Letting whatever he's about to say linger for a bit.

"We wanna take him in, raise him up. We know with you havin' school on your plate, you . . . you just got a lot going."

"You mean like adopt Taye?"

"We love that lil' kid. Brigitte always wanted to be a mama. And he loves us too. So, I told him I'd talk to you about it."

I take in a deep breath. "So, Taye knows about this?"

Samedi exhales the smoke. "He does."

"I—"

In all my shit, I didn't even check in to see how Taye's feeling about the whole thing. He and Mama Aya grew close while I was at school. He ain't said much since everything went down. I guess he's internalizing it. Shit, death is a bitch to process.

A laugh rumbles in Samedi's chest. "You ain't gon' lose him. And he will always be your brother. Just . . . it'll be a lot on your plate worryin' about him all the time. We can protect him. Give him a home. Give him what he needs."

And here is my next lesson: mastering the art of letting go.

To do that, I drink the last bit of Samedi's Cognac. Letting go manifests in a few drops of tears escaping my eyelids. Because how can I argue with that? Even though I want to. But Taye's well-being is the most important thing in the world right now. Questions have been filling my mind ever since everything went down. How can I really protect him? How can I provide the good life that he deserves?

"I ain't gonna be selfish," I tell Samedi, even though it's the hardest thing for me to do right now. "Maybe y'all can give Taye something I can't right now."

Samedi's hand is on my shoulder. Both of us, reflecting. "Focus on that school. It's good for ya. And I gotta feelin' there's more out there comin' our way," he warns.

When he says, "more coming our way," there's a feeling at the pit of my stomach, telling me he's not lying. "Ya mama is still out there, and she ain't gon' give up till she got what she wants."

That I know.

And that's what I'm afraid of.

Antwan appears in the yard. He doesn't have on his uniform and still sticks out like a sore thumb. When he comes up to me, he nods, taking off his sunglasses. "Malik."

"Hey, Antwan . . . ," I say back to him.

Sam shakes his hand. "Antwan . . . gon' in there, getcha a plate of dem red beans and rice."

His lips curl into a grin. "I'd like that very much."

One look at me, and he starts to say something. I give him a handshake, signaling that he's cool with me. He then crosses to the screen door and goes inside the house.

"Sam," Brigitte hollers from inside the house.

"Lemme get on and see what this woman wants before she gets on my nerves." He gets up. "You gon' be a'ight, nephew."

"Uncle Samedi." He stops, then turns. I stand up, feeling the weight of tears. "Just take care of him."

He pauses as I feel the lump forming in my throat.

"When school get in, you and Auntie Brigitte might have to fight him out of bed in the mornings. Then there'll be days when he beats you out of bed. He really likes Six Flags in Georgia. The Twisted Cyclone and the refillable cups are his favorites." Whew. Shit. The tears are hella heavy now. "You're gonna have bad days, but his laugh is gonna make everything bright again. Make sure he do his homework. Math ain't his strong suit. The birds and the bees . . . that's on you. Show him what it means to be a man. Because that's a spell I ain't learn how to cast yet . . ."

I try to control my breathing.

"He says he likes cooking. So, buy all the stuff," I continue, hesitating on my last thought. "Just promise you'll treat him right and love him like he deserves."

Samedi throws back three simple words. "I promise, nephew." He heads for the door, and then stops, turns. "But, nephew, you promise me one thing. One thing only."

I wipe the stinging tears from my eyes. "What's that?"

"Be a kid," he says. "Have fun, go to them college parties. Sleep in. Hell, get you some coochie. A lot of it." I laugh through the tears. He inches toward me. "Be a kid, because the world will fight to steal the innocence from Black boys like you, and you can't let it. You hear me? You can't let it. Move mountains, nephew. I restore all the good in you. I restore all the brokenness that's been passed down from your mother and your mother's mother. I restore goodness into you, nephew. I restore the innocence that was taken from you, nephew!" He slips into Kreyol. *"Mwen retabli li! Mwen retabli li! Mwen retabli li."*

The emotional walls come crashing down, and I just fall into Baron Samedi's arms, crying a silent cry.

"I got you, King. I always got you."

• • • •

After I sit for a few hours on the porch, a cloud appears over the bayou. Dark and pregnant with summer rain. Beams of sunshine hit in different spots, and ironically, it's hella shade across the bayou. After prepping for Mama Aya's repast and seeing all the family again, especially that Auntie Caroline, I sit on the porch, away from everybody, and just look at the sky.

I just watch it for a moment.

Must be God recognizing a brother's pain, because the bottom of the sky finally lets out. Pouring rain. The grass instantly becomes mushy, and the bayou overflows. Taye comes out on the porch. "You cool, Lik?" he asks under the symphony of rain.

"Yeah, I am." I rest my head on his.

"Nibo, you gon' eat these eggs scrambled?" Brigitte calls from the kitchen.

"Yes, ma'am," Taye answers back with a quickness.

I turn to him, looking hella confused. "Nibo? What the hell is that?"

"That's my nickname. You know everybody in a family got a nickname."

He ain't lying about that. "A'ight . . . Nibo."

In the front yard, that same black rooster me and Taye saw when we first arrived darts across the grass, trying to avoid the heavy rain. I look to Taye, who just shrugs.

"That's a long story."

"I'm sure it is." "Good Love" by Johnnie Taylor blares from inside the house. We both bust out laughing when we hear Uncle Samedi singing.

"Okay. I'm gonna go help Auntie Brigitte in the kitchen."

"All right."

His hug is what I need right now, and he disappears off into the kitchen. My phone buzzes.

When I look at it, my smile fades like the sun.

It's a text from Alexis.

Hey.

CHAPTER FORTY

WHEN THE CHICKENS COME HOME TO ROOST, THOSE BITCHES be saaanging.

Chancellor Taron stands on the balcony when I walk into his office. His eyes are lost as he stares out the window at the campus, deep in thought. And the text from Alexis still haunts me from a distance. Even left my read receipts on just to show her that I saw it, but I ain't answering it until I'm fucking ready.

I softly knock on the door. "Chancellor?"

He snaps to attention. "Yes, come in, Mr. Baron," he says, crossing back to his desk.

Soon as I sit in the chair in front of him, I notice that his office is put back to normal. Clean. Pictures of family and other educators on the wall. Curtains pulled back with the sounds of the drumline warbling in from the distance.

"How are you feeling?" he asks, breaking the ice first.

I try to steady my voice. "I'm . . . cool."

We sit in silence for what seems like eternity.

"You're wondering what will happen to Alexis?"

Part of me is glad he asked first because I don't have the strength to. "It's that obvious?"

"I know that look in your eyes right now. That hurt and that betrayal eating at every good memory you had with her."

Right. He probably had this same look with my mama.

Another beat of us just staring . . . breathing. Chancellor Taron leans back in his chair. A thoughtful expression washes over his face. "Well, as chancellor, I will have to expel her from Caiman University."

Expel. The word sounds so final.

"Mr. Baron, she exposed us, put innocent civilians in harm's way. Put you in harm's way." I look up when he says that. "I have no choice in the matter. She will be stripped of her magic and memory of this world."

I can't even argue. Truth be told, I don't wanna say nothing back, because there's not enough energy in the world to make me take up for her right now. My grandma is dead. My evil mama is somewhere out in the world, regaining her powers, still looking for that scroll. It's a lot on my plate, and forgiveness ain't on the menu.

"Naw. I get it, Chancellor."

There's a flash of softness in his eyes, like he feels bad for what he's about to say next. "The Kwasan tribe are not pleased with what happened. Now that the word is spreading that Mama Aya is dead"—the last part stings even more, and I shift in my chair—"they want to set some new boundaries. Some new rules regarding the university."

That feeling of dread bubbles inside me as my eyes move to the picture of his family behind him.

"It's going to take some time for your mother to regain her powers," Chancellor Taron continues, clocking the look of fear flitting across my face. "She's been subdued for so long. She's gonna need any and every bit of magic to regain her strength."

"I'm sorry," I tell him, feeling the lump forming in my throat.

"What are you sorry for, Mr. Baron?"

"Your family—I can't imagine what you went through."

A painful silence hangs in the balance.

"I believe you can to some degree."

He's right about that. These past few days, I learned that the ones you love, the ones you fight to the ends of the Earth for, can die to you in more than one way. It doesn't always have to be physical.

"Still, I'm sorry for your loss."

I stare. He stares back. Raw emotions clutching at him, but he breaks away from their grasp. He then starts to write on a piece of paper. The pen swishes and sways. After a second, he hands the paper to me. Unfolding it, I see the name DR. MOHAMMAD OJARAGI appear in black ink.

"What's this?"

"You've been through a lot. If anything, I understand how grief works. It can consume you if you let it." His tone laced with a painful truth. "We, Mr. Baron, may be blessed with magic, but we are still human. Your mental health is still real."

Conflicted emotions roll through me. "You want me to go to therapy?"

"Listen, Malik, given everything that's happened—and I know the only reason you came here was for Mama Aya—I want you to know that you're welcome here at Caiman. Always. And truth be told, I want to keep my eye on you. Protect you."

The look he gives me stops the argument from leaving my tongue, so I just nod. Can't even speak because there's too much going through my mind right now. "I want you to be prepared, Mr. Baron," he says. "But most importantly, safe."

He leans forward in his chair. "You belong here, at Caiman. You've always belonged, *Malik*. I hope you find it in your heart to forgive me for making you think otherwise."

Those words are like music to my ears. Singing me a tune I thought was lost a long time ago. And coming where I come from, you don't feel that feeling too often. You don't hear it too much, either.

I start for the door. Then I stop and turn back to Chancellor Taron. "Chancellor, can I ask you one more thing?"

"Sure, Malik, anything."

It's a beat before I say anything because I'm trynna figure out the words to say.

"You was in love with my mama, right?" The expression of guilt glimmers across his face. "I mean, you loved her more than anything. And you've been . . . protecting me all this time."

"What me and your mother had was complicated. Everything was because we knew every part of each other. She turned every tide in my heart. She was my anchor. I believed we were destined to be together." He pauses for what seems like forever. "This is the truth: I loved your mother with every fiber of my being, Malik. But she was just too broken to piece back together. She loved the darkness more than she ever cared for me, and I had to end it. And when I couldn't, I paid the ultimate price."

"I just don't understand why she's doing all of this," I say back.

"Your mother had her reasons, Malik. I've known her most of my life, and to this day I don't understand her reasonings behind the things she does."

His eyes drift to the picture of his wife and young son.

Another question hangs in the balance. Honestly, it's been embedding in my subconscious like a parasite ever since I first saw the picture of him and my mama together. "Am I your . . ." It's real hard for me to even utter the words. "Am I, like, your son or something?"

"Malik—"

"Just please, don't lie to me. Be real with me for one second. Because I can't take no more lying. Tell me I'm not grasping at straws here."

But before he can answer, the door to his office swings open. In comes Mrs. Empress Bonclair. Her heels click against the floor like sharp echoes, and suddenly the air turns chilly.

"Am I interrupting?" she asks with an unapologetic tone.

Chancellor Taron springs up like he's a dog on a leash.

"No, of course, not, Mother."

Instantly, I can feel the sharp smile from Mrs. Bonclair. It feels like a thousand paper cuts. "Well, well. Mr. Malik Baron, it is a pleasure to see you again."

"Likewise, ma'am," I say, putting on my code-switching voice.

She gives a dissolving grin. "My condolences on your loss. Ms.

Aya was a wonderful woman. There will never be anyone like her. The entire Kwasan tribe send their condolences as well."

She hella fake. Choosing my battles, I just smile back, biting my tongue.

"Thank you, ma'am."

"I'm sure she would be proud," she adds. Her eyes cut over to Taron, then back to me. "Son, there are pressing matters that need to be discussed about Dr. Akim and the Deacons of the Crescent."

Her eyes land back on me. Icy cold and a tight lip. "I wouldn't feel comfortable discussing it in front of a student."

"Yes, Mother, I understand." Chancellor Taron's eyes fall on me as I awkwardly open the door.

"Well, umm, Chancellor, I'll let you know about me comin' back to school." I turn back to Mrs. Empress. "It's really nice to see you again, Mrs. Bonclair."

"You as well, Mr. Baron. You as well. But you will be seeing more and more of me come soon." She turns to Chancellor Taron.

"Oh, you're gonna be teaching here?"

She crosses over to the window to look out toward the campus, her shoulders rising slightly as she inhales. "With everything that's going on, I believe that Caiman University needs a public relations makeover. Given that our admission has dropped twenty percent for the incoming freshman class. And now that the Bokors have gone public, not to mention whatever trouble that mother of yours might stir up . . ." She raises her hand, steely, making the curtains fall back down. I look to Chancellor Taron, who has a slight annoyed look on his face. "You may be on your way. I'm sure you have classes and some studying to do. We don't want you to fall behind."

I give a quick glance to Chancellor Taron. "Yeah, you're right," I say, still trying to be respectful.

"Oh, Mr. Baron?" She calls my name in a grim tone, stopping me from leaving. "I've been made aware of your use of unregulated Kaave magic. The Kwasan tribe can forgive a lot of things given the circumstances. But do know our patience is very thin."

That's definitely a threat.

Mrs. Empress gives a tight *get the hell out* smile. "Well, you have a nice day now."

"Y'all too."

When I step out of the door, I use a spell to give myself sonic hearing. Their voices come at me as if I'm underwater.

Mrs. Empress goes in. *"His mother escaped, and Mama Aya is now dead?! How could you let this happen?"*

"Kumale DuBois let this happen. I trusted him, and he is the one that released her. Not me."

Her heels click against the wood floor as she lets out a frustrated sigh. *"How many times have I told you, you should've just let the past be the past. You assured me that despicable woman would pay for her crimes!"*

A pause from Chancellor Taron.

Their entire conversation got me going back to that night when she was first exiled and Chancellor Taron was at the front, doing it all. My mama caused chaos, and standing here, I'm eaten away by guilt. And through it all, the question I've still got: Could Chancellor Taron actually be my father? Leave it to Empress Bonclair to swoop in before he could answer. But I guess after all the lies he's thrown at me since I got here, I wouldn't really believe whatever he had to say to that anyway.

Mrs. Empress continues her rant. *"Does it make you feel better having that boy here at this university?"*

"Mother—"

I figured she was gonna bring my ass in here.

"That boy will only bring destruction to you and this entire world. You've been warned time and time again, Taron."

I hear walking across the room. *"Well, the Deacons of the Crescent just went rogue, and now all the tribes got word, and—"* She stops herself. *"Son, we need to prepare ourselves for another war amongst the tribes. And if students continue to drop out, this entire institution will cease to exist. Do you want that?!"*

When Chancellor Taron doesn't answer, my heart drops to the bottom of my shoes.

CHAPTER FORTY-ONE

HURT PEOPLE HURT PEOPLE.

That's a lesson we all need to learn at some point in our lives. We're always taught the game of forgive and forget, but nobody never talks about how that shit just seeps into you, and the trophy you win is pain and enduring trauma that other folks put on you.

I mean, Kendrick said it best: *"We hurt people that love us, love people that hurt us."*

The sun fades, washing the campus in darkness and stars. A slow wind starts. This time it's not from me. Just the world's way of cooling off the heat of anger from my skin.

Everything goes quiet around this time. People back in their dorm or at the BCSU. On the edge of campus, there's a slight buzz ricocheting across the quad, accompanied by a soft hum of a streetlight that illuminates the evergreen crown of an oak tree. Its branches spread out like wings, waiting to wrap me up. Sitting here, I let my thoughts jumble in my head, mentally picking up the shards of my heart, waiting for her. The text that's staring back at me causes a roller coaster of emotions to rise up. Mental pictures assault my mind: Mama Aya dying, my mama turning evil, Professor Kumale. All of it just causes a river of teardrops to cascade down my face.

I can't help but let the hurt do its thing.

The sound of light footsteps tapping against the concrete snatches my attention. Under the streetlamp post, her beautiful shadow materializes in the spilled yellow light, curls glowing.

"Hey," Alexis whispers. I jump back, feeling the air trapped in my lungs. "It's just me. I promise, Malik."

With caution, I flick my eyes around. Untrusting. That PTSD is real, and I wanna make sure I'm ready to fight.

"Thanks for texting back," she says.

The words *I didn't want to* won't slip from my mouth. She comes over and sits by me, gazing out to the campus. The longer we sit here, I can feel her trying to hold back tears. Both of us processing, taking in a bit of space that's between us at this moment.

"Malik," she starts, voice buckling under the pain she's caused. "I'm so sorry."

It takes everything in me not to hate her right now.

But it's Lex. The girl I've loved since I was seven years old.

Somehow, we just start walking. Our feet lightly tapping against the hard concrete that turns into soft grass. We're by the edge of the bayou where the main part of Caiman U glitters like broken stars in the distance. The Spanish moss drapes around us, tickling the heavy silence between us.

"There's nothing I can say or do to ever make you forgive me, Malik, and I know that. I know that I hurt you. I know that I broke your heart."

The words finally spill out of me like water. "*Alexis,* why? I don't understand why you—"

I'm trynna find the words that I've been getting choked up on for the past few days. My inside twists just thinking about Alexis standing beside Donja and Professor Kumale. "Why did you do this, Alexis?"

Her hand tries to meet mine, but I recoil like it's poison. I sense her magic, and her shame ripples through me. "I just got so caught up, Malik. I got tired of just sitting around and not doing nothing, and when Kumale said he would help me after my parents died, I took his deal. But I didn't know the price, Malik, I didn't know about the—"

"You had to!" I cut her off. "You hurt a lot of people, Lex! And you . . . you lied to me. My grandma is fucking dead!"

The air goes out of my chest. "When I first got to the orphanage and Ms. Aida cooked us that big breakfast, you laughed and thought it was the nastiest thing when I put grape jelly on my eggs. You couldn't stop making fun of me for that. Then one day I come to the breakfast table, and I see you do it. You loved it."

She falls silent, palming the tears from her eyes.

"Everything in me from that night was so fucking scared, and I was alone. But that moment when I slipped out of my bed and sneaked to the backyard and saw you do magic for the first time, it helped me not be so afraid of mine. You did that, Lex."

"Malik—"

"I'm not finished. When you went away, my world crashed. I was alone for the past ten years, but I held on to you. I held on to you when I couldn't breathe. I held on to what we had for the past ten years. You was my anchor, Lex. And in those ten years without seeing you, feeling you, hearing you, I knew you'd be like the ocean, and I'd be the land. We'd always meet again at the shore. I loved you more than this."

I show her my crackling blue magic. Then I gesture to Caiman U and the bayou in the background. "I love you more than all of this."

"I love you too, Malik."

I erupt. "This isn't love! What you did wasn't love! If you fuck-ing love somebody, you wouldn't hurt them! I'm so fuckin' tired of people telling me they love me, when all they did was hurt me. Love shouldn't fuckin' hurt."

Through the heated stares and the strained breaths, I feel her hand on top of mine again. This time I let it stay. But the latch I have on anger right now is stronger than anything.

"That wasn't in my plan, Malik!"

"That doesn't matter, Alexis!"

My heart sinks. Full to the brim with rage. "I ain't gonna never be able to trust you again. You know that, right?"

"I just wanted to come by and see you before I'm off."

She leans her head on mine, shutting up the heartbreak in my bones. Our lips almost meet at the tangling of our hands. A heavy moment of hesitation. Finally, in a decisive move, she kisses me long and hard. Her soft lips cause my broken heart to drum against my chest. Our rhythm . . . off sync.

As I stare at my reflection in her eyes, the memories flood back into me. Us back in the orphanage, playing in the backyard. Alexis and me doing our magic by the bayou. Her and me sitting on top of the roof, looking up at the gaggle of stars. It changes to her driving away, disappearing into the distance.

All that's left are broken memories.

Right now, loving Alexis is like pouring salt in my cuts. I guess it's true what they say—you can't really fix a broken heart.

Her hands meet my cheeks, pulling my face in her direction. She stares deep into my eyes. "Remember when I said that your eyes can tell a thousand stories even without a word being uttered and that they can rewrite history if you let 'em? Never lose that, Malik," she whispers. Her cool breath softens the sting a bit. "I love you."

And just like the wind, she is gone.

• • • •

The sun hangs low in the sky while waiting for folks to show up for Mama Aya's repast. I take a sage broom, infuse the bristle with cinnamon and oils. And I just start sweeping out all the old energy and bad juju from back to front with a mumbled prayer from the Book of Psalms. No east to west or right to left, just like Mama Aya said when I first got here. I sweep the entire porch, the steps, and even the grass for, like, thirty minutes.

D Low, Savon, and Elijah appear in the yard, cackling to themselves. They see me sweeping. Elijah moves out the way with a quickness.

"Ummm, watch it now. I can't get my feet swept—ain't trynna go to jail or get bad luck."

We hug.

"Fall semester startin' next week. You comin' back, right?"

A beat as I let the question settle between us. "Depends. Are y'all playing me too? 'Cause I know Donja and Alexis was y'all's friend first."

"It's fucked up what they did." Savon kinda keeps their distance. "But we ain't with that shit. I don't bother anybody, and definitely ain't out here doing bane magic. It's too much, chile. I'm all about good vibes."

"Yeah, me too," Elijah agrees. "And plus, you know we gotta pledge; we're gonna be line brothas. We gonna be friends. And we want you to come back, Malik. Fuhh real."

D Low steps up. "I know it's painful right now. I know it hurts like a bitch. But you got us. We wanna help in any way we can."

"I'mma think about it," I tell them.

"Yeah, we ain't going away," Elijah says, laughing. "We gotta be a tribe for each other. And plus, you're stuck with us now."

"We got your back, roomie," D Low says.

We dap and hug. Then Savon and Elijah wrap their arms around me. "Thank y'all, for real. I 'preciate y'all having our backs with the Bokors."

"We did that, didn't we?" Savon jokes.

"Hell yeah, we did." D Low agrees with them with a kiss on the cheek.

"Y'all asses," Elijah groans.

"Don't be hatin', lil' brother," Savon says.

Brigitte peeks her head from the screen door. "They said y'all was here. Come on in this house and get you somethin' to eat."

A quick look to me for permission.

"Yeah, y'all go get you a plate."

They teleport right inside the house, laughing. D Low follows behind, but before he steps in, he turns to me. "Aye, we two Alabama boys out here being magical and shit, we can't let that go. Ya feel me?"

I just slowly nod.

"You gonna be a'ight?" he asks.

"I guess I ain't got no choice, right?" We both pause. "My mama is still out there, and she hurt many people."

"What we gonna do now?" D Low asks. "You gotta come back to school."

"Yeah, actually, I am. I'm gonna learn all I can at school," I reply, looking back at the house, hearing Taye's laughter coming from inside. "And protect those I love, because this shit isn't over. It ain't over."

He holds his hand out. "Whatever you need, I gotchu."

D Low hugs me long and hard. And I hug him back, tighter, feeling our friendship grow.

CHAPTER FORTY-TWO

A FAMILY THAT PRAYS TOGETHER STAYS TOGETHER.

That's what we do: party and carry on like life always do. Black folks gon' laugh at tragedy, because it is what it is. Some say that death is only the beginning. It don't bring no sadness, but joy. It's a celebration of one's life.

As I stand on the porch, watching the yard fill up with people, a jazz band appears, and they take out their instruments and start to play a feel-good song. Savon, Elijah, and D Low fall in line with one another, parading around the yard. Taye with his girlfriend, Sierra, looking all young love and shit. Happy. I smile as they yearn for me to join them. Shit. I do, and we all start to cut up around the yard, celebrating the life of Mama Aya. Auntie Caroline struts to the microphone, letting the whole bayou have it with her singing along to the tune "I Ate Up the Apple Tree."

All of Dessalines Parish is here, cutting a rug. Hearing so many folks speak about Mama Aya was truly inspirational. There were some tears. But more so funny and uplifting stories.

Me and Taye lead the family in the Electric Slide as the band plays Frankie Beverly and Maze's "Before I Let Go."

Her spirit is definitely felt today.

As the night falls, the rain starts. It drums on the roof of the house. I cut off all the lamps downstairs, dousing the house into darkness. I make my way upstairs, about to pass out. But first, something in me tells me to go to Mama Aya's room, which I've never been in before.

The door creaks open. It's wild. I can still smell her perfume. Her essence. A lulling, soft breeze from the rain enters the room, moving the old-looking curtains. A dim light on the nightstand bathes this empty cocoon in warm color. Right by the window, a small antique vanity sits.

The pain hits me from a mile away. I can still feel her presence. I sit on her bed and feel the softness of the fabrics. The million bed-padding pillows almost swallow up the headboard. The beige walls seem as though they're closing in. Just for a minute, I lie down and notice a black jewelry box on the vanity.

I make my way to it. Open it up and see a few rings and neck-laces. Or, in her case, talismans. Then I grab jewelry, and a surge of electricity shoots through my fingers, up my arms.

Her magic.

It glitters like chromes of light. My eyes search around, noticing the light settling on top of the same quilt Mama Aya was threading from before. She finished the stitched part of the Sankofa bird. Right on top, there's a folded piece of paper that has my name in gold cur-sive lettering.

Dear Malik,

I've wanted to write this letter to you for years, my grandbaby. When you were born, I knew greatness was in you. Even though your mama and I ain't see eye to eye at times, there was one thing we both agreed on, and that's loving you. Yes, your mother did love you; she just lost her way.

In my heart of hearts, I firmly believed that she loved you. And it was the evil that took over her heart and mind that prevented her from seeing it. But you came into this world loved. You will leave this world loved. Evil cannot take that truth away.

But there are more out there, baby. Dark forces. And I want you to be ready. I want you to be all you can be.

I bequeathed this letter as an inheritance. It will bless you, the same as my mama, Miriam, has blessed me. The magic of your ancestors. Passed down from generation to generation, dating back to ancient Africa.

Malik, baby, all I ask is that you don't lose yourself. Don't give in, and don't give up. Because when it comes to magic, it's real easy to do so. Take this letter to the tree in the yard. There you will find all that you need to be a better you.

One last thing: get your house in order, because you will be tested.

Love, Mama Aya

A teardrop falls out of my eye and lands on the edge of the paper. It spreads over the letter, edging to the creases of the fold. On the quilt, the shapes glow like stars. I hear her singing,

> *Way down yonder in de middle o' de fiel'*
> *Angel workin' at de chariot wheel*
> *Not so partic'lar 'bout workin' at de wheel*
> *But I jes' wan-a see how de chariot feel*

Wait a minute. I get it now. The song is not just a song, but it's a message. Hell, it's the rest of the map. It's the missing piece my mama couldn't figure out all those years ago. I start to sing the lyrics aloud. *Way down yonder in de middle o' de fiel'*. Suddenly, a pulsating ring of light makes the piece of paper and the shapes from the quilt flap wildly around the room like a butterfly. I follow it down the stairs and out the creaking screen door. It flaps around the yard, around the tree.

Angel workin' at de chariot wheel . . .

On my left, there's a chariot wheel wedged into the earth. I continue to follow the light. It circles the yard, weaving bits of shining chromed webs around the tree.

I got a mother in de promised lan'. Ain't gonna stop till I shake her han'.

Finally, it makes one last lap before it disappears into one of the shacks.

When I step inside, I feel the energy. It's heavy yet hopeful. Soon as my finger touches the wall, everything in this shack comes to life, blooming like the sun. Incantations are carved and etched into the memory of this place. So much energy, it glows like a thousand fireflies. I reach my hand into the hole in the wall, pulling back a . . . a scroll of paper?!

The same one that was blessed by my great-grandma's hands.

The Scroll of Idan.

Everything in me goes cold. I blow on the paper gently. A powerful gust of wind whips around me, turning into a flash of bright purple light. I'm reading the ancient language of our ancestors. The same piece of paper the original Divine Elam held in their hands. Feeling the Kaave magic. Ancient spells for controlling time, taming wild animals, transference . . . even becoming an orisha . . . all of it stares back at me.

My fingers softly graze the edge of the parchment. The paper feels light, but like a million pounds at the same time.

Words fly off the pages, tattooing themselves as illuminations on my arm. And the energy I feel from them is crazy. Hella powerful.

Soon as the words settle under my skin, the entire shack folds into itself. I'm lifted off the shuddering ground, into the spinning air as if it's independent from the earth. It radiates all over me. Power. Magic. Stretching my fingers, I'm snaked by a swirling prism of light.

Through the boscage, the bayou water shimmers under the moonlight with a misty fog. I whip my hand forward, making the water split down the middle. I think of the weeds bending. They do it on my command. The strings that dangle from the tree right by the house, I imagine the bottles swooping back up, piecing themselves back together.

They do.

A quick whip of the hand, and ripples of energy swell around the bottles. I hex them with a strong protection spell to ward off any evil that may come on this land.

And just like in my dream, I'm harnessing the wind and the storms. Clouds roll in. Thunder booms and lightning streaks across the dark summer sky. Coming at me like a rushing wind is a vision of the wind, the boat landing, my ancestors running through the woods, transforming into animals, others using magic. The same vision from when I was first baptized in my magic back in Mama Aya's sunroom.

And my magic goes supernova.

Leaving me in a sea of blackness . . .

• • • •

I blink back to consciousness, feeling myself slowly descend to the ground, right in front of the tree. My left hand meets the soft grass while my magic crystallizes like the blue of the ocean.

The tree closes itself up, leaves blooming to new life. A stream of smoke and white flash spurs from the darkness, taking shape as Mama Aya. Beside her are the flickering ghosts of Miriam and Ephraim. They all look at me with pride.

"My grandbaby," Mama Aya says, as if she speaks into a thousand microphones.

A river of tears stream down my cheeks. "I'm so sorry, Mama Aya. I'm—"

Her cool hand lands on my face. Instantly, I feel her warmth. All around us, I hear a chorus of the ancestors singing. *"Become yourself, baybeh,"* Mama Aya's spirit whispers.

I cling to her, trying not to lose it. "I promise."

The strength in my voice makes her eyes sparkle like stars. Miriam nods to me. So does Ephraim. Like a golden light, my ancestors doing the ring shout dance around the tree.

"You are our wildest dreams, Malik Baron," Miriam tells me.

And just like that, they all disappear in a cloud of smoke. Gone. "Goodbye, *Grandma*."

An apparition of my seven-year-old self manifests in her place.

His dark skin is illuminated by the spray of the blue light that covers the darkness of the bayou. An innocent grin stretches his face.

At first I notice he has the shimmering necklace of my mama's and her picture. As I walk up to him, he hands me the picture with a plaintive stare.

I squeeze it in my fist. It bursts into ancestral fire. One last glance at my seven-year-old self, face hardening with determination.

Slowly realizing . . .

She ain't our mama no more. She's our enemy.

I stretch forth my arms. He does the same, still fixing his gaze on me.

I nod. With the blue magical light circle around us, I finally let my inner child find solace in my spirit. I give him the safety that he needed and damn well deserves.

I let him live.

In a blinding blue light, he disappears into me.

My eyes flutter back open. I look around the land and at the house. My fight is not over. Nah. It's just beginning. The ancestors got my back. That's on everything I love. With these newfound powers, I have a whole family to protect from whatever else is about to come.

I'm ready. Because that little Black boy from Helena, Alabama, is no longer haunted by an outpouring of confusion, but a levee of weighted determination. He belongs here. His roots are here. He's part of something way bigger.

And the magic of resilience is in his blood.

EPILOGUE

BLACK BOYS LIKE ME DO HAVE MAGIC POWERS.

Everything I came to believe this past couple of months, I am finding that to be true every single day. But I will say: that saying of *with great power comes great responsibility* may be true, but I ain't ask for none of this. This responsibility was passed down to me. It's the cards that I've been dealt.

I teleport to the place that I've treated like it wasn't important to me. The place that's helped me beyond what I could ever imagine. But also, it's a place that helped uncover some deep, dark family secrets. The voices rise as I walk through the double doors of the School of Religion, into the safe place that I'm gonna call home for the next few years.

Caiman University.

It's gonna teach me to be ready.

Because a war is coming.

In a matter of seconds, I click on my playlist, turning on "Deja Vu" by Easy McCoy, and teleport all the way across campus to my first day of class for the fall semester. Through campus, it's busy. Everybody moving back into their dorms. Club sign-ups. Fraternities and sororities stepping in the quad. I stop, give a couple of daps to folks from my dorm, say wassup to Dr. Akeylah, who's talking with other professors. I even pass by Mrs. Empress Bonclair, and she watches me with those cold eyes. But I don't pay no attention to her.

Because Chancellor Taron's right: I do belong here at Caiman University.

Inside the big lecture hall, I see Savon and D Low are already in the chosen row, saving me a seat.

Just like my heart, there's an empty seat where Alexis was gonna be.

Me and D Low dap each other up. "Glad to see you back, bruh."

Passing by us is Dominique. She bats those eyelashes, real flirty. "Glad you're here, Malik."

"Aye, I'm ready to learn."

Savon cuts in. "Now, y'all heard we got a new adjunct professor comin' in. They've been a lil' *hush-hush* about it."

Elijah answers back, "Prolly some old head that's real boring coming to be an adjunct professor. The way things set up, might as well say good-bye to time traveling."

As they go into their own convo, I sit back, feeling my face crack a smile for the first time in weeks. This is my school. This is my fam. This is my life.

The doors to the classroom pop open. All our eyes turn to find a woman who I'm sure we never seen before. She enters with a majestic stride. A tignon wrapped around her head, and she's on her boss *ish.* She's a tall Black woman with a commanding presence, ready to teach the Blackgical minds of the South. Low-key, she gives me Viola Davis vibes. "Gon' head and get out a sheet of paper, because I'm sho you heard the stories of Salem in your schoolin'," she says to us with a deep country accent. "But lemme just tell ya—it ain't like how it is in them history books. They got everythin' wrong, and they know that. That's why they trynna erase our struggles. Our history. Our power. We can't let that happen."

The whole crew just look at one another with wide eyes.

"I go by the name of . . . Tituba Atwell." She faces me with a set of piercing eyes that chills my blood to ice. A whole buncha surprised whispers reverberate around the room. "And I'm here to teach you the *real* truth. Because this magical revolution that's comin' . . . will *not* be televised."

To Be Continued . . .

ACKNOWLEDGMENTS

Typing this, it's absolutely wild, and there are so many people to thank because *Blood at the Root* probably wouldn't have gotten this far without them. First, my ancestors. Thank you for fighting and guiding me along the way when I was so lost and discouraged. Thank you for affirming that this story would be seen, heard, and protected.

To my tribe: Millie, my Viola Davis, you are my best friend, pal, and confidant. Thank you for being a friiiiiieeennnd. You believed in me as a playwright the moment we met. You have changed my life creatively and personally. Thank you for dreaming with me and going along with my out-of-world ideas. I can't wait to write you the role that will get you that EGOT.

DeJuan Christopher—thank you for believing in me when I first sent a play. You talked me off the ledge of throwing it away. You've been like a brother to me. Our hours-long convos, the tears, the yelling, and the fights in Starbucks—you've been such a blessing to me. Thank you, bruh, for everything and for inspiring the character Baron Samedi. Jacquelin L. Schofield, you are Mama Aya. The way you brought her to life in the short film, I can't get your portrayal out of my head. I truly hope you can bring her to life when we do the TV show/movie. Thank you for the love and the phone calls, and just thank you for being you.

ThurZday, Thurz, you already know. Thank you for the debates, the passion, the tears, and especially for being on FaceTime with me as I wrote the book, revising it, and all the times I was getting it ready for submission. Thank you for the friendship, for challenging me, and for giving so much of yourself to me. I know we talk about one-sided labor friendships. But it's not that with us. Thank you for pushing through and anchoring yourself through our times in UMOJA. You already know. Hmmmph.

Oliver Smith-Perrin, you were the first one I told about *BATR*, when we went to Starbucks in Hollywood. Thank you for bringing Malik Baron to life in the short film. I appreciate you, bruh. Johnathan L. Jackson—thank you for reading the *Blood at the Root* pilot script. Thank you for the advice, the brotherhood. We literally sat on the phone for hours, wondering and frustrated about why folks didn't see the vision. Why we didn't get staffed on our favorite shows. But you did it. You held my dreams. I held yours. And now look at us.

Andi Chapman—thank you for the love, the prayers, and the calls. Thank you for your words of encouragement. Thank you for directing my plays with grace. I learn so much from you every time we work together.

To the entire cast of the *BATR* short film: Shandra Graham, Jemar Michael, Malik Bannister, Reshea Mackey, Terrence Prince, Atika Green, Jon Chaffin, Phillip McNair, Twon Pope, Joshua McNair, Dejean Deterville, thank you all for showing up during the wildest times in our lives—Covid-19, bringing these characters to life. We traveled all over LA to shoot this epic idea of mine, and y'all were troupers.

Margeaux Weston, first of all, thank you for your support and encouragement. You read the first draft of the *Blood at the Root* novel, and I was so dead set on self-publishing this book, and I was going to be on my way. You encouraged me to go traditional publishing and helped me every step along the way. You helped me shape the book to submit it to agents. Thank you for the phone calls, the laughs, the talks of our family's country ways, and the moments when I was frustrated during the querying process; you were right there.

Peter Knapp—sir, you are truly a giant! You have changed my life. Thank you for choosing and representing *BATR* and me as an author, listening to me, and guiding this story. You signed me in August 2021, and we got through it. When you first called me, telling me we had sold *BATR,* it took everything in me not to cry on the phone and make it weird. Ha ha. Thank you for believing in Malik Baron when many folks didn't. Thank you for believing in this story when we were amid rejection. You kept the faith. I kept the faith. I still, to this day, hope I wasn't annoying with all my emails and questions. But you have shown so much grace to this baby author who stepped into the literary world for the first time. You have been an amazing partner, and I can't wait to see what else we do together.

To my manager, Anastasiya Kukhtareva, thank you for giving me a chance. Thank you for reading all my scripts. Thank you for being a champion of my work.

Amy Wagner—ma'am! You don't know how much I appreciate you. I emailed you randomly, and you gave me a chance with my plays. I'm so appreciative of you. You're a rock star playwriting agent, and I can't wait to get *Boulevard of Bold Dreams* to Broadway.

To my a3artistsagency film/TV team—Martin To and Sally Wilcox, thank you for jumping on this ride with me. We got a lot of work ahead of us to bring *BATR* to the silver screen!

To my amazing editors, Liesa Abrams and Emily Shapiro— thank you for choosing *BATR* and changing my life. Your eyes literally shifted everything in my life for the better. Because of you, people will finally get to read about this Blackgical world. Thank you for letting me be me in the prose and dialogue and for not trying to make *BATR* into something it's not. You listened. You cared. You believed. Your excitement for *BATR* really got me through it all. Thank you for the emails. Thank you for the social media messages! I can't wait to continue to work with you on more YA stories. Let's make the change together!

To the entire Penguin Random House team, thank you for believing so much in this book. Because of you, *Blood at the Root* will reach many deserving readers. I can't wait to grow and explore with you. Thank you for making me feel at home. Fun fact: I manifested that *BATR* would be a part of Penguin Random House because back in December 2022, I kept seeing penguin decorations while driving in LA. And I swear I never noticed that many penguin Christmas decorations. Ha ha!

My two other amigos—Tre and Carlos. We came a loooooong way from Lee University and New Hughes dorm. Tre, we're in LA now, living our dreams as we said we would back in the dorms. Thank you for being the best friend I ever had. I'm so glad we messaged each other in 2012. Twelve years of friendship have been such a blessing. Carlos, you fool! Thank you for your friendship. Thank you for the spiritual guidance and advice. You inspired a lot of the Savon character. The one-liners. The out-of-pocket convos. We fight, we argue, but I know you got my back.

My Alabama fam: Torielle, you've been my best friend. You've been there. Thank you for helping me when I didn't have a dime to my name. We came a long way from those Kingwood days. Travis . . . I know life got in the way, but we still brothers. Love you man. Aaron Lewis—thank you as well. You the cousin who I can come to and ask questions about Helena, and you would know them all! To my high school theatre teacher, Mrs. C—thank you for believing in me. You were the first person to tell me that I was good at something, and you helped me realize I was a writer. I know I got on your nerves during theatre class, but you gotta love me! Ha ha!

To my mama, thank you for inspiring me. These characters. A lot of the sayings that are in the book come from you. I know being a single mother wasn't the easiest. And I wasn't the easiest child. But you're my mama, and I can't wait to retire you and buy you that dream home. My big sis, Shanna, thank you for inspiring the characters in this book. Thank you for listening when I complained about the submission process. You probably were like . . . *Ummm, I'm unsure how to help.* But you listened. Thank you for everything. All the sacrifices you made. I'll never forget it. To my nephew, this story is for you. I always want you to know that you have magic, beautiful

Black boy. I know I wasn't there because I was trying to make this dream come true. I love you, and I hope you love this book! Ha ha.

To my literary inspiration—the titan, August Wilson. I hope I'm making you proud. You have inspired me since I was seventeen. With your work, I had to confront the darkness of myself and illuminate it with love and light. Thank you for teaching me that my ancestors are the gems of the ocean. To Lorraine Hansberry—thank you for teaching me that characters can have the wildest dreams, even if it hurts the ones you love sometimes. I felt for and still do feel for Walter Lee Younger. Because like him, I *wanted* so many things. *A Raisin in the Sun* has blessed this little Black boy from Alabama. I will forever be grateful that I was sent to in-school detention. Ms. Knight gave me the choice to read a newspaper or your play, and I chose your play, which changed my life for the best.

To the best Twitter/TikTok followers—thank you for donating funds and for the likes, retweets, and love on social media. Because of your enthusiasm, this book caught the attention of publishers, and now look! I am forever grateful for you all.

I'm inspired by my fellow writers daily: Ryan Douglass, Ayana Gray, Antwan Eady, and I know you don't know me, but Tomi Adeyemi—thank you for inspiring me. I really hope we can meet one day.

To readers and future readers—thank you for picking up this book. Thank you for diving into the Blackgical world of Malik Baron. It means the world to me that you want to read about a Black boy from Helena, Alabama, who has magic powers. Far too often, we don't get to see characters like him in the young adult fantasy space. So I'm glad you all are gonna get to experience this. You're in for a wild ride!